THIS GREAT
HEMISPHERE

ALSO BY MATEO ASKARIPOUR

Black Buck

THIS GREAT HEMISPHERE

== A NOVEL ==

MATEO ASKARIPOUR

DUTTON

DUTTON

An imprint of Penguin Random House LLC
penguinrandomhouse.com

LIBRARY OF CONGRESS CATALOGING-IN-PUBLICATION DATA

Names: Askaripour, Mateo, author.
Title: This great hemisphere: a novel / Mateo Askaripour.
Identifiers: LCCN 2023050361 (print) | LCCN 2023050362 (ebook) |
ISBN 9780593472347 (hardcover) | ISBN 9780593472354 (ebook)
Subjects: LCGFT: Science fiction. | Novels.
Classification: LCC PS3601.S593 T45 2024 (print) |
LCC PS3601.S593 (ebook) | DDC 813/.6—dc23/eng/20231106
LC record available at https://lccn.loc.gov/2023050361
LC ebook record available at https://lccn.loc.gov/2023050362

Printed in the United States of America

1st Printing

BOOK DESIGN BY DANIEL BROUNT

For those who have always been deemed different
You will save us

I am invisible, understand,
simply because people refuse to see me . . .
When they approach me they see only
my surroundings, themselves or
figments of their imagination, indeed,
everything and anything except me.

—RALPH ELLISON

Invisible to whom?

—TONI MORRISON

2028

New York City, New York,
United States of America

PROLOGUE

GOOD MORNING, LADIES AND GENTLEMEN. I'M SORRY FOR THE IN-terruption, and I promise I won't take up too much of your time. As you can tell from my condition, I'm not here raising money for my basketball team."

Makeda scanned the train car for someone to make eye contact with. She grasped the pole with one hand and cradled her swollen belly with the other. The train's passengers—students rushing to class, exhausted construction workers on their way home, millennials heading to shiny start-ups—laughed at her joke. A year ago, she would have refused to play into a type—young, pregnant Black woman begging for money—but she no longer had the luxury of choice.

"Nor am I here with a sob story to guilt you into giving me a dollar. I am simply a woman down on her luck"—she gripped the pole harder—"who could use some help. Nothing more, nothing less. If you have money or food, I thank you in advance."

Releasing her hold on the pole, Makeda checked to see who, if anyone, was stirred by her honesty. As if on cue, one bearded Black man dug into the stained pocket of his work jeans and handed her a crumpled five. A young white woman unlatched her Louis Vuitton purse and held out some change. Makeda walked to her and let the woman empty the grimy coins into her hand.

"Thank you for the help," Makeda said.

The woman, oversize sunglasses and all, smiled and replied, "You're very welcome." Makeda knew that the woman had gotten the better end of the bargain—the feeling that you'd righted the entire world's wrongs for thirty-seven cents.

Five or six others made a contribution; among them was a pudgy olive-skinned boy with curly black hair who waved the crisp dollar his father had given him like a little flag. No matter the amount, Makeda thanked each and every one of them as she waddled down the aisle.

Their generosity didn't surprise her. She'd lived outside of acceptable, respectable society for over a decade. By now she knew that it wasn't an all-expenses-paid guilt trip that moved people, at least not them. No, these people of folded pizza slices, *Fuck yous!*, and brains hardwired with endless complaints—rising subway fares, the thick stench of piss and cigarettes, inhumane landlords—demanded bluntness and gorged themselves on cold, hard truth.

More strangers passed her money. Before shoving it into her bag, she quickly added it all up in her head—something *he* had said was a gift, but she never saw it as such; she had always been good with numbers, simple and true. $21.75. It wasn't a personal best, but enough to warrant a rest, especially in her condition, so she got off the train at Union Square.

Opting to take the stairs instead of the filthy elevator, Makeda paused every few steps, catching her breath. "You're a heavy one," she said, rubbing her stomach. Finally surfacing into the clear afternoon, she slapped the sculpture of Washington on horseback, as she always did, and sat on a wooden bench on the west side of the park—her favorite spot. Depending on where she focused her eyes, she could see Barnes & Noble, Whole Foods, and Mount Sinai. *There's nothing like spring in New York.* She closed her eyes, felt the sun's warmth on her cheeks, and inhaled deeply, hoping her baby, whom she'd taken to just calling "Baby," could smell what she smelled—that they could feel the sun just like she did.

"Excuse me."

Makeda's eyes jolted open. The white woman above her, who was at least sixty, dragged her eyes all over Makeda before spreading a thickly lipsticked mouth into a tight smile, which displaced the wrinkles to the corners of her lips. The red lipstick, sinister smile, and crinkly white skin reminded her of a vampire. But didn't vampires only come out at night?

"Yes?" Makeda asked, wondering if the woman's starched black pants were as uncomfortable as they looked.

"May I sit?"

Moving Makeda's large shopping bag to the side, the woman sat down before she could answer. She stared at Makeda's bulging stomach for seconds that felt like hours, then reached out and placed her cold hand on it.

"Please don't do that." Makeda angled her body away from the woman. White women were always fucking touching her—her stomach, her hair, her arms, her thighs—all without her consent. Long ago, she'd decided to not get mad about it. But they never learned. Instead of considering her anger, their instant frowns suggested that *she'd* deprived *them* of some God-given right. And who was *she* to tell *them* what *they* could and couldn't do?

"Oh." The woman pulled her hand away, quickly inserting it into her stiff red jacket pocket. "I'm sorry, but I was just on the train and was too slow with my bag to give you some money, so here." She held one of those green-and-peach-colored twenty-dollar bills between her fingers. A big spender.

A smile bloomed on Makeda's face, and the woman's gaze

immediately fell, like a loose telescope, focusing on her teeth. Makeda smiled even wider. She knew the woman was looking at her two front teeth, which pointed away from each other dramatically, as if they contained magnetic poles of the same charge. She was also missing the two sharp ones in her bottom row, a dentist at a free clinic called them *canines*, but she didn't care. She wasn't embarrassed by her teeth because they were *her* teeth, and that made them perfect; something *he* had helped her realize.

"Thank you so much. You didn't need to go to all this trouble, though."

"It's my pleasure. I'm Kathy," the woman said, and extended the same cold hand she'd just placed on Makeda's stomach. Makeda shook it and felt Baby kick.

"Ouch." She doubled over and took an extra second before getting up. After almost eight months, she knew what Baby's kicks meant—"I'm hungry," "Roll to your other side," "Play me some Alicia Keys"—but this one said: *"Leave, Mommy. Now."*

The woman smoothed the loose hairs popping out of Makeda's fraying braids. "You should relax. Babies don't like to be stressed. Also," she said, continuing to treat Makeda like the latest token Black American Girl doll. "I never got your name."

"Makeda," she responded, beginning to count down from thirty. *Twenty-seven. Twenty-six.* At zero, she'd leave.

Kathy stared into Makeda's eyes and cracked another tight smile. "I just love your names. There's always a rhythm to them, not like boring old Kathy," she said, laughing to herself.

A smooth breeze tickled Makeda's cheeks. It shook the newly grown leaves of the park's oak trees, ruffled the canopies of designer strollers that Black and brown women pushed white babies around in, and sent plastic bags of all colors and sizes soaring into the street like jellyfish. Men in tailor-made blazers and women in monochrome pantsuits laughed, bleached white teeth beaming for all to see, like they were in a Gap commercial. The *Truman Show*–esque scene reminded Makeda that her perfect day could still be perfect.

Five. Four. Three.

Makeda smiled. "Nice meeting you, Kathy. It's time for me to go."

"You know, there's a homeless shelter not too far from here."

This old bitch. "What makes you think I'm homeless?"

"Oh, I apologize. It's just that, I—"

She held up a hand. "No, I'm sorry. You're just trying to be kind. The truth is, I am homeless. But I'd rather be outside than in a stuffy shelter with unpredictable strangers. Especially when the weather is as beautiful as this," she said, making sure to punctuate her sentence with a laugh. Nothing made white people feel better than a Black person laughing. Besides, she didn't think she needed to mention the rest: that she met *him* at the Rescue Mission a year ago and fell in love, only for *him* to abandon her and Baby last month; that *he* even had the audacity to leave a coffee-stained Starbucks napkin in place of the money she'd been saving with the words *If you can make it here, you can make it anywhere, baby.*

Kathy wrinkled her nose as if a garbage truck had just passed by. "Well, I don't think that's the best decision for your baby, Mah-kah-dah. Being a mother is the most important job a woman can have, and I'm sorry, but I'm just tired of all of you having so many babies without a care in the world."

Makeda forced herself to take a breath—in through her nose, out through her mouth—then again, just as she'd watched *him* do whenever things didn't go his way, which was often.

"Have a good day." She took a moment to push herself from the bench, ignoring Kathy as she reached out to help her up, and walked away.

Passing the men hustling naive tourists and college students through lightning rounds of speed chess and artists hawking overpriced versions of paint by numbers, Makeda allowed the swarm of foot traffic to carry her across the street, all to a djembe drum's beat. Finally, she was spat out in front of her destination. The holiest of food stores: Whole Foods.

There was no place she loved more. It wasn't the gluten-free bread or cage-free eggs that drew her to the corporation masquerading as a mom-and-pop shop—it was the hypnotizing colors. Past the entrance, she rounded a tower of boxes with fat-free popcorn and stared at the lime-green, electric-blue, and neon-orange bottled teas and canned sodas sweating on their cold shelves. *I'll be back soon.*

Even though she didn't plan on buying any fruit, she took the escalator to the lower level and marveled at the bright, canary-colored bananas, waxy blueberries, and Satan-red strawberries all imported from subtropical parts of the country she'd never visited, but dreamed of seeing. At least once.

Baby kicked. "Okay," she said, gently knocking on her stomach like it was a door. "I get it." They were hungry. She went back upstairs, grabbed a strawberry cream scone from behind a plastic window, and settled on a coconut water she'd never had before, its glowing pink liquid irresistible.

Before entering a line, she considered each of the hanging signs above them bearing white arrows on red, blue, green, yellow, purple, and orange backgrounds. "What're we feeling today, love?" With no response from her unborn passenger, she closed her eyes and pictured a vast forest full of cabins, the sun filtering through pear-green leaves. *Green it is.* She smiled at the cashier as she parted with ten whole dollars, happy with how the day was turning out, despite that white woman's minor intrusion.

Instead of subjecting herself to a set of stairs that might as well have stretched as high as the Tower of Babel, she took an elevator up and settled down to eat her lunch. She watched the park through the store's windows and imagined that all of those people milling about only existed for her viewing pleasure; a thought that made her laugh, because, if only for a second, she believed it.

Then she noticed that Kathy was still on the bench where she had left her. Makeda's heart plummeted and her stomach turned, as though some interlocking mechanism inside of her was out of whack. She reminded herself that the white woman couldn't bother her now. Plus, from up here, she realized that Kathy's red and black outfit made her look more like a ladybug than a bone-chilling vampire, and everyone knows ladybugs are harmless. Only a few weeks ago, she had found a book at the Strand, *Insect Symbols*, which said that, in many cultures, ladybugs, also referred to as "ladybirds," were good luck, and that when you saw one you should make a wish.

She had learned to not put her faith in white people, but Kathy was no longer a menacing presence, she was now a sign of good things to come. Makeda closed her eyes, sweet cream icing still on her lips, like a funny mustache. *I hope that you'll grow up to be someone, Baby. Much more of a someone than me, with a real home, a real family, and a life that's all your own.* With her eyes still closed, she said, "Amen," but she didn't know why. A wish wasn't the same as a prayer, or was it?

When she opened her eyes, Kathy was gone. She wiped her mouth, tossed her trash, and took her time walking down the stairs, grabbing the wooden rail every few seconds so she could both rest and watch the people in line take their places under the colored signs, feeling an affinity for those who, like her, chose green that day.

"Got a name for the little one yet?" Her favorite security guard's deep Barry White voice always soothed her, as if he were serenading her with every word.

"Nope. I think I'll just wait until they arrive and name them whatever comes to mind. Could be Whole Foods, could be Manhattan, could be Subway, could be—"

"Slim."

Slim smiled wide enough to show that he still had all of his teeth. Makeda smiled back, wondering for the first time if he had a wife and children. She knew that he didn't speak to everyone like he spoke to her, and she saw him as a dad. "Now that you mention it, it could be Slim, yes. Has a nice ring to it. *Slim.* SlimFast. Slim pickings. Slim Jim."

He laughed, no longer paying attention to the exit, and potentially allowing thieves to escape with oat milk and veggie burgers. "Or just Slim. Simple."

"I'll keep it in mind, but no promises."

"Wouldn't ask you to make one," he said, saluting her as she made her way out the second set of automatic doors.

"Slim," Makeda whispered to Baby, on the verge of laughter. "Do you like that?"

"You have to go to a shelter tonight."

Makeda looked up and flinched. It was her ladybug. In front of her.

"Please leave me alone." Her mouth was paper dry. She side-stepped Kathy and turned left, toward University Place, but a hand on her arm held her back.

"I'll leave you alone, but not the baby. You've been on these streets for too long to know what's good for you," Kathy said, her grip growing firmer.

Makeda was confused, by the hand on her arm, yes, but also by the strength of this woman, charged with a power that flowed from somewhere else. "You're hurting me."

"And you're hurting the baby. We're going to a clinic to make sure it's healthy. *Now.*" Kathy's eyes were cold, and Makeda had seen cold eyes before. She wasn't being given a choice.

"Let go of me, or I'll scream," she said. She couldn't decide whether to punch Kathy in the face or call for help. Both could land her, instead of this "poor old white woman," in trouble.

"Go ahead," Kathy dared. "*Scream.* I'll tell whoever comes to help that you're endangering a child."

"Let go of me, you crazy *bitch*!" She yanked her arm out of Kathy's clamped hand. But the woman grabbed Makeda's hoodie with a force that nearly pulled her to the pavement.

"Someone help, please!" Makeda shouted. But this was New York, and though a few people walking by slowed down to watch, the chess hustlers and the hustled continued their games unfazed, and the tempo of the djembe drum picked up, with no one doing anything to help; *New York Tough* becoming *New York, tough* in a split second.

"You're coming with me." Kathy pulled Makeda toward the curb and held her hand out for a cab.

"Somebody!" Makeda screamed. "I'm pregnant! This woman is kidnapping me! Please!"

With a handful of her hoodie in Kathy's tight hand, Makeda dropped down on all fours, her heavy stomach touching the sidewalk. Cars raced by only inches away, a low rattle flowing throughout her own body. *Kick.*

A cab pulled up. "Get up," Kathy ordered.

"Please," Makeda wailed as tears traveled down her cheeks. Then she felt it, a slight pop, and warm wetness. Darkness spread across her gray sweatpants.

"Let go of her!" a man shouted, pushing Kathy away from her. Makeda looked up and saw Slim, not just a security guard but her guardian angel, his eyes wide open, jaw set, and no-doubt-bone-shattering fist cocked back.

Now a crowd had formed, the swarm of foot traffic buzzing with anger at this man threatening a woman. Okay, let's just call it what it really was: this *Black* man threatening this *white* woman. Kathy seemed to feel this, and looked from Slim to Makeda, perhaps wondering if her whiteness was powerful enough to outrank them both. Answer: it was.

"Lady," the cabdriver said, stretching his neck out the window. "You coming or what?"

Likely realizing there would be many other opportunities to save a Poor Black Child™ from its Neglectful Black Mother™, Kathy shook her head and got into the cab, her eyes stuck to Makeda's stomach until she disappeared down 14th Street.

"It's okay," Slim said, helping Makeda up. "We're going to get you some help."

He hailed another cab and joined her in the backseat. She grit her teeth against the pain and said, "NYU Langone, please. It's closest."

"It'll be fine, Makeda," Slim said, smoothing her head on his shoulder with one hand as she squeezed the life out of his other. "Don't worry."

She clenched her eyes as her belly tightened, then relaxed. "What about your job?"

"What, being a security guard?" Slim sucked his teeth. "That's my side hustle. I got a million of them."

Makeda smiled. She knew that all the pain she'd experienced in life had encoded itself into her DNA—sometimes she believed that she could actually feel it, like it was crawling just beneath the surface of her skin—but over time, and with *his* help, she had learned to graft optimism into her genes, too. This was why she wanted to speak, to thank Slim for being there for her, but all she could do now was clutch his hand and hope he knew just how grateful she was.

The cab came to a stop in front of the hospital. Slim jumped out, ran inside, and returned with a wheelchair and staff members, who bombarded her with questions: *What was her name, how far along was she, did she want to call the father?*

Makeda Solomon. Thirty-six weeks. No.

The doctor, Dr. Kim, welcomed her into the delivery room with unsettling enthusiasm.

"It's the big day, Makeda," he said, as if she were getting ready to deliver an important speech instead of a living, breathing, shitting baby. "Let's get to work."

After six hours, Makeda, sweat dripping from her face, looked at Slim, who had been holding her hand the entire time, and said, "Slim. I don't care if they're a boy or a girl. I'm naming them Slim."

He parted his lips and looked like he had just won an Olympic gold medal, maybe for shot put or wrestling; he was a big man, after all.

"Keep going," Dr. Kim said. "You're doing great, Makeda."

It felt like a stone giant was crushing her abdomen, a sensation that only intensified as the time between contractions decreased. She gripped Slim's large rough hand even harder.

"Makeda," Dr. Kim said, looking into her eyes. "Push."

She pushed, and pushed and pushed and pushed. The sound of her racing heart drowned out the world around her.

"Makeda," Dr. Kim repeated, louder now.

She gave one final push with everything in her, and she knew that her baby was here. Makeda, exhausted, smiled up at Slim, who still held her hand, but he was staring at Dr. Kim with a confused look, like something was wrong.

"What is it?" Makeda asked, her heart speeding again. "Let me see my baby, please."

Dr. Kim rose, silent. But there was nothing to see. Just a baby-sized indentation in the doctor's blue scrubs.

And then: the wailing of a child unseen.

2529

Forest Region,
Northwestern Hemisphere

CHAPTER 1

THIS TIME IT WOULD BE PERFECT. SWEETMINT KNELT DOWN, EYE level with the crisscrossing of string that hovered above her stove. She plucked it and then clapped her hands together.

"Holy Father," she said, raising her closed eyes to the cabin's ceiling. "Please let this work." With the biogas turned on and everything in place, she grabbed a knife from the kitchen table, took two steps toward the door—carefully ducking under more sets of string—and, in one swift motion, tore through the first string, which ran from the doorknob to the network in front of her.

A pitcher of sun-charged water dipped and poured into the open kettle on her stove, then a crudely carved wooden mallet swung from the ceiling and collided with the stove's red button, igniting the biogas. The weight of the mallet pulled on a group of interlocking strings, causing a spoon with a hole drilled into its handle to fall, dropping a pinch of needle leaf into a metal strainer that sat inside an herbcup. The cup, balanced by two thicker strings, soared toward the stove and stopped right as the kettle tilted and poured boiling water into it.

Sweetmint's nails were already chewed to nubs, but that didn't stop her from obliterating them even further. She turned off the biogas and counted out a full minute aloud. Then, holding the herbcup with one palm, she snipped the two strings that held it in front of the stove, removed the strainer, and took a sip.

"PERFECTION!" she shouted, throwing a triumphant fist into the air. It was the perfect amount of water. The perfect amount of needle leaf. The perfect length of string. The perfect-size herbcup. She took another sip, then ran from her kitchen to the other side of her cabin, careful not to trip on sawed wood, twisted metal, and other inventions-in-progress. She played a beat on the steel trunk that sat between two mattresses; her own unmade to the left, the other neat and untouched to the right.

Sweetmint shook her butt to the beat, but stopped when the sight of the untouched mattress sucked the joy out of her, as it always did. She threw herself on the couch, the sunlight from the window above warming her already warm skin.

"I did it. I did it. I did it," she said half-heartedly.

"Did what?" The voice came from the other side of her door.

"Good morning, Rusty," she said. "Come in."

"Sawukhoob, Sweetmint." The door opened, and his scentprint—rusted metal mixed with something more pleasing, like sweet potatoes roasted until the sap bursts through the skin—filled the cabin. Though she heard *his* footsteps, smelled *his* smell, and sensed *his* rumoya, or "cell spirit"—the life force flowing through all Invisibles, unique to each of them, influencing thought, feeling, and action—she couldn't see any physical manifestation of him. This made it impossible for him to hide the small box floating behind him.

"What's that?" she asked.

The old cushions sagged as he whistled and plopped his small but sturdy frame down next to her. She heard his locs swaying against the wall behind them, and watched as he placed the box, wrapped in rough brown canvas, on the trunk in front of them. "'Chunjani, Rusty?' 'Oh, mambonga for asking, Sweetmint. All is well. Freshpine and the little ones are healthy and happy. Glory, glory.'"

She threw her arm over his bare back, kissed his cheek. "I'm sorry. It's just, you know."

"I do. Your rumoya is nervous. But namruz is a big day. Maybe the biggest of your life."

"Exactly."

"Before I came in, I heard you say you did something? From the looks of the string and the cup of needle leaf on your table, I have a feeling you finally got your latest experiment to work."

"It's not an *experiment*. It's—"

"An *invention*." He let out a series of laughs that, to anyone else, would sound like a short burst of coughing. "I know, I'm just fooling with you. How many attempts did it take?"

She stretched her lower lip with her tongue, took a second. Then, "Twenty-seven. I could have probably done it in fewer if I'd drawn it out, but I wanted to see if I could do it entirely in my mind."

"And what actually goes on in your mind, when you're creating something?"

"Honestly," she said, looking up at the ceiling. "It's hard to say. It's like I go somewhere else, farther and deeper than anywhere I've been before, and when I'm there, I'm floating. I can view whatever problem I have as a puzzle. Then I begin to take it apart, piece by piece, and try to put it back together."

"Well," he said, his wide smile evident from his tone. "You truly have a gift given to you by the Holy Father himself. Glory, glory."

"Does this mean you'll let me try it out in your cabin?"

"Definitely not. You know Freshpine maintains total control over our khanaya. And the little ones would tear down those strings faster than you can say 'Chief Executive Rhitel.'"

"But what if I—"

He patted her knee. "Not this time, Sweetmint. But this"—he picked up the box, held it in front of her—"is for you."

She took it with both hands, slowly unwrapped the canvas, and found a mess of straw inside. "This better not be some sort of joke, Rusty. I don't have time for any of that today."

He was silent, but she knew he was smiling, waiting.

She pushed the straw aside, felt a warm piece of round metal. When she took it out, the wheat-colored device sat small in her large palm. A piece of metal with a ring attached jutted out of one side, and she pressed it, unlocking the lid and revealing the face of a compass; something most Invisibles didn't own or have use for.

"Mambonga khulu, Rusty," she said, doing her best to sound more grateful than confused.

He laughed. "You're wondering why I would ever give you a compass when our every move is tracked. But it's what it symbolizes," he said, tapping the glass, causing the needle to tremble. "I had to go downcity for something and met a man who customizes them. I told him I worked for a dippy collector and had him set the coordinates to Forest Twenty-Six, so no matter where you go, you'll never forget where you come from."

"I don't know what's more ridiculous, you lying about your work or thinking that I, having spent the majority of my twenty-four years here, would ever forget this forest." She bumped his shoulder with her own. "But either way, thank you."

"Khawamu." He got up and rubbed her head. "Well, I'll let you gather yourself before Daily Prayer. I love you, Sweetmint."

The words left his mouth and traveled the short distance to her ears, but she wasn't sure she'd heard them right. "What?"

"I said I love you."

She looked down at the compass, rubbed its smooth glass face, already connected to it. "You've never said that before."

"But you've always felt it, right?"

Sweetmint clicked the compass closed and looked up at him. "Funny that you chose today of all days to say that. When, you know, I'm the feast of the forest. But don't worry, Rusty, I won't forget you when I'm the first Invisible inventor hired by the Northwestern State."

He walked to the door, opened it, and paused. "You know," he said. "He'd be proud of you."

This. These words. He was gone, and after three years, he wasn't coming back. She knew Rusty didn't mean to hurt her, but then why bring him up?

"Doubt that," she whispered. "Working with dippies wasn't exactly what he had planned for me. Plus, I don't even have the apprenticeship yet."

"He wanted you to have the world, Sweetmint."

"Oh yeah? Then why did he keep me from it?"

"Who's to say what shape love takes?" He closed the door behind him, leaving her at a loss. But she couldn't try to process this. Not now. She drained the rest of the needle leaf, felt it splash down her throat, widen her veins, and turn her heart into one of the *thump-thump-thump*ing zaya drums the men in her forest played, then left.

The walk from her cabin in Donsee to the main square—a straight shot on Softstone Path through her dense forest—barely registered. She was so deep in her mind that she didn't even notice when Rusty's children called to her. Nor when the people who lived in the more clustered cabins of Nearsee stepped outside, many of them painted in various colors from head to toe, and stared at her.

She walked through the main square, passing the train platform, the men sitting on their two-wheeled carts, the women grilling their vegetables and tossing laughter and gossip back and forth, and the children playing games and whispering at her heels. A couple of fresh-faced hemispheric guards walked around, speaking with one another, but they were just scenery to her. She continued straight until she entered the church and, seeing that it was only moderately full, sat in a middle pew.

Now she heard them all. The whispers flying in every direction around her. Her forestfolk were likely just as surprised as she was that she had received this once-in-a-lifetime opportunity. She, who had always kept to herself, choosing to study rather than play sports or crowd into another girl's home to watch the display. She, who was at least a head taller than everyone else in her forest, and who had decided to walk unpainted. She, whom they loved to call so many names—their favorite was "ghihambi," which in Northwestern directly translated to "visitor," but really meant "stranger." It was what they called the DP missionaries who visited their forest to assess conditions and make sure they were proficient in the word of the Holy Father. But today, in the whispers that surrounded her, she heard something new, the sound of awe.

The pews filled and the church's wooden door shut with its classic *thud*. A girl to Sweetmint's left and a boy to her right fought with each other across her lap before their respective mothers did something she couldn't see, probably a pinch of the thigh or a twist of the ear; things she wished she had been able to experience. After a lifetime without parents, she'd learned that brief physical pains paled in comparison to emotional wounds.

Reverend Achte entered the church from a door behind the altar and slowly moved his old bones toward the wooden pulpit, his red-and-white-striped robe swishing with each step; its tightly woven mesh reflecting a sheen as pure and soft as his soul. At the pulpit, he raised his hand, silencing the congregation, then belted out a hearty "Glory, glory!"

"Glory, glory!" the church responded. Sweetmint closed her eyes, allowed the Daily Prayer's collective joy to flow through her, replacing her rumoya's nervousness with divine serenity.

"Welcome, my children. And what a glorious day it is indeed," the reverend said, his entire being charged with an aura of warmth that never failed to inspire goodwill in her and her forestfolk. Reverend Achte was the Holy Father's messenger who had served Forest Twenty-Six for over seven decades—at ninety, the oldest person most of them had ever met—faithfully guiding, loving, and protecting them from the tragedies he would vaguely reference that were happening in other, more distant regions across the Northwestern Hemisphere, or even close to their own.

"But before I get to why today is so glorious, I'd like everyone to open up their Chief Executive Rhitel Bibles." He lifted his own glass tablet above his head. "And please swipe to Proverbs 16:3." Everyone removed the flat glass slabs from behind the pews in front of them, opened their illuminated Bibles, and swiped to the correct page. Then, "Let us read it together. One, two, three. 'Commit to the Holy Father whatever you do, and he will establish your plans.' A simple order, yes? Give yourself to the will of the Holy Father in all of life, and he will bring you success. Glory, glory."

"Glory, glory," said the church.

"I share this verse with you all today, because one of our own has undoubtedly devoted themselves to the Holy Father, despite having experienced a life of hardship, sorrow, and abandonment. And it is from this devotion that the Holy Father has set her on a path that only the chosen few can ever walk on. Candace, please rise."

It was only when he said her state name that she realized he was talking about *her*. The people to her left had to move out of the pew to make way, and, walking to the front of the church, she focused on the floor, her heart *thump-thump-thump*ing all over again.

Reverend Achte extended his hands, searching for her in front of his pulpit. Once he made contact, he felt her arms and shoulders, cupped the back of her neck. "Raise your head, my child," he said. She brought her head back to meet his eyes; she was tall for an

Invisible, but he was severely tall, even for a DP. "Now, please face the congregation."

Sweetmint did as she was told, all five hundred of her forestfolk in front of her. The majority of them wore colored lenses and had the entirety of their skin painted in whatever colors conformed to their mood, the latest trends, or the longing to be something they were not. But others, like Sweetmint herself, opted to remain completely see-through—their distinct rumoyas emanating from the gaps in the pews—sitting there like missing teeth in a DP child's mouth.

"I am sure all of you know that in a few minutes, Candace will embark on a journey to Castle Tenmase, home of Mr. Croger Tenmase. For the younger ones," he said, nodding at the painted children in the pews, "Mr. Croger Tenmase, holding the official title of Director of Progress, is known by many names, such as 'The Chief Architect' and 'The Great Engineer,' because it was he, along with Chief Executive Rhitel, may the Holy Father bless his soul, who built the Northwestern Hemisphere into what it is today, revolutionizing all aspects of our great hemisphere when it was in utter disrepair.

"Candace is going to Castle Tenmase because she was selected, out of *hundreds* of applicants from recent Forestaeum Minor graduates, to be interviewed for a prestigious apprenticeship—the first of its kind, may I add—with Mr. Croger Tenmase. To study under him, learn about his hemisphere-changing inventions, and become a model Invisible for *all* in the hemisphere, not just Forest Twenty-Six or the Forest Region, to aspire toward."

Please let this end. Please let this end. Please let this end, she thought, clenching her eyes closed so hard that she gave herself a headache. Honestly, she didn't know how to feel. Whenever her forestfolk paid her attention, it was usually because of something bad, or because she had proven, once again, that she fit in about as well as one of those crazy Invisibles who thought wearing clothes, *actual* clothing, would earn them respect instead of an ocean's worth of humiliation.

She dared to open her eyes, and when she did, she almost tripped and fell backward. On all of the faces made visible by skin paint, eye lenses, and teeth covers, she saw something like pride. Maybe, and she knew she had to be careful here, but maybe she would have even said she also saw acceptance—that, for the first time, they didn't view her as a ghihambi, but a bukoneh. A mirror.

"So I would like us to pray for our Candace, or 'Sweetmint,' as you call her," Reverend Achte instructed. "Let us bow our heads, and please repeat after me. Holy Father," he said, the congregation echoing his words, "we are grateful to you for aiding our Candace in getting this far." He paused, allowing the hundreds of people to catch up. "And we know not only what this means for her, but also for Forest Twenty-Six, and all of the Invisibles of the Northwestern Hemisphere. Please grant her success today, but only if you see fit; if you deem her worthy. Nevertheless, we continue to be in your debt, for the light that you shine on all of us, every second of every day. Glory, glory."

"Glory, glory," the church said.

The doors opened, and instead of the normal spill of everyone rushing to work, school, or a detour up Twenty-Six Road, most people lingered, clogging the aisle that Sweetmint attempted to walk up. They grabbed her arms, yelling requests and well-wishes at her as children attached themselves to her legs like crusty lichen. "We always believed in you, Sweetmint!" "Please tell Mr. Tenmase that we'd like earspheres!" "If Mr. Tenmase needs domestics, my sisters and I are ready!" "That's a big castle he lives in, yes? I'd be happy to lend a hand tending to the brick, Sweetmint. Please pass it on. Mambonga."

She smiled, nodded, and let the crowd carry her from the church to the main square and all the way up the platform, where her train was already waiting.

"Sweetmint!" a voice called from below.

"Darksap!" she replied, turning in the direction of his voice.

"Good luck!"

"Mambonga!"

Finally breaking free, she entered the train, the soundproof door closing behind her. She had never been on a private train before. And, as funny as it may sound, the first thing she noticed was how spotless the beige floors were; no sticky grime, rough canvas wrappers, or spilled liquids clinging to her bare feet.

The light strips, too. They weren't on, since sunlight splashed through the doors' windows, but unlike the public trains she was used to, there was no yellow-brown film over the strips. Until then, she'd thought that's just how trains were supposed to be, including the splintered red and white wooden seats, the cracked windows that whined like a newborn as the car barreled toward its destination. Then again, DPs were known to be obsessed with cleanliness and purity. *Still, was this train special, or did all wealthy dippies have one just like this?* Even the air was different. Cooler, which made her think of the DP professors at Forestaeum Minor who would complain about the heat and lack of an indoor cooling system. *This must be what they were used to.*

Instead of entering the train and finding herself in the car's main cavity, as was the case with public trains, she stood in a chamber surrounded by four doors: the metallic one she'd come through, another in front of her, and one to her left and right—the latter pair made of wood so heavily polished that she couldn't tell what type of tree they came from. Maybe this was some sort of a test. It was Croger Tenmase's train, after all, and she knew he was capable of anything. Should she just stand in this in-between place? The ride was only about twenty minutes. The view through the door's glass in front of her wasn't bad, either; blue sky, tall trees with their green leaves, a thousand waving hands, all a blur.

To ruin with it.

She faced the door on her left and it automatically slid open. *Holy Father.* The walls were drenched in padded red velvet. One was decorated with paintings, and a window ran the length of the wall opposite it. Some kind of glass structure, dripping like hundreds of tears, hung from the ceiling, reflecting the sunlight that filtered through a roof made of purple-tinged glass. But what dazed her most was the hardwood dining table that stretched from one end of the car to the other, encircled by a dozen padded red velvet chairs. On the table were platters of colorful cakes and biscuits piled in tall cylindrical towers; trays of bizarrely dyed food—roasted purple carrots, bright-pink squash soup, grilled green corn—the steam rising off them; and shiny herbpots and pitchers decorated with intricate gold designs.

Sweetmint cautiously stepped inside the room, and a message appeared on the window closest to her: *Welcome, Candace. All of this is for you. Trust me, it's not poison . . . Or is it? CT.* She wasn't surprised by the message, his eccentricity was notorious, even to an Invisible like her. Her stomach curled into itself as she looked at the food; she'd only had that cup of needle leaf. *Well, if you say so.* She plucked a green biscuit from the top of the pile, bit into it, and moaned. *Squash, mixed with onions.* So moist; the biscuits she was used to were hard and crumbly. She grabbed a pitcher of carrot juice, poured a cup, and threw it back like she hadn't drank anything in years.

A cup of herbs and I'm done. But when she reached for the herbpot, what she saw reflected in its black and gold exterior made the biscuit and carrot juice begin to make their way back up her throat. *No. No, no, no, no.* She clawed at her neck, already knowing what wasn't there. The stainless-steel collar that those who went unpainted had to wear so hemispheric guards and Dominant Population men and women could more easily see and identify them. She must have left it in her cabin.

Sweetmint fell into one of the lavish chairs and beat her head with her palms. *You idiot. How could you have forgotten it?* Would this automatically disqualify her from the apprenticeship? Would they even let her interview? No doubt this was a sign that she couldn't follow the rules. You always had to wear your collar if you weren't painted, it was a fact of life. She'd had a checklist of things to do before leaving her cabin—lists were how she organized her thoughts— but the morning threw her off.

Sweat beaded her palms and the soles of her oversize feet. "Holy Father, please grant me your mercy. I need this," she said, slowly breathing in and out. It did nothing.

She thought back to everyone who had prayed for her. The people who really had no idea what it took for her to get to this point, or how difficult working with Croger Tenmase would be, but still believed she would somehow uplift them all just by being in the presence of a man like that. They had gathered around the fire the previous night and fed her—sweet potato pies, bowls of roasted vegetables, and bottles of homemade pumpkin, beet, and carrot juice. And all she could now picture was their well-deep disappointment; all she could hear was Rusty saying, "He'd be proud of you." No, he wouldn't. The Great Hope of Forest Twenty-Six—"a strange genius," as a few had called her—couldn't even remember her collar.

"You'll arrive in two minutes, Miss Candace," a relaxed, disembodied voice announced through an unseen speaker. Something else the trains she'd ridden didn't have. The thought of how DPs probably never missed their stops distracted her, then her own train silently slowed, arriving at her destination.

She willed herself up and stood in front of the metal door, fighting to slow her heartbeat. Before she could get a good look at the scenery in front of her, that same voice said, "Welcome to Castle Tenmase, Miss Candace," and the door opened.

The minute she stepped off the train, her bare feet met concrete that, despite the unforgiving sun, was somehow cool on her calloused soles. Below her, a checkered pattern of *C*'s and *T*'s were engraved in the platform. Suddenly, she yearned for the soft dirt and familiar trees of Forest Twenty-Six; to go back where she came from. But when she turned around and saw that the train's door had already closed, a freshwater stream of dread ran through her. *Stop. The only way through it is to do it.* She powered her legs down the platform's stairs, even as she saw what awaited her.

Two hemispheric guards—shibs, as she and her forestfolk called them—dressed in moss-colored mesh jackets and pants, stood in front of a black wrought-iron gate a handful of meters from her. Their matching caps with flat tops and stiff, rounded visors told her that they were low-ranking shibs. The worst kind, the ones who usually had something to prove.

When she was within arm's reach, the taller one with pale pink-white skin and too-green eyes stuck his hand out, stopping her, before turning to his fellow shib. "Charles, what day is it?"

"Monday, Braithwaite," the shorter one said. His face was redder, probably from too much time in the sun. Aside from Reverend Achte, she hadn't been this close to a DP in months and marveled at how sensitive their naturally pink-white skin was, simultaneously pitying them. Their visible skin wasn't only fragile, it also prevented rumoya from flowing through them, making them all body, no spirit.

Braithwaite raised his eyes to the sky. "Yes, that's what I thought. Is there a new rule that says unpainted vizzers are allowed to go collarless on Mondays?"

"Avert your eyes," the one called Charles spat, catching her staring at him. "Wow, this big one is bold, Braithwaite. But, no, I hadn't heard about that new rule. Do you think she thinks she's smarter than us?"

Her first thought: *Every young DP had didanlenses implanted into their eyes at birth, making it possible for them to see an approximation of us. Our temperature pulsing in a spectrum of colors. I know collars are the rule, but some leniency, please.*

Her second thought: *They either want a fight, or submission. Invisibles don't fight dippies, so . . .*

Her third thought: *Submission.*

She kept her eyes on their boots, the black plant leather so shiny it looked wet. "I'm very sorry. I don't know—"

"You don't *speak* unless we tell you to," Braithwaite said, his shadow stretching across the ground as he moved closer to her. She raised her head. If he was about to hit her, she'd at least want to see it coming, but this only made him go beet red.

"You know what?" he continued. "We should teach this vizzer a lesson, Charles. Let's paint her red, black, and white, in honor of our great hemisphere, which"—he raised and dropped his hand in front of her—"she obviously doesn't respect."

On cue, the sunburnt one wrenched her arms back. "Don't move," he whispered into her ear, his breath shallow. "We're going to get every centimeter of you . . . including the hot spot."

His partner went into a small concrete building bordering the gate and returned with a bucket and a paintbrush. He locked eyes with her and dipped the brush into the bucket. "I've always wondered what'll happen if you stick a paintbrush inside one of them. Will their insides change color? Will the paint turn see-through? Will we be able to see the paintbrush in their *patte?*"

"Only one way to find out," the other said, his penis turning rock hard in his pants, rubbing up against her.

"No!" she shouted.

She struggled against the shib's painful grip, and then he released her. "Braithwaite," he said. "Stop."

"Why?" he replied, red paint dripping from his brush. "Hold her still, Charles. She may be tall, but she's not that strong, is she?"

Charles nodded behind Braithwaite, in the direction of the gate. After Braithwaite turned around, he rushed into the building. There was a young DP, standing in the shade of a tall bushy tree with thick yellow leaves, watching them. He was far away enough for Sweetmint to assume he was another shib, maybe their superior, which is why when Braithwaite returned, he didn't have the bucket or paintbrush. The shibs stood side by side, straightened their backs, smoothed out their uniforms.

"Say nothing, vizzer," Braithwaite ordered.

The third one walked slowly toward them, his scent becoming stronger. Unlike the two in front of her, who gave off hints of sour pumpkins and rotten potatoes, this one smelled salty and sweet, like he'd just stepped out of the ocean covered in syrup. He wore a crisp, neatly buttoned white mesh shirt, collar open, sleeves rolled up; an equally well-fitting pair of dark brown mesh pants hugged his legs. Handwoven sandals, a sign of the rich and relaxed, adorned his feet.

He was tall, even compared to other DPs; his short blond hair and defined chin made her think he could be an actor in one of those programs her forestfolk went crazy for on the display—giving the moment a surreal quality, transporting her to a state of mind where rules ceased to exist and everything was possible. *What was the name of that program?* It didn't matter. What mattered is that he was now approaching, his casual stride at odds with what looked like concern in his eyes.

"Are you okay?" he asked.

The question stunned her; his differently colored eyes, one blue and one green, intrigued her. He looked to be about her age, too. She nodded.

He laughed, showing that even his teeth were perfect, per DP standards. A sign of weakness in her forest, as well as an insult they'd toss at their DP teachers behind their backs—"dandile," the one with straight teeth—but here, so far away from Forest Twenty-Six, his teeth looked exactly as they should. He *had* to be an actor.

"Good," he said. "You must be Candace."

"Mr. Tenmase," the shorter shib said, interrupting her daydream. He took off his cap, slicked back his hair; the taller one wiped sweat from his forehead. "She had no collar, no paint, and—"

The young DP kept his eyes on hers. "It's fine, Charles. I understand."

The two shibs, four interconnected lungs, exhaled.

"I understand," he continued, "that you have no regard for my uncle's guests, nor for women, especially one as beautiful as Candace here."

Wait, what? There was too much going on at once, even for her, who could map out inventions in her mind. Aside from this man, this *DP!*, calling her beautiful, she was even more confused about why he was defending her. She looked from the actor to the shibs and back to him, waiting for all of them to shatter with laughter and wreak ruin upon her body.

"You two are relieved of your duties."

"But, sir!" The green-eyed shib who, moments ago, was about to shove a paintbrush inside of her, stomped his boot. "You can't do that. We're State-appointed. Hemispheric Guard Director Curts himself assigned us to your uncle's castle."

The young DP turned to the shib, causing him to flinch. "Then I'll be sure he gets the word. But you two are going to walk up that platform, get on that train, and go back to whatever pathetic hole you call home and pray to the Holy Father himself that you're not sent to an underground office in the Waste Renewal Region. I hear the fumes alone rot your teeth."

"Come on," Charles said. He tugged his partner's sleeve and they both did exactly as they were told. The young DP walked to the concrete building near the gate, tapped its exterior a few times. The train's door opened and closed behind the two men. Then the train took off in the opposite direction from which she had arrived.

He extended his elbow toward her. "Come, Candace. My uncle is waiting for you."

Still in shock, she hesitantly grabbed his elbow—one of the rare times in her twenty-four years that she'd willingly touched a DP—and walked through the gate. Part of her was still waiting for him to drop the act; the other yearned to give in and play a part in this temporary delusion, whatever it was.

The checkered concrete gave way to a lawn that stretched in front of her and to her right, its prickly grass the color of pine needles. She faced left, to avoid this man's bicolored eyes, and found a dense forest at least half a kilometer away. It wasn't her forest, of course, but the sight of clustered trees reminded her that no matter what happened, she'd be back home, in her cabin, that night.

"Not going to ask me my name, huh?"

"I'm sorry, what?"

"I was making a joke," he said, his mouth spread widely, white teeth dancing in the sunlight. "I'm Sanford."

She nodded and looked away. He continued guiding them to what was hopefully the castle, even though there were only grass and trees in sight. Thoughts of his soon discarding the disguise and carrying out plans more sinister than the shibs at the gate crossed her mind, but she forced them away.

"Croger Tenmase is my uncle. Well, sort of." He paused, giving her space to fill, but she didn't. *When around DPs, never speak more than necessary.* Another fact of life.

"I'm from the Forest Region, much farther up north, and went to university, just like you," he continued. "But in downcity Rhitelville. Forestaeum Major. Uncle Croger was looking for an apprentice, and I applied. Then we sort of became like family. You're an orphan, right?"

It's not like she'd put that in her application, but of course Mr. Tenmase had conducted a background check. How could he not? She kept her eyes in front of her and nodded.

"Me too. It was . . ." He paused. "Not a great place to grow up. A lot of angry children and even angrier adults. But I did have one thing, though." He offered her another cup to pour an anecdote, affirmation, or even just a question into, but it remained empty. Still, he smiled, more to himself, it seemed, than her. "It was an illumination on my wall, of Croger Tenmase. I kept it up day and night—even had to fight other kids who tried to swipe it away because of the light. His face was the last I'd see before I went to sleep and the first when I woke up. It's what motivated me to escape, to be someone else, create a better life, where I was in control. But that sense of abandonment . . . It never really goes away, you know?"

Standing there, watching the words spill from his mouth like a waterfall she, too, contained, softened her. Here was a man, a DP of all people, who somehow understood the hole in her heart. It was then she realized that, no, he wasn't acting. He was opening himself up to her, unspooling a part of himself to show her that she could do the same, even if they'd just met. But all she could say was "I do."

She noticed the tension, the expectation of reciprocity resting in his body, finally release when his shoulders dropped, and he continued. "After my apprenticeship ended last year, Uncle Croger gave me his last name, so now instead of Sanford Sharpe, I'm also Mr. Tenmase. But please." He turned to her. "Don't ever call me that, okay? You can call me whatever you like, Sanford, Sandy, even koos, but not Mr. Tenmase."

A burst of laughter shot out of her mouth. She quickly brought her hand to her lips, embarrassed. "I'm sorry, Mr.— I mean, Sanford."

"What's so funny?"

"Did you mean to say 'khoost'?"

"'The skinned one,' right? What you call us in Vilongo? I actually prefer it to 'DP' or 'Dominant Population.' But what I don't get is why we're called the skinned ones, when you have skin, too. It's just that yours is see-through and ours is pink-white."

When she didn't answer, he bit his bottom lip. "Did I say something wrong?"

"No. It's just I'm impressed. That's all."

"Well . . ." He offered his elbow again. "I'm sure we're both full of surprises."

Surprises? That's the last thing I want. I need stability.

"Sanford." She ventured a question. "What is it that you do?"

"I make things happen."

The vagueness, after he was just so open, caught her off guard.

"You make things happen, okay. And what's it like—working with him?"

At this, he grinned. "Like walking through walls."

The lawn suddenly sloped upward, her thighs tightening with each step. She'd let go of his elbow midway up the hill, but before they reached the top, he winked and held his hand out. She climbed past it, arriving at the hill's crest, and felt like her head was floating away from her body. "Is this real?"

"As real as it ever was," he said, joining her.

Below them was a small valley blanketed in green, except for the castle, which rose out of the ground like a small mountain made of brick the color of DP blood. It soared four surreal stories high, dozens of opened and closed windows cut into its face like blinking eyes. Two round towers, pointed roofs like little caps atop their heads, stood on either side of the castle, with CaTiO3 solar panels, the same that her and her forestfolks' cabins utilized, strategically placed on them and the main structure. The Northwestern Hemisphere's flag—a physical Chief Executive Rhitel Bible, white and laid flat, set against a red circle on a black background—rippled in the wind.

It was only when she was in Sanford's arms that she realized she'd lost her balance and fallen backward, but instead of her crashing into the ground and rolling down the hill, he was there to catch her.

"Happens every time," he said as she stared into his pale pink face. The heat in her own likely registered as a deep red to his didanlenses, betraying her.

He gently set her back on her feet. "Ready?"

She nodded and, with Sanford by her side, put one foot in front of the other. The castle became larger with every stride; she smelled the earthy clay, sand, and iron that formed its bricks. Then, when they were at the bottom of the steps leading to its entrance, she stopped.

"Almost there," he said.

But she couldn't move. The castle's soaring double doors, made of wrinkleseed with a smell so strong and spicy that she could taste it, took her away from Castle Tenmase and dropped her back at Forest Twenty-Six. In front of her own cabin with a door made from the same wood, but felled, shaped, and sanded by the person she worked and failed to forget every day. After he'd put the door in place, he turned to her, and with a smile had said, "All done, Little Me. What do you think?"

"I think it couldn't be more beautiful," she replied, then and now.

"What?" Sanford asked, snapping her out of her memory. "Oh, yeah. I know. This place takes some getting used to." He took her hand, and she let him, pulling her back into a fantasy, now complete with a castle. "Listen, Candace. I'm sure all of this is a lot, but just know that here, you can depend on me."

She tried to speak, but a first-floor window creaked open above them. "Not this again," Sanford said, shaking his head.

"Not wh—"

"Coming down!" someone yelled, a thick rope flying out of the window. A DP appeared, back turned to them. He placed a foot on the window's ledge, then another, and carefully scaled down the red brick until he was a meter from the ground, at which point he kicked off the wall, let go of the rope, and landed directly in front of her.

He took a bow, and when he straightened himself, she immediately knew that this man was *the* Mr. Tenmase. He wasn't the type to appear on the display, so she'd only ever seen old illuminations of him; the stringy black hair he was now brushing out of his face, the wire-frame glasses that rested on his narrow nose, barely obscuring his high cheekbones. What an illumination failed to show was his faintly dimpled chin, the way he had a slender frame, but with sizable biceps that bulged against his black mesh sweater. Most surprising was that she towered over him.

"Score me, Sanford."

"Seven out of ten, Uncle. You stuck the landing, but looked shaky on the way down."

Mr. Tenmase threw his hands in the air. "Seven out of ten? Well, what do *you* know?"

He stuck a hand out, moving it around like he was searching for someone. When she realized that he had to be searching for *her*, she held her hand in his direction until he grabbed it. "Ah, there you are. I don't have didanlenses. You're also not painted or wearing a collar. I invented them for a reason, you know."

Her heart plunged into her stomach. "I'm sorry, Mr. Tenmase. I'll paint myself tomorrow, or I can do it right—"

"Nonsense," he said, patting her arm. "You probably won't even make it through the day, so let's avoid assumptions."

A dirt taste filled her mouth. She nodded and nodded and nodded, until she remembered he couldn't see her, and said, "Yes, Mr. Tenmase."

"Good." He turned to Sanford. "Go take care of your tasks now, son. And you"—still holding her arm, he craned his neck and sighed into her face—"let's get on with this interview, shall we?"

CHAPTER 2

YOU SEE," MR. TENMASE SAID, WALKING TOWARD HIS CASTLE'S left tower. "I didn't always live here. While most DPs prefer cities, I enjoy the solitude, not to mention the fresh air. An inventor needs to breathe. I suppose—" He stopped, stretched his arms out and spun around once. "Where are you?"

She rushed to his side. "Right here, Mr. Tenmase. I'm sorry, I didn't know if you wanted me to follow you or not."

"Candace, am I here to interview myself?"

"No, you're not."

"Keep up, then. It's easy to get lost out here."

They rounded the tower and the back of the property materialized like the illuminated pages her teachers gave her to read as a child. Clear water flowed in a stream separating the grass they stood on from the rest of the property; she could only make out a handful of gray and white buildings, but she knew, from what she'd seen at the top of the hill before she had fainted, that geometric gardens, glass houses, and other dazzling structures dotted the area all the way to the cliff and the ocean beyond it. Her mind was cataloguing every single thing she saw, creating a three-dimensional map that she could walk through on her own time, when they came to a short wooden footbridge.

"You're a quiet one, eh?"

"I'm sorry, Mr. Tenmase."

"Advice from an old man? Stop apologizing; it dilutes the strength of your words. Now," he said. "What is it that binds your tongue? Your professors swore you were never shy when it came to answering questions in class."

"It's just— I don't want to say the wrong thing."

"Sometimes saying nothing is worse than saying the wrong thing. Let's start with something simple: What do you know about me?"

A list appeared in her mind, full of bullet points, sub-bullets, and baby bullets beneath those. Inventions. Streets, parks, and buildings with his name. An origin story leading to the Hemispheric Rebirth, crowning him a hero, as well as giving him a list of titles that filled an entire page. But having him in front of her now, not a myth but a real man, made it difficult for her to know where to start.

"Though I am responsible for much of the hemisphere as you see it, Candace," he said, still standing at the foot of the bridge, "I have yet to invent anything that recycles wasted time."

"You— You're in your mid-seventies. Along with Chief Executive Rhitel, may the Holy Father bless his soul, you saved the hemisphere from inevitable ruin by inventing hundreds of technologies that allowed us to be self-sufficient. It is because of you that no one in the Northwestern Hemisphere ever starves."

He clasped his hands, brought his fingertips to his lips. "I'm disappointed."

Sweat covered her face, arms, and legs. She looked down at the stream moving below her and ached to dunk her head into it.

"Even the hemisphere's dumbest children could recite all of that," he said. "Tell me the things people say that you think I shouldn't know. The things that scare you."

Her rumoya was in conflict with her brain. She'd been taught so many points of etiquette when it came to interacting with men like Mr. Tenmase. How to speak, how to look, how to shrink. But he seemed a man for whom nerves were a biological flaw.

"That you're half crazy. That you never leave your castle. Honestly, my forestfolk don't even believe you're still alive, because we haven't seen you on the display in over a decade. There's even a rumor that you've created a tool that can lure Invisible children to your castle to pick their bones clean before tossing them into the ocean. It's why we call you 'Paklanzi.' *Bone Cleaner.*" She clamped her mouth shut.

He slowly raised his head and had enough spatial awareness to make direct eye contact with her. The sun had risen higher, spreading its heat across the property, but she was shivering. Anticipation punched against her rib cage, knowing what would come next. She was going back to Forest Twenty-Six.

A nod. That was it. Then he continued across the bridge.

Thank you, Holy Father. The farther they walked from the castle, the more she could see. A freestanding tower made of gray pitrock with a white dome stuck out of the grass like an index finger. To her left sat a rectangular prism made entirely of glass, housing plants whose wet dirt and chlorophyll she smelled, even from a meaningful distance. Clusters of other buildings and small wooden structures filled in the charming scene—his own terrestrial paradise. But if this was paradise, what did that make him?

Hands on his hips, Mr. Tenmase inhaled deeply. "Any questions about what you're seeing, Candace?"

"A million."

"Start with one."

"That glass prism. What is it?"

"A *greenhouse*, used for growing plants. I've been trying to grow flowers, but they die so quickly." His voice, weighed down with grief, trailed. "Have you ever seen one?"

"Only in illuminated pages. And even then, not many. They weren't useful, and what isn't useful is—"

"Unnecessary. Yes, I know how it goes. The hemisphere, this part included, was full of them five centuries ago. All different colors: red, green, blue, purple, yellow, you name it. 'A flower sprang from the dirt, and the blue sky rushed to meet it. But a child plucked it bare, and then began to eat it.' Do you know that one?"

"No, Mr. Tenmase. I don't."

"Chanter Krold, twenty-second-century poet. He was lamenting the loss of flowers. Imagine a world full of color. *Natural* color. Not dyed biscuits." He looked at her. "In my ideal world, flowers exist wherever the eye can see. Do you believe the world is ideal?"

She should have expected the abruptness, but she hadn't, her mind scrambling for something, the *right* thing, to hold on to.

"Candace?"

"It's not a horrible place, but it could use some improving."

"Improving how?"

"Well, the saying is true. 'No one starves in this hemisphere.' And in my forest, we have love, sports, family, community. Our basic and even abstract needs are met."

"But . . ."

"But, and I understand not everyone thinks like I do, but I know we Invisibles have more to offer the hemisphere. The majority of us are manual laborers, a selected few work as entertainers, teachers, assistant professors, and assistant reverends, but we have more to contribute. Much, much more."

His face was a stone mask with two unmoving eyes peering out at her; the seconds somehow passed slower and slower, giving her time to formulate an apology to Rusty and the others for failing.

Then the mask disappeared. "My thoughts exactly. It's easy to look around and have a clear view of humanity's present. But our future, since the dawn of man, has always been murkier. The bravest of us wade into the muck not knowing what we'll find; if, when bending down, our own reflection will be staring back or in its place an endless void."

The fact that she was still standing there was almost unbearable—his capacity to combine poetry and philosophy intoxicating. She didn't want to *work* for Mr. Tenmase, no. Sweetmint already knew, even then, that she wanted to *be* him.

"Anyway," he said. "It was toward the end of the twenty-first century that the temperature became insufferably hot and toxic for flowers and all animal life, and only hardier plants could thrive; certain vegetables, trees, shrubs, you get it. Drought, flooding, disease. The world was on fire for years, and we almost went extinct ourselves, until we made some lifesaving changes."

"I didn't know any of that. At least, not the way you said it."

"That's by design. But no need to worry yourself with that now." He nodded at the greenhouse. "I'd say we'll visit it later this week, but I'm not sure about you yet. In fact"—he moved closer, his firm gaze firing fear straight into her—"I don't know much more than what was on your application and a bit from your professors. Bright. Determined. A credit to her race. What else?"

"What else would you like to know, Mr. Tenmase?"

"Fill in the blanks." His eyes tore away from hers for a moment, then returned, accompanied by a self-satisfied grin. "No pun intended."

"I live in a cabin. A small one. By myself."

He twisted his head around as if he were looking for something.

"*Of course* you do. What, do you think I'm one of these DPs who know nothing about your people? I engineered this world, after all. Again."

"I've wanted to be an inventor as long as I can remember. Aside from having a family, it's the only thing I've ever wanted."

"Why?"

"Because I feel freest when I'm creating something, when I crawl into that space inside of my mind and find myself . . ."

He continued staring up at her. "We're finally getting somewhere, don't stop now."

"Floating," she said. "When I'm in that place, the world becomes quiet, the pain no longer exists, and I feel safe. Like anything is possible. It's the only part of my life where I have any control—where no one can ever abandon me."

"Who abandoned you?"

Her legs threatened to fail her.

"Candace." He reached up, placed a hand on her stiff shoulder. "Who abandoned you?"

"My brother," she whispered. "Three years ago."

"And."

"And I don't know where he went, or if he's even alive. As stupid as it sounds, there's a part of me that thinks if I become a big Invisible inventor, the first of my kind, then my parents, wherever they are, will want me. My brother, wherever he is, will come back."

"Where's his collar? You're aware that the State uses them to track you, right? They're not just to see those who"—he waved his hand in front of her—"are of the unpainted variety."

"Yes, I know. He left it back at our cabin. Hemispheric guards came looking for him, questioned me for hours, and took it with them."

"Leaving collars behind must run in the family," he said, winking. "But thank you for finally telling me something I didn't know."

She had never opened up so fully to a stranger, especially not a

DP. Between him and Sanford, she felt exposed, a raw wound in the wind.

"Here," Mr. Tenmase said after they exited a sculpture garden, bringing them to a row of tall bushy trees. He drove his hand into a crack between two of them and, after rustling around, pushed. A dull *click*. "Go ahead."

"Go ahead where?" The click sounded like a door unlocking, but the tree wall looked exactly as it had a second ago. She lightly pressed the two trees in front of her and they swung back, revealing a narrow dirt path with a similar ring of trees behind it.

"A maze," he said from behind her.

"What for?"

He shoved her inside. The door clicked shut behind her. "You have five minutes to find its center."

Blood rushed through the veins in her head, making her lightheaded. Sweetmint looked to her left and right, saw no difference in the two paths, and glanced upward, only finding the treetops framing a patch of blue sky. She fought the severe urge to faint.

"Four minutes and fifty seconds, Candace. If I were you, I'd make a choice, though not even trying is also a choice, of course."

She ran down the path to the right and rounded a bend. To her left was a diagonal path that maybe led directly to the center, but that'd be too easy, so she kept to the right. But after a dizzying series of lefts, rights, and more rights, and more lefts, she was completely lost.

"What time is it?" she screamed. Here, in this maze, on this property, over two hundred and fifty kilometers from Forest Twenty-Six, she was completely alone. The seconds slipped through her fingers. She went down the path she'd just taken. Air rushed from her lungs as her pulse raced faster and faster. *I can't do this. I can't do this. I can't do this.* She dropped to the ground, her bare back on the warm dirt.

"TO RUIN WITH IT!"

Staring at the empty sky above her, she thought of her forest-folk. They should have never believed in her, and she hated them for it. Their lives weren't easy, but at least tree fellers, tunnel diggers, domestics, cleaners, and every other role where you performed a defined function came with clear instruction. This. This was something else. They had no idea. They couldn't.

The sun moved above her, shining directly into her eyes. She turned and rested her cheek against the dirt. Then she smelled something new. The dirt that she lay on was dry and looked the same on every path she'd walked, but a meter or so beneath her was an almost undetectable, but very real, dampness.

Why is this wet?

She sat up, brought her nose so close to the dirt that she inhaled its particles, and coughed until tears struck the ground. *What is this?* Closing her eyes, she relaxed each of her limbs, allowed herself to fall into the darkness, plunging farther and farther until she stopped and became suspended in midair; until she floated. *The dirt is wet because the trees were just watered. No, it would dry in minutes. The dirt is wet because of humidity. No, it never reaches that deep.* Without arriving at a perfect answer, she decided to follow the smell, to let her curiosity take control.

Sweetmint jumped to her feet, but remained low, hands on her knees. She made a left, then another, until finally, after rounding one last corner, she saw Mr. Tenmase sitting on a long white chair at the edge of the first pool she'd ever seen in person, his face cast upward, basking in the sun's intensity.

Unable to stop herself, she fell to the blue and white tiles at the pool's edge, cupped her hands, and plunged them into the cool water before bringing it to her mouth. It sent pleasant shivers down her back. She looked at the water, thought how beautifully the sunlight danced on it, like a sheet of gems, then threw back another handful, and another, and was close to a fourth when Mr. Tenmase touched his soft hand to her back. "That's enough. You'll get sick."

"I'm—" She swallowed the apology. "Did I make it?"

He laughed, his cheekbones rising to the same level as his mudrock-colored eyes. "You did. Two seconds later, and it would be a different story; a different future for us both. How did you find your way out?"

"Moisture. One path had more than the others."

"Ah, that's true. From the pipes used to cool the pool. They do run beneath the maze."

He was right next to her, but he sounded a kilometer away. "Can I please sit here for a second?" she asked. "My head feels like it's about to split open like a squash."

"Well, you don't get squash soup without some squashed squash, yes? But, no, no time to rest. You, my dear, have one more test."

One more? Every cell in her body was exhausted, but she got up, wobbly on her legs, and followed him to the rear of the castle. They ascended a set of stairs that led to a balcony overlooking the back of the property, its gray concrete slightly crumbled from the humidity, and entered the castle on what must have been the first floor. Cool air kissed her face, the first time she'd been in a home with regulated temperature. She thought about the thin line between the natural and unnatural, how for whatever was gained in these minor comforts, something was also lost.

Paying no mind to whether she was behind him or not, he led her through a series of darkened hallways. The thick carpet soothed the soles of her feet; the chiller air helped her breathe easier. She'd made it inside the castle, the most difficult part behind her. *One more test and I'm there.*

Sunlight burst through a door Mr. Tenmase opened. She closed her eyes and followed him inside. When she opened them, she didn't have time to sort and analyze the immensity of what she saw, because standing in the center of the sprawling room was someone she'd never expected to meet again.

"Set it down there, Abe," Mr. Tenmase instructed the short, chubby Invisible holding a gold tray with an herbpot and two cups. The man, his entire body painted white, stood with his head bowed, but when he raised it, catching sight of Sweetmint walking toward him, she saw the recognition play out step-by-step: eyebrows narrowing in confusion as he identified her scentprint, his eyes widening in disbelief, a smile flashing across his face, and the final swallow as he restored his expressionless mask of servitude.

If she hadn't been so dazed from the morning's events, she would've picked up his stinging, metallic scentprint from outside the door. Five years was a long time to not see someone, but she could never forget his smell, though she didn't remember it being so offensive. His rumoya, usually exploding with passion, had never been so subdued, so flat and restrained. It was as if someone had taken a hammer to who he was and beaten him into an entirely new shape.

"Ms. Candace," Abe—scent name: Irony—said submissively, with the faint, highbrow accent of a DP from the Forest Region, like Mr. Tenmase. This was no longer the man who would laugh for hours around the fire; the man who always made sure she had a seat close, but not too close, to the warmest part, handing her a glass of mixed juice and a bowl of freshly charred vegetables, maybe even a sweet he'd sneak to her away from the eyes of the children who ridiculed her.

"Abe."

His gaze dropped to her dirt-covered fists, and she relaxed them, loosening her throat. "We thought you were in the city."

"City?" Mr. Tenmase said, removing the herbpot's top, inspecting its contents. "No, my last domestic, a wonderful woman named

Ilara, sadly had to return to your forest for one reason or another. But she recommended Abe here, and he's been with me for the last five years. If I'm lucky, he'll be here until the day I die."

Ilara? I've never heard of an Ilara.

Abe dipped his head. "The luck would be mine, sir."

Oh. The longer she stood there, the more certain she became that it was Abe himself who held the hammer that had hewed him into an entirely new being. But what was worse: Being the one who wielded or the one who was wielded upon? She wanted to smash his face with her open palm, to wake him up from whatever delusion had poisoned him. But she couldn't. He had to sense the rage in her rumoya, and that was enough. For now.

"That'll be all, Abe. Thank you." After he left, Mr. Tenmase patted the seat on the couch next to him. In front of it was a small, well-worn table, made from broadsaw wood, and an equally weathered armchair.

She took a seat and glimpsed one of the paintings on the walls around her. A tall man wearing black boots and a beige uniform held a large golden cup with red liquid being poured into it from a glass bottle angled over his shoulder. It was obvious that an unpainted Invisible held the glass bottle. Before she could further investigate how this made her feel, the pain from an entire individual's existence being reduced to a tilted bottle, Mr. Tenmase handed her a cup.

"Now," he said, pouring a steaming black-blue scentless liquid into it. "Before you drink this, I have to let you know that, while I am a man of science, I am also a man of faith, which the world of the future will be founded on. Not just faith in the Holy Father, but ourselves, and each other. Do you understand me?"

Not at all, but she nodded.

"This"—he touched his finger to the rim of her cup—"is your final test."

49

She looked into the cup, then up at his expectant eyes. "But what's in it?"

He waved his hand in the air. "I could tiptoe around it, but there's no use in that. It's something I cooked up that we used during the Rebirth . . . on rebels, of sorts. It seeks out impurities in Invisible blood, and if it detects an unruly, treacherous disposition, it'll kill you. At least, there's a seventy-five percent chance of it. Drink the Kool-Aid."

"What's Kool-Aid?"

"An incredibly unhealthy beverage people consumed by the liter centuries ago."

"Oh."

None of this made any sense to her. She thought she'd be judged on her ability to reason and innovate her way through problems, not by reckless tests of loyalty. Did he think he could just treat her like some worthless Invisible girl with nothing to lose? That she was, like the Invisible in that painting, no more than a prop to be positioned and toyed with? Her life, even if it didn't look like it, was worth something. She was worth something.

"I'm sorry, Mr. Tenmase, but I won't drink it." Her hands trembled as she set the cup back on its tiny plate on the table in front of them.

"You believe in the Holy Father, don't you? If you're meant to be my apprentice, and if your intentions are truly pure, then he'll ensure your protection. Plus, even if your blood is rebellious, you have a twenty-five percent chance of survival. I'd hardly say that is even a real risk. Better than five, or three, or one."

"But," she said, her tone growing weaker from the realization that the future she'd been so close to holding had fallen from her hand. "My life isn't a game for you to play with."

He folded his leg on the cushion and angled toward her, his knee digging into her thigh. "Yet what are you doing, Candace? You are living in a cabin, alone, waiting for a brother who won't return." His knee shifted, hurting her. "I know you want more, which is why you are here. Risk is the prerequisite for the life you seek. Safety is the enemy. Now isn't the time to think, now is the time to act. And act bravely! The future is paved by the brave, you know."

His words, so many words, pummeled her. Hundreds of thoughts took off on the dirt paths of her mind; wind rushed through the leaves rustling in her heart. Yes, she *did* want to play it safe. But it was this same desire that always told her to listen to her brother, and now he was gone. This same desire to never be late to Daily Prayer, school, or university. To never react no matter what her forest-folk said or thought about her. To take it, and take it, and take it, because taking it was what it meant to be Invisible, and only the foolish dared to dream bigger. Dreaming was synonymous with suicide for her and her people because so few survived it. Still, she had always done everything right, and what did she have to show for it except a broken heart and an untouched mattress? Why was she even here, in The Great Engineer's castle, if she wasn't prepared to risk, *really* risk, it all?

She sat there a moment, the faint crashing of waves the only sound permeating the room. Then Sweetmint found her bag, reached into it, and touched Rusty's compass. *Holy Father, please allow me to make it back home this evening. Alive and breathing.*

Her hands, no longer trembling, grabbed the cup. She closed her eyes, threw the warm liquid back, and sent the cup to the ground, shattering it in two on the carpet as she rocked back and forth, waiting. She felt the strangest thing just then. A new feeling whose presence was foreign to her. She wasn't afraid. No, it was the opposite: she was more alive than she'd ever been before.

When nothing happened, she opened an eye and found Mr. Tenmase's reddening face. No longer able to hold it in, he let out a high-pitched wail of laughter; his knees rising into his lap as he fell backward onto the couch. Eventually, he straightened himself out, wiping tears from his eyes as his laughter faded into a final sigh.

"That," he said, still working to calm down. "That was just warm water with blue dye, my dear."

"Why," she asked, frozen. "Why would you do that to me?"

He leaned his head back, folded hands resting on his stomach. "Because I had to see how far you would go to be here, that's why. And you passed with flying colors. The only other person to ever actually drink the herbs was Sanford!"

The door swung open and in walked Sanford, an actor entering his scene on cue, beaming. "Did she drink it?"

"She did!" His uncle clapped his hands together.

Sanford rushed to her side. "Congratulations, Candace." He shook her hand so hard that she thought he would break it. "And welcome."

She wasn't sure what in the Holy Father's hemisphere had happened, or whether the entire day was a nightmare she'd soon wake up from. But on the chance it wasn't, it sounded like she'd passed the interview, that she was officially the apprentice of Croger Tenmase, The Chief Architect; a hemispheric hero. As the reality of this set in, she did the only thing she could do.

She laughed.

CHAPTER 3

IT WAS THE ANNUAL PAINTING—THE DAY THAT EVERY INVISIBLE across the hemisphere was required to paint themselves and sit for a capture so that the State could keep their records up to date—which meant there was no time for anything. Sweetmint had been awake for hours; first, lying on her mattress, then touching herself, then, when she had nothing else to occupy her thoughts, staring at the empty mattress on the other side of the trunk. It looked as it always did: lumpy, with the canvas sheet that she washed weekly *just in case.*

The smell of corn porridge and syrup from nearby cabins filled her nose, signaling that she had only about fifteen minutes to get ready before making it to the train. But the smell kept her stuck to her mattress, thrusting her backward in time, to two decades ago, her tiny legs aching from walking dozens of kilometers.

"Where are we going?" she asked, the soles of her feet bubbling with blisters.

"Home," her brother replied, wrapping his hand tighter around her own.

She had never been outside for this long, nor surrounded by so much darkness. It felt like she was moving in place. They weren't allowed outside after dark, even if the orphanage's outdoor area was an enclosed courtyard with only one way in and one way out. And on the rare occasions she'd go to her dormitory's window to see what the world did look like when the sun went down, the light strips shining hazy blue-white from the four buildings surrounding the courtyard made it almost look like it was still daytime, except that the sky itself had fallen. This was probably why her nightmares were often bathed in blue. But out here, there was only black; the dirt they'd been walking on for hours, hard in some spots, soft in others; and dry leaves *crunch-crunch*ing as her brother led her to nowhere.

"But we left Clasped Hands," she said. "That was our home."

He stopped. She couldn't see him, but when he placed his soft hands on her arms, she knew he was kneeling in front of her. Soft hands that, in less than a month, would grow firm. At eight years old, a full four years older than her, he was already tall enough to have to kneel to be level with her.

"That was not our home, Candace. Those people, Mrs. Clutchen, Mr. Waxsmith, Miss Hollyfield, all of them—they weren't our family."

"But—"

"There is no 'but,' Little Me. You can't trust dippies, ever. And we're never going back there, okay?"

"What about . . . What about finding our parents?"

"We don't have parents."

She started to cry, heavy breathing forcing its way out of her mouth, her body shaking between his hands.

"Stop crying," he ordered. "Do you trust me?"

"Yes," she said, wiping her face and trying to stand still.

"Then there's no reason to cry. Don't you hear those people?"

"What people?"

He placed a cupped hand to her ear, told her to be very, very quiet. At first, there was nothing, no wind flowing across the empty field they walked through, no *cling-clang*ing of forks, knives, and spoons kissing the shiny white plates back at the orphanage; no children singing their bedtime hymns. But when she closed her eyes and relaxed her face, the sound of people speaking, far off in the distance, appeared.

"Who are they?" she asked.

"Well," he said, standing and tugging her along. "We're going to find out. And if they're nice, we'll stay. That will be home, but only if you like it."

They stumbled through the field until a fire appeared; hundreds of people sat around it, talking, singing, sharing food. She tried to run toward them, but he told her to slow down. When they reached the circle, the people stopped, and a man smelling of rusted metal approached them. The first thing he did was hand each of them a bowl of roasted vegetables and a glass of water. Then he told them to sit and join in, if they'd like. Another man called Candace over. "I'm Abe. And this is my brother, Rusty," he said, dust rising in the firelight as he patted a seat on the tree trunk next to him. Candace and her brother, each busy shoving fistfuls of vegetables into their mouths, gulping water to get it all down without choking, didn't respond. But that didn't stop Abe from singing, laughing, and making jokes.

That night, Rusty—state name: Kandolo; along with his wife, Freshpine, state name: Martha—made space for them in his cabin's living room and said that they'd sort everything out in the morning.

"Big Brother?" Candace whispered, facing him on the straw-filled cushions used as a makeshift bed.

"Yes, Little Me?"

"Is this home?"

He was quiet, and she thought he'd fallen asleep, but then: "I think so."

Days later, the four of them sat around the table and laughed as Rusty told them stories and Freshpine spooned corn porridge and syrup into wooden bowls. It was the Annual Painting. But instead of Mrs. Clutchen lining the children up and painting one of them red, the next white, and the third black before repeating the colors of the flag, Rusty and Freshpine asked what colors they'd like to be, if they wanted any special designs. Candace said orange with purple dots, her brother said pure black. It was then that Rusty gave her the scent name "Sweetmint," and her brother "Sweetsmoke," based on their scentprints; something Mrs. Clutchen said was just in their heads, like rumoya, their sixth sense. At the Annual Painting, the shibs noted that she and her brother had been reported as missing, and when Rusty said he'd take care of them, a senior guard shrugged and said, "More free beds for Clasped Hands" before updating their records.

The weight of her memory hollowed her out, made her want to lie in that exact spot on her mattress forever, but then she remembered how incredible the last month with Mr. Tenmase had been. She got up, stretched her hands toward the ceiling, brought them to her toes, and held it.

Six long steps later, she was in the kitchen, bent down, hands reaching into the cabinet below the sink, feeling and then finding a small can. She set it on the table with a *thud*, its contents thick and congealed, and popped it open with a blunt knife. The paint's dense, burning smell punched her in the face; she felt her eyebrows to see if they were singed; all hairs were fortunately accounted for.

A paintbrush was harder to find, but she eventually spotted one wedged between her bathroom toilet and the wooden wall behind it—dipping and swirling it in the can until it turned from the dark green of shaded leaves to the lighter yellow-green hue they took when the sun filtered through them. She propped one foot on a kitchen chair and drew the brush from the top of her foot to her knee in one long stroke, careful to cover as much of her skin as possible. Once the front and backs of her legs were complete, she worked her way up her stomach, past her chest, across her face, and did everything she could to not break down when it came time for her back; something he had always helped her with.

To her relief, there was a knock at the door. With it, the smell of burning paint riding on the sweet syrup of Darksap's—state name: Cinque—scentprint. "Come in," she said, quickly swiping the paintbrush up and down her butt cheeks.

He opened the door, but remained at the threshold, his shocked white-lensed eyes aimed at her own.

"What?" she asked.

"It's strange."

"What is?"

He closed the door, took a step toward her. "Paint or no paint, you're just as perfect."

"Thanks, friend."

His purple-painted face sank at the F-word, but quickly regained its composure. "You missed the fukhaba game last night. I scored three goals just for you." He forced a laugh.

"Ah," she said, nodding. "You want me to stand on the sidelines and cheer you on like a good zanifa. I get it. I suppose I should make sure there's food on the table for you when you get home from work, too, right?"

"Well, tree felling is hard work." He grinned, then reached up, moving a loose strand of hair out of her face.

"I told you to try university."

"Would've never got in. More hands"—he cradled her cheek with his palm—"than head. Plus, I wanted to help my uma, uba, and younger brother and sister have a more comfortable life."

"I know," she said, admiring his sense of duty. How mature he seemed just then.

"But back to what you were just saying, about wanting food on the table when I get home and 'a good zanifa.' No, Swint. Whatever makes you happy makes me happy. And I know the traditional life isn't for you. We—"

"The purple is a little loud for my taste, Dapp," she said, removing his hand and quickly changing the subject.

He turned his painted body around, and she glanced at his new muscles surging and swelling; his shrub-like hair a perfect sphere. There was something different about him; an attractive confidence moved through his rumoya that wasn't there before. What had changed?

"I don't know how people paint themselves every day," he said. "I mean, it's nice to switch it up every once in a while, but more and more of us are going painted these days."

"Times are changing," she said, returning to the moment. "It's like if you don't have a silicone bag, an immaculate coat of paint, or know what so-and-so said on last night's program, you're not real."

He raised his eyes to her own. "You're the realest person I know."

"Time to go," she said, motioning toward the cabin's door.

Blinking left eye, right eye, left eye, right eye, he said, "Forgetting something?"

Ruin! She dove into her bathroom and returned with a lens case in her hands. When she tried to put one of the orange lenses in, it dropped onto the table.

"Here," he said, dipping it back into the solution, then placing it on his fingertip.

"I can never do this on my own," she said, inhaling his sweet breath as he placed the first lens in. Everything, she saw now, was more defined on him. Somehow, over the past month, he'd grown up on her.

"It's all about patience." He grabbed the second lens. "When you know something is a fit"—he angled it toward her eye—"and you're open to it"—he popped it into place with ease—"you'd be amazed by how good life feels."

She sat there, staring into his white-lensed eyes, both of his hands on her shoulders. There was a longing in his gaze, as if he wanted to entwine his entire being with hers, and have her entwine her entire being with his; the exceptional fit, as he'd just mentioned, crafted in a way that could only be nature's doing. She felt his hunger pulsating through his rumoya, and he must have also felt a newfound curiosity thrumming through her own.

"Why are you looking at me like that, Dapp?" she whispered.

"Because I know what I want, and I'm no longer afraid to let it be known."

Sweetmint looked out the window, then back at him. "Let's go."

He held the door open for her and they set off on Softstone Path, toward the station. Doors opened and closed in the distance, people chattered in the main square, and children screamed, but there was a solid block of silence between them, until Darksap said, "I still don't get why you live here, in Donsee, especially with your fancy apprenticeship."

"What do you mean?" She closed her eyes, the sun's warmth reaching through the canopy above, caressing her cheeks.

"This." He waved his big hands in the air. "You're so deep in the forest with only a few other cabins around. Need I remind you that 'Donsee' comes from the fact that, from the main square, people 'don't see' those who live here? I mean, don't you get lonely?"

Of course I do. It's all I know.

"I like the space. And the silence. It helps me think. Plus"—she bumped his shoulder with her forearm—"it's never stopped you from turning up at my door whenever you feel like it."

He shrugged. "Seeing you is my favorite part of the day, Swint."

The farther they walked, the smaller and more crowded the cabins became. Unlike her own, these, in the area they called Nearsee, were painted in loud colors—one had a neon-yellow roof, a blue window frame, and a pink door—or covered with weatherproof canvas resembling the exterior of the glass buildings DPs lived in in downcity Rhitelville. It was these people who painted themselves every day, went to Twenty-Six Road to throw their hard-earned rhitellings away, and dreamed the deepest dreams of waking up with skin that wasn't see-through.

An air of festivity floated through Forest Twenty-Six's main square. Women, who had risen before the sun, stood behind blackened grills fanning smoking corn, squash, zucchini, and potatoes. Others wore canvas aprons, stained from their morning labors, and held glass flasks of vegetable juice for sale. Children, bodies painted all different colors, tried to hide and chase each other, while teenagers, working hard to be above it all, flirted with one another away from their parents' eyes. The forest's men gathered in groups, some sitting atop their two-wheeled carts, while others stood, discussing important matters or exchanging dirty jokes; all of them stuffing their cheeks with pumpkin seeds before spitting and turning the square's dirt into a pockmarked field where nothing would ever grow.

A dozen shibs remained motionless on the platform, in front of the train's closed doors. Their moss-colored mesh uniforms pressed to perfection; armed with whips and the power of the hemisphere. Their faces made no attempt to betray what all of the people below them could feel: hate, disgust, annoyance. Still, they were just doing their jobs, and not every shib was mean-spirited. Who knew what type of mayhem would exist without them?

Without warning, Darksap's little sister and brother pulled him away from Sweetmint; his eyes on her the entire time. She saw Freshpine across the square, and searched for Rusty, her typical Annual Painting partner, the one who held her hand during the toughest parts, but he was nowhere to be found, sending her nerves into a frenzy. *He'll be here soon. He has to be.* As she waited, people still came up to her, subjecting her to their daily demands—for her to get someone a job, pay for something, or pass on an "ingenious, one-of-a-kind, moneymaking" idea to Mr. Tenmase—so she walked up the platform's stairs, stopping midway to keep a distance from the shibs above.

"Where's your shadow?" a voice said behind her, followed by a choir of laughter.

She didn't need to turn around to know who it was.

"Probably massaging his neck from having to find Sourmint's eyes." Sweetmint cringed at the name. "Or maybe she stepped on him with those wooden blocks she calls feet."

"I hear she's so tall because she has dippy blood. I mean, look at how straight that slicked-back hair is."

"And that *paint*." The speaker sucked her teeth. "Even the sun fears ugly, and I see *no* light on those missing patches!"

Sweetmint jerked backward as one of the Rainbow Girls grabbed a fistful of her hair. She swung around, hand pulled back, ready to attack, but before she could find out which of the seven girls did it, Darksap was already standing between her and them.

"Move," she said through gritted teeth.

He gently grabbed her wrist, lowered it. "Ignore them," he said, raising his voice. "They're just jealous."

Red rolled her brown-lensed eyes. "Jealous? Don't make us laugh, Darksap. Our stomachs can only take so much."

The train doors opened, snapping the square's chaos into order. Men, women, and children formed three neat lines in front of the platform's stairs; the shibs nodded for them to ascend, one by one. She remembered the days when everyone would shove to get a seat, and she also remembered the day a shib killed a man with his bare hands for accidentally knocking him down the stairs. That was a decade ago. Since then, straight lines, bowed heads, and pure silence.

She anxiously scanned the train for Rusty but didn't see him, so she and Darksap found two seats in the middle—back-aching, cushionless seats that were the complete opposite of what she'd become used to—but quickly gave them up to an elderly couple, two of the last to enter.

"It really doesn't matter," Darksap said. "A five-minute ride up north is nothing."

She nodded, her mind still on the platform's stairs, the feeling of her neck snapping unfurling throughout her body. She wanted to fight back, but she couldn't. She'd seen the Rainbow Girls transform their hands into blunt objects and their elbows into sharp knives, as if they were trained. It was probably a necessity of their job, and she didn't want any of that.

"You know not to pay them any attention, right?"

"Who?" she asked.

"Red and them."

She forced a tight smile and turned her back to him, hoping to lose herself in the blur beyond the door's dirty windows. But his warm hand found her own. She immediately pulled away.

"What's wrong?" he asked.

"This," she said through a sigh, slowly facing him, slouching to get closer to his ear. "This is wrong."

"I don't understand. He's been gone for three years, Swint. And he's not around to chase boys away anymore. You're free to be whoever you want to be now. To be with me." That hunger was back in his rumoya; the longing in his eyes. "I'll never try to change you—to ask you to be someone you're not. This could all be so simple if we only let it."

Distractions are the death of all doing, Little Me. The death of all doing. Words her brother had ingrained in her, but it was more than that. Her rumoya, the life force that influenced all aspects of her being, including her heart, couldn't be controlled. In this moment, it just didn't beat for Darksap. He was too soft, too tame, too kind. If she gave him a chance, he'd just revert back to that, when she wanted—no, needed—more. Someone who had the power to surprise her with actions, not words.

Her hand on his shoulder, she said, "I care about you so much, Dapp. You're one of the most gentle and incredible men I know, but, to be honest, I just don't see you that way. I also don't even have time for romance, not with all of my work."

Beads of purple sweat dotted his forehead. She wondered if his previous show of bravado would finally break, see-through tears welling up in front of his white lenses, but all he did was blow out a long stream of air and smile.

"I understand. I am gentle, you're right. But I can also be a fighter, when there's something or someone I care enough about to fight for."

Before she could respond, the train stopped, and the doors opened.

"Everyone out!" a shib ordered.

CHAPTER 4

THERE WAS AN ART TO SURVIVING THE ANNUAL PAINTING. DRIVEN by collective fear, you exited the train as quietly as you entered. You didn't linger on the platform stairs, especially since a sea of DPs lined the concrete walkway from the train to a massive warehouse called the Barn. Of course, the shibs would have a hard time keeping the crowd from trying to pull out every follicle of your hair, but that was to be expected. Remain calm. And if something, like a small black bottle, heads straight for you, as one does toward Sweetmint's face right now, well, you better learn how to move like Mandla. But never, ever, stop walking.

"Look at that big one!" a DP child shouted as he pointed up at Sweetmint.

"Don't look at him!" an older woman ordered. Her pale blue eyes and straw-colored hair matched the child's. "A brute if I ever saw one," she added, baptizing Sweetmint, Darksap, and the little ones around them with spit.

Parents did their best to shield their children from flying objects and liquid that reeked of urine, as Rusty had done with her time and time again, but nothing would ever protect them from the memory of their first AP. An unfortunate rite of passage that would linger in their hearts forever. Her brother combated this by stoking a blazing hate of his own—for DPs, the world around him, and anyone who had ever betrayed him—but she could never do the same. It just didn't take, and she didn't think they were *all* bad, just a small, rotten percentage. For her, the main challenge was to not let their hate make her hate herself.

"Different year, same Barn," Darksap said as they neared the windowless concrete box.

She tilted her head upward, the Barn's roof soaring so high into the sky that she couldn't see its end. The gray concrete pillars were still there. As were the bronze statues of naked DP men holding torches, Chief Executive Rhitel Bibles, and swords. Red and black flags fell from the sky on the left and right of the building's exterior; Chief Executive Rhitel's humorless brown eyes, perpetual pout, and long face watching every single Invisible who entered. Yes, it was all the same. Except Rusty had always been there, making a joke to calm her. Now, without him, the proceedings contained a pervading sense of unease, making it harder for her to walk.

The shibs continued to push and prod them into the Barn's doors that led to dimly lit tunnels. Higher-ranking shibs, wearing black mesh uniforms and white caps, were stationed throughout the tunnel, white-gloved hands curled around flesh-tearing whips.

"You know the drill!" a shib behind them said, his voice echoing all around them. "Remain in your line, and all will be fine. Step out, and we'll make you shout."

Darksap chuckled. "You ever ask yourself who wrote that?" he whispered.

"*Sh!* Let's just make it through without any problems."

The tunnel spit them out onto a floor blasted with bright white light. No matter how many years you did this, you always winced once you walked out.

"Tell *them* that," Darksap said, pointing his chin at the thousands of DPs sitting behind tall glass panels in row upon row that stretched high above the floor. Some passed food back and forth, others pointed slabs of capglass—specialized glass for taking captures and moving illuminations—sharing the scene with friends who couldn't make it, or recording them for posterity, likely labeling the fond memory with "AP '29." Children ran down the stands, fogged the glass with their breath, their fingers drawing smiley faces that disappeared within seconds.

"You ever wear clothing?" Darksap asked. "Seems like your body would choke beneath all of that cloth, even with the mesh and perforations. You know—"

She grabbed his hand. He sharply inhaled, stopped speaking. A couple hundred red and black wooden stools were positioned around the floor's edge, directly in front of the glass separating them from their audience. A shib stood next to each stool, ensuring that there were no issues as Invisibles stepped forward in their input line, sat for their capture, then joined their respective output line—a solemn dance of forward steps, down and upward movements, and more forward steps.

Some people claimed they could smell long-lost kin; a stray scentprint, too familiar to be foreign, riding on the air. But given the strict lines and watchful eyes of the shibs, it was impossible to ever walk up to someone and ask, "Are we related? Do our rumoyas converge at some unknown ancestor?" So close, yet so far. The pain of unknowable histories never stronger for some. Not Sweetmint, though.

An hour later, it was almost their turn. The young woman in front of Darksap—black and white stripes stretching from the crown of her shaved head to her tiny feet—shook as she sat in front of the wall. A group of DP boys and girls pointed and laughed, and an illumination appeared on the glass, along with her name, age, occupation, and locale: HANGBE, SEVENTEEN, HAIRDRESSER, FOREST ELEVEN. No wonder her black-painted palms looked so smooth. Soft hands for soft clients. Sweetmint imagined that this young woman, whom she didn't know, worked in a hair salon in downcity Rhitelville. A DP owner would give her two or three rhitellings per client, while they pocketed fifty. A fact of life. But it beat being a domestic or working at Rhitel Burger.

"Smile for us, vizzer!" a boy with too-red cheeks ordered Hangbe. "Come on, you filthy *fenster!*" another said, opting for the equally hate-filled word for Invisibles, but in Vikench, the hemisphere's heritage language.

Hangbe's entire body trembled. She looked up at the shib, who was a bit short for a DP, for help. He smirked and said, "You heard them. Smile for the capglass, vizzer."

Her black and white face paint began to run, yet she still forced her lips upward, revealing neon-green teeth covers. Only then did the shib tap an icon on the glass wall. A three-second countdown appeared, followed by a flash, and she was done. Hangbe rose and joined an output line leading back to the tunnel.

Darksap let go of Sweetmint's hand at the absolute last second before he stepped forward and lowered himself onto the stool. The children pointed and jeered, but he remained still, his purple-painted face a practiced veil of detachment. She wondered where his thoughts were right now. Even though they never discussed it, every Invisible had a private place in their minds they retreated to. It was a matter of survival.

The same boy who'd commanded that Hangbe smile slapped the glass, dull thuds dissipating into the air. Darksap didn't react. The boy slapped harder, and harder, again, and again, his face transforming into a ferocious sneer. The other children joined in, and older DPs looked down at Darksap, irritated. Couldn't he see that he was there for their entertainment?

His details appeared on the screen: CINQUE, TWENTY-FOUR, TREE FELLER, FOREST TWENTY-SIX.

The shib looked at them, then brought his face centimeters from Darksap's. "What's wrong with you, *Chin-kwee*? Do you not like children?"

Nothing. Not even when he jabbed his finger into Darksap's arm. The shib looked up at the children, shook his head. "Sorry, boys and girls," he said, tapping the glass display's icon. "This one must be too stupid to understand what we're saying. Their brains are half the size of ours, you know."

A flash. Darksap stood and brushed his hand against Sweetmint's own as he walked to the output line.

Long gone was the boy with the red cheeks, probably bored. The group that now faced Sweetmint was made of all girls, eyes and mouths wide open. Brown, red, and blond ringlets curled down their faces like the reverse trajectory of smoke as they whispered to one another and pressed their tiny palms against the glass.

"She's so big," one said.

"Look at her hair. It looks like my mommy's."

"Her feet are giant, too. *Wow.*"

Sweetmint saw in the glass's reflection that the shib was distracted, so she looked at the girls and stuck her tongue out. Even though it was unpainted, she was sure that they had didanlenses, which was confirmed when one shrieked and the entire room stood still.

"MOMMY! MOMMY! MOMMY!"

Her mother, a twig-thin woman with skin so pale that you could see a river of blue veins beneath it, raced down the stands and grabbed her crying daughter. "What is it?" she asked, lifting left arm, right arm, inspecting every centimeter.

The shib turned around, his full attention on the mother and child. "What is it?"

"It—" The girl pointed at Sweetmint. "It stuck its tongue out at me!"

The shib yanked her up by her arm and soon she was surrounded by a group of them, whips drawn. One raised his, but she was immediately pulled backward. Darksap thrust his body between her and them, his powerful hand wrapped around the shib's wrist as he struggled, mid-swing, to bring it down.

"Khathazeki nakon," he said, eyes still on the shib. But worrying was exactly what she was doing.

"This vizzer's speaking Vilongo!" another shib shouted before two of them pushed Darksap stomach-down to the ground. Four separate boots pinned his wrists and ankles. A knee crushed his neck.

"He can't breathe!" Sweetmint shouted.

A whip whistled with delight as it sailed from high above and connected with his back—skin tearing as easily as a dry leaf, chest paint exposed through the gash. Within seconds, the floor was slick with purple-tinged blood.

DPs crowded the glass. Some rejoiced with each strike of the whip to Darksap's back, gripping their children's shoulders, forcing them to watch. But there were also those who turned away.

A separate group of shibs had restrained Sweetmint the second they began to whip Darksap, preventing her from kicking, punching, and biting. The only other person from her forest who would have tried to do the same, Rusty, was missing. If they killed Darksap, nothing would happen. For them and the hemisphere, life would go on as it always did. But not for her.

"Stop it!" she shouted again, but the shibs didn't even look in her direction. Though he wasn't moving, they continued to whip him, taking turns, as if they were using his back as a drum for their murderous music. There were five of them around him and at least four holding her. She'd been screaming for minutes, and that wouldn't stop them, these mad musicians. If anything, her voice was the background vocal they sought to add texture to their constant, consonant violence. She tried to float, to map every option with her mind, but couldn't. Then she remembered that, at Castle Tenmase, she wasn't Sweetmint—the feeble, agreeable Invisible these men now subdued—she was Candace. The inverse of impotence.

She stopped struggling and rose to her full height. "If you don't stop *right now*, I'll notify Mr. Croger Tenmase. My employer."

They didn't stop, but one, who might have been the leader, turned around and laughed at her. "You don't know Croger Tenmase."

"I do," she said. "Didn't you hear that he has an Invisible apprentice? That's me. Not a servant, not a gardener, and not a cook. An *apprentice*. And if you don't tell these men to stop, on the Holy Father I will have him notify Hemispheric Guard Director Curts of what happened today, which I'm sure won't be good for anyone involved."

He held her stare a moment longer, likely calculating a series of probabilities and potential losses both personal and professional. She could tell she'd planted a seed of "what if?" in his mind, and once that took root, anything was possible. Then he turned to his men and said, "That's enough, gents. We don't have time to waste on these vizzers. Not today."

One by one, the shibs, sweaty and satisfied, curled their whips and returned them to the belts on their hips before dispersing the crowd, creating order out of chaos.

Her best friend lay on the floor, his cheek in a pool of blood, his back hacked up like the trees he brought down every day. But before she could curse the men who had done this and their entire lineages, he cracked open his swollen eyes, looked up at her, and grinned a bloody grin.

"Told you I'm a fighter."

CHAPTER 5

CANDACE GOT OFF THE TRAIN WITH A POWERFUL STEP. BEFORE HER feet could touch the checkered concrete, Karl, one of the shibs Sanford had replaced the last two with, gave her his hand, helping her down the platform's stairs.

"Good afternoon, Ms. Candace."

She let go of his hand. "Good afternoon, Karl. Thank you."

"Good afternoon, Ms. Candace," Lionel, the other shib, echoed as he tipped his cap.

Their eyes lingered a second longer than usual, no doubt surprised to see her painted from head to toe.

"Everything at the Annual Painting go okay?" Lionel asked.

She flinched as the morning's scenes pulsed in her mind like a steady heartbeat. Darksap's raw back. Everyone helping him onto the train. His parents each taking a shoulder as they walked him to their cabin to heal him. A man on the train, Burningwood—state name: Cetewayo—accusing her of putting everyone in harm's way with that childish poke of her tongue. She was still disappointed and confused by Rusty's absence; maybe he had been in another line, and then in another car of the train, and they had just missed each other. But that had never happened in previous years. Was he avoiding her?

"Yes," she replied, retreating out of the memory, returning to the gates of Castle Tenmase. "Nothing interesting to report."

"You know," Karl began. "I used to work the AP before this job. Seemed like something always went wrong, and that—"

"I'm sorry, Karl," she said, nodding at the locked gate. "But I'm already late as it is."

Karl cleared his throat, glanced at Lionel, then back at Candace. "Orders are orders, ma'am. You know that. It'll just be another minute or two."

Ma'am. The first time one of them had called her that, she thought they were mocking her. She'd arrived at Castle Tenmase for her first official day, and those two other disgusting shibs were gone. Sanford had asked her if she liked the new ones, and when she said yes, he only nodded. It touched her that he did that for her. But he was also the reason she was standing in front of the gate now, the afternoon sun grilling her green scalp to ruin.

Lionel pointed beyond the gate. "There he is, Ms. Candace."

Sanford stood at the top of the hill, like some kind of anointed being, then took his time walking toward them—ease, as if it were bound to his very blood, in the swing of his arms, the toss of his head, the movement of his legs. He had escorted her from the gate to the castle every morning for the last month—he'd instructed the shibs that *he* had to open the gate for her—and she still wasn't tired of it, the effort he took to begin her days at Castle Tenmase with intention and a private moment, just for them.

"Hey," he said, as if he were meeting her for the first time. He was handsome, according to DP standards, but this—the way he looked at her, how comfortable he was being himself—captivated her.

"Are you going to let me in?" she asked.

He undid the lock and extended his hand toward her, but she just walked past him.

"You're green," he said, catching up to her.

"I've always wondered what they taught you in those fancy DP schools, Sanford. Yes"—she raised her forearm—"this color is called green."

He brought his hand to his heart and stumbled. "Ow, Candy. It's just different, that's all. And," he said, slowing down, "a little triggering."

"Triggering how?" she asked, also slowing down.

"This woman at the orphanage, Mrs. Burnstock. She liked to bake bread and dye it green, the same shade you're wearing now."

Candace shook her head. "That sounds lovely."

"It does, right? The thing is, if you were bad, she'd remove the bread from its tin, still hot as if it were right in the oven, and press a corner of the tin to your stomach. Your skin would bubble, and there'd be a strange smell, of freshly baked bread and burnt flesh, in the air." He inhaled, then shivered. "It's like I can still smell it now."

"Oh," she whispered, picturing the boy who lived inside him, and all of his pain, similar to her own. Without thinking, she brought her hands to his shirt, lifted it up, and saw the faint, angular scars across his skin, tracing them with her fingertips. "I'm sorry, Sanford."

He grabbed her fingers, held them for a second—the heat of his stomach transferring to the heat of his fingers and to the heat of her own—then pulled his shirt down and laughed.

They climbed the hill in silence. Once they reached the top—the vast, self-regulating world of the castle below them—he caught her arm. "Are you okay?"

Instinctively, she yanked her arm out of his grasp in the same way she'd done when they'd restrained her at the Barn. She touched her lips, forcing herself to breathe, to remember that those shibs who hacked into Darksap's back weren't Sanford and Sanford wasn't those shibs—that they really weren't all the same.

"I'm sorry," he said, both hands raised.

"No, it's fine. It's just that, every year, the AP reminds me of a lot. And I feel certain losses more deeply."

"You're talking about your—"

But she didn't want to talk about anything or anyone. Sweetmint, and all of her troubles, didn't exist at Castle Tenmase. Candace wasn't a prisoner of the past, she was free, so she took off down the hill, her large legs taking equally large strides, leaving Sanford to say, "Hey!" and chase her to the bottom.

Sweat rained from his brow when he reached her, turning his button-up see-through. "You're fast."

"What she is, is late!"

She looked up and found Mr. Tenmase's head, wide eyes and flared nostrils, sticking out of the window. She ran up the steps, pushed open the heavy doors, took the main stairs two by two, turned right, left, and a final right, then stood in front of his study's closed door.

"If you're waiting for an invitation, you'll be sorely disappointed," he said from inside.

Candace opened the door and was surprised to find the room in such a state of disarray. Mr. Tenmase, like every other DP, adhered to a strict code of cleanliness and order. "Even one item out of place is a holy disgrace," her schoolteachers used to say. But now, now his desk was cluttered with yellowed papers—paper! How outdated—hollowed rocks, cracked in half like a pumpkin, revealing a world of shimmering purple crystals; pencils, measuring sticks, and other antique artifacts whose names she didn't know.

Paperboard boxes flew in every direction. He flung steel trunks open only to kick them out of the way, and they crashed into the walls with vibratory violence.

"Why are you late?" he asked, continuing his frantic search.

She stepped inside, careful not to trip on a box, and took a seat on the uncomfortable couch in the room's center. The same one that she'd drank the blue liquid of death on. It was now her favorite.

"The Annual Painting, Mr. Tenmase. I reminded you last week. It's the same day every year, and—"

He pulled his head out of a box, squinted at her. "Are *you* educating *me* on the Annual Painting? Candace, who do you think designed it? The concept, the building, the theater seating, every single aspect?"

"So you're the one responsible for my friend getting his back hacked up by the guards this morning?"

"I'm afraid I don't know anything about that. But, yes, these things happen. It is public spectacle, more than anything else, that saves society from itself. Let me remind you: we're not just in here tinkering with gimcracks and knickknacks. We're in the world-building business, so put your petty grievances aside when you walk through that door."

These things happen. In moments like this, it was clear her famed mentor was a DP. But for her to get to where she needed to be, she had to understand—understand, *not* accept or embrace—that what happened to Darksap was a by-product of a larger social apparatus, which Mr. Tenmase was slowly revealing to her.

"So, what are we doing today?"

"Same thing we do every day, Pinky. Try to take over the world."

"Who?"

"Another time. You recall our discussion from last month, yes?"

"We've had many, Mr. Tenmase. Which one?"

"The chief purpose of our work, my dear pupil. The invention of a lifetime."

Of course. *The Big Reset.* On her first official day, Mr. Tenmase had sat her down on the couch to review the rules of their engagement. He took the armchair, which he said was made of natural leather, from a long-extinct animal, the predecessor of the plant-based material she was familiar with. "Hence the flaking," he added, brushing pieces of the black-brown material to the floor.

She'd grabbed her glass tablet, swiped the display, and began to take notes, but he reached over and, with a hand on top of her own, said, "Number one, never write anything down. You must keep it all in here," tapping his temple.

"I can do that."

"Good. Two, what we do here stays between us. I don't want you running back to your friends in your forest and gossiping about me, where I live, and the work we do."

I don't have many friends, Mr. Tenmase, so that won't be a problem. But she just nodded.

"Three, and this is important: don't get too close to my nephew. He means well, but he has too many wild bones inside of him, which often leads to trouble. Trouble you can't afford."

She nodded again.

After the rules, he explained that she'd be paid one thousand rhitellings per month—"and don't even contemplate negotiating"—which she didn't believe until he walked to the wall, swiped his hand, tapped his fingers, and said that the first month's pay was now in her Invisible Discretionary Fund (IDF) at the Invisible Bank of the Northwestern Hemisphere (IBNH). When she got home later that night, anxiously bringing her account up on the wall, it was all there, instantly making her one of the wealthiest Invisibles in Forest Twenty-Six.

For this amount, and the opportunity to learn from the man who made the hemisphere, she was expected to go to Castle Tenmase every weekday right after Daily Prayer and do absolutely anything Mr. Tenmase instructed her to do: mixing different-colored liquids, polishing unidentifiable brass instruments, collecting herbs from the castle grounds, even checking the pool temperature. Slowly, but surely, he promised, he would introduce her to technologies that Invisibles had only heard of or seen from a distance, eventually allowing her to assist him with his own inventions. The apprenticeship would last for a year, then she was free to either stay on or part ways in search of something else. But she already knew she'd never leave.

"You see," he had said. "I'm working on the invention of a lifetime, and you're going to help me create it. I'll explain more in due time."

"Can I have a hint?"

"I call it the 'Big Reset.' The greatest gift the hemisphere needs, even though it doesn't know it yet. But we do," he said, tapping his temple again. "We, The Great Knowers. The Prime Movers. The Protectors of Progress. Understand?"

"To be honest, not really. But I'll learn quickly."

He held his hand out. "Don't let me down, Candace."

She took his hand into her own. "I won't, Mr. Tenmase."

Hurtling back into the present, Candace got up off the couch and walked over to his desk, surveying the mess. After some light digging, she found an earsphere and inserted the small rubber sphere into her ear. A mini display that only she could see, full of virtual icons, appeared in front of her.

"Sure you don't want to read a physical book?" he asked. "They're restricted for a reason. But in here, you can read to your heart's delight, soaking up unthinkable information."

"No, thanks." The earsphere, with its infinite connections that were off-limits to Invisibles, was a far more appealing portal than dusty and decrepit pages of paper. She'd never even seen a physical book before coming to Castle Tenmase, and thought them, and their contents, to be stale. "Maybe another day."

Her eyes lingered on an icon with "NWN" in red and black lettering for half a second, causing the Northwestern News to pop up.

Scenes from Annual Paintings across the hemisphere filled her vision. She quickly flicked her eyes and saw a boxing match. A heavyset DP man, wearing only red and white shorts with matching high-laced shoes, pummeled another in red and black shorts as a bloodthirsty crowd raged in the background. When the round ended, an unpainted, collared Invisible jumped onto the elevated square, mop in hand, and wiped as much sweat and blood from the canvas as possible before the match resumed.

Bored with the violence, she flicked her eyes to a commercial. It was Drams Jams Ivy, the beloved Invisible singer—painted completely white and wearing a white suit—spinning around while praising a cleaning product. "If you got a girl, make sure she gives Mooncurl a whirl." *Wink*. She hated to admit it, but she loved Drams Jams Ivy, even though her brother used to call him "the strongest weapon the dippies ever manufactured."

Another commercial with Drams Jams Ivy came up, this time for Rhitel Burger. Rhitel burgers with pink buns, green fries, orange syrup shakes, and blue smoothies floated across her eyes, and her stomach gurgled. Her train had arrived with its daily spread, no two days' menus ever the same, but everything that happened at the AP had made her lose her appetite, until now.

"Mr. Tenmase?" she asked, watching Drams Jams Ivy bite into a Rhitel burger.

"Yes?" he replied from the far side of the room, plunging his hands in and out of a series of circular bins, head tilted back, feeling around inside as if his fingers contained eyes.

"Is there a Rhitel Burger around here? I'm pretty hungry."

He stopped his search, but remained crouched, a machine ready for activation. "Can-dace," he said, snapping her name in two. "Please don't tell me you eat Rhitel Burger."

"Um, sometimes."

Slowly, as if working to contain a strange rage, he stood, walked over to her, and removed his glasses so she could see directly into his eyes, the gray color of mudrock, which was plentiful in her forest.

She backed up into his desk, nowhere else to go. "What is it, Mr. Tenmase?"

"Listen to me closely. Rhitel Burger is mass-produced poison, manufactured in the Healthcare Region. Promise me you won't eat it again."

"You can't be serious." She laughed, thinking it a joke. "The commercials always say how nutritious it is. I mean, even Chief Executive Rhitel, may the Holy Father bless his soul, eats it."

"What's the average Invisible life span?"

"Around eighty years old."

"And DPs?"

"One hundred twenty. Give or take."

"And why do you think that is?"

"I don't know." She couldn't believe she'd never thought about it before.

"Of course you don't. That's by design. Always pay attention to the question behind the question, Candace. Ever notice how your people get tired after eating Rhitel Burger?"

She thought about the people in Nearsee, close to the main square, who shoveled down those expensive fries in pure ecstasy. But this food fatigue wasn't anything unusual. They even had a word for it, "burgered." Yes, she did feel burgered after eating it, too, which she'd done more over the past month than she ever had before.

"There's a reason Rhitel Burgers only exist in Invisible locales, just like PatchMarts, but none wheresoever we DPs live. Rhitel Burger, which I can assure you The Chief Executive has never tasted, is as harmful as it is tasty."

"How would you know it's tasty if you've never had it?"

Now he winked; the net of tension that had grown tight around her body loosened. "You know why. I invented it."

The second she thought she had a hold on who this man was, she discovered more that threw everything into question. He was impossible to map, but, to give form to the formless, she kept a tally of items related to her mentor in her mind. AP—*bad*. Rhitel Burger— *bad*. Trains—*good*. Earspheres—*good*. Glass tablets—*good*. How he treated her—*good*.

Then, "Fact or fiction: I care too much about you to let you poison yourself."

"Fact."

"So, no more Rhitel Burger?"

"Okay, Mr. Tenmase. No more Rhitel Burger."

"Thank you," he said, bowing. "Now, ready to see what I've been searching for?" He clapped and danced across the room until he reached a half-torn box from which he pulled a long white object with a black stick protruding from its top. Sitting down on the couch, he gestured for her to join him, then placed the object on the table in front of them.

She leaned in. "What is it?"

"A *cell phone*. More specifically, a Motorola DynaTAC 8000X."

"Cell phone," she repeated, giggling. The names he told her for these historical artifacts always felt like bells going off in her mouth, their uses equally hilarious. *Roomba. Snuggie. Shake Weight. K-Cup. Swiffer. Swiss cheese.* She still couldn't wrap her head around that last one. Why would anyone ever buy anything with holes in it, and how could holes increase its value? The perforated and mesh clothing DPs wore was a practical exception; unlike Invisibles, they'd never been good with heat.

"Go on," he said. "Pick it up."

She gripped the blocky object, testing its weight. "It's like one of Castle Tenmase's bricks." Her fingers moved across the glossy buttons, the oblong hole at its bottom, the perforated material at its top. "What is it?"

He shrugged. "You tell me."

"A weapon?"

"You're not entirely incorrect. But not in the way you're thinking. It was a communication device, the first commercially available product of its kind. All the way back in 1983."

"*Holy Father.* That old?" She flipped it around, observing the flat white back. "But what's this made of?"

"*Plastic.* A synthetic, versatile, and virtually indestructible material used for centuries that had a wide range of applications, but devastated the environment. You've never heard of the Plastic Wars of 2100?"

"No," she replied, embarrassed.

"That was—"

"By design?" she asked, looking from the cell phone to his face.

"Now you get it. The Plastic Wars of 2100 were part of a larger war between the Environmentalists and Modernists. The Environmentalists were against the use of plastic, the Modernists were not. It was a very bloody conflict that lasted for half a century, with Invisibles being used on both sides. In the end, the Environmentalists won, making concessions for rubber and silicone, but it was too late."

"Too late? How?"

"You've already witnessed the effects. Those metal structures way off in the ocean? They literally suck water to keep its levels down, then purify and redistribute it across the hemisphere for farming, waste renewal, drinking, and even that pretty little pool in the back. The point is, the material in your hands was outlawed. Most of it was shot into space so that it became someone else's problem."

"How . . . advanced."

"Truth be told, back when that cell phone was made, people

thought we would be far more technologically advanced than we are today—teleportation, underwater homes, immortality, that sort of thing. But war and famine reset the world many times over. And we"—he shook her hand—"are not only going to be at the forefront of the next reset, we're going to invent it, together. We will reset the way people live, think, love."

She set the cell phone down and rubbed her temples, but her head still felt more crowded than the public train she used to take to university. No room to move, no room to breathe, no room to be. According to Mr. Tenmase, they were playing centuries' worth of catch-up. She fluctuated between feeling empowered and optimistic and helpless and depressed. In a way, too much information, too fast, could be toxic.

"Now," he said, pointing to the cell phone. "We've already studied enough modern technology, including today's impromptu nutrition lesson. But to build the future, to reset the world with new technology and new ways of thinking, we need to reconstruct the past. To better ascertain just how we got here today. Understand?"

"I think so."

"Good. Let's begin."

Mr. Tenmase laid out three different tools on the table—a hammer, handsaw, and screwdriver—and asked her to pick which one she thought would best enable her to open the cell phone. After much deliberation, she fell back on her intuition and selected the correct tool, the screwdriver, then set about disassembling the device, eventually revealing an entire world of green, yellow, and silver circuitry. Hours later, all of the cell phone's guts were on the table, the use of each board, chip, and component made clear. The people of the past could be so primitive, but also ingenious in how they never stopped pushing the boundaries of what was possible. This cell phone a prime example.

"How do you feel?" he asked.

Her back was sore from leaning over the table for what felt like an eternity. She relaxed into the couch, folded her hands, and turned around to watch the sunset through one of the back windows, the sky a hand-whipped mix of pink, purple, and orange. "Exhausted, but also full. Like I've just eaten one of the biggest meals of my life."

"This was just an appetizer, my dear," he said, slapping his knee. "And you devoured it with grace. There's nothing you can't do, Candace. Nothing you can't have, so long as you stay focused on the bigger picture."

"I will, Mr. Tenmase." Her lenses, dry from the day, irritated her. "Mind if I take my lenses out and wash this paint off?"

"It's your body. You'll just be getting on the train, and it's not as if Karl or Lionel will bother you for your collar."

Rising from the couch, she twisted left and right, touched her toes. Before she could straighten out, the study's door banged open and Abe rushed in. His white-painted chest heaved as if someone were chasing him.

"Abe?" Mr. Tenmase asked. "What's all this drama for?"

"The—" He drew in a lungful of air. "The display, sir."

Mr. Tenmase swiped his hand across the wall; the Northwestern News appeared in full color.

Anna Franklin, the regional reporter for the Northwestern News, stood in front of the Executive Estate. She moved her short brown hair out of the way, revealing an earsphere, and nodded. Her thin frame looked like nothing more than a skeleton wrapped in tight pink-white skin, but the way her gaze pierced through the display caused Candace to step closer. The reporter now wiped tears from her eyes.

"For those who are just tuning in, today is a tragic day. Not only for our great hemisphere, but the entire world. I regret to inform you that Chief Executive Rhitel, may the Holy Father forever bless his soul, The Great Liberator and leader of this unrivaled hemisphere, has been murdered."

Candace turned to Abe, who had his eyes on Mr. Tenmase's still back. She placed her hand on the older man's shoulder, steadying herself, steadying him. "Is . . . is this true, Mr. Tenmase?"

She felt him breathing in, holding the air for many seconds, before gradually letting it out. He repeated this again and again, then slowly sank into the couch. "It must be," he whispered.

"I'm sorry," she said. "I know how close you two were."

"A long time ago, yes," he replied, head in his hands.

"But how is this even possible? Someone getting into the Executive Estate and murdering him?"

"I haven't a clue. Something like this, or anything close to it, was supposed to be impossible."

"What can I do, sir?" Abe stood behind his employer, ready. "Anyone I need to get on the earsphere?"

Mr. Tenmase reached his hand backward, patted Abe's arm. "No, nothing right now. Let's just wait and see what they say."

Shibs, toting golden weapons she'd never seen before, moved behind Anna Franklin. Politicians in tight-fitting perforated suits passed in the other direction. Elderly holy figures, mesh robes flowing behind them, pressed glass tablets—featuring Chief Executive Rhitel Bibles—against their chests as they appeared and, upon realizing they were on display, immediately disappeared. The reporter, slightly more composed, brought a finger to her ear and nodded.

"We're receiving information right now," she said, nodding again, then looking into the capglass. "Authorities claim that the number one suspect is an Invisible, Shanu, pictured here at twenty-five, three years ago."

Candace saw the Invisible, his skin painted a shade of red so dark that it looked as though he were covered in DP blood. Defiance, obvious for anyone to see, burned behind his yellow lenses with the intensity of a sun that would never set. She didn't understand what she was seeing. A jaw, one that could have been carved from the world's strongest wood, was still visible underneath a beard. Thick lips that pressed into each other. Sand-like stubble covering a shaved head.

"Sweetsmoke?"

Abe ran toward her as the world spun. Too slow, only the carpet was there to soften the blow.

"Candace?"

"Sweetmint, wake up."

Her head was swirling, but she forced her eyes open, did her best to center them on the two men above her.

"There you are," Mr. Tenmase said.

From the hard, lumpy cushions beneath her, she knew she was on the couch. "How long was I out for?"

"About fifteen minutes," Abe replied.

"Yes, not too long, but long enough for Abe to fill me in. The Invisible, Shanu—he's your brother? The one you said went missing?"

Her mind was a blur. She closed her eyes, bit down hard.

"It's probably best you go back to your forest, Candace. I'm sure someone from the State will visit you soon, and I can only advise you to tell them the truth: that you haven't seen him in years and don't know where he is."

Anna Franklin was still speaking in the background. "Heads of Hemisphere from the Northeastern, Southeastern, and even the Southwestern have offered their condolences. Hemispheric Guard Director Curts will make a hemispheric address in thirty minutes, but he has already assured us that he will capture this Invisible before the five-day mourning period is over and elections are held. More to follow, and may the Holy Father bless the Northwestern Hemisphere."

"Now and forever," Abe whispered.

Sweetsmoke's face appeared on the display again, SUSPECTED MURDERER OF CHIEF EXECUTIVE RHITEL scrolling in white letters beneath it. Candace leaned over and vomited sour-smelling liquid all over Mr. Tenmase's pants and shoes. Instead of moving away, or shrieking in disgust, he leaned toward her, held her still-green hair back. "Let it out, my dear. Let it all out."

Abe rose and hurried to the door. "I'll go get something to clean this, sir."

"I'm sorry." She wiped her mouth, rendering it see-through and therefore slightly more difficult for Mr. Tenmase to locate as he brought a glass of water to her face. But he found it, tilted the glass toward her lips, and she slowly drank its contents before shoving the glass away.

"He didn't do it, Mr. Tenmase." She tried to stand, but he guided her back to the couch. "I know he didn't. Shanu's not capable of murder."

"You haven't seen him in three years, Candace. In my many decades of life, I've learned that you never know what someone is capable of until the opportunity presents itself."

"No," she said, righting herself. "*I* know what my brother is capable of. It doesn't matter if I haven't seen him in three years or thirty. He was always a bit radical, sure, but this—he would never kill someone . . . and I need you to help everyone else see that."

Abe entered with a towel, a spray bottle of cleaner, and a bucket of water, but Mr. Tenmase, eyes still on Candace, said, "Give us a minute, Abe. Please."

"Yes, sir."

She watched her mentor watch her. "I'm afraid I don't have the power you think I do," he said. "When something like this happens . . ." He looked up at the ceiling. "Well, *nothing* like this has ever happened. But what I'm trying to articulate is that the machine is already in motion, and it won't stop until it's fed."

"*You* created this machine, Mr. Tenmase," she said, stabbing the air near his face. "All you need to do is get Hemispheric Guard Director Curts on the earsphere and tell him to stop. Tell him that there has to be another explanation, and we'll figure it out together."

His slender hands gripped the drinking glass tighter, and he looked into it, as if it might contain the answer.

Pure horror crept across her mind, like dense fog in the early morning. "They're going to hunt him. Even though he's innocent, they're going to hunt my brother and do indescribable things to him for all the hemisphere to see. Just like Forest Seventy-Eight."

"You don't know that." He reached his hand out, but she slapped it away.

"It's *you* who doesn't know anything, Mr. Tenmase." She stood, her body pushed and pulled in a million directions. "What was all of that talk hours ago, about how valuable I am to you, how much you *care* about me?"

"Candace."

"No!" She looked down at him. "All of this talk about the work we're doing together, the world we'll create. None of it matters if it's a world without my brother in it. None of it. You're *The Chief Architect*," she spat. "The Great Engineer. So if you're so in control, so smart, why can't you see that I need your help? You don't care about me, you're just another DP living in a fantasy!"

He jumped up, his face, despite their height difference, as close to hers as possible. "You're angry? Good. Use it! You're sad? Even better. Channel it! You feel *betrayed*? Turn it into an extra limb and harness it. Do you think you're the first person to feel these things? This castle"—he picked up an earsphere—"these inventions. They're the stuff of sadness. The artifacts of anger. The by-products of betrayal. You must rise above the nonsense that threatens to pull you under, Candace. Rise above, and exploit its value."

"Nonsense?" she said. "My brother's innocence isn't nonsense,

Mr. Tenmase. All I'm asking is for you to pick up the earsphere and make one call. That's it."

"It's not that easy. One day, when you're fluent in the ways of men and power, you'll understand."

Abe returned with the bottle, towel, and bucket still in hand. "Everything okay?"

Her silent standoff with Mr. Tenmase stretched on until Candace finally shook her head and said, "I'm leaving."

"Fine. See you tomorrow. *On time.*"

Marching through the door, she heard Mr. Tenmase say, "Let her go. And please prepare some herbs for this evening's guest."

There was a small group of shibs by the gate now, reinforcements, probably, who eyed her with suspicion as she walked up the platform's stairs. The train's door opened, but she didn't enter, not yet. Suddenly, the air was more stifled, the lights brighter, and the future never hazier. Except for one thing.

I'm going to find you, Big Brother. No matter what it takes.

CHAPTER 6

LOCAL MANAGER II STEPHAN JOLIS TOOK HIS TIME WALKING DOWN the platform's stairs. A crowd of hemispheric guards lowered their heads when he approached, and one rushed to unlock the front gate of Castle Tenmase.

"Would you like me to accompany you, sir?" the guard asked, likely thinking that he could use this opportunity to get ahead—something that Jolis found both disgusting and admirable.

Jolis moved the one-point-nine-six-meter structure that was his body through the gate, past the HG, then stopped. He turned around and found the young guard's eager blue eyes, which were identical in color to his own and reflected the same desperate hunger he'd had years ago.

"Accompany me?"

"Y-y-yes, sir," the boy, probably fresh out of the academy, replied.

"And what makes *you* think that *I* need to be accompanied?"

"No, um . . ." He looked down at his black boots, glistening with moonlight. "I meant no offense, sir. But with what happened to The Ch-ch-chief Executive, may the Ho-ho-holy Father bless his soul, you can't be too sure."

The twenty-eight-year-old local manager raised his index finger, beckoning the HG to come closer. His face lit up, and with only a few long strides, he stood in front of Jolis, completely blocking him from the other guards' views. "I'll be happy to—" The boy coughed and bit his tongue at the same time, a red trickle spilling down his lip. Tears welled up in his eyes; he no doubt wanted to scream, but Jolis knew that sound wouldn't be able to travel up his constricted chest, out of his puckered mouth.

With the boy's balls in his grip, he brought his lips to the young guard's ear, whispering, "Just checking," before crunching them further. "We're at war, and every self-respecting DP man is going to need a pair of these to survive. Understand?"

Through clamped eyes and a clenched jaw, the boy nodded, then collapsed when Jolis released him.

The political hopeful closed his eyes, inhaled the night's humid, salt-filled air, and crossed the lawn. At the top of the hill, he saw Castle Tenmase, most of its rooms dark except for Croger's drawing room and a dining room. The castle itself—lit by a combination of automated torches running across its brick facade, electric spotlights shining from the ground—glittered like the short dresses made of tiny diamonds that upscale girls wore out in the city. He'd had a few of these girls, but there was something about them he couldn't stand: it was like they were made of nothing but air.

Walking down the hill, he thought about how marrying one of those girls would probably be a good move; someone obedient, who fit the type that the hemisphere expected him to be with. But should he find one and marry her in five days, before the election? That would be too obvious. No, he'd do it after he won. *If* he won. She would be tall, with skin the color of porcelain, and a mind just as fragile—easier to dissuade from having children, making the most—

The doors swung open as he was mid-thought, not even realizing he had already reached the castle. Standing inside was Croger's fat servant with a pained look on his face, when he had nothing, nothing at all, to complain about. "Good evening, sir." He stared at Jolis with his usual look of apology. If Jolis had told him to get on all fours and allow him to ride him until his knees gave out, he'd do it. That type of servitude, that type of submission, was infuriating.

"How many times do I have to tell you? If you can't keep your dirty vizzer eyes off me, I'll rip them out."

The servant dropped his eyes to the floor. "I'm sorry, sir. Mr. Tenmase is waiting for you in his drawing room. May I take your jacket?"

"And let you actually touch me?" He dusted off his coal-gray suit as if this sorry excuse for a man *had* placed his grimy little hands on him, then walked up the main staircase, his mind racing faster with each step. Once he reached the drawing room's door, he closed his eyes, forced his thoughts to slow down, and focused on why he was there: to find a way forward.

He opened the door and there was Croger in his usual armchair, reading. "Did you come from the train alone?" the older man asked, his eyes still on whatever rotting relic he held.

It was in this drawing room, three years ago, that Jolis first saw a physical book, and he still wasn't used to the sight of it. Having grown up with illuminated pages displayed across walls, desks, and later glass tablets, he hadn't even known they'd existed.

"I did."

"That was foolish of you, Stephan. I'm sure one of the men outside would have accompanied you. We can't take any chances now."

He grinned. "One did try, but I politely said no."

Croger side-eyed him, gestured for him to sit. "Not there," he said, pointing at a dark spot on the couch.

Jolis patted the couch, found a dry area, and sat. "Do I want to know why part of your couch is wet, Croger?"

"Questions are to fools as silence is to the wise. A means of getting by, getting by, getting by." He reached across the table, gripped the handle of a white herbpot with red, white, and black flowers painted on it, and poured Jolis a cup of rhitelmint and sweet majortel, from the smell of it.

"It's nothing, really. Abe just cleaned it."

The taste of mud filled Jolis's mouth. "I can't stand that vizzer. You tell me to be careful, yet you have one of them"—he pointed to the drawing room's door—"living with you. He could cut your throat in the night, and it'd be hours before Sanford finds you." Jolis's friend poured a cup for himself and laughed.

"Abe? He's the most faithful person I know. I treat him with respect and even gave him an errand pass so he can come and go as he pleases when I don't need him. He poses no threat."

"You're so sure. Ever hear the saying 'Hubris beheaded the hemispherian'?" Jolis leaned back on the couch, the steaming cup of herbs and saucer resting on his knee. "And what about the young one you've allowed into your house for the last month? You think she's not going back to her forest and plotting how to steal your precious paintings, tools, and all those worn-out physical books you're not supposed to have in the first place?"

"Candace isn't a thief, Stephan. She's a model apprentice and instrumental to my work." He set his herbs down on the table. "But we have more important topics to discuss. Where would you like to begin?"

Such a simple question, yet it required a colossal effort to answer. Jolis sipped his herbs, allowed the hot liquid to make its way down his throat and loosen all the tension stored in his limbs.

"We've spent years getting ready for the day The Chief Executive, may the Holy Father bless his soul, died. But I never pictured it happening so soon. And not in this way. A vizzer pulled this off, can you believe it? They wouldn't even know the sun was out if we didn't make them go to Daily Prayer, or how to get anywhere if we didn't tell them where to go, or what—"

Croger grabbed Jolis's knee. "It's tragic, Stephan. But in tragedy there is opportunity. And here is yours. The debates begin tomorrow, and you've already been voted as the Legacy Coalition's candidate. As long as you don't self-sabotage, by the end of the week you will be the next Chief Executive of the most powerful hemisphere on the face of the Earth. I can't understand why anyone in your position would look so forlorn."

"I'll tell you why," Jolis said, slamming his fist on the table, cups rattling. "Williams Washington."

"Have sense, Stephan. You mean *Local Manager IV* Williams Washington?" Croger swatted his hand in the air. "He's nothing more than a stand-in. And this new Community Coalition is made up of silly men who wouldn't have dared band together when The Chief Executive was alive. Stop fretting."

Jolis jumped to his feet, pacing around the room. "You're not in the Gallery. You haven't seen the group of men walking out with him growing larger over the last couple of years, even if they never formally called themselves the Community Coalition. He has sympathizers, Croger. Men The Chief Executive, may the Holy Father bless his soul, didn't even know were betraying him because they were such good actors, fit for the display. I'm sure we'll see them in the next *Never-Ending Glory*."

"Do you know what a *bug* is, Stephan?"

"No," he said, turning around. "But I'm sure you're about to tell me."

"I didn't think so." He grinned. "Folks in the midregions are spared lessons in historical organisms."

Years ago, these minor jabs at Jolis's upbringing would result in raised fists, an unrestrained eruption of fury. But when he realized how key Croger was to his destiny, and that The Chief Architect was more friend than foe, he learned to calm down. They still stung, though.

"They were little winged beings. Minor annoyances," Croger continued. "Sometimes they'd fly in your face or prick you with tiny needles in their bottoms. But if and when they did, all you needed to do was simply flick them away . . . or crush them."

"Washington is not a *bug*, Croger. He is a man."

"You'd be surprised at how fine the line is between those two things."

Jolis shook the air with his massive hands. He wanted to scream, to rip Croger's paintings from the walls and shatter the castle's glass windows, but he settled for kicking a few paperboard boxes on the far side of the room.

"Ever since I walked into the Gallery, I knew he'd be a problem. Just from the way he moved, I could tell he was ambitious. And then"—hands on his hips, he raised his face to the ceiling, laughed—"he started to propose all of those ridiculous ideas. You remember, don't you?"

"Yes, I—" But Jolis wasn't listening.

"The removal of city passes for vizzers. The ability for them to attend DP universities. Higher pay, voting rights—*voting rights*, ha!—increased focus on regional mortality rates. We laughed at him day in and day out, and the only reason The Chief Executive, may the Holy Father bless his soul, didn't have him executed for treason is because he knew none of it would ever actually happen. He, in his older years, thought leniency led to loyalty. But now look, this man is going to put his ideas on display for five whole days and who knows what will happen?"

Croger was at his side now, neck snapped back so he could lock eyes with his protégé. "Are you about done?"

The young man's arms were shaking, a thick vein protruded from his neck, and all he wanted to do was bang his fists until something broke. The thought of everything they'd worked for being undone by Washington, a coward dressed in local manager's clothing, made him consider, only briefly, killing him.

Continuing to try to catch Jolis's shifting gaze, Croger said, "Do you remember when we first met?"

Jolis squeezed his eyes shut at the stupidity of the question. How could he not? He'd been in downcity Rhitelville for the whole of twenty minutes. Enough time for him to walk into a clothing store and, when the attendant was distracted, steal a beige linen short-sleeved button-up and a pair of pants to match. It was exactly what the model wore on the store's illumination on its glass window, and he looked so . . . at ease.

He'd tucked the shirt and pants under his armpit, vanished from the store before anyone noticed, then found a bathroom in Rhitel Park and quickly changed, tossing his dirty T-shirt and pants into a trash can on the way out. From there, he made his way to the Gallery of Rule; men in ironed suits with perfectly clipped hair smiling and laughing as they walked up the marble stairs, past the rounded columns, and through the open doors. Suddenly, a tap on his shoulder.

"If you're going to steal from Ferdinand's, might I suggest that you remove the evidence before wearing?" The man tore a canvas tag from the shirt's collar, and when Jolis spun around, he was face-to-face with an older man who had an energy just as youthful and electric as his own.

"I—" he began, ready to defend himself against this accusation, but the man held up a slender hand.

"Our little secret. But tell me, what business do you have here, at the Gallery of Rule?"

There was something abnormally tranquil and compelling about this stranger. He brought to mind a mighty river. "I don't have any, sir, but I'd like to."

"Croger Tenmase," the man said, extending his hand.

Jolis stood there, staring into his eyes, unsure if he was falling into a trap or toward the future. Was this *the* Croger Tenmase? But he didn't succumb to fear; he'd risked it all since he was a child, and risk, he knew, was a requirement for success. "Stephan," he said, shaking the man's hand. "Stephan Jolis."

"Well, Stephan. I was going to go up there"—he nodded to the Gallery door—"but I think my time would be better spent with you. Are you hungry?"

A smile tore across his handsome face. "Starving."

Now, years later, Jolis stared into those same eyes, still full of power and possibility. But look how far they'd come. "You called me a 'glitch in the system,'" he said to Croger.

"I didn't know what else to call this daring young man who'd somehow survived in a desolate part of the midregion for so long that he wasn't even registered with the State. You looked so hungry, but in that hunger, I saw someone who would do whatever it took to be in control of their own destiny. Why else do you think I nurtured you, helped get you elected, and guided you through every obstacle to here, so close to the door of the Executive Estate?"

"Because you want something. But I'll admit that, after three years, I still don't know what that something is."

Croger banged his fists on Jolis's chest, some actual force in them. "You are the disruption we've needed for a very long time, my boy. Can't you see? You are going to blow up the whole system. You, with your incendiary ideas, will push the machine past its breaking point." He shook his head, as if Jolis still wasn't getting it.

It was hard to follow his mentor when he got on this philosophical track. But he did like the sound of "blow up the whole system." Winning was the focus, everything else was just the details.

"What's our angle?" Jolis asked. "We only have five days."

The door creaked open. Abe poked his oversize head inside. "Do either of you need anything?"

There was no stopping him. Jolis rushed to the door, wrapped his hand around Abe's throat, and spit into his face. "Hasn't your master ever taught you to never interrupt DPs?"

"For the sake of the Holy Father, Stephan! Let him go!"

Abe looked up at Jolis pleadingly. "Please, sir," he whispered, using what little air he could gather in his lungs. Jolis let go, shoved the servant outside, and slammed the door shut.

Back in his armchair, Croger took a sip of herbs, nodded at the closed door. "There's your angle."

"What do you mean?" Jolis smoothed his suit, flattened his hair, and wiped sweat from his face as he returned to the couch.

"I think it's safe to say that you and I don't share the same views of the world, Stephan, yes?"

"You do have your . . . sensitivities."

"Do you ever look around and think, 'With every advantage that humanity has been afforded, *this* is the best we dreamed up?'"

"It's hard not to," the young man said.

"Exactly. Utopias aren't possible, nor are they desirable. But a system, a machine, that has the ability to improve upon itself as necessary, with the goal of human progress—kindness, empathy, respect—*that* is ideal. And it is completely possible."

Jolis narrowed his eyes. "I'm not following you, Croger."

"With my help, Rhitel reshaped the world in his image in less than a century. Now I'll do it in a quarter of the time."

"Don't you mean we?"

"Yes, of course. *We.* The truth is that our hemisphere's current concerns—interhemispheric relations, Invisible rights, DP supremacy—it's all the same from where I sit. But invention, the Big Reset, *that* is what excites me. And a creation of that magnitude requires suffering, great change, and great pain. The explosive kind, which is where you come in."

Jolis took a sip of his herbs, lukewarm now. "How?"

"You're going to channel the hatred you have for Invisibles, evident by how you just nearly murdered my servant, into victory. The hemisphere is hurting and craving someone to blame, so who better than this Invisible they say is suspect number one? You will make Leon Curts's hunt your hunt, use the murder as your platform, and build on the fire that is already burning"—Croger rounded the table, placed his palm on Jolis's chest—"in your heart, the hearts of the men of rule, and the hearts of every DP in the Northwest."

"But I can't stand him. If Leon was any softer, he'd be a sack of jelly."

"Any successful partnership thrives on a modicum of humility, Stephan. You and Leon, our *esteemed* Hemispheric Guard Director, can suspend the enmity—along with your ad hominem aspersions—for a few days, can't you?"

It was so simple he hadn't even considered it. All he had to do was be himself. Double down on his rhetoric, hone the hatred, and forge an alliance with Leon, no matter how forced it was, to help him find this dangerous murderer. Or at least pretend to for as long as it served his own purposes.

"I can see the seeds sprouting," Croger said. "We also have an insurance plan. Do you know what that is?"

"You already know I don't."

"Centuries ago, before we had the preventative medical measures we do now, celgens and other rapid-recovery technology, disease was rampant in this hemisphere and beyond. If someone fell ill, they had to pay in order to get better, or else they wouldn't be helped. An insurance plan was something you paid monthly so that you could receive help whenever you needed it."

Jolis thought about it for a second. "That sounds made up. That a society would endanger its own population instead of ensuring it was as strong as possible." Then, "What's *our* insurance plan?"

"The Invisible, Shanu? My apprentice is his sister."

"You have the murderer's *sister* working for you? Are you out of your mind?"

"I have it under control. All I'm proposing is that we can use her, if necessary."

"Use her how?"

"Oh, in a myriad of ways. To draw Shanu out. Aid Leon. Something else. What is it that you always like to say? 'In changing times, only the useful survive'?"

Jolis bit his knuckle, the corner of his lip curling upward.

"Good," Croger said. He walked over to the wall, activated the display, and joined Jolis on the couch. "Now, Leon is due to speak any minute. Let's sit back and watch our future unfold."

CHAPTER 7

THE TRAIN PULLED INTO FOREST TWENTY-SIX. ALL SEVEN OF THE Rainbow Girls stood on the platform. Blue admired her nails. Green and Indigo were arguing about something. Violet touched up her lips. Yellow helped Orange flatten the tiny edges that framed her face. Red, seeing Sweetmint stumble through the train's doors, peeled her lips back in a tight grin, teeth covers glowing under the platform's light strips.

"Wow, Green." Red grabbed her shoulders from behind. "Looks like Sourmint is coming for your spot."

Green let out a solitary sound, something between a laugh and a sneeze. "As if."

Sweetmint tried to move past them, but Yellow, at least half a meter shorter than she was, pushed her back. "Not so fast, Sourmint. No 'ebusukhoob,' or anything?"

"Good evening," she replied, just wanting to get to her cabin, close the door, and sleep for as long as possible. To put an end to this never-ending day.

Orange sucked her teeth. "How rude. Think you're better than us? Must be all that dippy blood." She reached her long-fingered hand up and yanked Sweetmint's hair, hard.

Not this, not now.

"Heard about Sweetsmoke," Red said, shaking her head.

At this, Sweetmint shoved Orange away. "How?"

Red reached into her red silicone bag dotted with real *and* really expensive diamonds. She held a fist toward Sweetmint, then unfolded it. An actual earsphere, highly illegal for any of them to use, let alone possess. "Just one of the many perks of what we do. But you wouldn't know anything about that. Sourmint, the innocent one, who only ever did what her big brother told her. Who's never even lived."

She wanted out. She had to get away. But her body, immovable, had other plans. She knew the Rainbow Girls could sense the fatigue, fear, and confusion that radiated from her rumoya, yet there they were, circling her, closing in.

"It's *such* a shame about Sweetsmoke," Blue said, head tilted back, eyes on the night sky. "He was so zuhle. Strong, silent, and just *sheee*. A real marfana. They don't make them like that anymore."

Orange closed her eyes. "And those lips." She clapped her hands together. "Like two fat sweet potatoes on top of one another! I'd wait for the AP every year to get a good look at them. Yum, yum, yum."

"You know," Indigo began. "I always wondered about him." She turned to Sweetmint. "Did he not like women? He never paid any attention to us. And if he didn't like us, there *must* have been something wrong with him. A hamban, probably."

One. Two. Sweetmint stood in front of Indigo, her shadow turning the plump Rainbow Girl's skin so black it was blue. "Sweetsmoke never wanted any stupid injakas like you. Why would he? Your legs have touched more men than the sun. Now let me through."

They set their bags down, removed their teeth covers, and stood, waiting to see which of them would do the honors of hitting her first, when bright lights appeared; all of them, Sweetmint included, flinched as a train silently pulled into the platform.

"Time to go," Red said with a wink.

The girls bumped Sweetmint as they broke away and entered the train, but Red, the last one, put a hand on Sweetmint's shoulder. "Want to come? It may do you some good. With a fresh coat and a few tight braids, I'm sure some of the less particular men would love you."

Sweetmint looked down at Red's hand, then to her face, and spat onto the platform. "I wonder what your dead mother would think if she saw you now, Sharpleaf. That's the name she gave you, isn't it? Before you started to paint yourself and do what you do."

Red's cheek twitched. For a moment, Sweetmint regretted her words, but then Red's full lips parted into a smile. "She would think I'm a survivor, *Candace*. Just like every other self-respecting Invisible in the hemisphere with the courage to see the world for what it really is." She stood on her toes, closer to Sweetmint's ear, and whispered, "But the better question is: What. Are. You?"

With the Rainbow Girls gone, she was finally able to leave. Light and sound filtered through the tiny crowded homes she passed in Nearsee. Children laughed. The smell of Rhitel fries drenched in salt seeped out of their cabins. For a few minutes, all she saw through the windows lining Softstone Path were entire families, fully painted, eyes glued to their displays. She wished she could escape—to be them, even for a few hours. There was one sure way to do that: PatchMart never closed, and was only behind her and up Twenty-Six Road. But no.

She started to run. Halfway between the main square and her cabin, she hooked her foot on a loose root, tumbled, and lay flat on her back. Tears flowed down both sides of her cheeks; she pounded the dirt as hard as she could with the backs of her fists, wailing.

When her throat was raw and her eyes ran dry, she opened them, the night sky an ocean of stars. There, directly above her, were the Three Teachers. It was Sweetsmoke, so long ago, who had first pointed them out to her.

———

"One, two. Good," Rusty said, dirt shifting on the ground as he moved his feet. The sun cooled to orange as it retired for the evening, spreading light wide across the field that Rusty and Sweetsmoke sparred in. Sweetmint's four-year-old self sat in the comfort of Freshpine's lap, both of them watching the men move, grunt, and strike. Men, because even though he was only eight, Sweetmint had never known her brother to be anything like a boy.

"Move," Rusty instructed, the sound of his hand slapping against Sweetsmoke's head making Sweetmint flinch.

"But I can't see you," Sweetsmoke replied, the too-big boxing gloves rising and falling in front of his face.

"What's your point?" Rusty hit him again. "You think that you can see the enemy? Those dippies in the Executive Estate, making all the decisions. Have you ever *seen* them?" Something popped in the air, and Sweetmint knew that it was Rusty's open palm connecting with Sweetsmoke's cheek. "Have you?"

"No," her brother said. He jabbed his left hand as hard as he could, but Rusty wasn't there. The momentum carried him forward, and Rusty pushed him to the dirt, parts of his sweating face, chest, and legs becoming visible with the dark particles of earth.

"There's a war happening, Sweetsmoke. And I know you know this, otherwise you wouldn't have come here. You'll either be ready or you won't. Because when the time comes, you'll have to do whatever it takes to protect the people you care about."

"That's enough," Freshpine said. "Time to eat and sleep."

That was during their first few months in Forest Twenty-Six. Before Rusty and Sweetsmoke built the cabin that she and her brother would live in for over a decade and a half. Before Rusty obtained a special travel pass and began entering Sweetsmoke into boxing competitions, which would take her brother to forests up and down the region, pitting him against larger boys, who would beat Sweetsmoke senseless until they couldn't. During the day, Rusty taught him how to properly fell a tree—in the evenings, how to fell a man. Their guardian was never like this with her, which made her view him as two people: her Rusty, and Sweetsmoke's Rusty. One soft, one hard, but both loving.

Back then, she was always having nightmares. About what, she couldn't remember. The screaming, sweating, and jolting up from the makeshift bed she and Sweetsmoke shared in Rusty's cabin hurt her neck for days. But her big brother was always there, already awake, taking her into his arms, his newly rough hands running their fingers through her hair until her breathing steadied and she drifted back to sleep.

But that night, sleep kept its distance. Her heart pounded harder and harder, and Sweetsmoke, already tall, got up from the cushions and touched the tips of her fingers with his own.

"What?"

"There's something I need you to see, Little Me." He continued to rub her fingers until she finally grabbed his hand.

The forest was silent at that time of night. The only light came from the full moon and the stars above, reaching through the dense broadsaw trees, falling in thin bright streams around them.

Still holding her hand, he brought her deeper into the forest, to the same small clearing where he had endured Rusty's sound-splitting slaps the day before. "Here." He sat down in a thick patch of grass and patted the empty space beside him.

With his forearms as a pillow, he stretched out, an indentation in the moonlit grass outlining the shape of his body. She lay her head on his chest, her tiny self folded into his own.

"No. Look up."

She turned her head and saw the stars, some as large as pebbles, others flickering dots that seemed unsure if they wanted to take part in this world. "So? They're just stars."

"Oh yeah? That's what you think. Look." He beat his hand in the dirt beside them, his arm now visible, and reached his finger into the sky.

"You don't see them? Those three stars there." He pointed. "The ones in a row from top to bottom." He found her hand, uncurled her small finger, and guided it to the stars. "See, one, two"—he lowered her finger—"three. And then there's one"—he brought her hand to the left—"there. And another"—he brought it to the right of the trio in the center—"there."

"Oh, I see them!"

"Good. So those three in the middle, those are Invisibles, called the Three Teachers. And the ones to the left and right, those are dippies."

She sat up. "What do you mean? They're stars."

Pieces of grass stuck to his head like a crown. "That's what you think, but they're not. A long time ago, the Three Teachers were three Invisibles who didn't like the ways dippies were treating us, so they decided that they needed to teach Invisibles how to become better, stronger, and smarter in order to defeat them."

"Defeat them? Why?"

"Because they don't like us, Little Me. Trust me. No matter what you see or hear, they will never like us. And that's what happened to the Three Teachers."

He angled his face back to the stars above. "The dippies didn't want them to help the rest of us, so they threw them up, all the way up high, into the sky, and they got stuck. Right there. Then the dippies sent two more dippies, the two other stars, to hold a big see-through net, so the Three Teachers never fell back to Earth to help us."

She thought this over. "Are they sad up there?"

"Maybe." He pulled her back to his chest. "But they're still able to talk to some Invisibles here, so it's not all bad. More teachers are on the way. But you have to be hard." His chest filled with air, raising her head, then he let it out. "With me, Rusty, and Freshpine, you can be soft. But with everyone else, be hard. It's the only way for us to change the world."

"Who says?" she asked, propping herself up on an elbow.

"Rusty, okay?"

"Okay."

With that settled, she lay back down, pressed her ear to his beating heart.

"Big Brother?" Her voice was already faint, entering the world of dreams.

"Yeah?"

"Are we ever going back?"

"To the orphanage? No."

"So what do we do now?"

"We live, Little Me. We live."

———

She lay there now, in the middle of the forest not far from that thick patch of grass they had slept on twenty years earlier. Every part of her body was in pain from her fall, but her heart hurt worst of all.

"How could you leave me?" She gazed at the Three Teachers, waiting for an answer, but they just silently shined above her.

She rolled onto her side and pushed herself up. There was nothing in her cabin except loneliness and hurt. But to her right, deeper into the forest, a giant fire burned, giving off a welcoming glow. And though she couldn't see them, she knew who was there.

As she turned off Softstone Path and entered Wrinkleseed Row, sharp twigs, crinkled leaves, and small rocks stuck to the soles of her feet. The moon, always sympathetic, shone brightly through the canopy. She placed her hand on rough tree trunk after rough trunk, careful not to lose her footing, but as she got closer to the Baz Buthani, their gathering space, her stomach turned. Something was wrong. An absence of music from the men's zaya drums, chumo flutes, and takitshe rattles. A lack of the usual laughter, singing, and shouting.

All she heard was conversation, hushed tones ringing loudly in her ears.

CHAPTER 8

HEMISPHERIC GUARD DIRECTOR CURTS RUSHED INTO HIS BATH-
room and locked the door. No slipups, not this evening. He
swiped his hand across the mirror in front of him. 19:20 appeared in illuminated white text. *Almost time.*

His hands shook as he removed his peaked Director's cap, thin
fingers running over the hemisphere's gold seal, the twisted gold
braid bordering the short visor. *I'm just a man*, he sang at medium
volume. *A man looking for a place to roam. A man who does his best, to
make the world his home.* He flipped the black cap over, admired the
printed capture stuck to its inner roof: Della, his wife, smiling; her
long skinny arms wrapped around his daughter, Eva, who was
laughing from a tickle attack, golden curls falling in every direction
like spools of sunshine.

A man like most, whose heart comes at a price. He plucked the capture from inside the cap, sighed with relief when he saw the small
square wrapper taped behind it. His supply, hidden in his office
safe, was finished, as was the home stash, and he needed a patch
more than ever. *A man*, he finished the verse, *who understands that
every man has his vice.*

It was as though he and Drams Jams Ivy, despite coming from two completely different worlds, were the same person. The singer's lyrics always calmed him. Plus, Curts had been selected each year to be lead vocalist in school, so he knew that he could more than carry a tune. And it was at a Drams Jams Ivy concert that he'd met Della—all of this history converging into the semblance of happiness, but not enough to obliterate the doubt that, like an old-world virus, back when viruses existed, fought its way into his bloodstream.

He unbuttoned his jacket, carefully folding the black uniform with the wide red stripe, and placed it on the toiletry stand. After loosening his tie, removing both his button-up and undershirt, and stacking them on top of his uniform, all that was left was his skinny bare chest, its paleness glowing under the bathroom's light strips. Finally, he grabbed the white patch, pulled off the protective layer, placed the adhesive side to his chest, and pressed with two fingers to expedite its effects.

Curts ran the faucet and splashed his face one, two, three times. When he raised his head—observing premature stress lines on his forty-three-year-old face—the patch kicked in. His hands stilled, his chest expanded, and the lines on his face seemed to do exactly what the *R* on the patch promised: they relaxed. A hard task for the primary enforcer of hemispheric law, the one who possessed unparalleled access to intelligence—spirals of files with files with files—on just about everyone and everything. A man whose power was derived from the backing of The Chief Executive whose life was just ended, throwing Curts's own position into flux. Never mind that now.

Nobody got time for me, but that's okay, 'cause I got no time for nobody! He sang, far louder than before, grabbing a wooden comb and swaying from side to side as he ran it over his hair. *Everybody want to wait and see, and that's okay, 'cause I got something for somebody!* Holy

Father says— He heard his earsphere vibrating in his jacket pocket. With one quick swipe across the mirror, he saw the word HOME, and tapped the screen to accept, but only on audio.

"Hello, Del?"

"Hi, Daddy."

"Oh!" He laughed. "My small potato. How are you, dear?" He ducked through the ring of his undershirt and tucked it in.

"Scared, Daddy. Today Klara and I were watching *The Adventures of Angela Rhitel*, and the news said that The Chief Executive, may the Holy Father bless his soul, was murdered by a vizzer."

He paused his buttoning, closed his eyes, and counted to three. "Eva Curts. How many times have I told you to never, ever, use that word?"

"But Klara—"

"We *don't* use that word. It's hurtful to Invisibles, and we never want to hurt anyone, like Amahle, whom we love, right?"

"Yes, Daddy," she said, sounding on the verge of tears. "I'm sorry."

"I know you're scared. But trust me, everything will be okay. Okay?"

The line was silent, then, "Oh-kay, Big Potato. Here's Mommy. I love you."

"I love you, too. *Mwah.*"

"Leon."

"Del," he said. "How are you, love?"

"Fine, hon. Eva's scared, but I told her there's nothing to worry about. Did I lie?"

He tucked in his button-up, grabbed his jacket. There was a knock at the door.

"Hold on, Del." He muted himself. "Yes?"

"Sir." It was Hemispheric Guard Deputy Director Mund.

"One minute, Lucretia."

"They're waiting for you, sir."

"I'm well aware, but that doesn't change the fact that I'll still be out in one minute."

He heard her retreat and shut his office door. Unmuting himself, he said, "Del?"

"I'm here, honey. But go. The hemisphere needs you. I love you. From here to forever."

"From here to forever," he said, and hung up. He wished she were with him now, her fingers caressing his chest, her lips grazing the back of his neck, the funny little jokes and naughty desires she'd whisper into his ear. But he had to be strong. For her, Eva, everyone.

One last look in the mirror. He put on his cap, remembering, at the last second, to pocket the patch's protective layer before leaving. Again, no slipups.

Curts exited his office and began rehashing the scenario, just to be clear before he spoke. What did he know? There was a paper note, which was strange enough on its own, supposedly written by the Invisible, Shanu, taking credit for The Chief Executive's murder. Experts quickly noted Invisible blood on it, and confirmed that it did, indeed, belong to him. An Invisible who had disappeared three years ago and somehow continued to evade Curts and his guards. He'd thought that the man was dead or had breached the hemisphere. A fatal miscalculation.

But what was his motive? He was just a normal tree feller. An orphan, yes, but he had a younger sister. His forestfolk claimed that he was hardworking, a skilled boxer, and was mostly an outsider, but dedicated to the few he considered family. "An occasional public outburst," one told his men, but Curts knew that was normal. Through no fault of their own, these Invisibles were emotionally stunted. This one had received a work dispensation, which allowed him to circumvent formal schooling, but he had no criminal record to speak of.

When he rounded a corner, Lucretia was there, standing outside the conference room door. She brought her hand—ring finger curled toward her palm, covered with her thumb—to her forehead. "There you are, sir."

He returned the salute. "Here I am. Any new information?"

"No, sir."

The Director gestured for her to enter, and he followed, the entire room falling silent.

A wooden podium to the left. Two dozen cushioned chairs filled with various politicians, high-ranking hemispheric guards, and reverends to the right. Invisible children, painted in the hemisphere's red, white, or black, carried trays of chilled juices, steaming herbs, and small, brightly colored sandwiches. On the far right, in the podium's direct line of sight, was Anna Franklin—her captureman next to her, programming the thick piece of capglass rigged to a tripod that would broadcast Curts's speech.

One, two, three, four. One, two, three, four. One, two, three, four. He counted when he couldn't sing, the repetition quelling the chaos swirling inside of him. With the help of the patch, his nerves settled down.

Curts moved toward the podium. At the same time, a reverend extended his hand to address another, knocking a cup of dark red juice off an Invisible child's tray and spilling it onto Hemispheric Guard Associate Deputy Director Ribussce's pants and what looked like freshly shined boots.

"You little vizzer!" he shouted, rising to his full height, over two meters tall. He kicked the boy in the stomach, sending him and his tray soaring backward, where Curts stood.

The Director picked up the black-painted boy, surprised to see how still he was, as if the kick to his stomach was well deserved. Ribussce lunged for him, but his superior stuck his hand out. "That's enough."

The large man paused, nostrils flaring. "You're too lenient," he spat. "And that needs to change."

Holding his stare, Curts said, "Clean yourself and take a seat. Now."

Ribussce let the moment stretch as everyone in the room waited to see what would happen. Then he smiled the smile of a man who had a plan to placate until he no longer had to, patiently waiting in plain sight until the perfect time to strike. "Yes, *sir.*"

I'll need to watch him more closely than ever.

Curts took his position behind the podium, swiped a few random illuminated pages across the hardwood for effect, and touched his hand to his chest to ensure the patch was still there, its sedative contents seeping into his bloodstream. Once all was in order, he saluted the audience. "May the Holy Father bless the Northwestern Hemisphere."

"Now and forever," they replied in unison, saluting him back.

"Let's get right to it. As you all know, Chief Executive Rhitel, may the Holy Father bless his soul, was murdered earlier this evening. He was smothered to death in his bed. Our primary suspect is an Invisible, named Shanu, who has been untracked for three years now. We'd believed that he had escaped to the Southwestern Hemisphere, but obviously that is not the case."

The men in the audience shifted in their seats, but it was the only woman aside from Lucretia present, Anna Franklin of the Northwestern News, who spoke. "Excuse me, Hemispheric Guard Director Curts, I—"

"I'll take questions after my prepared remarks, Ms. Franklin."

"Of course, but, if you'll allow me, I'm wondering what makes you think you'll catch him now, when, as you said, he's been untracked for three years?"

He was tempted to double down and deflect, but this was an easy one. "Up until this point, Shanu was just one of a handful of

Invisibles we were pursuing across the hemisphere, and today"—he made eye contact with her captureman's capglass—"he is our main priority. Not only that, but every Northwesterner has now seen his face, making it harder for him to move undetected."

The regional reporter nodded.

"Law and order are what make the Northwestern Hemisphere what it is. This Invisible has committed the highest act of treason possible, but it is important for us to remember that Invisibles, including him, rely on us for protection against their baser natures. We have spent the greater part of a century coexisting, and I will not allow this to ruin all that Chief Executive Rhitel, may the Holy Father bless his soul, has built. So tonight, I am here, vowing to all one hundred and fifty million Northwesterners, both DP *and* Invisible, that I will capture Shanu within five days, before the Chief Executive election."

"Pure truth!" a local manager from the Train and Technology Region shouted.

"Heed him!" a reverend, based in the Healthcare Region, added.

The politicians, guards, and reverends who filled the room nodded to one another. Despite this tragedy, Curts still had their support, which meant he had the support of every Northwesterner who mattered. A deep sense of relief placed its hands on his shoulders, slowly pulling away the blanket of fear that cloaked him. He was the Hemispheric Guard Director of the Northwestern Hemisphere, one of the most powerful men in the most powerful hemisphere.

What was one Invisible?

"I'm sorry," Anna Franklin said, every head turning in her direction. "But how did an Invisible whose last known occupation was tree feller break into the Executive Estate undetected, work his way past dozens of personnel, including your hemispheric *and* golden guards, enter The Chief Executive's bedroom, may the Holy Father bless his soul, smother him, and then escape?"

Sweat gathered in Curts's armpits, dampened his forehead. So much for the patch. He took a sip of water, his hand shaking as he lowered the glass.

"And how," she continued, "do you even know it was him? Or is he just taking the blame because he's one of the few Invisibles you've never caught? According to my records, no Invisible has ever been untracked for this long."

He couldn't tell her the truth. That the surveillance display cut off at the time of the murder, making it impossible to see when and how Shanu had entered The Chief Executive's bedroom. That there had not only been a breach in their supposedly unbreachable security under his watch, but that he—whose eye was said to touch every field, factory, and forest in the Northwestern Hemisphere—also had no idea how the Invisible did it.

"We," he said, coughing. "We're still investigating and gathering all the facts. But it is important to note that Regional Hemispheric Guard Director Tumber has resigned in light of these events, and—"

"Director, our Chief Executive, may the Holy Father bless his soul, was *murdered*. We want the facts. And we want them now. Otherwise, what's to stop someone, anyone, from attacking us? This hemisphere's eminence draws not from its interhemispheric relations, but from the belief that to attack us would unleash an unparalleled and unrestrained fury that . . ."

He couldn't hear her anymore. His hand was shaking even more vigorously now, and he tucked it into his jacket pocket. In front of him was a small ocean of expectant and increasingly suspicious eyes. Della was watching. Eva was watching. Every single Northwesterner's attention was on him; what he did now would set the tone for what would come next. Lunacy or lawlessness. Chaos or calm. Discipline or destruction. As if they were playing out before his eyes, he could see them both happening, side by side.

"*First*," he said, his voice blasting through the room. "I don't think your questions are appropriate, Ms. Franklin."

"But—"

"There are no buts. Second, let me remind you that your job is to report the news, not to conduct yourself as a member of the Gallery of Rule. The last time I checked"—his eyes fell from her face to her crotch—"you didn't have the proper equipment."

The men laughed, easing his anxiety.

"Third, we know it was him because there was a note—written on antique State stationery—claiming responsibility, with a blood sample that matched what we have in our Hemispheric Hematic Directory from when he was at Clasped Hands Orphanage. Fourth, his handwriting matched occupational documents bearing his signature. Need I go on? All of this is irrefutable evidence, and whether that satisfies you or not isn't my concern. My sole focus is catching Shanu and bringing him to justice, either through death or rule. Regardless, law and order will prevail, and every Northwesterner will be able to sleep soundly once again. Though our Great Liberator, may the Holy Father bless his soul, is gone, in five days a new man will sit in his chair, stewarding this great hemisphere toward an even brighter future. Thank you."

Applause echoed off the conference room walls. Every man except Ribussce stood to shake Curts's still-trembling hand on their way out and reminded him that he had their full faith in finding "one troublesome vizzer." Crisis averted. He smiled, he laughed, he thanked them for their support, and then they were all gone, except for three people: Lucretia, Anna Franklin, and her captureman.

He wanted to corner Anna, to demand an explanation for the little stunt she'd just pulled, but he didn't have time. Tragedy always revealed a person's true colors, even if it was someone who'd called themselves your friend for years. *I'll deal with her later*, he decided.

"Sir," Lucretia said, joining him at the door.

"Convene the Public Force."

"On it."

Minutes later, he was in a one-person elevator, plunging from his office to a small windowless room hidden in the depths of the Executive Estate. The doors opened to a long wooden table with a dozen chairs set around it. Lights with actual bulbs, a remnant of the past, flickered from the ceiling until they settled into the reality that, yes, they were being put to use again. The air, trapped in the room for at least a month, was stale, the humidity so thick that you could taste the dirt beyond the concrete that surrounded them.

An elevator on the other side of the room opened, and in walked Lucretia with twelve Invisible men and women behind her. These men and women, handpicked by Curts himself, were his secret weapon. He remembered Lucretia's disbelief when he first told her about the Public Force, only because he needed someone other than himself to manage them. It took some time to convince Chief Executive Rhitel of her utility, that she could be trusted, but he did. And it, she, had all paid off.

"I trust no one saw them exit the private train," Curts said.

"Of course not, sir. I cut the surveillance and brought them from the train to the elevator. Plus, red drops."

"Good work, Deputy."

A smile appeared and died a necessary death in one quick twitch of her face.

"Sit," he instructed.

He saw eleven chairs slide from the table, heard the Invisible skin kissing the old leather all at once. Curts and Lucretia remained standing, and though he couldn't see him, he knew that the Public Force's leader, Captain Kandolo, was, too.

"Ready when you are, sir," Captain Kandolo said.

The Director looked at him for a second, trying to see if he could get a whiff of what he'd said caused people in his forest to call him "Rusty," but, no, he couldn't. The red drops worked.

"Thank you, Captain," Curts said. "We don't have much time, so I'll be brief." He searched out each of the Invisibles' faces, but the red drops also rendered his didanlenses useless. Gone were the perceivable heatmaps of their bodies; all he had was moving sound and shifting air.

"You all know why you're here. What happened today is the by-product of our incompetence. Political tensions, both domestic and beyond our borders, are rising. Northwesterners, from here all the way to the Farming Region, are scared for their lives and the lives of their children due to one Invisible. And it's all because we haven't been able to find him, despite recently ramping up our efforts."

"What are our orders, sir?" Captain Kandolo asked.

"Return to your respective regions and undercover positions. Ask questions, listen for information, and ascertain if anyone has seen him. For those of you working in DP homes or businesses, discuss Shanu with your employers, so long as it doesn't raise suspicion. At this point, it's not ridiculous to assume he's being helped by DPs. For all we know, he could be living in downcity Rhitelville in someone's closet." He assumed each of them were nodding. "Does anyone have word on if the Children of Slim have made contact?"

"Lieutenant Imbuka," Captain Kandolo said.

Curts couldn't see her, but he once had, and remembered that she was small and heavyset with tightly braided hair that crisscrossed her head like a farmer's field. A chair across the room moved backward; he heard the sound of planted feet, standing at attention.

"No word, Director. They're searching for him just as fiercely as we are. Once I gain their full confidence and meet those of higher rank, they'll bring me to their safehold, where I'll be able to learn more."

"We've spent decades trying to find it. If you pull this off, Lieutenant, I'll make sure that your children's children's children will never want for anything. Understood?"

"Yes, sir. Thank you, sir."

The Director nodded, then faced Captain Kandolo. "And you, does his sister still trust you?"

"More than ever, sir."

"Good. I plan to also have a word with her soon. Let order prevail."

CHAPTER 9

WHEN SWEETMINT FINALLY BROKE FREE INTO THE OPEN SPACE, the fire was in its blazing glory. A wide circle of fingerwood trunks surrounded it with one hundred or so people sitting on them. Plates of warm food floated in their laps, cups full of juice hovered in their hands—she couldn't see all of her forestfolk, yet she knew all eyes were on her, their collective rumoyas congealing into a state of anxiety.

"There she is," announced a child's voice on the far side of the circle.

Freshpine, still wearing her light yellow paint from the morning, walked over to her. "Sweetmint," she said, touching the back of her hand against her cheek. "Are you okay?"

She rubbed her arm, looked from the plates and cups turned in her direction back to Freshpine. "No," she whispered. "Where's Rusty?"

"I'm not sure. Darksap said he returned on the train with them, but then had to go back and get something. Work has been demanding more of him lately."

Sweetmint turned to leave. Ever since she and Sweetsmoke had happened upon the same place she stood now, Rusty had been there, grounding, protecting, and translating the ways of the world. His absence, just like at the Annual Painting that morning, made her feel rootless—a tree tipping, clumps of dirt clinging to its exposed veins, with only one destination. She wouldn't let the others hear her splintering, witness her imminent fall.

"Come," Freshpine said. She grabbed Sweetmint's hand, led her toward the fire and the silent crowd before pulling her down onto a trunk. A distinct smell of damp earth moved in her direction, along with a plate full of roasted corn, sweet potatoes, grilled onions, and a cup of carrot juice. It was Wetmoss—state name: Nandi—Darksap's mother.

"Mambonga."

Wetmoss, still painted like the rest of her family, nodded and returned to her trunk. Darksap sat there, his lensed eyes illuminated by the firelight trying to tell her something. But what? Despite her uneasy feeling, these were still her forestfolk, who just last month were praising her as if she were the Holy Father himself.

"Well, since no one else wants to speak, I will." Burningwood. The man on the train who had accused her of endangering her forest at the Annual Painting. He had removed the gold paint he'd worn that morning, but his voice—rough, like tree bark—was one of a kind. His plate rose in the air as he stood.

"Soon enough, shibs will be crawling all over our forest. Terrorizing us to find Sweetsmoke. And I say we do whatever we can to help them, so they leave us alone."

Hemispheric Guard Director Curts's address must have been on their restricted displays. The State making sure that Invisibles, too, knew what was at stake; how much they had to lose if her brother wasn't found, or given up, as soon as possible.

The fire grew in intensity, a charred log cracking every few seconds, bursts of sparks flying into the air. There was some whispering, but no one joined Burningwood, so he continued.

"Look at us." He placed his plate on the ground, directed his voice around the circle. "How many of us are even here, right now? Eighty? Years ago, our entire forest would have been here, sharing stories, singing, eating, and rejoicing in what little we have. And now look. In our forest, a quarter of us are patchers, half of us want to be dippies, another quarter care as much as a river rock, and then there's us, those trying to preserve a way of life that has aided us for over a century, even after we lost our elders in the Shipping; after Rhitel came to power, disappeared all Invisibles over the age of five, and forced mere children to carry what remained of our culture in cracked cups. Vilongo. Music. The knowledge of our forest and its medicine. But so much more was lost.

"Still, we have weathered the changes in Chief Executives and increasing sanctions, avoided massacres that have befallen others. Yet *her* brother." He raised his voice, leveling it at Sweetmint from across the circle. "Is the reason why we will be burned to the ground, just like Forest Seventy-Eight." Many sucked their teeth or whispered a prayer.

"He didn't do anything!" she shouted, standing now.

Burningwood's laughter scraped the air. "I don't expect you to know better, what with your new life serving Croger Tenmase. No, I take that back. If there's one thing you should have learned by now, it's that it doesn't matter what your brother did or didn't do. If they say he did it, he did it."

At this, the people of the circle slapped the trunks they sat on in agreement. Even children joined in, mimicking their parents and siblings. The fire's flame grew higher—the women were supposed to maintain it, but it went ignored. The cool truth of this moment, of this betrayal, whipped across Sweetmint's entire body.

"Where is he?" someone to the right of her asked.

"Yes," Burningwood said, rounding the circle, getting closer. "Where is Sweetsmoke?"

"I—I don't know." His scentprint, of *burnt*, not burning, wood flooded her nose and forced its way down her tight throat. He was right in front of her.

"I know we're not dippies living in a castle, Sweetmint, but do you take us for fools? You're telling us that your brother, the one whose back you clung to like tree sap, has never contacted you, not once?"

"Not once," she whispered, still trying to figure out how she went from accomplished to accomplice so quickly.

Thick hands latched on to her arms, twisting her skin. "Tell us the truth," he demanded, his insistent, thundering voice making her think she *had* done something, that she *was* just as guilty as her brother.

Darksap's scentprint appeared beside her. An axe floated in the air, its wooden handle reflecting the fire's shifting hues.

"Stand down, Burningwood."

Not letting her go, the older man laughed his grating laugh. "Or what? You're going to chop me down like one of your trees? How dare you raise your hand to an elder. And a weapon."

Darksap's rumoya was a mix of fear and anger, but also resolve. Burningwood had to have sensed this, that Darksap actually could, and would, sink that axe's blade into his body if he didn't let her go.

"Enough," someone said from behind her.

Rusty walked toward them, his scentprint more pronounced with each step.

Thank you, Holy Father, Sweetmint thought.

He gently removed Burningwood's hands from her arms before guiding Darksap's axe down.

"She's going to get us all killed," Burningwood said.

"No," Rusty replied. "Your hostility will. Now is the time for us to stick together. If Sweetmint knew anything, she would tell us. Wouldn't you?" he asked her.

"Of course." A lie.

"Good." Rusty directed his voice to the people around the fire. "I think it's time we all went home. We don't know what's on the horizon. Rest. Tomorrow is another day, and we'll all need our strength to face whatever comes with it."

The women grabbed the buckets of dirt and dumped them onto the fire. Smaller groups formed, no doubt already discussing what had happened, what was happening, and what would, or should, happen. Before she could give in to the downward spiral of despair, Rusty took her by the arm, steered her toward the forest.

"Where were you?" she asked, her question's edge blade-sharp.

"I'm sorry. I forgot some tools in the Upper Forest and had to get them. We're fined if they're found lying about. You know dippies and their need for cleanliness." He paused. "I only found out about Sweetsmoke when I reached the square. Then I ran here."

"And what about this morning, at the AP?"

"The State is more focused on increasing regional output than ever before. So much so that a few of us, me included, were asked to sit for our capture at the worksite instead of the Barn." He stopped walking. "I'm so sorry I wasn't there. For you and Darksap."

She palmed her forehead, embarrassed by how angry she was at him, overwhelmed by the reality descending upon her. "I just don't know what to do, Rusty. He didn't do this. He couldn't have. Part of me thought, maybe even hoped, that he was dead, because why else wouldn't he come back to me?"

"He had a lot of anger, Sweetmint," he said, rubbing her shoulder. "Especially after what happened at the boxing trial. But you're right, he would never do what they say he did. It's unthinkable. I'll do all I can to help him, but you have to promise me that if he contacts you, you'll immediately tell me. No one else. I can't do much, but people owe me favors, so maybe I could smuggle him out of the region or the hemisphere before it's too late."

"You would really do that?"

His rough hands cradled her face. "How could you even ask that? You are as much my daughter, and he is as much my son, as my own blood. But you *have to* promise that you'll tell me."

"I promise."

He invited her in for herbs, but she said she wanted to rest, so they parted at his cabin. "I love you, Sweetmint. Trust no one," he'd reminded her, her arms wrapped tightly around his back, her head resting on his powerful shoulder.

She walked straight into her cabin and activated the display, shuffling through dozens of icons until she located the red and black one with "NWN" on it, and tapped. The Northwestern News came up, and with it was a repeat of the Director's hemispheric address. One swift swipe on the wall lowered the volume, as if that would somehow protect her from what he was about to say, but his words were like a scream: "So tonight, I am here, vowing to all one hundred and fifty million Northwesterners, both DP *and* Invisible, that I will capture Shanu within five days, before the Chief Executive election." Then, five words that thrust her outside of her body: "either through death or rule."

So this is it. She fell back onto her mattress, stared at the polished pieces of broadsaw stretching across her ceiling. Lying there, hearing "through death or rule" on repeat for an hour on end, she thought back to how her brother had said that they weren't orphans because their parents had died, they were orphans because their parents had abandoned them. No matter how much she pleaded or cried, he wouldn't tell her more than that they were "alive and lived in the city." This forced her to make up a story about them: two Invisibles who had somehow worked their way among the privileged few allowed to live in proximity to the DPs.

If she could find them, maybe they would be impressed by all that she had done and would want to help her find Sweetsmoke.

They would apologize for giving them up; her mother and father would explain why and beg for forgiveness. She was willing to forgive them, the three of them hugging, like a real family. And then her parents would use their resources to save their son. These thoughts made her lighter, carried her spirit up from her mattress and into the world of dreams—the only respite from the reality that tried, with all its might, to hold her hostage.

CHAPTER 10

BROTHER BLACKSTONE AND SISTER BLACKSTONE STOOD AT THE door of the Future Room, watching the babies sleep. Moonlight spilled through dozens of ceiling windows onto their wooden cribs—the only signs of their presence low snoring and the intermittent rustling of the tiny blankets they rested on.

Sister Blackstone took his hand, squeezed. "How do you feel?"

Her husband squeezed back, and leaned forward, kissing her forehead. "I feel good, my root. Better than good, actually."

"Shall we go address the Children?"

He found her lips once, twice, three times, and laughed. "Or we could . . ."

"After our work is done." She pulled him away from the sleeping babies, through the darkened tunnel, and into Tintaba's cavernous womb. The light strips ringing the cave's main gathering space pulsed blue all the way from the base to the domed roof, dozens of meters above them.

Despite recent developments, the Children of Slim pushed carts into and out of the thirty-six tunnels, laughing, playing, and preparing for this evening's address.

"Go on," Brother Blackstone said. "I'll join you in a second."

"Okay, my soil." She kissed his cheek, then disappeared into the mass of people—partially visible from the gray cave dust that rained down upon them.

Brother Blackstone looked out into the cave, feeling love, pride, and power for his people. Here, in Tukhali Intaba—Hollow Mountain—more commonly called Tintaba, was a happy rebellion; one that had been quietly building for decades, founded on subverting oppression not just in the Northwestern Hemisphere, but worldwide, with joy as its driving force. Not everyone here held the same view, but most did. And now, finally, was the moment they'd been waiting for; a prophecy fulfilled. *Cheer blood.*

The Children of Slim stopped their work and entered the tunnels empty-handed, then returned with wooden chairs, which they placed in circular rows around the stage that Brother Blackstone now walked toward. Tears fell from his own dust-covered face as he ascended the stage, passing the five people who sat there. Sister Blackstone stood, linked her index finger with his own, and walked alongside him.

When they reached the stone podium, he closed his eyes and said, "Children of Slim, how are we?"

"SOLID!" the crowd below him shouted. They, too, understood the meaning of this moment, and they—these Factfolk from across the hemisphere, around the world—would do everything in their power to make the most of it. Factfolk, not "Invisible," because their existence was a fact, plain for all to see.

"I said, 'Children of Slim, how are we?'"

"UPRIGHT!"

"And? Please don't tell me that's it, my siblings. Give me one more."

"HAPPY!"

He opened his eyes, hundreds of dust-covered faces smiling up at him and Sister Blackstone. They knew he and she were no better than they were, just a woman and man in the right place at the right time, whose ideas helped to push them forward, whose open-mindedness allowed them to overcome infighting, and whose vigilance ensured their protection, no matter how hard Curts the Patcher and his predecessor tried to locate and eradicate them. Brother Blackstone loved his people for loving him and Sister Blackstone no more and no less than each other. But when they became the leaders of the Children of Slim and tried to destroy the stage they now stood on, lowering it to the same level where everyone sat, the people objected. Not all old things must go, they said.

"Happy," he repeated, his voice tremendous. "The foundation of our movement. Though the dippies degrade us, though they work as hard as possible to make us hate ourselves, we, the Children of Slim, know that genuine joy is more dangerous than hatred. Cheer blood?"

"CHEER BLOOD!" the people responded.

"Cheer blood, indeed," Sister Blackstone said. "The blood of our ancestors that flows in our veins and bolsters us today, toward the inevitability of freedom. Real freedom, for *all* Factfolk. We know our siblings in the Southeastern Hemisphere, in particular, have it even worse than us. But we must turn to the now, to today. As word has passed around, The Chief Executive of Evil has been murdered."

While some of them were likely happy, no one expressed it. The Children of Slim had wanted a reckoning for Chief Executive Rhitel. Yes, he had died a gruesome death, but death was too easy a sentence for a man who sowed seeds of hate across an entire hemisphere.

Brother Blackstone continued. "Authorities claim it is Brother Sweetsmoke. Some of you may remember that I'd once tried to recruit him, and he declined, stating that his rebellion would be a rebellion of one. Then, three years ago, he vanished. None of our siblings here or beyond our hemisphere have ever come across him, yet the sadistic State says it was him, a letter in his handwriting and his blood serving as proof.

"Though we've always had other plans for Rhitel, the prophecy is playing out right before our eyes. As Father Slim said before his death, one of our own would die, then return to slay an unslayable foe. And that person would be chosen as our Illuminator—to lead us out of the darkness and into luminescence. Brother Sweetsmoke *is* that Illuminator."

"Siblings across the hemisphere have been activated," Sister Blackstone said. "As well as dippy allies. To make it clear for all here, our aims are threefold. First, to prevent the election of Local Tormentor II Stephan Jolis, a man who is far more wicked than the previous Chief Executive of Evil. If he is elected, he won't make it past his inauguration.

"Second, to further destabilize the State through coordinated attacks on the hemispheric sites they hold dear, fueling the fear and pushing them to make rash decisions—some that may harm our people in the short term, but will also cause the dippies to lose faith in their leaders, making the Fundamental Flip more possible. Chaos is convenient for those who can control it.

"Three, to find The Illuminator before Curts the Patcher does. This means we have five days to locate him, bring him into our fold, and dissuade him, whether peacefully or not, to cease being a sole actor. Our efforts *must* be united in order to be effective."

"Five days until the end of the world as we know it," Brother Blackstone said, smiling. "The day of the dippy is over. But enough of strategy and solemnity. Tonight"—he quickly spun around—"we dance. Cheer blood?"

"CHEER BLOOD!" the people responded. They stood and linked their index fingers with one another, holding them high. Music, made from instruments both wood and wind, flowed through the cave's walls, and soon the Children of Slim swayed, their own anthem, "Flip the World and Sing," soaring from their mouths as they beat their feet, joined by the seductive harmony of happiness. The promise of a new world—shaped by their tired and hopeful hands— was no longer just the soft clay of wishes and dreams, but now, after all this time, quickly hardened into fact all around them; a mountain of their own making.

CHAPTER 11

KNOW YOU'RE OUT THERE," SWEETMINT SAID. HER COLLAR'S WARM metal clicked in place as she fastened it around her neck.

"Then don't keep me waiting."

She opened her cabin's door, and Darksap stood there, his body covered in the light dust of earth.

"What's going on?" she asked. "You're filthy."

"Come." He reached his hand out, and though she was confused and a bit concerned, she still grabbed it. Darksap's hand was swollen and raw, as if he'd just come back from work, even though it was morning. His rumoya was peaceful, radiating a calm that flowed into her own. "Do you mind closing your eyes?"

"Where are you taking me?"

"Just close your eyes. Please."

She closed them and gripped his hand tighter as he led her—based on the dense smell of foliage and the growing sound of the river—behind her cabin, in the opposite direction of the main square and church.

Soon her feet found soft, lumpy dirt, as if it had just been tilled. He guided her over this field, or whatever it was, then stopped.

"Now open them."

The area they stood in was part of Fingerwood Field, named as such due to the swath of fingerwood trees that stretched from here all the way to the bank of the Phakishe, their main river. It was a place where she and Darksap used to play when they were younger, the few times she could escape Sweetsmoke's watchful eye. They would end their games running, hand in hand, to the river, then, without any countdown, jump into it, never letting go.

But now, this portion of Fingerwood Field, a handful of square meters, was empty of its namesake; in its place rich black dirt turned over so it felt like velvet to the touch, and formed into rows with vegetables of all kinds, from the looks of it, already beginning to sprout. She turned to Darksap, struggling to say something, anything.

"Dapp?"

"Yes?" He laughed, not surveying the field, but smiling up at her, waiting.

"Did you?"

"Yes."

"But . . ." She bent down, touched a narrow coiled stalk of corn emerging from the ground. "How?"

"I started last month, once you got the apprenticeship. And I picked this spot so it would receive the maximum amount of sun, even with the other trees around. I'd come here before work and fell the trees myself. Then I began to plant all of your favorite vegetables."

"Why? Why did you do all of this . . . for me?"

"Honestly, I was having the hardest time trying to figure out what kind of gift to give you, to show you how proud I am of all you're doing, and this made the most sense. I, um"—he coughed, seeming less sure of himself now—"I hope you like it, Swint."

She thrust her hand into the dirt, feeling its protective warmth.

Then he knelt down next to her, placed his hand over her own, and allowed it to sit there, in the plush earth, his chest to her back, his breath on her neck. "I would turn this entire world into a garden for you," he whispered into her ear. "And it still wouldn't be enough."

Her eyes were closed as he spoke, and she felt Darksap and her growing into one then, afraid of how porous the boundary between the two of them had become. With each passing day, he was proving to be less of who she thought he was. Now she began to view him more as a man who acted than was acted upon. And this, this garden, this breaking of earth in order to make space for something new—it was the kindest thing anyone, other than Sweetsmoke, had ever done for her. But she couldn't give in to this . . . whatever this was. No, not now. Not when Sweetsmoke needed her.

She pulled her hand from the dirt and stood.

He did the same, his face powdered light brown, hoping, wishing. But for what? Something more, she knew that. More words. A stronger gesture. An affirmation that, like this garden, she, too, wanted new life to grow between them. Then he leaned toward her, his lips leading the way, but she turned from him.

"Mambonga, Dapp," she said, as if speaking to a woman selling vegetable juice in the square. "Mambonga khulu." Her eyes were on the field, but when enough time had passed, she faced him again. "Ready to go?"

Darksap took a breath, then said, "Sure," his voice showing no sign of defeat, but rather a sense of optimism that had suddenly spread to her. A lesser man would have beat his chest and begun listing what *she* owed *him* for that which she hadn't even asked for, trading patience and reassurance for pressure and heavy-handedness. But not Dapp.

Men, women, and yawning children joined them on Softstone Path before entering the mass in the square. The ration train was at the platform. Shibs tossed straw bags full of vegetables to the heads of the households who didn't grow their own food, like Rusty and Freshpine did, and either didn't want to give in to the allure of Rhitel Burger or couldn't afford it. Even though Burningwood's words at the Baz Buthani had been spoken without mercy or care, his observations about the forest were right. Fewer people wanted to eat food they had to prepare on their own, rationed or self-grown.

No longer trusting the food that the shibs handed out, she decided to stop taking rations and all DP-prepared food with the exception of Mr. Tenmase's. Maybe she was being paranoid, but these days, paranoia was a form of protection. Plus, she could ask Rusty for some of his harvest while she and Dapp worked to get her—or was it their?—own set up. She'd even help with the rising grow tax that he complained about every year.

Small talk and whispering, likely about her and Sweetsmoke, floated through the air as people slowly filed into the church on the opposite side of the square.

"You okay?" Darksap asked when they were a few meters from the church's doors.

Anxiety rose from her stomach to her chest. She looked up, attempted to take in the entire church, and failed. When she and Sweetsmoke had first entered the forest, walking into the clearing and finding all of those people, she could see the silhouette of the church's black metal cross piercing the sky, the Northwestern Hemisphere's flag flapping in the night.

The next day, Rusty had brought them to Daily Prayer, something they'd done in a small church inside the orphanage, but this—a four-level fingerwood structure with peaked solar-paneled roofs and a dozen pillars shooting out of a pitrock foundation—this was a home fit for the Holy Father. Looking at it still grounded her now, as it did back then, even though Sweetsmoke told her that Rusty told him that the Holy Father wasn't their father. He said that the DPs made him up because they were afraid of dying, and that this fear took the form of a mysterious man who would punish anyone, especially Invisibles, who weren't as afraid. But she didn't believe him. The thought that this was all some random, purposeless accident—impulsive children making a cosmic mess with no adult supervision—terrified her. Yes, the other side of faith was fear, but so what.

"Swint?"

They stood at the threshold, Darksap looking up at her.

She forced a smile and stepped inside.

The pews were full. Every member of the forest was there, even the ones who had fallen victim to the patch. As she and Darksap made their way to the only available seats in the front, she felt hundreds of eyes on her: the ones from the Baz Buthani, the Rainbow Girls, Rusty, Burningwood.

Reverend Achte stood tall at the front of the church and nodded at everyone until the doors shut. His bright smile, the smile that you couldn't help but return, was now a grim line.

"Glory, glory," he said, lacking all emotion.

"Glory, glory," the church responded, hesitant.

He lowered his head, took an unnaturally long inhale that shook his whole chest, then let it out as he looked up at them. "Today is a somber day. Not only has our leader, Chief Executive Rhitel, may the Holy Father bless his soul, been murdered, but it has been committed by a man who once sat in this very room."

She squeezed Darksap's hand, he squeezed back. Staring ahead, her eyes locked on to the wooden wall behind the reverend. Intricate carvings of biblical scenes covered it from left to right: a flood rising above cursed people, idol worshippers turning into dust around a fire, a boy, his face similar to Chief Executive Rhitel's, aiming a slingshot at an Invisible opponent.

"We all knew Shanu. And while he would attend Daily Prayer, in here, just like you"—he raised a shaky finger toward the church—"it was clear he had a darkness in him. That he wasn't a true believer in the Holy Father, in community, in service. His questions and out-bursts signaled as much." The weathered man brought a hand to his heart. "Candace, you are present, yes?"

"Yes, Reverend Achte. Right here, in the front. Next to Cinque."

His eyes pointed in her direction. "Yet here we have Candace. A shining hope for this forest. One who has made all of us proud and, I am sure, all of you proud to be Invisible. She is the embodiment of the rewards you are all capable of reaping if you only submit to the higher powers, both divine and Dominant. Glory, glory."

"Glory, glory," she and her people echoed.

"Please stand," he said, extending his hands.

With a warm, calloused hand on her arm, Darksap urged her upward, and her body followed. Reverend Achte opened his arms to her as she stepped toward him, waiting, expecting. They touched—she allowed his frail limbs to wrap around her, wishing she could stand there forever, feeling, for a moment, that every-thing would be okay.

"There, there." He released and rotated her so she faced her forestfolk. He gestured for a guard to hand him his glass tablet, then, with his illuminated Bible open, held it in Sweetmint's di-rection, pointing to one of the pages. "Please read this section, my child."

"Th-ere-fo-re," she began, her voice shaking so badly that the word broke into four. "Each of you Invisibles must put off falsehood and speak truthfully to your Dominant neighbor, for we are all members of one body."

"Everyone, please give Candace a round of applause."

The church clapped half-heartedly. Yes, something had shifted in a big way.

"Candace," Reverend Achte said. "Do you know where Shanu is?"

"No, Reverend."

"And if you hear from him, you will alert us, for the good of this forest and your forestfolk?" The question hung in the air, gaining mass, then, "Think carefully now, my child. You are in the home of the Holy Father, and he knows when your words are dressed in falsehoods."

She dropped her head, scraped her toenail against the wooden floor, hard.

"Candace?"

She turned to the reverend, saw time etched in the lines of his face, his eyes patient, yet assuming. It pained her to lie. Thoughts of internal damnation turned her breath shallow, the room spinning around her, but then she saw Darksap, an image of his silently and steadily felling those trees in Fingerwood Field *for her* appearing in her mind, and it gave her strength. Even if she did believe in the Holy Father, there had to be more to this world than obedience and submission. There had to be.

"Yes, Reverend."

"And you all . . ." He faced the church. "If you know anything about Shanu's whereabouts, will you, as it says in Ephesians 4:25, 'put off falsehood and speak truthfully to your Dominant neighbor'? Will you remember that we are of one hemispheric body and do everything it takes to protect it?"

"Yes, Reverend," the church replied, their desperation, their desire to go back to their quiet, simple lives of only a day ago, screaming through the syllables.

"Glory, glory. Candace, you may be seated. Now, let us pray. For the Northwestern Hemisphere. For Chief Executive Rhitel, may the Holy Father bless his soul. And, most important, for Shanu's imminent capture."

But she didn't pray for any of those three things. In fact, she didn't pray at all. For the first time in her life, she couldn't. Instead, she pictured herself as the flood that would destroy the cursed people, the fire that turned the idol worshippers to dust, the rock in the slingshot, reversing its trajectory into the eye of the DP who thought he wielded it. These visions scared and confused her; she had to make sense of this spiritual discord, and do it fast.

That's what she focused on as she lay on the lavish bed in Mr. Tenmase's train. Once she got comfortable with the daily spreads of food he provided, she ventured to the compartment on the opposite side of the car. There, she discovered a bedroom bathed in sunlight, crisp white sheets on a too-soft mattress, pillows that made her head feel like she was soaring through the sky, and even a small wooden desk in the corner with a chair that seemed to be made exactly for her body.

Lost in comfort and thought, she didn't notice when the train began to slow down. It wasn't until it came to a full stop, dense forest to the left and right, that she realized something was wrong. It's not like these trains ever broke down.

"Hello?" she called.

She left the bedroom and entered the *dining car*—Mr. Tenmase referred to it as such after she embarrassingly called it the "eating place." She turned her head around to see something, anything, that would help quell the panic rising in her chest, the growing tightness of her collar. *I'm not dying here*, she told herself, though the air was getting warmer, thinner.

"Hello!" she screamed, the word echoing off the walls of steel and glass. "Can anyone hear me?"

Then, shuffling. One of the doors was opening. She rushed to a window, saw a group of shibs, all in their moss-colored mesh uniforms, except for one, who wore black, a wide red stripe running down his center. Two shibs lifted themselves onto the train and then grabbed the hand of the man in red and black, pulling him up.

There was nowhere to run. She backed away from the window too quickly, caught the edge of a dining table chair, knocking her off balance and onto the floor. Her head smacked against the carpet with a flat *bam*. The next moment, the man in red and black was above her, his face more frightening than she had thought it would be. His eyes expressed concern, but the way his mouth curved into a genuine frown reminded her of when she last saw him, on the display the previous night, speaking of "death or rule."

"May I help you?" he asked.

She tried to sit up, fell, then, accepting defeat, nodded. Hemispheric Guard Director Curts, along with one of his men, placed a hand underneath each shoulder, carefully helping her up and into the nearest chair.

"Water," he said.

A shib poured a glass for her and Hemispheric Guard Director Curts held it to her lips.

"Drink."

Her neck already stiff, she tilted it as far back as she could, took a few sips. "Thank you, sir."

"Khawamu."

She blinked hard, trying to unscramble her thoughts. She must have misheard him. Surely he said "You're welcome" in Northwestern, not Vilongo.

He laughed. "When I started out, I worked in forests like yours. The people taught me some Vilongo."

"Oh."

"You must be wondering why I'm here."

"You're here because of my brother, sir."

"That's right." He sat in a chair opposite her. "As you know, he committed the worst act anyone, Invisible or Dominant, can. And it's on me to find him before someone else does." He leaned toward her, lowered his voice. "The truth is, I'm here to help him, Candace. When I find him, he'll receive a fair trial and likely serve out a life sentence at His Executive's Prison. But if I don't"—he closed his eyes, shaking his head—"some DPs are downright barbaric."

Scenes of her older brother being hanged, dismembered, burnt alive, or some other sick manifestation of justice punched across her mind. She looked out the window, all of that forest, so much space in this world, yet nowhere to run. Nowhere to hide. But Sweetsmoke had. The thought produced a smile that she immediately wiped away.

"What do you want from me, sir?"

"Have you heard from him?"

"No, sir. And I hope not to. As you know, I'm Croger Tenmase's apprentice, which means I have my hands full."

He held his eyes on her, letting the seconds dwindle. *One, two, three. One, two, three. One, two, three.* "For all I know," he finally said, "you helped him commit the murder."

She opened her mouth, but he rested his hand on her shoulder. "Don't worry, I know you didn't. You were at Croger Tenmase's when it took place. We also searched your home and found none of his DNA. But I'm simply conveying the narrative people could choose to run with as time progresses."

Was this a threat? She really couldn't tell. He, like Mr. Tenmase, was a man constructed out of contradictions: one second speaking Vilongo, the next speaking of violence.

"If he contacts you, tell the first guard—I mean shib, as you call us—tell the first shib you can find, okay?"

"Yes, sir."

His lips parted in a way that felt too forced, unsettling her. "Good. I know you'll do what's right. From what I hear, you always do."

He patted her knee, then walked toward the open door. His two men jumped down, but before Hemispheric Guard Director Curts followed suit, he stopped. "Candace?"

"Yes, sir?" she asked, staring at his back.

"If I were in your position, I'd do anything to try to save my brother. The person who was the only real family I ever knew.

Believe me, I understand the duty to family." He paused. "Maybe better than most. But please listen to me clearly: there is no saving your brother. Leave the law and order to me and just focus on your work with Croger Tenmase. Despite how things look now, your future is as bright as it was before. Trust me."

He jumped down, the doors closed, and the train continued to Castle Tenmase, the only evidence of their meeting the pounding in her head.

If Karl and Lionel suspected her of anything, they didn't let on. The same pleasantries were exchanged. A few light jokes. Lionel looked up at the sun as the three of them waited for Sanford to appear on the hill before strolling toward them. Did they not watch the display? Or maybe they were instructed to act as normal as possible.

Sanford opened the gate, a solemn, guilty look on his face. Only once they were out of Karl and Lionel's earshot did he turn to her. "You okay?"

"What do you think?"

"Right, stupid question. I mean, how are you?"

"Same answer."

They ascended the hill in silence. Today she didn't stop at the top; the only thing she wanted was forward motion, the unstoppable force of momentum and inertia. But before she could begin her descent, he grabbed her hand, tugging her toward him.

"I'm not in the mood for whatever this is, Sanford."

"I'm not them, Candy. All of those people who want your brother dead and think Invisibles only exist for our benefit. You know that, right?"

She looked into his eyes, his face contorted with pain and some marrow-deep need for her to release him of a thousand faults. Sanford was right. He wasn't spewing hatred and abusing Invisibles for his own entertainment, but, at the same time, he wasn't doing anything to stop it.

"What do you see when you look at me?" he asked. When he didn't receive an answer, he closed his eyes and said, "I feel your fear. Your anger. The all-consuming sense of helplessness. As if all of this is just happening to you for no reason other than that it can."

"How . . . How could you know all of that?"

"Because," he said, his eyes still closed, "I don't need to see you to see you, Candy. We're from different places, but have felt many of the same things. And I want you to know that I am not the enemy."

Her hand turned to fresh dough in his own. She knew she had to be hard now, harder than ever, but there was something about him that rounded the sharp and smoothed the jagged—that made her want to relax, really relax, and allow his world to swallow her whole.

"Do you feel that?" he whispered.

"Feel what?"

"Like we're the only two people in the world."

She did, and it terrified her. This ability he had to block out all of the bad. Life could be so easy, if she let it. If she permitted herself to escape into him, into Castle Tenmase. To agree with someone like Hemispheric Guard Director Curts that Sweetsmoke and Sweetsmoke alone was responsible for his own actions, as well as the consequences that followed. But blood wasn't something you could run from.

"I need you, Sanford," she said, squeezing his hand. "In a big way."

He parted his lips. "I need you, too, Candy," he breathed out, closing the small space between them.

"I want to find my parents so they can help me search for my brother, and to do that, I need a city pass."

He flinched and let go of her hand. "You know I can't do that."

"Of course you can. I just need it for a day. All you have to do is—"

The little color he had drained from his face. "I know *how* to do it, but I can't. If the HGs ever found out and traced it to my uncle . . . it would be more than a slap on the wrist."

"You're my only hope. And I'm not just saying that. I literally have no one else who can help me find him. Maybe once we locate him, but not until then. So please, I'm here asking you, begging you, as someone who I know cares about me. Who actually sees me."

"I do. I swear I do."

"Then *help* me." She turned her back to him, wiping away tears.

There was nothing more to say, but after the silence became too deafening, he said, "I'm sorry. I really am."

No matter what he said, these DPs were all starting to look the same. Empty promises. Invisible faces. The only truth you could count on was that they always, without fail, put themselves first. She walked down the hill, cursing herself for believing she could count on him. It hurt to know that someone could look at you the way he looked at her, like his heart kept beating just so he'd get another chance to see her, and then not show up when she needed him most.

Inside Castle Tenmase, it was business as usual. Mr. Tenmase led her to an underground level she hadn't known existed. When the light strips turned on, she saw a grand red and white metal frame with wings, a fan attached to the nose, three rubber wheels for support.

"An *airplane*," he said. "Used to transport people from one place to another via air."

She wanted to take it apart, to understand it from the inside out, and then allow it to carry her far, far away. But she just sat on the floor and brought her knees to her chest.

Oblivious, Mr. Tenmase walked toward it, ran his hand over its glossy side. "Still in good condition, after all of these centuries. If you can believe it, this is a much smaller version of the model that hundreds of people would fit into. We'll bring them back after the Big Reset, but with compressed biogas for fuel. The sky will be full of them, flying this way and that. You ever see anything fly? No, I haven't either. Nothing except leaves riding wind. But I can imagine it. Looking up at all that motion. Untethered. And this—"

She tuned him out, his words reduced to noise. There was no mention of her brother. Of "death or rule." None of it, she realized, affected him. Here, in this precious castle, he, like Sanford and even Abe, escaped the world and its ugliness. Tinkering with the past, tinkering with the present, tinkering with the future, his true home the abstract depths of his own mind. Always protected, always safe.

"What do you think, Candace?" he asked, spinning the fan at the front.

When she didn't answer, he finally turned, saw her on the ground. "Is this some new thing the young people are doing? Sitting on the floor? If so, I'd be happy to remove the couches and armchairs from the drawing room." He laughed.

He's really laughing. With everything going on.

"It's just hard to focus on any of this right now," she whispered.

"I understand," he said, kicking one of the tires. Then he clapped so loudly that she jumped; the sound reverberated across the concrete room. "How about we play some tennis?"

"Tennis?"

"Yes, what do you think that green court in the back with the long net is for? Surely you've seen tennis on the display. The Invisible league is quite strong, especially this year."

She shrugged, depleted. "I've seen it. I just don't know if this is the time for it."

"Time for it? Candace, there's *always* time for tennis. As Drosher says, 'Sport moves the heart like gravity pulls the river. An unseen terminus, but the power is never withheld.'"

Of course. How could I be so foolish? There's always time for tennis when you're a DP.

CHAPTER 12

GRAND MAGISTRATE ROYGER RANG THE BELL, AND THEY RELEASED The Hooter. She emerged from a door on the Gallery's floor, beneath the ninety-nine directors and local managers in the wooden stands. Slick with black corn oil that dripped with each step, the young Invisible moved toward the floor's center. She stopped between the two empty podiums that Local Manager II Stephan Jolis and Local Manager IV Williams Washington would soon occupy.

Jolis knew, from how her yellow-lensed eyes darted in every direction, that this was her first time. She raised her hands in the air, sliced them downward, and the blaring trumpets and firing percussion of "The Holy Call of the Hemisphere" pushed its way through the Gallery's speakers, surrounding the hemisphere's most powerful men in an onslaught of sound.

Raise the banner! Though darkness is ahead, through the might of the Holy Father, our light shall always spread.

Grand Magistrate Royger and his auxiliary magistrates on the elevated bench clapped to the beat of the hemispheric anthem. The men in the stands rushed down the aisles, no care being paid to the wrinkling of their suits, and chased The Hooter.

From the mountains of the west, to the forests of the east, what so proudly we hail, is the taming of all beasts.

The woman ran to the far corner of the room, past the magistrates' bench. A director, from the Clothing Region, reached her before anyone else. He wrapped his arms around her and raised her into the air, but she slipped away, dodging a dozen men, who slapped her bottom, grabbed her tightly coiled hair, and punched her in the back. One of these punches landed with a wet *slap*, but she didn't stop running.

Clear the streets for the hemispheric guards, who protect our hemisphere from all potential threat. From the cradle to the grave, in our blood our future's kept!

Eventually, she ran the length of the stands, parallel to the wooden railing, and seeing Jolis standing in the shadows, she stopped.

"Help me," she begged, struggling to catch her breath. Though it was only for half a second, the way she looked at him, it was like she recognized him. He couldn't stand it. They were nothing alike and never would be. Everyone had a role to play, and her role, in this moment, was to entertain these savage men of rule.

He grinned. "Help yourself."

A dozen hands tried gripping her shoulders as she made a final effort for a tall wooden door leading outside, to the heart of downcity Rhitelville. But it was locked. She banged her tiny fists on it, whimpering a thousand prayers, until the men, out of breath and patience, yanked her away from it. They threw her onto the floor and groped her in every way; Grand Magistrate Royger's black robe flowing and short wig of white hair shaking, as he and his magistrates sang along.

We all stand prepared, for any fight the hemisphere demands. For what is a man that truly can't protect his beloved land? With the grace of the Holy Father, and the strength of Rhitel, the submission of the Invisible and the Dominant Population's swell. All who oppose us, shall meet a most disastrous end. A wailing of the trumpets, screaming, "Defend! Defend! Defend!"

Her screams, stabbing into the air with an agony that almost made Jolis wince, punctuated the anthem's end. As the music faded, Grand Magistrate Royger stopped clapping, smashed his hardwood mallet on the bench three times, and the men, satisfied, returned to their seats. They slapped hands, wiped themselves of sweat and oil, and beamed as they put on their jackets.

The Hooter lay still in the middle of the floor. Two guards grabbed her hands and feet and carried her back through the door she had entered from.

Finally. These introductory antics did nothing for Jolis, but at least they primed the men with a primitive fervor he could take advantage of. He felt a deep aversion for this excess, the lack of discipline, the basic pleasures these men succumbed to—including the magistrates, the highest legal authority in the hemisphere, hand-picked by Chief Executive Rhitel himself to judge matters of hemispheric importance, pass and nullify laws, and, like now, preside over elections. Even so, everyone knew they were just another finger on the hand that Rhitel had ruled with. When Jolis came to power, there would be nothing like what he just saw. Change is too serious for games.

"May the Holy Father bless the Northwestern Hemisphere," Grand Magistrate Royger said.

"Now and forever!" the men joyfully replied.

"Local Manager II Stephan Jolis. Local Manager IV Williams Washington. Please approach your podiums."

Jolis advanced to the center of the room. Washington took his precious time walking down the stairs, shaking hands with his twenty-seven supporters. Many of them were traitors who had defected to the opposition upon The Chief Executive's death. Like Jolis, he hadn't participated in the chasing of The Hooter.

The man moved slowly, surely, as if his feet took great pleasure touching the ground. His hair, an equal shade of brown to Jolis's, was unruffled. No sweat clung to his alabaster skin, a twin to Jolis's own, and his suit hugged his tall, lean body in the same way. They could be brothers. But despite their striking similarities, there were clear differences. Soon enough the Gallery would know this without a shadow of a doubt.

The men on both sides clapped, whistled, and screamed for their respective candidates. Grand Magistrate Royger extended his arm and the room fell silent. "Here we are. Two young men vying for the most powerful seat our world has to offer. Now, the majority of you are too young to have experienced an election, but it's quite simple: Local Manager II Jolis and Local Manager IV Washington will engage in four days of debate centered on topics most salient to our hemisphere. On the fourth day, you exalted men, not the doltish populace, will submit your votes via earsphere. On the following day, we will inaugurate our new Chief Executive."

Before they began, Grand Magistrate Royger called for refreshments. A group of Invisible teenagers, earmuffed and painted in the hemispheric colors, entered with trays piled high with biscuits, herbpots, and tall glasses of juice. Washington, accepting some beet juice, went as far as touching the Invisible servant's shoulder in appreciation. One approached Jolis and he hissed at him. When the boy didn't hear him, Jolis kicked his shin. The boy took the blow, as if he expected it. Then he stared into Jolis's eyes for a second longer than he should have, and produced the faintest grin before walking away, which, Jolis had to admit, he respected.

"Fine, fine," Grand Magistrate Royger said, an oversize canvas capture bearing Chief Executive Rhitel's sober face and ever-watching eyes on the wall behind him. "You all have your treats and sweets as a reward for this morning's exercise." The seventy men on Jolis's side laughed. "And without further ado, we'll begin today's debate, which is on the topic of trade. Local Manager IV Washington, Local Manager II Jolis has been most amicable and given you the choice of who goes first."

Washington turned in Jolis's direction. "How nice of him." His supporters sneered with the same look of self-righteousness. Jolis wanted to drown every last one of these men who thought they knew better, who thought they were tapped into the ways of the world, when they were each just rotten trees in need of felling for the seeds of the future to take root. These wastes of— *Stop*, he heard Croger say in his head. *Stay calm.*

"I'll go first," Washington said.

"Proceed."

"But instead of trade, I propose we discuss the subject that's most critical to our hemisphere's future."

"Which is?" the Grand Magistrate asked with a hint of annoyance. He wasn't one for theatrics, at least once proceedings began, and Washington was already getting under his skin.

"The fate of the Invisibles."

"This is absurd!" one of Jolis's supporters yelled, pointing his hand in Washington's direction. "Who does he think he is?"

Grand Magistrate Royger whispered with his magistrates, then peered down from his bench. "What do you think, Local Manager II Jolis?"

"I think that, for the first and last time, Local Manager IV Washington and I agree."

"It's settled, then. Local Manager IV Washington, you may begin."

Washington took a sip of his juice and casually wiped his mouth with a napkin, as if he were at home, or in the park, or wherever he relaxed and concocted his watered-down plans. This display of laid-back behavior made Jolis want to break his drinking glass on Washington's podium and stab it through his heart—purple juice and blood spreading across his chest like a nightmarish sea.

"A brief history lesson," Washington began. "We all know that Invisibles are second-class hemispherians who contribute to our society through manual and nonmanual service roles, while also acting as our own measuring stick of how good and noble we are. But for those like myself who have studied the archives, you know it wasn't always this way.

"No, before Chief Executive Rhitel came to power, may the Holy Father bless his soul, our hemisphere was a far more egalitarian land. Invisibles and DPs coexisted peacefully, the laws were fairer to *all* people, and we even had Invisibles right here, in the Gallery of Rule, sitting"—he faced the rows of men behind him—"in the very seats you now occupy, gentlemen."

"TRAITOR!" one of Jolis's men screamed. Others joined, chanting, "TRAITOR! TRAITOR! TRAITOR!"

Men on Washington's side stood, ready, but sat down after he raised his hand.

"Order!" Grand Magistrate Royger shouted. He banged his mallet. The sharp crack of wood on wood ricocheted throughout the Gallery. By the third *BANG!*, the men had quieted down. "Local Manager IV Washington, you're permitted to speak as you may, but please do try to maintain some decorum fitting a DP regarding sensitive subjects."

The spineless local manager nodded at the Grand Magistrate. "Of course. The point here is that if we were to move to a more equitable society, where Invisibles are allowed to participate not as products but as people, The Chief Executive, may the Holy Father bless his soul, would still be here. Thus, my plan is simple: we don't give them everything at once, that would be foolish. Instead, we systematically grant them rights, which would improve their livelihood and enrich our hemisphere financially, culturally, and spiritually.

"This means." Men on both sides began speaking over one another, the volume in the Gallery rising. "This *means*,"—Washington spoke louder—"giving more than a lucky few the opportunity to work in industries untethered to regional production, removing the Invisible tax on their wages, as well as the grow tax for those who seek to raise their own food; eliminating travel passes, integrating the educational systems—"

"And let them *baisok* our women and daughters while we're at it, right?" another one of Jolis's men cried in partial Vikench—fist in the air, red-faced, neck tendons about to burst.

Keep going, Washington. Jolis kept a straight face, but he was sliding across the dance floor of his mind.

"This Invisible, Shanu," Washington continued, "is the manifestation of three-quarters of a century's worth of pain, degradation, and humiliation inflicted upon the Invisible by the DP, making *us* not *them* responsible for The Chief Executive's murder, may the Holy Father bless his soul. And if we don't correct the errors of our ways, there will be more murder, because there are surely more Shanus in every region of our beloved land. Thank you."

Grand Magistrate Royger banged his mallet again and again, but only when a group of guards approached the men of rule, whips drawn, did they finally settle down.

Happiness washed over Jolis like a bucket of cool water. Every drop of doubt he'd had was gone. From the hushed tones behind him, he could sense that even the men on Washington's side might have thought their man went too far.

"Local Manager II Jolis," Grand Magistrate Royger said. "Your rebuttal."

Jolis dropped his head, allowed an uncomfortable silence to

permeate the room; the only sounds a stray cough, an overly loud sip, expectant tapping of hands and feet on wood.

Turning to face the dozens of seated men behind him, he said, "What a sad day it is when a candidate for Chief Executive has to stoop so low that he blames The Chief Executive, may the Holy Father bless his soul, our Great Savior, for his own murder. Unlike Washington, I'm not here to talk *at* you, I'm here to talk *with* you. And I know I don't speak as eloquently as him, with every word worth ten rhitellings, or with the highbrow regional accent that many of you are used to, so I'll say it as plainly as I know how: if you follow this man"—he stabbed his hand in Washington's direction—"life as we know it will be destroyed. Do you want Invisibles to become your neighbors? For them to sit in a classroom next to your precious sons and daughters? To, may the Holy Father forbid, join us in this Gallery and act as though *they* know what is right for our hemisphere? Take a moment and let that sink in, because *that* is the world that Washington aims to create.

"This man would have you believe that Invisibles are mistreated, which is why Shanu murdered Chief Executive Rhitel, may the Holy Father bless his soul. He would have you believe that *we*, as he so clearly stated, are to blame. But I can assure you that Shanu is a deranged killer, *not* a victim. He is an exception, for now, but will certainly become the rule under Washington's plan. This is not an opinion"—he thrust his finger into the air—"but a fact. And to prove it, I'll go straight to the source."

Jolis walked off the Gallery floor, entered the antechamber, found the Invisible boy he'd kicked in the shin, and gestured for him to follow. The boy, still wearing his earmuffs, complied without question.

When he returned to the floor, the men began whispering. "What is this?" Washington asked, holding his open hand out to Jolis as Jolis and the Invisible faced the magistrates' bench. "Grand

Magistrate, this is not only turning these proceedings into a farce, but it is also cruel."

"Local Manager II Jolis," Grand Magistrate Royger said. "I trust there's an explanation for this."

Jolis, an unstoppable train, pounded the podium. "There's been so much talk of Invisibles this morning, Grand Magistrate, that I figured we should hear from one ourselves, to better understand their state of mind." He saw that the boy was no longer the grinning, confident young man from before. His small taut body was shaking, eyes focused on the floor directly in front of him.

"What is your name?" Jolis asked after removing his earmuffs.

The boy mumbled something too low for anyone other than Jolis to hear.

"Speak up," he said, resting his hand on the Invisible's trembling shoulder.

"L-l-langa, sir."

The local manager nodded. "Nice to meet you, Langa. How old are you?"

"Fifteen, sir."

"Fifteen!" Jolis looked around the Gallery. "We can all remember when we were fifteen, the trouble I'm sure we all got into." He turned back to Langa. "Now, Langa, do you know how to read?"

The young man cleared his throat, nodded.

"Well, let's see." Jolis pointed to an illuminated page on his podium with some of his notes. "What's this say? At the top."

"The. The sh-sh-sh—"

"Take your time, it's okay."

"The surest path to destruction is by compounding weakness with weakness."

Jolis held his hands out in both directions, turning from the magistrates' bench to the rows of men. "Thank you, Langa. Another question: Have you ever been hungry and not had food?"

"No, sir. In my forest, Forest Eighteen, we have a lot of food. Even two Rhitel Burgers." His eyes widened with desire. "It's my favorite."

"Of course it is. So, you've never been hungry and not had food, because no one starves in our hemisphere. And you know how to read. Now, what's your favorite thing in the world to do?"

"To box with my friends, sir. One day, I'd like to be a professional, like Mandla. He can knock anyone out." He threw a few jabs. "And he's also from Forest Eighteen."

Jolis laughed. The men in the Gallery, on both sides, nodded at Langa's answers, his unfiltered enthusiasm magnetic. "I've watched Mandla in person, at Rhitel Arena. Have you ever seen him fight there?"

The boy shook his head.

"I know tickets can be expensive, but I'll get you some, for you and your friends. How's that sound?"

He grabbed Jolis's hand, jumping up and down and up and down. "Thank you, sir! Thank you!"

"My pleasure," he said, removing his hand from the boy's, wiping it on his suit. "But two last questions. Do you feel oppressed?"

The boy looked up at Jolis, his eyebrows curving and bending across his red-painted forehead. "Oh-pressed, sir?"

"Yes. It means that you can't do what you want because people are stopping you from doing it. Do you feel that way?"

"Sometimes, sir. Yes."

"See!" one of Washington's men shouted, vindicated. Washington grinned.

"How?"

"If I haven't finished my schoolwork, sometimes my parents don't let me see my friends. That's when I feel oh-pressed."

The men, including the magistrates, did little to hold their laughter in, but Jolis held up his hands, silencing them for another minute.

"We've all been there, Langa. Trust me. Last question: What do you think about what Shanu did? The Invisible who murdered Chief Executive Rhitel, may the Holy Father bless his soul."

Langa rubbed his chin for a minute, long enough for Jolis to think that he'd made a mistake in putting the fate of his argument in the hands of a fifteen-year-old Invisible. Every man leaned toward them, there, in the center of the Gallery. Jolis looked at Washington, found hope in his eyes, his slightly open mouth.

"I think." Langa rubbed his chin harder, wiping away some of his face paint. "I think that he's made it harder for the rest of us. Shibs"—he coughed—"I mean hemispheric guards, have come into our cabins to ask us a lot of questions. We're getting stopped on the way to the train, even on our main road." He looked up at the Gallery's ceiling. "It's not fun, and I hope that Shanu is caught so life can return to normal for us."

Jolis's leg, which he'd realized was shaking, stilled. "Me too, Langa. Me too. Thank you for your time. And I'll make sure you get those tickets to Mandla's next fight."

The boy showed his wide smile to everyone in the Gallery as he walked away, back through the doors he'd entered minutes ago. He would remember this moment forever: the time that he spoke in front of the most powerful men in the hemisphere, and they listened.

Jolis wanted to jump for joy, to take his clothes off and run, like The Hooter, around the entire Gallery screaming, "VICTORY!" But he just stood to the side of his podium, facing Washington. "Need I say more?"

Hands banged the wooden railings, a sign that the men were with him. He closed his eyes, heard the roaring of soft skin on hard wood grow, and imagined the sound forming a large hand that would scoop up his body, lift him to the ceiling, through the roof, and all the way to the Executive Estate, dropping him directly into

The Chief Executive's seat. There would be no going back to being nothing, no more running. The world, at last, was about to be his.

"That concludes today's debate," Grand Magistrate Royger said above the rumbling. "Thank you for such a spirited and innovative"— he nodded at Jolis—"back-and-forth. I think I speak for all when I say we look forward to tomorrow. Now, let's bring in The Defiled. We've all earned a little fun."

CHAPTER 13

THE TENNIS COURT SAT ON THE FARTHEST EDGE OF THE PROPERTY, close to the cliff separating land from ocean. A three-meter-high black chain-link fence stood at the border, preventing people from falling to their deaths while trying to return back-breaking serves.

Abe was already standing under the shade of an umbrella near the court's entrance when Candace and Mr. Tenmase approached; a cart with glass bottles of water and purple-colored towels beside him, two rackets in his outstretched hands. "For you, sir." An all-black one with *CT* written in red at the center for Mr. Tenmase. "And you, Ms. Candace." She took the all-white racket with the bright red handle and stepped through the entrance, bracing for the soles of her feet to be singed. But the green and blue court was cool.

"What's this made out of?" she asked, waving her racket across the ground.

"A special metamaterial I invented ages ago," Mr. Tenmase replied, passing her as he walked to the opposite side. "Passive radiative cooling. Instead of absorbing sunlight, it reflects it back into space." He palmed his throat. "We use a different version in your collars so that they don't burn your necks. I assume you know how to play?"

Her mind left the court, traveling backward through that morning's events. From Sanford to Hemispheric Guard Director Curts to Reverend Achte to . . . Darksap and the garden; the heat from his chest against her back, his breath tickling her neck, the way his words dripped into her ear like the sweetest syrup.

"Candace?" Mr. Tenmase said, throwing and catching an orange ball.

"Yes, sorry. I know that I need to get the ball to bounce inside your red lines in a way that you can't return it. And you'll try to do the same, right?"

"That's the gist. And you serve behind your farthest red line, the *baseline*, anywhere in your right corner. You start."

Abe tossed her a ball. She gripped it, threw it into the air, and when she brought her racket down, it connected with a ton of nothing. The ball hit the ground, bounced a few times, rolled away.

"That's okay," Mr. Tenmase said. "Again."

Embarrassed, she retrieved the ball, went back behind her baseline. She bounced it once, caught sight of the red baseline, and the image of Shanu, the one shown on the NWN the night before, burst into her mind. She raised her racket, ready to hurl it across the net.

"What are we even doing here?" she yelled.

He bounced from his left foot to his right, knees bent, racket twirling. "Don't ask ridiculous questions. We're playing tennis."

She let the racket fall from her hand. The waves thrashed beyond them, their percussive collisions only heightening the moment's rising absurdity.

"Pick it up," he ordered. "Pick it up now."

"Not until you tell me why we're playing tennis when the entire hemisphere is searching for my brother. You haven't said anything," she screamed at the top of her lungs. "*Nothing* at all about it!"

He unbent his back, walked toward the net, and gestured for her to meet him there. She didn't know him to be a violent man, but there, with that racket in his hand . . . anything was possible. In her experience, men never ceased to surprise you with their creative capacity for destruction.

Shielding his eyes as he stared up at her, he flared his nostrils, inhaled, and released. "I'm not a heartless monster telling you to *just get over this*, Candace. But fact or fiction: your brother abandoned you."

She didn't respond, fearful that she would say or do something she couldn't take back.

"Fact. Instead of holding on to the past, you need to move forward so that we can create the future, not be held captive by it. How many times must I say it? You are destined for greatness. The Big Reset is impossible without you, and—"

"Greatness means nothing if I can't help the ones I love, Mr. Tenmase." That sound, of the waves crashing against the shore—an endless cycle of cleansing through violence and relief—filled in the gap of silence that followed. "I don't know why my brother left, but I have to find him. I *have* to. Can't you see that I don't have a choice?"

"You always have a choice," he said, shaking his head. "Life's limitations are only ever due to a lack of vision."

She waved her hand in front of him. "Those are just pretty words, Mr. Tenmase. If you help me, I'll work for free. I won't take weekends off. I'll"—she looked down at the ground, her shadow nonexistent—"I'll even paint myself white and be one of your servants, like Abe. Anything, anything at all, if you just do *something*."

"Whether you believe me or not," he said, tapping his racket against her arm. "I care about you, Candace. That is why you're not in His Executive's Prison right now, locked up like some common criminal. Or shipped off to the Waste Renewal Region, turning feces into soil and urine into fountain water. Count your blessings, because you have more than you're aware of, and I am the unseen merchant of your luck."

"But—"

He stretched out his arms. "We're here, playing tennis, because the key to being an inventor, the type who sees the world as it is *and* as it could become, is to remain loose in the face of chaos. To remember that the essence of creation is play. What do you think the Holy Father was doing when he formed all of this?"

Play. Candace was quickly learning that for her and her people, reality was a punch in the jaw every second of every day. She gripped her racket, wanting to strike him in his smiling, pink-white face so he could know what it felt like, just once. Sometimes that was all it took to understand. Instead, she ran behind her baseline, and he did the same.

"If you manage to beat me," he called from across the net, "I'll give you something special. Something that no other Invisible has ever possessed. At least legally."

Tossing the ball into the air, she raised her eyes to meet it, swung her racket, now an extension of her arm, and sent the ball sailing through the air, directly into the box closest to the net. It bounced toward Mr. Tenmase, but was too fast and high for him to return it. They continued that way for an hour—her smashing balls with furious screams, Mr. Tenmase mostly missing them.

"Okay, okay," he finally said. "I give up."

She wouldn't admit it, but she *did* feel better. The running left and right, jumping, crouching, and sweating—giving into her anger and abusing the ball—helped her to forget everything. Even if just for an hour. She laughed as she grabbed a towel from Abe. *This is what it must feel like to be a dippy.*

"Come," Mr. Tenmase said. "Time for your prize."

They walked to the west side of the property and stopped at the greenhouse, an all-glass structure twice the size of her own cabin.

Through the glass she saw clay pots sitting atop wooden tables; little hills of dirt clumped up across the floor; a coiled white hose just to the right of the door, which Mr. Tenmase now held open.

"After you."

She entered, ran her eyes up and down every centimeter, but failed to find anything special.

"This is my favorite place. Aside from the toilet, it's where I do my best thinking."

"What a pleasant image."

"Anyway"—he stepped past her, wiped some dirt from a faded wooden table—"I'm trying to grow flowers in here, but the overly hot air dries out the dirt before the seeds can germinate, and the soil is too acidic. The humidity needs to be increased, but I'm making progress."

She gasped when he picked up a pot from beneath the table and held it in front of her. "Look," she whispered, slowly bringing her finger to the small hairy green stalk with a crown of sorts at its top. The flower, with its delicate yellow petals surrounding a dark brown head, beckoned her. There was something oddly brazen about it; the way it was so unabashedly loud, unable to hide its brilliance or blend in. She felt intimidated, jealous even. "What is it?"

"A hardier variety of specimen that does well in this heat called a *sunflower*. I've been patiently growing this one for almost two months." He set it on the table, stepped back, and placed his hands on his hips, nodding at his plant like a proud father. "They never make it this far, but if she can, then I think I'll be able to get her to full maturation, and hopefully do the same with others."

Candace couldn't take her eyes off it. She'd never seen one before, not really. Just spare, hand-drawn illuminations in school. This, though, was something else—its existence undeniable.

She turned to him. "Why?"

"Why what?"

"Why spend all of this time trying to grow a flower when the world has been fine without them?"

He met her eyes and laughed. "Beauty for beauty's sake is always worth it. *That*, my dear, is the true purpose of invention: to create something beautiful and rare, even if it doesn't last." He placed the sunflower back and pulled a small glass bottle from a shelf, setting it on the table. Inside was a clear liquid, with red dots floating in it, and a dropper.

"Your prize."

"*This?*" She picked it up, brought it close to her face.

"Don't sound so glum. What you're holding there is so potent and so powerful that Chief Executive Rhitel forbade it from public use. Its primary function was to neutralize your scentprints, making it harder for Invisibles to recognize each other in the event of an uprising. But when we discovered that it also dropped your temperatures to the point that we couldn't see you with didanlenses, it was classified as a State weapon."

"A weapon?" She twisted it around and around, the red dots suspended in a slow spiraling motion.

"That's right. But a hemispheric guard must have leaked it on the unseen exchange. Now there are a dozen dangerous derivations of it, colloquially referred to as 'red drops.' Very expensive."

"Why are you giving this to me?"

"Because I know I can't stop you from doing whatever you're going to do, and while I'm not going to intervene, maybe this," he said, snatching it from her, "will come in handy. But you *must* be careful with it. One drop will keep your temperature down and scent clear for fifteen minutes, but more has the potential to kill you, or anyone you give it to."

She grabbed it back, held it up to the light, mesmerized by the dancing red dots. "And this isn't a joke, like the blue herbs?"

"Far from it. But you need to promise me two things. First: you won't tell anyone about it or share it with others."

"I promise."

"Second: everything has to go back to normal. No more sulking. When you're here, you're here. Our work comes first, and you leave all the noise behind once you step off the train. Deal?"

Hope coursing through her veins, she wrapped her arms around his brawny shoulders, rested her head against the back of his neck, and was surprised when he hugged her back.

"Deal."

CHAPTER 14

CURTS LAY ON HIS OFFICE CARPET, EARSPHERE INSERTED, EYES darting in every direction as he worked through round after round of math sets that became increasingly difficult. The activity eased the drilling in his head, but he knew it would return soon. A patch would solve it.

Twenty-four hours and nothing to show. No credible leads. No Shanu. Nothing. He'd visited the Invisible's parents, located through an old DNA match, and was surprised by who they were. Curts could have exposed them, paraded them on the Northwestern News and used them to lure Shanu out, but they certainly didn't know where their son was, nor did they want anything to do with him, so it was no use. They'd made that clear almost three decades ago.

The bright lights of the Executive Estate's lawn penetrated his office, casting furniture-shaped shadows across his body. *Maybe if I stay as silent and as paralyzed as possible, something will happen. A sign from the Holy Father, if he's even out there.*

A greater man wouldn't wait for a sign, he would go out in search of it—create one, even. But he was beginning to doubt his abilities. He felt small, like the child who was called soft and weak by his parents because he loved to lie outside for hours finishing complex math problems, because he would vomit when he saw someone backhand their Invisible servant in the street, because he preferred penning poetry to punching peers. Even now, after proving himself to anyone who mattered, he was hiding in an office.

All of his usual tasks—tracking rare subversives and escapees, reviewing new hemispheric guard training regimens and visiting academies to inspire the next generation of guards, interfacing with every major administrator of regional prisons—were suspended due to the pursuit of Shanu. But the larger concerns remained, such as infiltrating the Children of Slim and bringing them to justice, especially if they were working with Shanu himself.

His earsphere vibrated. He hesitated, then picked it up.

"What is it?"

"Well," Stephan Jolis said, "don't sound too excited, Leon."

He didn't respond.

"Okay, we can get straight to it."

"I'd appreciate it."

"It's no secret that we're not the best of friends. We've been cordial enough, due to our common friend, and now that he's gone, there's not much of an incentive to keep up appearances."

"I thought you said you were getting to the point, Stephan."

"Listen, we have our different methods, but we're ultimately on the same side. Chief Executive Rhitel, may the Holy Father bless his soul, is gone. But we're still here, with a hemisphere to rule. Together."

The drilling in his head increased. He sat up, massaged his forehead, but no luck. "What are you proposing?"

"Only that we work together. You need to catch this viz—Invisible, as you like to say—in four days. And I need him caught in four days. Preferably on the fourth day."

"You act as if I can put him in a box with a bow on it."

"That'd be even better, but I'll take what I can get. Let's just keep each other informed of what we hear and make sure we both come out on top. When I win, your position will remain secure, and I won't get in the way of your"—he paused, letting Curts know that it was killing him to have to do this—"unique form of maintaining law and order. Deal?"

He needed every ally he could get. Especially one who had a strong chance of being the hemisphere's next leader; someone who, in a way, already held his life in their hands. Yes, compromises had to be made, but Stephan's entitlement, lack of self-awareness, and sheer audacity was sickening.

"Do you remember that comment you made at the Rebirth Anniversary celebration a couple months ago?" Curts asked.

"Can't say I do. But if you're really going to bring up—"

"It was a joke, actually. You said—in front of my wife, The Chief Executive, may the Holy Father bless his soul, my deputy, and others—that instead of dessert, they could all take a bite out of me, because I was more jelly than man. 'Not one solid thing to him,' you added."

The line went quiet. Then, "I really don't remember that, Leon. But what do you want me to do about it now?"

"Apologize. Then beg. Beg me to keep you updated on the search for Shanu, to let you in on the files and files of information I have on people, like your opponent, Washington, or even surprising details I've discovered about your mentor, Croger. An entire vault of intelligence that I, and I alone, can access whenever I need to put someone in their place."

Stephan laughed. "You want *me* to beg *you*, of all people? You're so weak. If it weren't for gravity, you'd be floating somewhere on the other side of the universe, weeping about a joke some 'mean politician'"—he made his voice whiny now—"'made about me.' Holy Father, Leon. You're—"

Curts pointed his pupils at the call and ended it. Almost immediately, a message from Stephan appeared: *The strongest of enemies were once the best of friends, Leon, and the opposite is also possible. You'll come around eventually. You have to.*

Before he could reply, his office door swung open, the lights flickered on, and in walked the former Chief Consort Rhitel. Even if she were Invisible and he could only see the pressed beige mesh cardigan, four buttons running down each side, blouse, and matching skirt, which stretched far past her knees, he would know it was her.

"Brauna?"

"It's still Chief Consort Rhitel to you, Leon." She surveyed the room, her nose wrinkling in pity or disgust, he couldn't tell. "Get up."

He did as he was told.

"Stand here." She pointed directly in front of her.

Like an obedient child, he stood exactly where she'd pointed. And then he received the slap of a lifetime. The night sky appeared in his eyes, spinning round and round. He staggered backward, but she grabbed his collar, steadying him.

"This little vizzer that murdered my husband is still free, and you're in here, what? Enjoying a pot of herbs and a biscuit?"

"Chief Consort, I—"

"Look at me, Leon. Listen to me closely." She had a long finger in his face, so close to his eyeball that it took up most of his vision, the room reflected in pale pink nail polish. "You are a spineless, sorry excuse for a Northwesterner. I never liked you. My husband never liked you. My daughter, in particular, young as she is, detests you. But you kept things running smoothly, until you didn't. Let me speak plainly: someone is hanging in four days. Whether you're looking up or down is entirely up to you."

She left as quietly as she'd come, leaving him to question if she'd been there at all, or was just a figment of his failure.

He clenched his eyes, fighting to stop the drilling that spread from his head into the spine that he did or didn't possess. *No, no, no.*

"Sir?"

Lucretia brought a glass of chilled water to his lips, her warm hand on his neck, easing his head back, gently pouring the liquid. He hadn't even heard her enter, one of her many talents.

"Breathe, sir. Just breathe. Everything will be okay."

When he first met her a decade ago, it was obvious that she wasn't a pure Northwesterner—with her slightly tanned skin, red hair, and green eyes—despite her family living in the hemisphere for well over a century. Probably mixed with some Southwestern, he'd guessed, and she confirmed as much after he'd hired her. She said she was afraid he'd use it against her. He wouldn't have, but Chief Executive Rhitel expressed concerns. Curts, determined, fought for her and won.

The Director knew she was meant for more the moment he found her in the Rubber and Silicone Region's academy, nicknamed "Manville" because of how testosterone-fueled and uncivilized the hemispheric guards who came out of it were. But there she was, the only woman among dozens of men. A woman both respected and feared by her male cohorts due to her quick, acidic wit, alarming proficiency with knives, and rugged beauty that belittled all who laid eyes on her. Except Curts: a newly appointed, fresh-faced Hemispheric Guard Director who needed competent people he could trust—someone with something to prove. Lucretia was one of them.

She did her best to smooth out the wrinkles in his shirt. "I take it that wasn't a cordial catchup with the Chief Consort, sir?"

He brushed her hands from his shirt and stood up. "No, it wasn't. Any news?"

"We're on it. Guards across the entire hemisphere are interrogating Invisibles, and Shanu's capture—the one he took at the Annual Painting three years ago—is being shown on the display every hour."

He tucked in his shirt, removed a comb from his chest pocket, and ran it over his hair. Still uneasy, he sat on the couch. "What about the other hemispheres?"

She lowered herself on the couch opposite him. "Head Rector Yaima said, and I quote, 'I plan to continue living for a long time, so I won't do anything to stoke revolution amongst our Invisibles who are happy, healthy, and wholly satisfied.'"

"Smug Northeasterners." He couldn't stand their sanctimonious arrogance. "And obviously the Southwesterners won't help."

Lucretia nodded. "Supreme Advocate Cadorno's people didn't even respond to our request. And Key Defender Laanm said he would be glad to help us once we remove our trade embargo."

His head fell into his hands, a thousand hammers striking against his skull. "Stephan is too much of a bumbling, egotistical isolationist to do that," he said, his voice muffled. "Washington would, but his chances of winning are slim, even if I do feed him some particularly damaging evidence against Stephan. Either way—"

"It'll be too late. Unless we can somehow have Jolis pledge to open trade *if* Laanm helps us. But we don't even know if Shanu is actually there. If he's anywhere, it's—"

"The Southwestern Hemisphere. Yes, I know. Is Ribussce doing anything of note?"

"Not that I can tell. These days I hear he makes the rounds at the clubs, striking fear into every Invisible woman he encounters. If there were ever a man who was disgust embodied, it's him."

"Even so, keep an eye on him. He's a serious and treacherous threat, especially since he has his aunt's ear, and if the former Chief Consort is anything, she's a woman of swift and decisive action." His earsphere vibrated on the ground. "Give me a second," he said, scooping it up.

A message from Del, asking him if he was any closer, and when he was coming home. He couldn't face her and Eva. Not now. *Working late tonight. See you when I can,* he wrote, eyes scrolling across the screen of light. *Love you from here to forever,* she immediately responded.

"Everything okay?" Lucretia asked.

"No." He rubbed his temples, felt the walls closing in all around him. "But it will be once we catch him."

He went to the back corner of his office, retrieved a fresh jacket, and carefully straightened his cap in the tiny mirror that hung inside his closet's door. Enough was enough.

"New plan," he said, spinning around to face her. "We tried to play nice, but it's led us nowhere."

"What do you propose?"

"Instruct guards across the hemisphere to begin rounding up Invisibles at random. Don't physically harm them, but detain them longer than necessary, without food or water. This will help them understand that until Shanu is found, their lives will be turned upside down."

"A balanced measure, sir. Anything else?"

"Yes. Message Captain Kandolo and impress the urgent importance upon him of Lieutenant Imbuka's locating the Children of Slim's stronghold. Also inform him that if he doesn't start to produce results, his forest will lose the protection that his position affords it; that we will tear it down like Forest Seventy-Eight."

"But," she said, narrowing her eyes at him, "you're bluffing, right?"

"For now."

The memory of what his predecessor did there, the example he set for every Invisible in the hemisphere, sent a cold shiver up his possibly nonexistent spine.

"Lastly, reach out to all regional reporters, starting with Anna Franklin, and notify them of the one-hundred-thousand-rhitelling bounty on Shanu's head if found alive, fifty thousand if found dead.

For both DPs *and* Invisibles. Make sure they broadcast it across Invisible and DP display networks nonstop."

"Yes, sir. I'll get on it," she replied, her face hardly containing its excitement.

This was part of his job, too. To reinvigorate, not only himself, but those, like Lucretia, who looked to him for leadership. Winning was a matter of will, not circumstance. Stephan had taught him that.

He finished checking his reflection in the mirror, turned around, and placed his hands on her shoulders. "No one, especially an Invisible, is going to triumph over law and order. Now go."

Not wasting another second, she saluted him and headed toward his office's door.

"Lucretia."

"Yes, sir?" she said, pausing.

"Don't let me down."

"Never, sir."

He walked to the corner closet farthest from the window. The opened doors revealed a metallic elevator, on which an illuminated display appeared. After tapping in his code, the doors opened, and he took the elevator far, far down, all the way to a train only he and The Chief Executive had access to.

A dusty film covered its steel exterior. Inside, he set his destination, and the train pulled out. He removed his jacket, boots, and cap, neatly arranging them before lying down on a bed. Four hours to rest and think. Four hours to cover thirty-two hundred kilometers. Four hours until he reached forbidden salvation.

"You'll arrive in ten minutes, Hemispheric Guard Director Curts," the train announced, waking him from a dreamless sleep.

He leapt to his feet, opened a closet near his bed, and removed a set of clothing. Dark blue mesh T-shirt, loose-fitting beige pants, scuffed, handwoven sandals, and a hooded jacket with perforated illustrations covering every centimeter. Once he was changed,

Curts gently rubbed light brown paint across his face, neck, and hands.

"Plant Parish Fifty-Eight, Waste Renewal Region," the train said, slowing to a stop.

With precision, he pulled off the nonstick backing of a beard, held it up to his mouth, matching its corners with the contours of his face, and slowly pressed it to his skin, making sure it looked as natural as possible. Then he grabbed tufts of hair that matched his own but were longer, and carefully clipped them in, piece by piece. He checked his reflection in the mirror, flinched at the man staring back at him. If he were in the Forest Region, he'd stick out like an Invisible in a suit. But here, in the Waste Renewal Region, where some of the hemispherians maintained a more rustic way of life, he'd more than fit right in.

He'd disappear.

CHAPTER 15

SWEETMINT WENT OVER THE PLAN AS HER TRAIN RACED BACK TO Forest Twenty-Six. Get to the city. Find her parents. Convince or guilt them into helping her find Sweetsmoke. All in four days. But how? Her forestfolk were against her. The Director of the all-powerful Hemispheric Guard *personally* told her to give up. Mr. Tenmase, a man far wiser than she was, also said it was useless. And an entire hemisphere of people wanted her brother executed. *Holy Father*. This was impossible.

The train arrived, interrupting her thoughts. Of course the Rainbow Girls were there. Violet and Yellow stood on the platform, laughing. Orange, Indigo, Blue, and Green walked arm in arm as they entered the main square from Twenty-Six Road. But Red sat with her head in her hands on a bench by herself.

Ignoring the giggling and hushed tones pointed at her like tiny knives, Sweetmint rushed down the platform, but she stopped when she heard muffled sniffling coming from where Red sat. She wanted to ignore it; Red was her tormentor. But seeing her there like that, the other girls just going about their business as if nothing was the matter . . . She recognized a familiar form of loneliness.

"What happened?" she asked, the glow of the platform's light strips traveled through Sweetmint's body and reflected off Red's skin, making it glisten.

"Go away, Sourmint. You reek of burnt dirt."

Forget this. She moved toward Softstone Path, but then her heart jolted with the memory of how every time she'd told someone to go away, she'd meant, "Be there for me." Sweetmint sat down on the bench beside Red, chuckling as the other Rainbow Girls narrowed their eyes at her.

"What are you laughing at? I said, *Go. Away.* Or are you too big and dumb to listen?"

"Probably," she replied, "since everyone these days is trying to tell me what to do, but I'm only doing the opposite." She tilted her head to the sky and saw the Three Teachers watching from above—a sign that she was right where she needed to be. "But I'll just sit here with you until your train comes. Unless you want to tell me what's wrong."

Red finally lifted her head. Black paint from her eyes and red paint from her face streaked down her cheeks, blurring her typically immaculate paint job. Her lips were gorgeous tonight: a deep purple dusted with tiny diamond-like gems, some of which now stuck to her palms.

"You wouldn't understand."

"Let me guess, dippy let you down?"

Red nodded, her face a tree the *exact* moment before it falls with a thundering *BANG!* Then, a quivering mess of snot and tears. Her arms latched on to Sweetmint, stunning her, but she did the only thing she could think of. She brought Red's head to her chest, rocked her side to side, saying, "It's okay. It's okay. It's okay." Just like Sweetsmoke had done with her.

Shouts of masculine joy erupted in a house near the main square—probably a group of men watching a fukhaba or boxing match. A few painted people turned off Twenty-Six Road and passed them, canvas bags of Rhitel Burger in their hands, on their way home to Nearsee. Two patchers stumbled toward Orange, Indigo, Blue, and Green, dusty hands gripping cracked glass tablets, likely stolen, begging for a money transfer, but the girls just waved them away.

"He said he was going to leave his wife for me. And when I asked *when*, for the hundredth time, he finally said, 'The only way you'd ever live in my home is as a servant.'" She found a tissue, blew. "I tell the girls to never believe anything these stupid men say, to maintain control so they can get whatever they want, and here I am, the dumbest of them all."

She rubbed Red's soft, luxuriant poof of hair. "You're *not* dumb. You were in love. And that's special, even if he was an amgolo."

"That's what you say."

"You know," Sweetmint whispered. "*I've* never been in love."

"What about Darksap?" Red asked, blowing her nose again.

"What about him?"

"He stretches toward you like a tree to the sun."

"Maybe." She shrugged. "But I don't have the time for romance. Plus, he knows me too well."

Red righted herself, grabbed another tissue, wiped her face. "Take it from me. The ones who know and still adore you are the only ones worth keeping."

A train was pulling into the station. The other girls turned to Red. "I'll be there in a second," she said. "Go inside."

She reapplied black paint to her eyes, touched up the blotchy spots on her face, and dipped her lips into a metal tin with those powdered gemstones inside. "How do I look?" she asked, raising her face to Sweetmint.

"Like you're too good for him."

Red grinned, her lips sparkling in the night. "I never thought I'd say this, but you're right, Sou— Sweetmint."

"Don't get soft on me," she joked, then paused to observe Red, fully restored to her normal splendor. "I just don't know how you do it. Going to the city every night, and—" *There it is.* She leaned back on the bench and mouthed *Thank you* to the Three Teachers.

"Everything okay?" Red asked.

"Please know that me being nice to you had nothing to do with what I'm about to ask, okay?"

"Okay. But make it quick. The train won't wait forever."

"I want to go to Minx with you. Tomorrow."

Red jumped up and laughed so hard that the other Rainbow Girls pressed their painted faces against the train's window to get a better look.

"You want to *what*? I hate to break it to you"—she swiped her hand in front of Sweetmint, as if it were obvious—"but you don't have what it takes to do what we do."

Sweetmint leapt to her feet, placed her hands on Red's shoulders. "*Please.* It's for Sweetsmoke," she said, speaking faster. "I can go to Minx, meet one of those big important shibs you're always talking about, and convince them to give me my parents' address and a city pass."

"And what will you do when you get to the city? You don't even know an avenue from a street."

"I'll figure it out, Red! One step at a time. This is how inventing goes. Sometimes you plan it out, and other times you don't. I have no other choice."

Orange stood in the train's doorway. "Red! We're going to be late. Come on."

Red glared in her direction. Orange shrank and sat back down next to Indigo.

"Listen," she said, facing Sweetmint. "If Sweetsmoke is behind all of this mess, maybe you should just leave it alone. I've never seen dippies this afraid of one of us. And that makes *me* afraid. It'll only lead to trouble."

"It already *is* trouble. And I'm trying to do something about it. Will you help me or not?"

Blue banged on the train's window. "Come on, Red!"

Red pointed her chin at Sweetmint. "You know what we do?"

She nodded.

"And you know that I'm going to have to show you how to walk like us, talk like us, *be* like us?"

"I do. I can do it."

"We get back in the mornings, a few hours before Daily Prayer. I'll stop by your cabin tomorrow. But if you actually do come to Minx with us, and something goes wrong, I don't know you. Okay?"

"If something goes wrong, I'm on my own. Got it." She wanted to hug Red and squeeze the life out of her.

"Fine. See you tomorrow." Red's hips swayed as she made her way up the platform.

"Red?" Sweetmint called, right before she entered the train.

"Holy Father. What now?"

"Thank you."

CHAPTER 16

"SIR," SOMEONE SAID, SHAKING CURTS AWAKE.

When he came to, the world spinning in slow motion, he saw an Invisible woman in front of him. A dim light strip glowed across the ceiling, making it difficult to see which color paint she wore; her body temperature, though, registered orange to his eyes. In her hands was a cup of steaming herbs.

"What?" He sat up, patting his false beard and long hair, which he found glued to his cheek. "What time is it?"

"Seven in the morning, Mr. Durrum. Here." She placed the herbcup into his hands, wrapped his fingers around it so it wouldn't drop. "Drink this, please."

He was still in his private room, drapes blocking out the sun's violent light, soundproof walls making everything quiet. The proprietress helped him off his back, set him down on a couch.

"Your earsphere has been vibrating on the table for a while now, sir. Shall I get it for you?"

"Yes, please," he whispered, his throat and body still feeling the effects of the many patches he'd done last night.

She dropped it into his hand and then left the room.

"Lucretia," Curts said, his voice clawed raw.

"Sir." He sensed her eagerness. "I've been trying to reach you. We have something."

He stood, his body a coiled spring. "Out with it, Lucretia. Time is of the essence!"

"Shanu's collar pinged the network and—"

"Pinged the network? We recovered it from his cabin three years ago."

"I know, but we just got a ping. Maybe the collar we took was somehow a replicate, I don't know. This ping was from Upper Iron and Steel. Based on the coordinates, it looks like he's deep in a mine."

"How do you know this isn't a trap?"

"It's connected to a heat source with a heartbeat. Maybe he's hiding. Or he's hurt. We're on the way there now, but I've already instructed local hemispheric guards to secure a fifteen-kilometer radius around the mine. Regional Hemispheric Guard Director Melor is on it."

Curts swore as he tried to find his pants. It was twenty-five hundred kilometers from this plant parish to Upper I&S. At least three hours.

"Listen to me carefully, Lucretia. I'm coming, but it will take me a while to get there, so you need to lead the capture. You, not Melor or anyone else. Actually, keep him away from this all. I don't want any regional interference. Do you understand?"

"Yes, sir. I'm ready."

"I know you are. Make sure no one enters or exits the mine. If he pops out, take him alive. If he remains down there, just wait for me. And if he's somehow armed, have the golden guards shoot to kill. This can all end today."

"Understood, sir." She paused. "If I may ask, where are you?"

He finally located his pants, thrust a leg through. "Up north, in the Diamond Region, on a tip from Captain Kandolo. It didn't turn out to be anything, though."

"That's disappointing. See you soon, sir."

"See you soon."

Tired of fighting his way through semidarkness, he yanked the drapes open, the sun's harsh light filtering in through the wide translucent-green window. The proprietress had already folded his clothes in a neat pile near his bed, for which he was grateful. She and the others, though they only knew him as "Mr. Durrum," took care of him with the utmost attention to detail.

"Isisa," he called. Immediately, the door swung open, and the proprietress appeared, painted a bright orange that matched the color his didanlenses had registered in the dimmer light.

"Thank you for folding my clothes. And for the herbs."

"Of course." She bowed.

"But this," he said, pointing to a large canvas capture on the wall of Chief Executive Rhitel staring at him, one he'd taken down the previous night and flipped around. "Next time don't put it back up if I take it down, okay?"

"Yes, Mr. Durrum. My apologies."

"It's fine. A pack of the usual, please. Three dozen."

"Right away, Mr. Durrum."

Patches in hand, the herbs working their way through his system, he left the patch den, the white light of day finally touching his face. He drew his hood as he stumbled through the crack-bricked streets, Invisible women pushing carts yelling, "Freshhhhh juice! Cactus, eggplant, and squash! Freshhhhh biscuits! Salviatel, sweet pepper, and rhibas! You know what we say, don't waste the day! Freshhhhh juice! Freshhhhh biscuits!"

He kept his head down, but color flashed in his peripheral and he slammed his back against the closest wall, chest tight; small children painted in fluorescent colors chased each other past the mudbrick dwellings and stores made of concrete and glass lining the main street. A patch would help settle his nerves, but there was too much on the line for him to be in an altered state of mind.

As he continued toward the station, he noticed a group of guards, all of them young, with unbuttoned uniforms and capless heads—lips snarled as they spoke with one another and surveyed their surroundings. They must have been reassigned to the Waste Renewal Region from another, due to bad behavior or because they were "in need of toughening." Still, the blatant contempt for their dress was unacceptable. But in that moment, he wasn't the Hemispheric Guard Director. He was no one.

"Stop," one called to him as he passed the group, his body transforming from warm flesh to cold metal with a single word. But he kept moving. Then a hand on his shoulder, a hard pull, spinning him around, face-to-face with a squat guard whose entire face converged into one mean, blunt point.

"You didn't hear me talking to you?"

"I—" he croaked, throat full of sand.

"Dropped this," the guard said, holding up a patch that must've fallen from one of Curts's pockets. He grabbed Curts's hand, placed the patch in it, and closed it for him, as if he were a child who had dropped a play toy. "Have a little respect for yourself."

The smell of rotted waste filled his nose, though he knew it was all in his head; this region's filtration and disinfection system was the best in the hemisphere, for good reason. But he swore the stench was forcing its way up his nostrils, down his throat, and into his very blood. He should've just said, "Thank you," turned around, and headed straight for the station. But that odor, that lack of order and cleanliness. It was an abomination.

The guard, probably thinking he was just some patcher, shook his head and walked away.

"Do you," Curts said, clearing his throat, speaking louder. "Do you always dress so sloppily?"

Now the guard stopped—the sun's glare reflecting off his sweaty red neck—then swung around, stomping toward Curts. "How dare you, you sorry excuse for a DP! You just earned yourself a day in His Executive's Regional Prison. You worthless, ungrateful—" He raised his fist, blotting out the sun, and Curts tensed before the flesh-to-flesh collision, but another guard appeared, guiding the man's fist down, and said, "Disturbance at the plant. Let's go."

"I'll remember you," the guard said, finally tearing away and joining the others.

Curts made his way to the station, disappointed. A large part of him wanted to feel the fist against his face, the crack of fleshy bone—to, if only for a second, be stripped of his title, his rank, and all of the pressure that came along with it that pounded and pounded and pounded him deeper into the ground until dirt burst from his eye sockets. But then he remembered what awaited him, and kept on, becoming the Director once again.

He called his train and thought about how maybe Shanu was growing arrogant, having evaded him for this long. *A man's hubris is his enemy's best weapon.* The hemisphere wanted blood, Invisible blood, and Curts would soon give it to them. Given the transgression, the Grand Magistrate would likely sentence Shanu to be strung up in the dead center of Rhitel Square, to the Eternal Elm, planted almost eight decades ago, when The Chief Executive came to power. His body would be dropped from a sturdy limb, then sway back and forth, just like how Curts pushed Eva on her swing behind their home. But most magnificent of all was that the Director's reputation as the hemisphere's protector would be untarnished once again, forever gilded in lustrous gold.

CHAPTER 17

O
H," SWEETMINT SAID. SHE HELD THE DOOR OPEN AS SHE TOOK IN
Red's frizzy hair, missing lip paint, and lensless eyes that resembled glass orbs; a faint pink glowing from the red paint on
the back of her head.

"What?" she said, pushing her way inside. "Didn't think I'd
show?" She dropped her bag and a small bucket of paint onto the
kitchen table, poured herself a glass of water, downing it in one gulp.
"Holy Father." Her still-red eyelids opened and closed twice, and
she shot Sweetmint a look of disbelief. "*This* is how you live? Where's
the colored canvas? A couch with a metal frame? Something, *anything*, that doesn't feel like it's from the early 2300s?"

"I mean . . ." Red took a few steps, placing herself in the living
room, and pointed at the two bare mattresses on the ground. "You
don't even have a bed. I don't know how Sweetsmoke raised you, but
these conditions are worse than how they live in the midregions."

Sweetmint didn't expect to feel embarrassed, but she did. Of
course she knew that the way she lived wasn't modern, but, really,
it seemed like Red was making it a bigger deal than it was. Still, if it
wasn't a big deal, why did Red's reaction now prompt a field of
questions inside of her, like why *was* her cabin so sparse? Why, after

earning all those rhitellings from Mr. Tenmase, had she not actually spent them on herself? Maybe, it occurred to her, she wasn't as advanced in the ways of the world as she thought.

"Are you here to help me get ready for tonight, or are you here to redecorate my cabin?"

Red laughed, her rumoya vibrant, electric. "You'd be surprised by how little difference there is between the two. But today, we're just starting with you, which"—she slid her eyes up from an approximation Sweetmint's feet to the crown of her head—"will be a tough job, even for me."

Hesitation axed into Sweetmint's heart, rendering her silent. Red walked over, found her hand, and sat her down at the kitchen table. "This won't be easy, but life has never been easy for any of us, right?"

Sweetmint looked at Red, who now knelt in front of her. It was hard to believe that Red, *the* Red, was in her cabin, holding her hand and helping her.

"Right," she replied, squeezing Red's hand, letting out a gust of air.

Red smiled and opened the can of paint on the table. "Okay, this morning is just a test run, so you're more comfortable in your role for tonight."

"Role?"

"Correct. Role. Like Callie Enroh in *Domestic Diaries*. Now let's start with your look. Get up."

She did as she was told. Red dipped a paintbrush into the fresh can, swirled it around a few times, and brought the warm silver paint full of glitter to Sweetmint's collarbone. The synthetic smell of long extinct fruits—sour and sweetness woven together—was strong enough to make her head spin, but she couldn't pass out. Not now.

"Instead of making you a Rainbow Girl, you're going to be our special guest. *Glitter.*"

"Glitter," Sweetmint repeated. Red drew the brush across her neck and chest with grace and ease as natural as a river.

"You already have dippy features, which is good. The high-ranking shib I'm going to introduce you to tonight prefers his Invisible women to resemble dippies. Most dippy men at the clubs don't, but this one does. So this straight hair"—Red removed a smaller can of paint from her bag, dipped a fresh brush into it, and, now on her tippy-toes, brought its pale yellow to Sweetmint's head—"will work wonders on him."

"Who is he?"

"I told you," Red said, making sure not to miss one strand of Sweetmint's slicked-back hair. "A high-ranking shib. Do you know many of them?"

Sweetmint coughed.

"That's what I thought." She set the brush down, hunted around in her bag, then presented a gold lens case in her open palm.

Deciding not to annoy her with any more stupid questions, Sweetmint struggled to put the light green lenses into her eyes and, after Red's assistance, blinked a few times. "How do I look?"

"Hold on, hold on, hold on, Stella Irons. Open your mouth." She thought of the singer, wondered if whatever Red did to her made her come close to that level of beauty. Her stylist inserted white teeth covers, said, "Now close it," then brought a cylinder of soft pink lip paint to Sweetmint's mouth.

"Okay!" Red clapped her hands. "Go find a mirror and try not to weep from what I managed to do with"—she pointed a finger at Sweetmint's face, drawing circles in the air—"*this.*"

Sweetmint flinched when she saw herself in the bathroom mirror. "No. Way."

"*Way,*" Red said from the kitchen. "What do you think?"

She puffed her pink lips out. Poked her glittered cheeks. Rolled her light green eyes around. Patted her blond hair, hardened by the paint. "You *are* good, Red. I can't even recognize myself."

"I'm not good, Sweetmint. I'm the *best.* Before I started working at Minx, I worked downcity, styling dippies. That injaka of a boss didn't like that her clients, *and* their husbands, preferred me over her, so she fired me. To ruin with her, though. Look at me now."

But Sweetmint couldn't look at her, she was too busy looking at herself. Or, not herself, but someone she could escape into. At least for a night.

She smelled Darksap before she heard his knocking, and she froze. "One second!" she called from the bathroom, but it was too late. When she stepped into the kitchen, he was there, standing with Red. All she could see was his collar floating in the air, sense his rumoya bristling with shock.

"What?" was all he said.

"Hey, Dapp."

"What are you doing, Swint?"

Red wrapped her arm around his shoulders. "What does it look like? She's trying on a new look. Is that okay with you?"

From the way Red's arm fell, she knew Darksap had shrugged it off. Hard. "Why are *you* here?" he asked.

"You know," Red said, "one day you're going to realize that there are those, like you, who just go through life allowing things to happen to them. And there are those, like us"—she walked over to Sweetmint, locked hands with her—"who make things happen."

Sweetmint pulled her hand out of Red's. "This is all just a game, Dapp. Red offered to give me a makeover, so I said, 'Sure, why not?' I'll take it off and see you at Daily Prayer, okay?" She didn't like to deceive her oldest friend, but she couldn't allow this to escalate. Tonight was the focus.

The air grew so thick from Darksap's silence that she felt it pressing against her skin and moving down her throat, threatening to choke her. "*Oh-kay?*" she repeated.

"Yeah," he finally said, bursting the bubble of tension. "Okay. I'll see you." He walked out. Red closed the door behind him, then spun around.

"*What* was that? I mean, the marfana almost exploded when he saw you, and not in a good way."

"You were sort of mean to him, Red."

"Mean? Life is mean. Come on. Plus, if he loves you, he should want you to change, grow, experiment. *Live.*"

Love? She let it go with a sigh. "What's next?"

"The act."

"The act?"

"The act."

"And what does 'the act' mean?"

"Have you ever had sex?"

The embarrassment she'd felt when Red first entered her cabin was back, but now it was mixed with something else: a small ache in her heart, the low thrum of anger in her blood. She wanted to say, *No, Red, I haven't had sex. My brother told me boys were a distraction for me, girls a distraction for him; that I had to strengthen my mind as he strengthened his body for an "eventual day of reckoning." Crazy, confusing talk. And, yes, I want to have sex. I have urges just like everyone else. But that's the last thing on my mind right now.*

But all she whispered was "No."

Red tilted her head to the side. "Hm, that's what I thought. But it's fine . . . I don't think you're going to have to do that tonight. Plus, being sexy has nothing to do with sex."

"Really?"

"Really. Now pay attention, okay? I'm only going to explain this once."

Red threw so much at her in such a short amount of time that she felt like she was back at Forestaeum Minor. Except instead of being surrounded by columns of polished wood and dozens of students vying to prove they were the smartest in the group, she was in her tiny cabin, learning how to walk at a slow pace with her back straight and head held high, "like a dippy," as Red said.

Patches were another subject. "You hold it like this." Red held a used one between her fingers. "And make sure only half of it actually sticks to you. That way you won't feel the effects as strongly, but the men will think you're on one. They want you to be a little phala." *High*. Something she had never been and hoped she could avoid.

Smiling. Flirting with your eyes. How to slightly bow when addressing the clientele. When to laugh, whisper, and, most important, touch. Unlike her university classes, she stumbled through every lesson, and Red reprimanded her at least fifty times, but then they had to leave for Daily Prayer.

"Listen," Red said. "I'm not going to lie to you. It's not perfect by any stretch of the imagination. What we do and how we do it . . . it's all instinct that you gain from experience. And you"—she touched the tip of her finger to Sweetmint's newly blond hair—"are more head than heart. But you're also a brave injaka, so you just might pull it off."

Brave. A word no one had ever used to describe her. But then something Mr. Tenmase had said entered her mind. He was discussing a random Northeastern war she'd never heard of, one that expelled the DPs' distant cousins from that hemisphere and forced them into the Southeastern. "On the other side of bravery is stupidity, and most men don't know where they stand until it's too late." *Good thing I'm not a man*, she thought as she rushed to the sink, scrubbed her hair, face, and skin.

Red threw the cans of paint, the lenses, the lip paint, and the teeth covers into a straw bag and shoved it beneath the couch. "I hope you're ready. Because if you're not, and these people find out what you're up to, they won't lock us up. They'll kill you *and* me. Fun, right?"

"Yeah," Sweetmint said. "The definition of it."

CHAPTER 18

THE TRAIN STOPPED AND CURTS JUMPED TO HIS FEET. DESPITE HIS adrenaline, he must have fallen asleep. Looking out the window, he could only see scorched earth the color of sand in every direction, cracks winding across the surface like parched lips.

When the door opened, he looked down and saw a two-meter drop to the ground. Turning his back to the open door, he got on his stomach, hung from the threshold until his feet were only a handful of centimeters from the cracked dirt, and jumped.

Something, or someone, shuffled on the other side of the train. "Come out with your hands up," he ordered, hoping that his tone would communicate that harming him would be the biggest mistake of their life. For the first time in a long time, he wished he had a weapon. "I said come out. Now."

An Invisible woman and girl, as skinny as the dirt beneath them was dry, emerged from around the train to his right. "We're here. For you, sir," the woman said. Their bodies registered as a green yellow—strange, given how hot it was.

He held his hand up when they were a meter from him. "Stop."

They immediately dropped their heads. "What do you mean 'here for me'?"

"The other shibs. They told me that if I brought my daughter. Next time, we could get even more rations. This is the ration train, yes?"

It was obvious to him that she wasn't accustomed to speaking Northwestern. Her accent, heavy with the mixed rhythm of Vilongo and Vikench, caused her words to come out choppy, like the violent waves far out in the Northwestern Ocean. He wasn't sure what he was hearing, but he had an idea, and it made him sick. The midregions were synonymous with hard living, much harder than you'd find in a place like the Forest Region, with its proximity to the seat of the hemisphere's power, but this—women trading themselves and their children for extra food, and hemispheric guards preying on them in such a disgraceful way?—no, this was too much.

"Come here," he ordered. They walked toward him, and he knelt down, eye level with the girl. "What's your name?"

She looked at her mother, who nodded. "Lerato, sir."

"Nice to meet you, Lerato." He stood, faced her mother. "This isn't the ration train, and I don't have any food. I'm sorry. But here."

He inserted his earsphere, scanned the woman's face, which brought up her information, including her Invisible Discretionary Fund at IBNH, and transferred one thousand rhitellings.

"There are now one thousand rhitellings in your IDF. I hope it helps."

The woman, Liyana, the display said her name was, looked at her daughter, then back at Curts, and began to cry. He took a handkerchief from his pocket and handed it to her. After she finished wiping her tears, he said, "I need you to do two things for me."

"Anything, sir."

"Promise me that you won't give yourself, or your daughter, to any more guards for food. I'm going to find the guards who operate the ration train here and make sure they never wear the uniform again."

Liyana nodded, her scrunched face doing its best to fight back more tears.

"The second thing is that I need you to take me to the mine. Can you do that?"

"Yes, it's not that far. From here. Do you see that cluster? Of homes?" She pointed to the south of where the train had come from, and he saw rounded metal structures reflecting the brutal sunlight in the distance.

"Steel City Five," she said. "Our home. After that, the mine. But no one goes there anymore. Except, there are many men now. They came from a train on the other side of it."

I must have misprogrammed the coordinates.

"Please, take me."

"Follow me," Liyana said, taking the first step, when a gust of wind forced dust into the air, attacking Curt's eyes, nose, and throat.

He bent down, coughing, crying, struggling to breathe. Liyana went back to him, used her teeth to bite off his black sleeve, then wrapped it around his nose and mouth.

"There. That will help. You're not used to the dust, like us."

"Thank you," he said, still coughing. Little Lerato grabbed his hand, tugged him in the direction of her mother, and the three set off.

They reached Steel City Five, a collection of steel homes that resembled half-submerged barrels, each with a wooden door and a few front-facing windows. He'd never seen these structures before and wanted to ask how they defended against the sun's heat, but he couldn't give in to his common curiosities. There was a small main square and what he assumed was the church at one end of it, as well as the typical buildings that always stood out from the rest in any Invisible section—PatchMart, Northwestern Boutique, Rhitel

Burger—but aside from a trio of hemispheric guards who saluted him, no one was outside. The only proof that Invisibles lived there were the pulsing orbs that stared at him through the dusty windows.

"Where are all the people?" he asked as they left the homes behind them.

Without breaking her stride, Liyana said, "We go out for work and church, then stay inside. Sometimes the guards will let us do more. Most of the time not."

This is cruel. How could he not know about this? It was Hemispheric Guard Associate Deputy Director Ribussce who oversaw Hemispheric Dwellings and Improvement, which included the ration trains, so none of this exactly surprised him, but still. Seeing savagery in the flesh was hard to ignore. Reform would happen, after they found Shanu.

In the distance, he saw a circle of golden and hemispheric guards. When they were only a handful of meters from them, Liyana stopped, picked up Lerato, and said, "We will leave you here, sir. Thank you. Again. For all."

"Thank you, Liyana. I'll fix everything here. I promise."

She looked at him, her face a swirl of colors, and Curts thought he saw a faint smirk. He couldn't fault her for not trusting him, but she'd see he was one of the good ones.

The Director kept on, and when the guards realized it was him, they saluted and called for Lucretia. One handed him a purebreathe. He removed his ripped mesh sleeve, now beige with dust, and replaced it with the dark green mask that both filtered out the dust and purified the air. Finally able to breathe easily, he broke through the ring of guards. Beneath them was the largest hole he'd ever seen; so large that it felt like it had its own gravitational force. Who knows how they did it. A bomb? A thousand Invisibles digging nonstop for weeks? Some outer space collision?

Inside the hole was a series of ringed pathways of rock, hemispheric guards studding every level like alternating black and olive dots on one of little Eva's dresses. Lucretia made her way up, sweat shining on her forehead, her formfitting black uniform no doubt absorbing the sun's merciless heat.

A green shed-like structure sat in the crater's center. Curts assumed it held an elevator, or a ladder, leading deeper and deeper into the Earth's dark esophagus.

"Sir," Lucretia said, huffing as she reached the surface. She saluted him; he reciprocated.

"Update."

"Well . . ." She looked back, taking a step forward, most likely to avoid the crater's vertiginous pull. "He's certainly in there. When we surrounded the headframe, he said he knew that we were there, that he could smell us. I know you told us to wait, but we called for him to come out, and he refused. He said he didn't do anything wrong, that he wanted his sister."

"Sister? It has to be him, then, asking for Candace, Croger Tenmase's apprentice."

"Yes, but he won't come out. From the sound of his voice, he's down on the first level; the only way there is to somehow force the cage back up. The alternative is to convince him to come out."

"Do we have choke pods?"

"Of course."

"Drop a point-seventy-five down the shaft."

"May I recommend a point-five, sir? It'll still do the trick."

"Fine," he said, admiring her humanity. "Also, when this is all over, have Ribussce give me a list of every guard that works in this region. It's rife with corruption and I won't allow it to continue, which means Regional Hemispheric Guard Director Melor is fired. You and I are also going to have a talk about how you let this slide through the cracks."

Her confused look let him know that she wasn't aware of what was happening; the shame that spread in her eyes told him that she would take responsibility. "Yes, sir."

Lucretia used her earsphere to communicate with the guards in the crater's center. One removed a ball from his vest, held it in the air.

"Go," she said. With perfect aim, he threw it into the headframe.

Within seconds, they heard the screaming. Then the pulling, clinking, and clanking of metal. The cage filled the headframe's empty space, and the boy with the collar came stumbling out, a cloud of blue smoke making him look like one of those imaginary beings Curts had seen on animated programs in the archive.

The boy fell to his knees as the golden guards formed a circle around him, their weapons pointed at him like fatal, accusing fingers.

Lucretia pressed her finger to her ear. Then, "He's unarmed."

"Bring him up," Curts ordered.

The men each grabbed a limp blue limb and rose through the crater, ring by ring. Curts didn't know how it was possible, but the sun burned even brighter.

The four guards with the boy reached the surface; Curts pointed to a metal chair. The boy screamed in agony when they placed him on it, the smell of burnt skin entering the air, and used ropes to tie his wrists and ankles.

"Give him two hydropatches."

A guard slapped a light blue patch on each side of the boy's neck, ensuring he wouldn't pass out—at least, not from dehydration.

"I didn't do anything!" he shouted, his shaven head, round nose, and high cheekbones covered in blue dust.

"We both know that's a lie," Curts said, kneeling eye level with Shanu. "Now tell us how you ended up all the way over here, in the midregion."

"I was born here," he said, wincing, his skin being melted off by the searing chair. "I'm a midregioner. And this inactive mine is where my girlfriend and I like to meet, since it's the only place we can get any privacy. But she never showed. I was still waiting on the first level, then I smelled your men. That's it."

"You're lying."

"On the Holy Father, I'm not. I don't know who you think I am, but I'm not him."

Curts inserted his earsphere, brought up the capture of Shanu from three years ago, and couldn't tell if it was or wasn't him. These Invisibles, with their changing paints and hairstyles, were hard to distinguish one from the other. He'd usually do a quick facial scan for confirmation, but if someone could reconfigure a collar, who knew what they were capable of.

"Take a blood sample and check it with the Hemispheric Hematic Directory."

A guard did as he was told, handed the piece of glass stained with see-through blood to Lucretia, and she inserted it into her modified glass tablet. "Sir," she said, raising the device. It read SIYANDA, TWENTY-FIVE, STUDENT, STEEL CITY FIVE.

Damn it! He was so close. But this Invisible had to know more than he was saying. Curts pressed the boy's wrists into the chair's metal arms, his blue-tinged skin sizzling for all to hear until his screams swallowed the sound whole.

"Who are you?" Curts asked.

"You saw. I'm Siyanda."

The Director pulled his hand back, smashed his fist into the boy's handsome face. "Who do you work for?"

"I'm a student," he said, twisting his head left and right. "At Ironaeum Minor."

Curts seized his bulging throat. "Are you with the Children of Slim?"

The young Invisible struggled to respond, but Curts heard a rumbling that sounded like "Who?"

He pushed the boy over, kicked him in the head, the sound of boot on bone a hard knock on a hard door, and shouted, "Tell me!" *Bang.* "Tell me!" *Bang.* "Tell me!" *Bang.*

By the time he was done—his shirt unraveled and soiled with dirt, face glistening as if he'd just stepped out of the shower, peaked cap on the dusty ground—the boy was unconscious. Curts looked up and saw dozens of guards staring at him, a variety of expressions splashed across their faces: violence-driven lust, confusion, fear. No one had ever seen "The Saint," as he knew they called him behind his back, like this; especially not Lucretia, who looked down at her glass display, then up, eyes bulging.

"Sir," she said, turning the glass to him. It was a map of the hemisphere, dozens of orange dots blinking across the surface.

"What is this?"

"It's at least one hundred other new pings of Shanu's collar in the hemisphere. Just like this one."

He looked down at the boy, still unconscious, and told a guard to untie him and get a celgen to heal his wounds.

His earsphere vibrated. Hemispheric Guard Associate Deputy Director Ribussce. "Ribussce is calling," he said to Lucretia. "Do you know what for?"

She shook her head.

"What is it?" he asked, picking up.

"I thought I should call you directly, *sir*," Ribussce said, jubilant. "While you idiots were being sent on an Invisible chase, Shanu blew up a wing of the Executive Estate."

CHAPTER 19

"SWEETMINT," RUSTY SAID, GRABBING HER HAND AS SHE STEPPED onto the train.

"Rusty?" His hand was cold and slick with sweat, his rumoya giving off straight fear.

"Has he contacted you yet?"

"No. I would have told you. Why?"

"Time is running out. For all of us."

"What do you mean 'for all of us'?"

"Just be sure to let me know if you hear from him as soon as possible." He pulled her into a tight hug, his entire body trembling. She had never seen him like this, and now *she* was even more frightened. Only when the doors began to close did he let go. Turning around, she saw his collar still shaking on the platform where she'd left him.

What was that? She dropped into one of the velvet chairs and looked down at her hands, dots of glitter still stuck between her fingers. Stray strands of faint yellow hair rested on her collar, proving that her morning with Red was real, that Glitter was real, and that the danger that lay ahead of her that night was realer than real.

Too much was piling up too quickly, and it threatened to drown her if she wasn't careful.

As the train sped toward Castle Tenmase, the outside world a blur, she thought about how Darksap, after seeing her with Red, hadn't spoken to her at Daily Prayer. He'd sat beside her, as silent as the sun creeping over the horizon, though she felt his desire to say something. Was it better that he bit his tongue, or would she have respected him more if he gave shape and sound to what was on his mind, in his heart? She really wasn't sure of what was happening between them—confused by how parts of her that were once closed off were slowly beginning to open, making her feel loved and wanted in a way she'd never felt before—but it didn't matter now.

Now the only thing on her mind had to be her plan. Make it through the day at Castle Tenmase. Become Glitter and get what she needed at Minx. Meet her parents, convince them to help her find Sweetsmoke. Locate Sweetsmoke and smuggle him out of the hemisphere with Rusty's help. Only then could she breathe easy, only then could she move on, have any real future.

She grabbed a pink biscuit, tore off a piece of it with her teeth, and tipped back a steaming cup of brightspice. Not the best thing to drink when you're already having trouble slowing down, but she didn't care. She'd rest for days, weeks even, once this was all over. The herbcup fell from her hand at the sound of measured clapping—POP . . . POP . . . POP—coming from the other end of the car.

"Wow," the familiar voice said, though she couldn't place it. "I can feel all the plotting through your rumoya. It's invigorating."

He walked toward her, dry soles padding over soft carpet. Then it clicked.

"Abe?"

"Sawukhoob, Sweetmint." He placed a hand on her shoulder. "Sorry about the herbs. Didn't mean to scare you."

She reached out, patted his flabby arms, soft chest, and stopped at his round stomach. Yes, it was him. "Why can't I smell you? Or sense your rumoya?"

"Red drops, but I'll explain everything later. I disabled the train's audio monitor and we don't have much time. Tenmase isn't who he seems, Sweetmint."

"That's a bit obvious, isn't it?"

"He's bad. The worst kind of dippy: those who feign care for us, not as a matter of heart, but of convenience, of corrupt calculation. As we speak, he's working with people, like Local Manager II Jolis, to find Sweetsmoke and use him as the final puzzle piece to get Jolis elected. After that . . . it's all over. We become real slaves. Every man, woman, and child put to manual labor until we drop dead—selective steriliza-tion, breeding, advanced torture, just like in the Southeastern."

She couldn't stifle the laughter that rose from her stomach and flew out her mouth, pummeling him in the face. "It seems," she said, catching her breath, "that your rumoya still gifts you with an incredible capacity for storytelling."

He grabbed her forearm, his two hands locked on with no signs of letting go. "I *know* what this sounds like. What you must think of me. But believe me when I say that who I am at Castle Tenmase is an act. I became his servant on purpose, to learn whatever I could about his plans and use them against the State."

"And why should I trust you, Abe?" She yanked herself free from his grasp. "You could be lying to me, luring me into some trap."

"It's too much to explain now, but we're on the same side as you. And we want you to join us. If we can find Sweetsmoke before the dippies do . . ." His voice trailed off. "We've waited decades for this. The dippies are scared and weaker than ever. Part of the Executive Estate was even just blown up!"

"The Executive Estate? What do you mean?"

"At the end of the day, I'm going to give you herbs that will make you sick for a few hours. Ask Tenmase if you can take the day off tomorrow, and he'll say yes, so long as he doesn't suspect anything. Then tomorrow after Daily Prayer, get on the train. It will look just like this one and take you north, far up north, where we'll be waiting for you."

"That all sounds fine, but I don't need you, Abe. I have my own plans."

"Listen to me!" he shouted. "This is not a game. You only get one shot at this, and we're taking it. I promise you that we, more than anyone else, are capable of keeping Sweetsmoke safe."

She weighed his words. She didn't really understand, but she knew that he was being sincere. "It's funny."

"What is?"

"Your brother believes that he's the only who can keep us safe."

He went quiet. Then, through clenched teeth, said, "Don't trust him, either."

"I trust Rusty more than anyone else. He's the only person who never left me. You did. Sweetsmoke did. But not him."

"I understand. Just come tomorrow and it will all make sense."

Her head ached, the throbbing intensifying as blood rushed throughout her internal circuitry. Her plan was becoming derailed, but maybe that was a good thing. She'd still go to Minx and get what she needed. Then she'd follow Abe's lead before finding her parents. As he said, time *was* running out, the ticking like one of Mr. Tenmase's restored timekeepers, so loud that her heart mimicked its rhythm.

"Okay," she said. "I'll do it."

"Good," he replied, exhaling. "Very good."

"But, Abe?"

"Yes?"

"You said '*we're* on the same side as you.' Who's we?"

"Oh." The train slowed down as it approached the castle. "You'll see."

CHAPTER 20

JOLIS, THROUGH INTIMIDATION AND BRUTE FORCE, FINALLY GOT on a train, albeit with two guards ensuring his safety. He wiped a film of sweat from his forehead, leaned back in his seat. Grand Magistrate Royger would give him a slap on the wrist for being late to the second day of debates, but how could he have known what would happen? Control was his comfort zone, but sometimes he had to accept that fate had a mind of its own.

It all happened so fast. He'd planned an impromptu meet and greet with hemispherians visiting the Executive Estate and recruited Anna Franklin to broadcast it on the NWN. Some of the men of rule would view it as an obnoxious display of ego, but so what? Ego was the fuel of the future. "And folly," an imagined Croger whispered in his ear, but he ignored him.

As he told the public, he was there "to connect with the people, not the politicians." The role he was playing—a relatable, yet removed, common man—had been a difficult one to master at first, but these days it was as natural as putting on his sleek suits and shiny shoes. A new skin so convincing that he sometimes forgot he was acting.

He had walked down the curved set of stairs, smiling and waving all the way to the bottom. The men, women, and children had hugged him, shook his hand, and even cried in disbelief that they were meeting the man who could actually become the next Chief Executive. He knew it was an experience of a lifetime for them—being in the restricted area behind the Estate, the proximity to power—and would use that. HGs pushed people back, but he gestured for them to let the crowd consume him, becoming the backdrop for his interview.

Anna Franklin, playing her part, had asked him why he was there and not at the Gallery of Rule, to which he said, "The high and mighty men of the hemisphere can wait. I am the people's leader." He paused to shake hands and pat the heads of those around him. "Long gone are the days when our hemisphere was ruled by men that you"—he looked directly into Anna's captureman's capglass—"only knew as illuminated light on the walls of your homes. Chief Executive Rhitel, may the Holy Father bless his soul, did everything in his power to bring this great hemisphere out of the ashes, a hemisphere where no one starves, and now it's time for a new day where we will—"

The applause from the hundreds of people around him had drowned out his voice before he could finish. He allowed it to wash over him, cleansing every ounce of doubt he'd had. Suddenly, the people's approval was met with a quick, deafening crack—like a century-old tree falling to the forest floor, or the tip of a whip connecting with Invisible flesh—followed by muffled screams as the ground beneath them shook and shifted. Jolis had clenched his eyes shut, jabbed his fingers into his ears, and couldn't see or hear what was going on. Once the shock wave had passed, he smelled the smoke coming from behind him. His ears kept ringing, but he managed to open his eyes; over his shoulder, smoke, thick, billowy, and black, rose into the air. Guards who had recovered from the blast herded the crowd across the lawn, away from the Estate and down a set of stairs hidden inside the lawn itself.

Anna Franklin was on the ground, struggling to get up. He ran to her side, grabbed her elbow. "Are you hurt?"

"I'll live." She winced as he helped her onto her feet. "What was *that*?"

"I don't know." He looked back at the Executive Estate. The smoke was thinning out and disappeared within a few seconds. "An explosion of some sort."

"Do you think it was Shanu?"

Jolis stroked his chin. "I have no idea. But it's a knockout of a way to get someone's attention. Curts will figure it out."

"You have a lot of confidence in a man who can't even catch one Invisible." Her eyes were focused on the Estate as more guards arrived and assumed their positions. "If he doesn't find Shanu—"

"He will. He has to."

She stared at him, confusion written on her face, then her lips twisted into a bloody grin. "Either way, this all works out for you, right?"

"We'll see. But thanks for coming, Anna." He placed a hand on her shoulder, her white blouse stained green from the grass. "And sorry about this."

"Why are you sorry? It's not like you did it." That tenderness and understanding. He'd missed it, but they both knew that he was a man whose train only had space for one.

"I know, but I let my arrogance get the best of me. If I hadn't asked you to come, and if I hadn't gotten all these people out on this lawn—"

"Then they would have been in there when the explosion, or whatever that was, went off." She took his hand into hers. "Call it what you want, but you saved hundreds of people, Stephan, and I'll report it that way."

"Arriving at the Gallery of Rule in one minute, Local Manager II Jolis," the train announced.

He noticed that his hand was curved in the same shape it had been when Anna held it, and he let go. The black underground of the tunnel whooshed past his window until the station's bright light greeted him like a new day. Jolis felt something sprout inside of him then: a feeling. It made him giddy with hope and he wanted to stand up and spin around as fast as he could, just as he had done when he was a child and no one else was around—the rare moments when he didn't have to act older than he was. If someone asked him to bottle up that feeling, slap a white label on it, and give it a name, he would have called it "joy." A thing he hadn't experienced in a long, long time.

CHAPTER 21

Brothers and sisters,

Despite the explosion at the Executive Estate, Local Tormentor II Jolis walked into the Gallery with an extra pep in his step, pleased because every attack on the hemisphere only bolsters his own platform. The other men of rule, including the magistrates, retained their bloated air of pomp and entitlement, especially since no one had died. Grand Magistrate Royger even thanked Jolis for his "publicity stunt," since it kept Charred Dippy off today's menu.

Yesterday's disgusting delight was The Hooter, which, as you instructed, I chased down with a vengeance so as not to raise any suspicion about whose side I'm on, given that I do sit in the rows behind Jolis, and he has always counted on me as a trusted supporter. Hiding my hatred of that man and all he represents has been the greatest act of my life. May I win a Rhimmel Award at the next ceremony. That was a joke, by the way.

Today, Brother Drams Jams Ivy—painted white from head to toe—entertained the men so well that most had tears embarrassingly spilling down their pink-white cheeks and chins like baby drool. I, of course, was also moved, but more so by the knowledge that our Brother Ivy has infiltrated the highest rungs of society, earning a rarified status, despite often being assaulted by those who don't understand his true revolutionary purpose. Still, through a strange alchemy, he has the unparalleled ability to make all of the pain and pretense of our world sound resplendent.

The topic of debate for today was trade. Local Tormentor II Jolis went first, outlining three key changes to his despotic predecessor's xenophobic mandates to, as he claims, "ensure the safety of our hemisphere, an expansion of our moralities, and the prosperity of future Northwesterners." I've summarized them as follows:

1. Require all Heads of Hemisphere to apply further restrictions on their Invisibles, treating them "as the laborers they're meant to be, instead of fake equals." The gall!

2. Increase our own hemispheric output by requiring *all* Invisibles to do manual labor and nothing but manual labor. "Sunsuckers," one of the dippies' many pejoratives for you, will no longer attend Invisible schools or have a choice whether they walk painted or naked (they'll all be painted, but [!] can choose the color). However, they will still be allowed to take part in sport, given its

physical nature and how much the dippies enjoy watching Invisibles sweat. The hypocrisy is startling.

3. Limit the number of Invisibles who can travel by train, with only domestics (a manual job, he clarifies) given that privilege. Invisible homes will also be standardized so that dippies can monitor them and regulate their diets, leisure, and breeding more than they already do. He expressed disagreement with continuing to curb Invisibles' physical maturity through Rhitel Burger and other means, asserting that "if we gain a stronger hold on their minds, the strength of their bodies will only be used to our benefit." I'd like to get hold of a hammer, then his head.

Jolis ended by saying that trade with other hemispheres is something he can take or leave, since our hemisphere is his only concern. From the way he ended his speech, he looked like a man on fire. I wanted to extinguish him with my spit, but had to bang the railing in support of him like everyone else on my side, so I opted to picture my fist crashing into his face rather than the hardwood. It was oddly satisfying, and I highly recommend it.

Washington, our tall, unruffled contender, attacked Jolis's lack of experience and proceeded to argue for compromise with other hemispheres over conflict, spurning his opponent's "bombastic bravado and bluster," while also highlighting how vague his midregion origins are. Washington went as far as to say, "I could poke fun at how he speaks with the simplicity of a child who has just learned the alphabet, but I won't." Ha!

His main argument is that it is hatred, which Jolis is the embodiment of, that has caused the actions of someone like Shanu. "Instead of providing the calming waters that our hemisphere is thirsting for, [Jolis] will only add fuel to a fire that is destroying our land, region by region."

More concretely, his plan consists of reopening the borders that have been closed for three-quarters of a century, including transoceanic railways. People from other hemispheres, "pink-white, tan, and yellow-brown DPs, along with all Invisibles," will be welcomed in the Northwest, fostering cross-cultural interactions, which is in alignment with the Fundamental Flip.

He even spoke of the possibility of somehow introducing real, organic livestock back into the world, "so long as it's controlled," and then ventured to say that flowers are being grown in the Southwestern Hemisphere. "All different types of them. Red, blue, white, purple, orange, yellow. Beautiful specimens of nature that we haven't been able to grow and sustain for over four centuries."

If you ask me, it was the mention of flowers that did him in. Regardless, Jolis pounced on his idealism and the Gallery awarded him with howls of laughter. If you could have only seen it! Washington *finally* began to sweat, his light blue shirt darkening with each passing second. He loosened his orange tie, aired out his crimson suit, and looked lost, lost, lost.

It is with an herbcup overflowing with regret that I say Local Tormentor II Jolis won the day again. There, on the Gallery floor, his lips twitched in satisfaction, and it seemed that he had come to know, perhaps for the first time in his young life, that there is no drug as intoxicating as purpose.

So, despite the turn of events, I still end today's dispatch with a smile, because it is we who hold the hemisphere's fate in our hands, and it is we who will deliver every Invisible from despair. I can only hope that you feel my commitment in every line; that you know though I am a dippy, every aspect of my heart is see-through.

> May the rebellion stay happy,
> Brother Lesbod

CHAPTER 22

"THERE," RED SAID, APPLYING THE LAST TOUCH OF PINK LIP PAINT. "Just like this morning. Have a look." She held up a small mirror and Sweetmint turned her head left and right.

"Perfect."

Red grabbed a Rhitel fry, opened her mouth wide, and inserted it with the same care she used to paint Sweetmint's lips, careful not to mess up her own. "Of course it's perfect," she said in between bites. "Now, have some of these."

Sweetmint stared at the Rhitel fries, burger, and shake on her kitchen table and wrinkled her nose. "No, mambonga. That stuff's poison."

"Poison, hm?" Red took a small bite of her burger, sipped her unnaturally blue shake. "Well, poison never tasted so good. But, trust me, you'll regret not eating."

"I'll take my chances."

"As stubborn as a fire is hot," Red said, moving the food aside. "Okay, now run me through the plan again."

"*Again?* We've gone over it two dozen times," which was true, adrenaline making her more alert to all of the ways that tonight could turn into disaster.

But Red just stared at Sweetmint, her neon-yellow eyes two tiny blinding suns. They had become something like friends over the past twenty-four hours—or at least something less like enemies. Still, Red retained her power of making Sweetmint feel like the smallest speck of dirt.

She wondered, for a second, what Red could've achieved if she'd been given the opportunity. In a different world, she would have been Chief Executive, and a good one. Young women across the hemisphere would watch her on the display and believe that they, too, could be her. Or if not be her, they could at least love themselves without hesitation, regardless of what they chose to do with their lives. Then the second passed and she was back in her cabin, and Red was waiting.

"I'm your cousin who usually works at Ladette's and is getting a feel for Minx, because I'm considering a switch. I have to be flirtatious—with my eyes, lips, and the way I move my hips—but not present myself like a woman who is easily attainable. I also have to ride a fine line between being submissive and powerless, but not come off as desparate. And, above all else, I must never panic, even if the shib I meet tonight wants . . ."

"To have sex with you." Red gripped Sweetmint's shoulders. "Even if this big and powerful shib wants to have sex with you, don't panic, and remember that you are always in control, even when they think they are."

Sweetmint stood and faced the two mattresses on her living room floor. The prospect of Sweetsmoke's spending a night in the cabin that he and Rusty had built, from fingerwood trees they felled, gave her the strength she needed. "I'll do whatever it takes," she whispered.

"Good." Red handed her a small silicone bag. "This is for you. Put whatever you need in it for the night, anything that'll make sure nothing goes wrong."

"Thanks." She threw lip paint, eye and teeth covers inside, plus Rusty's compass, for good luck, and one extra item: a weapon of sorts. *Just in case.*

"Now, I've told the other girls that you'll be joining us tonight, but don't be surprised if they're a little resistant."

Resistant, Sweetmint realized once they'd made it to the square, was putting it lightly.

When they saw her, Orange, Violet, and Blue walked over and laughed for a good minute. Indigo, Yellow, and Green joined them, and Orange said, shaking her head, "Red, you have *got* to be kidding us. This? I don't even know what to call this."

Blue waved her hand in front of Sweetmint. "Yeah, even I'm beyond stumped. I mean, it's like one of those tall trees with rot that lets you know to either chop it down or stay away . . . *Far* away."

"Is that Sourmint?" Green asked, getting closer. "The high-and-mighty injaka who has looked down on us and what we do since forever? Holy Father, I must be dreaming."

"Okay, okay," Red said. "Enough. You know what's going on. Sweetmint wants to see what it's like to be us for a night, to get her mind off Sweetsmoke and everything, so let's finish with the teasing. Tonight, she's one of us, and her name is Glitter."

The six of them did as they were told, but remained colder than cold. As Red promised, when Sweetmint faced the platform's glass display, her new name, GLITTER, appeared, along with MINX next to VALID DESTINATIONS. She had been worried that she'd step on the train and shibs would arrest her for traveling without the proper pass, but Red had somehow made it work.

It was going to be a short ride. Only about ten minutes to a part of Rhitelville that Red said "isn't exactly Downcity, where all those uptight dippies live, but it's close. It's basically Midcity, and beyond that is Upcity, which has fewer buildings, more green areas, and homes instead of apartments. Word is Drams Jams Ivy lives there. And then there's Sambrick Village across the river to the west." She pointed in that direction, even though they were in a dimly lit tunnel. "Capital Gardens is across the other river to the east. The houses are even bigger there than in upcity. It's where someone like Hemispheric Guard Director Curts lives."

"How do you know all of this? The only maps I've ever seen show the hemisphere's nine regions, our forest's location, and the general area of Rhitelville and its landmarks, but all—"

"Of the other places around it, or even within it, are left empty. Yeah. I've not only *seen* more detailed maps, but I've also been to a few of those places. Some of the men you meet at Minx, they . . . like house calls. But only when their wives and children aren't home."

"It's weird," Sweetmint said, shaking her head.

"What is?"

"They're so obsessed with cleanliness. And they beat it into us from a young age. 'Clean home, clean soul,' 'Washed face, holy grace,' and all of that. Yet, it's like they're so—"

"Messy?" Red laughed. "You don't know the half of it, injaka. But you're about to get a peek. Believe me."

As the train slowed, the other girls checked their painted faces and hair, covered teeth, and lensed eyes in the dark reflection of the windows. Then it stopped, and just like when she'd look out into the orphanage's courtyard at night and think the sky had fallen, blue light shone from every direction, making it hard to know whether she was flying or drowning.

CHAPTER 23

THE TRAIN DOOR OPENED TO SKY MANOR'S UNDERGROUND PLAT-
form as the elevator doors were beginning to close. "Hold it!"
Jolis shouted. He rushed out of the train and a hand appeared
between the wooden doors, forcing them to slide back open.

"Oh," a tall man in a dark brown suit said, straightening his
glasses. "It's you, Local Manager II Jolis. How are you?"

Jolis stood at the man's side and stared at the closing doors before turning to him. "I'll be a lot better when you call me Stephan,
Miller. I've lived here for two years, been over to Maisy and yours
for dinner, yet you still talk to me like a stranger. What's that about?"

Miller coughed, adjusted his glasses again before straining an
awkward smile. Jolis knew he was afraid of him. Another man
would have felt sadness then, for the way a certain spirit—especially
one of single-minded determination—repelled friendships. But he
didn't. All men weren't created equal. And friendship was the biggest distraction ever invented.

"I'm sorry," Miller said, not meeting Jolis's eyes. "It's just that . . .
I don't know." He forced that same stiff smile. "How often does one
speak with the next Chief Executive?"

The local manager shrugged. "True, but I'm sure we'll still see each other around. You've increased forest processing output for the last couple of years, right?"

He nodded just as the elevator stopped on the fifth floor. Jolis slapped him on the back so hard he had to steady himself so he didn't fall through the opening doors. "Then it sounds like you're due for a promotion! I'll make it one of my first tasks when elected. How's that?"

Miller turned around, exposing two rows of immaculate teeth; finally, a genuine smile. He grabbed Jolis's hand, pumped it up and down so many times the local manager's wrist ached. "Thank you, Chief Executive! Holy Father, wait until I tell Maisy. I've wanted this for some time now, but you know how it is. We all need to wait our turn."

"I do. And your turn is now, Miller. Anything else I can help with?"

Before he said, "No," Jolis noticed his suddenly downcast eyes and pursed lips. He took one step toward him, so close now that he was almost pushing him out of the elevator. "What is it, Miller? You can tell me."

The tall man scratched his eyebrow, looked over his shoulder, then turned back to Jolis, but still didn't make eye contact. "It's this vizzer, Chief Executive," he whispered. "Maisy and the kids are sick about him. Even I'm nervous. What happened at the Executive Estate this morning, all of it. I mean, we live in the tallest residential building in downcity Rhitelville . . . What's to say he doesn't try to blow this up next?"

Fear. It made Jolis want to slap Miller in his chiseled pink-white face as hard as he could. A man ruled by fear wasn't fit to be called a man at all. But his anger soon transformed into a desire to drop to the floor and laugh so hard he would throw up. One Invisible was making every DP from the Forest Region in the east to the Farming Region in the west dirty their precious pants. Yet Shanu was, to Jolis, a savior. And he needed him to get to where he was going. After that, he could go up in sweet smoke.

"Hemispheric Guard Director Curts is on it, Miller. Please believe me when I say we'll murder every last vizzer until he's captured and executed. Tell Maisy I say hello."

"Good night, Chief Executive. Thanks again."

Jolis got off on the top floor. As he did every night, he took his time walking across the short hallway's green carpeting, taking in each of the five illuminations displayed on the walls: a connected forest landscape with only a dirt path, trees, and sunlight reaching the capglass over a mountain's peak. The pentaptych was titled *Invisible Running*, and the man who captured it claimed that in each frame there actually was an Invisible running, but that it was up to the viewer to believe it, which Jolis did. He knew all too well that almost everyone was running from something—usually themselves.

He waved his hand across the door at the end of the hall and it slid open. The clear *swoosh* always made him smile. When he first moved in, he had swiped the door open and closed for an hour just to hear it, thinking of how little attention people pay to the sounds that accompany changes in their life status. The hacking of an axe, a river running in the distance, fire crackling, and then, for some, *swoosh*. Or no sound at all.

Twenty minutes. He kicked his shoes off onto the gray tiles and tossed them and his clothes into a hidden chute that led to a cleaning station. Within an hour, the same chute would return his wrinkled clothes and dull shoes, looking brand-new. Yes, all of this had taken him some getting used to. But it was easier than he'd thought. What does sudden access to excess do to a person? Usually, it softens; for Jolis, it launched a bitter taste into his mouth that he'd never been able to shake, a taste that, not so deep down, kept him forever hard and focused.

Finally entering the main space, he looked left—made sure the recessed sitting area was tidy, not one multicolored pillow out of place, his hulking petrified tree stump sitting on its pedestal in the center—then right, to the kitchen. The shiny black marble called to him, saying, "Chef Stephan, come and use me," but it was too late for food, especially because he wasn't one for quick snacks. For him, cooking was both his greatest pleasure and the highest form of art. If he'd taken a different path, he would own a restaurant in the heart of downcity and source the most delicious ingredients from across the hemisphere, crafting culinary experiences no one had seen before. Maybe it was still possible—these days, politics and business were one and the same.

His stomach rumbled, and he had to get ready, but he was still thinking about the cautionary tale Croger had told him earlier that day, when he went to the castle to celebrate toppling Washington in the Gallery. According to him, he shared it to remind Jolis of the lengths one had to be prepared to go in order to gain power, as well as all that others would do to take it from you.

Seventy-six years ago, Chief Executive Rhitel's predecessor, Chief Executive Sambrick, planned to back another candidate, Local Manager XII George Elmor, someone far more liberal and balanced. But supposedly, when Rhitel found out, he smothered Sambrick—his mentor and friend—then, after also murdering Elmor and his wife, he seized the chief executiveship for himself. As the story goes, Elmor had a child, and no one knows what their fate was.

Jolis thanked his friend for the revised history lesson, but, honestly, it did nothing to humble him. Instead, he was emboldened, because what no one, including Croger, knew was that he already *had* killed to get to where he was. *And*, he thought, inhaling his home's luxuriously cool air, *I would do it again if I had to.*

To ruin. En route to the bathroom, he tapped the wall a few times, and the sweet voice of Stella Irons streamed into the apartment.

Grateful, grateful, grateful, she sang, the hammering of iron and steel serving as the song's percussion. The thrumming of a bass grounded the performance as a soft piano floated just below a voice that was far too mature for a woman of eighteen. *Grateful for the moment, yes, I can say that's true. Grateful for the oceans, of every shade and hue. Grateful for the world, how good is it to me? Grateful for your warmth, leaves oh so grateful for their tree.*

Her lyrics weren't that impressive, but what drew him to her was her story. A small Invisible girl coated in dust, mining for ore, entertaining her family and friends with songs of salvation, when, one day, a supervisor overhears her, records a bit of her singing for his wife, who then urges him to pass the recording to her brother, a man responsible for finding talent to wow the masses, and turns this Invisible girl from the Iron and Steel Region into a hemispheric sensation. In her voice he did hear the gratitude she sang about, but also a sorrow as bottomless as the Earth is round. No, there was no time for melancholy. Not now.

Naked as the day he was born, he rushed into the glass chamber at the center of his bathroom. Soap-infused water jetted out of a dozen holes all around him, then pure water, and finally hot air. Clean and pure in thirty seconds. *What a marvel.* A hemisphere, when it came to hygiene, truly without a peer.

Nails clipped. Hair combed. Teeth brushed. Eyebrows plucked. He threw on a navy robe, grabbed a sniffpatch from the dispenser above his bathroom's counter and slapped it into his armpit. Once he was sure it had seeped into his bloodstream, he shimmied back into the main space and slid the glass doors open to the balcony.

Steel me, Stella sang pleadingly. *Steel me with the force of your love.*

He triggered a round piece of glass that enclosed his balcony from top to bottom, then programmed it black so that no one would be able to see inside. Just as he bent down to inspect his small herb garden, caressing the little leaves, a woman's illuminated face appeared on the glass below the railing. *Perfect timing.* One tap gave her elevator access. Then, a minute later, a knock at the door. Facing the entrance now, he tapped the balcony's nearest wall, and his apartment door slid open. *Swoosh.*

Standing in the doorway was one of the most unbelievable pieces of art he'd ever seen. Painted scenes of outer space covered her breasts, vivid rivers flowed from her stomach to her vulva's green hair, which served as the bushy tops of two trees that stretched down her thighs until they exposed brown painted roots on her feet.

In that moment, he wasn't the next Chief Executive. He was just a man; a man who was beyond hungry.

Famished.

CHAPTER 24

THE TRAIN DOORS OPENED, AND THE GIRLS WALKED OUT. *WHOA.*
Standing in front of a glass elevator were two of the tallest
Invisibles Candace had ever seen. One was painted glimmer-
ing gold from head to toe; two long braids running from his forehead to the back of his neck. The other was his mirror image, except
silver. But what alarmed her most was that they wore suits, black
ones, like DPs. Typically, the sight would be laughable, but the size
of their arms, chests, and necks let her know that they could, and
probably had, hurt men with ease.

But when they saw Red, their solid faces slipped into watery
smiles. "Red!" the golden one said, swooping his mountainous body
down to hug her.

"Sanele! Where have you been all week? We've had to put up
with those smelly young marfanas who don't know how to treat a
girl." She punched his arm, and he held it as if she'd stabbed him.

"Ow! Go easy on a marfana. Anele over here"—he stuck his
thumb out toward his brother—"hurt his leg trying to dance like he
was a young one, so he wasn't able to come in for a few days. You
know I'm his uba and uma, so I had to take care of him."

Anele, whom Orange, Indigo, and Green stared up at with lust, just rolled his silver-lensed eyes and laughed. "This marfana. Red, you already know that his breath stinks from all the trash he talks every day."

Hands on her hips, Red stepped closer to Sanele. "I don't know, Anele. Your brother's breath sure smells good to me."

Every Rainbow Girl let out an *oh* and an *ah*. Candace understood that Sanele liked Red, or vice versa, or both. The playful back-and-forth put her at ease until Sanele turned to her. "And who's this?"

"Where are my manners? This"—Red yanked Candace from the back of the group to the front—"is my cousin Glitter. She usually works at Ladette's and is thinking of making a move to Minx."

Anele inspected her. "I go to Ladette's sometimes, but I've never seen you there. I would have remembered it."

Red laughed. "Of course you wouldn't have seen her, you big jisolo. My cousin works in a private room on the top floor"—she flicked her finger up—"with dippies who shell out more rhitellings than you or I have ever seen. Just to spend time with the one and only Glitter."

Candace's heart was beating so loudly, she swore they could hear it through her ears. She had to calm down so her frantic rumoya didn't give her away. Anele, maybe just thinking she was the nervous type, shrugged, his black jacket stretching to its limit. "Makes sense. I'm usually on the middle floor, with the fine women"—he winked at Indigo—"who don't mind spending time with a lowly marfana like me."

Thank you, Holy Father. Thank you, Three Teachers. Thank you, thank you, thank you.

"Lowly is one way to put it," Sanele said. He waved his hand, decorated with many rings, in front of the elevator's glass doors. They slid open. "All aboard." Then, once everyone was inside, "Where to first?"

"The first floor for Glitter and me," Red said. "I want to give her the full tour. And"—she turned to the other girls—"we'll meet you on the top floor, okay?"

They nodded in unison.

Seconds later, the doors slid open, and Red, seeing that Candace hadn't moved, pulled her out of the elevator. There was just too much to take in. The light strips—dark reds, blues, and yellows flashing from every direction, bouncing off the black tiled floor—made it difficult to focus. The music, a bass so heavy that it shook her heart, paired with strange yet rhythmic sounds of glass breaking, metal clanging, and wood cracking, all without vocals. *Who are these people?* Invisible women with half of their heads shaved, the other half's hair straightened or in braids. Some of them looking as if they were dipped in metal, like Sanele and Anele; others covered in glossy black paint, resembling burnt pumpkin seed oil; all of them stuck to sweaty DP men dancing, rocking, and swaying to the seductive beat.

"You're into it, huh?"

"What?" Candace was so consumed by it all that she had forgotten Red was there.

Red touched her tapping foot with her own, bumped her butt against hers. "I've never heard music like this before," Candace shouted above it, slightly embarrassed by her body's uncontrollable gyrations. "Or seen anything like this. It's—"

"A lot," Red said, speaking into her ear. "I know. But not for Glitter. This?" She spread her DP-blood-red-painted hands in front of her. "This is where Glitter lives."

She's right. Tonight, Candace doesn't exist. I'm Glitter. I'm Glitter. I'm Glitter. She repeated it in her head like a prayer; a hymn to hum.

Before she knew what was happening, Red pulled her through the mass of sweat-soaked people and they arrived in front of a bar. DP men sat on stools in front of the mirrored bar top; a blue neon light strip bordering the wide mirror behind it turned the men's pink-white skin ocean blue. Invisible women assumed a variety of positions: standing next to the men, talking; or sitting in their laps, laughing.

She and Red moved to a less crowded space, and Red pushed her onto a stool before sitting on one herself. "So, this is the light floor. Aside from dancing, it's where dippies come to enjoy light patches, the ones that make you feel good and bubbly, like these." She pointed to the dozens of multicolored dispensers attached to the mirrored wall behind the bar. An older woman—yellow gems covering her entire body, even her large puff of coiled hair—stood in front of it. When she wasn't gossiping with the women or flirting with the DP men, she was retrieving patches for them from the dispensers.

"It's where a lot of them start their nights," Red said. "Unless they're hard-core patchers." She nodded at the elevator across the room. "*Those* will go straight to the second floor, or higher, for the harder stuff."

But her mind wasn't there, with Red. She was in a place she'd never been. A new world of possibility where people moved for no other reason than because it felt good, and because they could. She wanted this form of escape, to let go and give in to every desire Sweetsmoke never allowed her, that she'd never allowed herself—"Ow!"

"Focus!" Red yelled into her ear, pinching her thigh. Hard.

Glitter slapped Red's hand and tried to rub the pain away, but it lingered. "Okay, I'm sorry. So what are we doing here? Where's the shib you said would help me?"

"Does Drams Jams Ivy do a show before warming up his voice? Does Mandla fight before loosening up those sexy arms and legs of his? No, so *slow down*. You need to practice. Understand?"

"Not really."

Red pointed to the other end of the bar. "You see that dippy, the one all by himself?"

She tilted her head, and there he was, the pink-white skin of his bony face and hands sticking out of his blue mesh sweater and reflecting the neon blue of the bar, as if he were covered in a light coat of paint.

"Yeah, I see him."

"Good. All I want you to do is go up and talk to him. Make him like you and get used to the clientele. That's it."

"But what do I say?" The bass felt heavier now, the music sounded louder, the lights flashed harder. "I'm . . . I'm nervous."

Red scrunched up her face. "What? Glitter doesn't get nervous. Plus, you don't *say* anything. At least, not first. Remember your training. Now go over there and make me proud."

Glitter got up, legs wobbling all the way, and stood next to him, not sure what to do. Red motioned for her to dance a little bit, so she rocked her shoulders up and down, but felt too self-conscious and tree-like. Not caring, the man instantly turned to her, a white patch stuck to his throat. "Well, hello," he said, stretching his lips so widely that they seemed to disappear behind his head. "You look absolutely delicious."

A wave of nausea crashed and rolled around in her stomach. It worked its way up into her throat, but she forced it down with a grimace. He must have taken it as a smile, because he moved nearer, his lips so close she could smell the steamed potatoes and garlic he'd had for dinner.

He shut his eyes, inhaled until his chest was full of her scent, then let it out, bit by bit. "The things I would do to you." His lips, a cool blue from the lights, grazed her ear. "And you're not even my type. I like my women shorter, with big hair, but"—a sweaty hand slid down her shoulder blades, rested on her bottom—"you'll do."

It was a strange feeling. She was only standing there, yet this man—who, for all she knew, worked in a building in downcity Rhitelville, had a wife, children, and enough rhitellings to buy all of Forest Twenty-Six—was a servant to her body. Skin, blood, and bones, just like every other woman in the hemisphere, except, and now she smiled at the thought: *My skin, my blood, and my bones are Invisible. I am the forbidden, and in here, the forbidden reigns supreme.*

The woman behind the bar approached him. He took his hand off Glitter as he ordered another patch. By the time he turned back around, she was already at the other end of the bar with Red, laughing as he twisted his head in every direction, searching. They hit the dance floor, their two bodies—one tall and dusted in glitter, the other short and covered in red—folded into each other, soft skin touching as the music worked its way through their limbs. When sweat began to stick to them, Red nodded to a quieter corner of the room.

"Good work, Glitter! You pushed him right up against the edge of his desire and left him there. You know, you could have told him to do anything just then, and he would have done it. Money, jewelry, anything. How does it feel?"

Powerful. In these men, on the dance floor and seated around the bar, she saw reflections of every DP she'd ever known. Reverend Achte, schoolteachers and professors, Mr. Tenmase, even Sanford. They all carried themselves with a sense of superiority, of entitlement. But being here, watching these men of the so-called Dominant Population foam at the mouth for women they considered less than, served as proof that there were two sides to everyone, even her. The person you were in the light of day and who you were in the darkness of night—true natures revealed in the contrast. DPs weren't clean, she realized, they were just experts at hiding their dirt.

"Like I'm receiving an education," she replied.

Red smirked. "Because you are, and from the best teacher. These

227

dippies, you see how childlike they are? Just looking for a different version of their uma's pibele to suck. And *these* are the men running our hemisphere, which is why they're so dangerous."

Glitter turned to her. "I didn't know you'd thought these thoughts, or had these feelings."

"Don't sound so surprised that there's more to me than what's between my thighs, injaka. But we can talk politics when we make it out of here. Time to go up."

They moved to leave, but someone pulled Glitter's hand. "Who—" She turned and saw Sanford, his hand locked around her wrist.

"What are you doing here, Candy?"

Before she could answer, Red was already between them, her palm against Sanford's chest. "Look but don't touch, handsome. And I don't know who 'Candy' is, but this is Glitter."

He tried to find Glitter's eyes over Red's head, but she looked away. What was *he* doing at Minx? Would he tell Mr. Tenmase? How could she explain this away? It was odd to see him standing there, the only bubble they'd ever existed in, Castle Tenmase, now popped, making it more difficult for them to relate, to project their fantasies onto each other. Actors without a backdrop.

"Candace," he said. Another Invisible woman, brown, beige, pink, and white painted on her like layers of a cake, was trying to tug him back to the dance floor, but he didn't move. "Candace, look at me," he repeated. "I don't know what you're doing here, but you should go." He reached for her, but Red playfully caught his hand, intertwined her fingers with his own, and guided it back down. Undeterred, Sanford kept his eyes on her. "This isn't a place for you."

She finally faced him and said, "But I'm Glitter, love. I don't know who Candace is," before walking away, arm in arm, with Red.

"*Who* was that?" Red asked, laughing.

Glitter shrugged. "Someone who thought they knew me."

CHAPTER 25

JOLIS SLID HIS FINGER DOWN THE NEAREST WALL, LOWERING Stella Irons's singing. Only when he nodded toward the woman standing in his doorway did she walk toward him. Her face painted black; a large white star over her left eye, minor constellations orbiting it. On her head sat tight, mushroom-like knots of spiraled hair. Yes, she was one of the most captivating women he'd ever seen, but the frantic eyes, the tiny, timid strides she took, spoiled it.

When she finally reached him, he raised her chin, staring directly into her eyes, and whispered, "Is this your first time?"

Unable to make eye contact, the young woman tried, and failed, to swallow.

"What's your name?" he said, soft and sweet.

"S-s-starlight, sir."

"No need to call me sir. But what's your *real* name?"

She hesitated, then, "Jabulile."

He laughed, but stopped after she slightly twisted her head away from him, scared. "Then why aren't you cheerful?"

Her trembling ceased and her moon-colored eyes finally met his gaze. "You speak Vilongo?"

"Just a little." He paused, giving her more time to relax. "Did they tell you how I like it?"

She nodded.

He pointed her to the guest bathroom, in the bedroom near the kitchen. A minute later, her feet were padding over the kitchen tile, and he called, "In here," from his bedroom. He smelled salt and syrup when she entered, which made him only want her more; it was her natural smell—the scent she'd hidden underneath the paint.

"I'm here," she announced.

"You're here. Come." He stroked the empty side of the bed next to him. "Would you like something to loosen up, maybe a patch?" he asked after she lay beside him, a shallow, body-shaped indentation on his sheets.

"No, thank you."

"How was your night?"

"Fine."

Finding her forearm, he dragged a finger across it. "Just fine? Come on, you've got to give me more than that."

"Well," she said, turning to him. "I spent most of it at Minx, and—"

"Sorry," he interrupted. "Do you work at Minx?"

"Oh, no. I just went with some friends."

The tension that had drawn his skin tight undid itself. He'd always told the agency to never send any woman who worked at Minx or the other clubs. For safety, of course. There were too many variables, too many possibilities of coming across someone from the past. These special moments were for short-term carnal pleasure, even though, sure, he was sacrificing long-term romantic happiness. But life, he knew from a young age, was a series of sacrifices, and if you did it right, if you achieved what you were supposed to, then the sacrifices ceased to matter as much.

Lost in his head, he missed what she'd just said. "What?"

"I said it was weird, though. Minx."

"Weird how?"

"Tense. The girls said some of their clients were on edge because of Shanu, the Invisible. But they also said it was an opportunity to make more money, easing the dippies' fears and whatnot, you know?"

"Yes, I do. The hemisphere is built on people like that, who can always adapt, no matter what. But what about you? You just started doing this work, but what's your dream?"

A short shrill laugh rushed out of her mouth.

"What's so funny?" he asked.

"Look at what I do," she said, heat radiating toward him. "How can I dream?"

"Everything you do is a stepping-stone, like boulders to get you from one side of a river to the other."

"And what do *you* know about stones and rivers? You, in this building. With these sheets"—plucking them—"with the world at your fingertips." She sat up, grabbed his hand, and held it up for him to see. "So soft, as if you've never had to do any heavy lifting at all."

Jolis turned his hand around, admiring the smoothness of his palms. "You would be surprised. But I was serious. If you could do anything, anything at all, what would it be?"

She sank deeper into the bed, resting on her side again. "That's easy. I'd be an artist. Everything you saw on me, all the paint—I did it myself. I've painted ever since I was a girl in the Rubber and Silicone Region, swirling twigs in the muddy swamp water and drawing whatever came to mind on myself and my little sister. Trees, people, imaginary beings."

"That's beautiful. Maybe I can help you earn some money that way. I have friends who enjoy physical art, or might want the walls in their homes painted. You know, some people have parties where they want their Invisible workers to look a certain way, so you could make a whole business of going from place to place doing that."

"And why would you do that for me?"

"Why wouldn't I?"

"Because men like you don't help women like me for free."

"You've never met a man like me, Jabulile."

Her hand, dripping with that smell of salt and syrup, met his cheek. She brought her lips to his own, then to his ear. "You're strange," she whispered.

Gone was the trembling girl who'd walked into his apartment. This boldness that surged through her fingers, lips, and snapped across her skin made him harder than hard: swollen.

"Strange," he breathed out, grabbing a handful of her knotted hair, yanking. "How?"

She wrapped a hand around his testicles and tugged, hard, forcing a grunt out of him. "Most men like you want their Invisible women painted from head to toe. But you," she said through clenched teeth. "My boss told me I'd have to come here painted, then shower and remove it all before joining you in bed. Why?"

He pressed his hand to her chest, guided her onto her back. Her rising pulse connected with his own as he dragged his fingers across her collarbone, then past her breasts, chest, and stomach. He gripped her thighs and raised them, kissing their soft inner flesh until his lips reached her vulva.

"Because," he said, staring where he knew her eyes were, "I want you as you are."

She twitched when he placed his broad tongue on her clitoris. Her slow, heavy breathing told him that she was enjoying it, making him want to come then and there. She could be free with him, and he, falling deeper, could be, even if only for a moment, his true self.

The licking, flipping, digging, and kissing yielded a pool of sweat that stained the sheets. Her head finally rested on his chest as she said, fighting to breathe, "I would have done that for free."

"And I would have paid double."

Moonlight fell through the bedroom's glass wall, bathing them in a light bright enough to reach through the darkened windows. He planted a solitary kiss on top of her head, those tight, braided knots having loosened, spilling all over now.

"What's your name?" she asked, her arms wrapped around him, exhaling into his chest, words shaped by a smile he didn't need to see to know was there.

"Andrew."

"Andrew, hm? Well"—she held him tighter—"I'm going to call you Mr. Invisible. Because you're the only dippy who seems to see us."

"I like that."

"Me too." She sat up, ran her fingers through his hair. "Do I need to go? Or can we lie here a bit?"

He usually didn't let women linger—the pleasure came from the impermanence. But she touched something in him he'd been missing.

"We can lie here."

Fatigue submerged him into sleep and spat him onto a stage, dancing, with thousands of people in front of him. He had a partner: a small woman covered in white dust, whom he knew was Stella Irons, but resembled Jabulile more. She ran across the stage toward him and jumped. Her chalky body floated in the air and he planted his feet, stretching out his arms to catch her, but when her body made contact with his, he shattered into billions of pieces—so tiny that, even if a million people spent a million years picking up every shard, he would never become whole again. The crowd stood up, ear-piercing applause echoing throughout the theater as they chanted, "Mr. Invisible! Mr. Invisible! Mr. Invisible!"

There, broken beyond repair, the distinct smell of noburn wood—herbal, spicy, with bits of smoke—assaulted his nostrils, awakening him. He opened his eyes and Jabulile was on top of him, hovering; his cutting knife, with the noburn handle he'd crafted himself, just above him.

"May the rebellion stay happy!" she shouted.

He caught her wrists in time, forcing her off him, throwing the knife across the room and choking her with every bit of his strength, channeling the brief but real pain of betrayal. He didn't know who had sent her, but he was embarrassed that he'd let his guard down. That he was so close to losing everything when he was so close to winning it all. Now she would only serve as a reminder to trust no one.

The seconds of struggle felt like centuries. After she went limp, he picked her up, gently cradling her in his arms. He walked across his apartment, then threw her small body down the same chute he used for his dirty clothing, forcing himself to forget the time they'd just spent together, how free she'd made him feel. None of it was worth it. Not really. And if she died, no one would even care.

That was the way of the hemisphere.

CHAPTER 26

RED LED GLITTER TO A SPIRAL STAIRCASE ENCLOSED IN GLASS
next to the bar. All the noise from the floor became distant, and
every time her foot touched a step, it lit up in a different color.

"It's noiseproof in here," Red said from the stairs above her.
"This is one of the only places where we can speak without being
listened to."

"Listened to?"

"What?" Red looked down at her and laughed. "You think the
State doesn't know what goes on here? Who do you think runs this
place? We're just lucky we have that patcher as shib director. Before,
that woman behind the bar, Nofoto, said there used to be raids all
the time, just for fun."

She'd seen shibs on the light floor, dancing in full moss-colored
mesh uniform, patches no doubt under their shirts and pants. The
hypocrisy was alarming; their hemisphere flew a flag with The
Chief Executive Rhitel Bible laid open on it, yet sanctioned places
like Minx, which they would consider the embodiment of sin. And
was Red talking about Hemispheric Guard Director Curts? A
patcher? No one was who they said they were, nothing was as it

seemed. The thing that scared her most, though, was that DPs could do whatever they wanted without any accountability. How could someone ever form a conscience without consequences?

They came upon a doorway. Red stopped at its threshold, stepping aside on the tiny landing so Glitter could have a look.

DP men and Invisible women sat at dozens of white-clothed tables with candle flames flickering an array of colors between them. The men gulped down strangely hued liquids—glowing golds, pulsing reds; brown, sludge-like substances—that trickled down their cheeks and onto their tucked-in napkins. Every table was crowded with plate upon plate of vibrantly dyed foods that they forced with awful urgency past their stained lips without stopping until, Glitter saw, they were near the point of choking.

Red's mouth was slightly open as she gazed at the equal parts repulsive and impressively gluttonous scene. "Is this some type of restaurant?" Glitter asked.

"Basically. Dippies put on patches that alter their taste buds, and the flavors of the food become stronger than anything you or I have ever tasted. The women are just their dinner dates and never have to take their clothes off, because by the time the men finish their meals, they're too full to do anything other than sleep. It's a good trade."

"Why aren't there any dippy women here?"

"Isn't it obvious?" Red said, shaking her head at Glitter as if she'd asked the dumbest question in the world. She turned back to the flavor floor and sighed. "Minx, and really every other place in this great hemisphere of ours, isn't for women, Glitter. These men come here for a fantasy, and dippy women would ruin that. Plus, dippy women are too fragile. But, between us, they can also be quite vicious. I know some girls who have made house visits to dippy women, and they said their men are a walk by the river in comparison."

"Dippy women . . . requesting Invisible women . . . for house calls?"

"Don't be so simple. Women and women. Men and men. It all goes on behind closed doors. No matter what that Bible says, it's as natural as green leaves on brown trees. But if a man *really does* want a dippy, he can go to Siren Mansion, where The Defiled work."

"The—" She caught herself, but it was too late. Red already knew how much she didn't know, there was no point in hiding it. In the past, a lack of knowledge, about anything, would send her down a spiral. But she was discovering that not knowing was okay, and embracing that was a strength. "What are 'The Defiled'?"

"One of the hemisphere's not-so-best-kept secrets. Leviticus 21:13–14. If a dippy woman gets divorced, she's considered spoiled, or 'Defiled.' She can never marry again and is basically an outcast. Most of them end up working in clubs, like this, or even travel, sometimes as far as other regions, to meet private clients. There's a whole network for them. It's not a bad life, really."

A man directly in Glitter's line of sight took a bite of whatever was on his plate, its juices running down his chin, and closed his eyes in ecstasy. She imagined that this was what a man having an orgasm looked like. His legs twitched, his arms shook, and the woman across from him seemed bored—at least until he opened his eyes. Then she smiled, touched his hand, and encouraged him to drink, to eat; the world was his feast.

"Anyway, I just wanted you to see this." Red raised her head toward the top of the staircase. "Let's keep going."

On the third floor there were no bizarre colors, food, or unrestricted states of bliss. Just a dim yellowish-white light that shone from slim rectangular panels running across every wall. Smoke sauntered through the room, probably pumped through the ceiling, making it harder to see.

A bar sat in the same place as on the first floor. A woman covered in black paint—cracks exposing her true skin—moved behind the bar, pulling patches out of dispensers and passing them to the working women, who then joined men lying on beds inside of white-clothed canopies, of which there were at least a dozen set up in front of every wall.

"Well, it doesn't look like they serve food here," Glitter said.

Some of the canopies were open; men with unbuttoned shirts rested on their backs, plenty of pillows around and below them glowing the soft yellow of the room's lights. Their shoes, as if these DPs were in their own homes, placed side by side on the glass floor outside of the canopies.

"What a smart girl you are, Glitter. You sound just like my sarcastic friend Candace."

Friend? So they *were* friends.

Red winked. "Now's your time to shine. You did great on the light floor. Now I want you to get comfortable getting even closer to them."

"Forget that," she said. "Let's go straight to the top. I'm ready."

"Really?"

"Really."

They walked to the front of the room and waited for the elevator; working women floated back and forth from the bar to the beds, being whatever the men needed them to be. Glitter thought about who they were outside of this bizarre building—mothers, daughters, and sisters with their own dreams, desires, and aspirations. She prayed that it was worth it. But she also knew that sacrifices are hard to quantify.

"Why are we taking the elevator?" she asked.

"Because you won't want to see the fourth floor."

"What's on the fourth floor?"

Red hesitated. "It's just really intense. Women in cages. Wrists and ankles strapped to wheels. Heads and hands locked into wooden frames as men do things to them."

"Things?"

"Yeah. Slap, spit, whip. The fun stuff."

Glitter curled her hand into a stiff fist at the thought of women being wounded as DP men grunted in glee. "They must be getting paid more rhitellings than anyone else in the building."

"I know it's hard to believe, but those particular women enjoy it."

The elevator arrived and Sanele was inside, grinning. "Having a good night, ladies?"

"Now that you're here," Red said, rubbing his bulging arm.

"Don't tempt me, you know I'm at work right now."

"Oh, I know." She batted her eyes as she looked up at him. "But we are, too, so it's fine. Penthouse, please."

"You got it. And you . . ." He turned to Candace. "Enjoying your first night at Minx?"

"I am," she said, the doors closing. "Thank you."

Two floors later, Red stretched on the tips of her toes, kissed Sanele's golden cheek, and walked out with Glitter right behind her, rocking her hips side to side like she'd done this a thousand times.

"Looks like I don't have to pull you around anymore."

"Looks like it."

It was the smell that hit her first: a mix of damp leaves, sweat, and urine. Then her eyes adjusted to the blackness of the room. Sets of chairs and small tables were positioned around the edge, a single dark blue light panel placed above each one. Glass bottles sat behind a bar in the back—probably fermented grains and vegetables, she guessed, from the sharp smell stinging her inner nostrils.

Men seated in antique leather chairs, glasses in their hands and brown, smoking sticks between their index fingers and thumbs, radiated an assuredness that frightened her. Every set of chairs and tables was placed near the gaping mouth of a dark hallway, only compounding the feeling that she was in a nightmare set in an underground station. She turned around, hoping to find Sanele still inside the elevator, but he was long gone.

"Glitter, stop," Red ordered.

She looked down, saw Red's fingers digging into her shaking wrist.

"Now is *not* the time for nerves," she whispered. "You see that man over there?" She pointed across the room, to the right of where they stood. All Glitter could see was the silhouette of a seated man. Unlike the others, he was alone. "That's the man you came to see."

No. She wanted to run. There was something about him, how he just sat there, only moving to slowly bring the smoking stick to his mouth or take a sip of his drink—how none of the women dared approach him—that made the tiny hairs on her body stand up. She couldn't see his face, but she had never been more certain of anything before. No matter how powerful she'd felt moments ago, how badly she wanted to save her brother, cowardice, that familiar yet unwanted guest, crept into the room and stood beside her. She found her fingers wrapped around the compass Rusty had given her, praying it would somehow transport her back to Forest Twenty-Six.

Red grabbed her arm, dragging her across the blue-black tile to the man. "Nice to see you again, Hemispheric Guard Associate Deputy Director Ribussce. How are you?"

He looked up from his seat. Finally, Glitter could see his closely shaved face, every feature perfectly sculpted in symmetry and severity, as if from a tall block of stone. Up close, she noticed how his chest and arms tried their best to break through his uniform. All she could think about was how easily he could snap her neck.

"This one for me?"

"She is," Red replied, working extra hard, Glitter thought, to sound upbeat. *Is she also scared?* "Do you like what you see?"

"Turn around."

With a push from Red, she did as he said. He slapped her butt cheek, she cried in pain, and he held his hand there, shaking it up and down. He did the same with the other cheek, but this time she just sucked in air through her teeth, clenching them in anticipation.

"Back around now."

She faced him again. Tilting his head, he said, "You look more DP than vizzer."

"Yes," Red said. "We always say that if she wasn't Invisible, she would probably live in Rhitelville, or somewhere else in a big, fancy—"

He raised his hand. Red stopped speaking. "Leave."

She squeezed Glitter's hand and disappeared. It was then Glitter wished, with all that she had in her, that she had grabbed a patch from one of the bars downstairs. Surely it would numb her to the terror she was experiencing now.

"Come," he ordered, standing up. *Holy Father.* This man was a full third of a meter taller than she was. His black mesh uniform, three red stripes on its left side, reminded her of the one she'd seen Hemispheric Guard Director Curts wear, confirming his status. This man, even if he wasn't so powerfully built, could do anything, including murder her, and no one would ask any questions.

Hemispheric Guard Associate Deputy Director Ribussce stepped into the darkened hallway, his uniform perfectly blending into the night-black tunnel. When he stopped and said, "Don't make me repeat myself," it was as if a monster made of sound or air, not a man, was speaking.

Hand to the wall to steady herself, she followed him down the hallway until he stopped and pushed open a door revealing a room suffused with hazy red light. She turned around, back where she'd come from, and saw only darkness.

"Close the door."

She did as she was told and, even before facing him, heard the weight of his body drop onto the bed, the sole piece of furniture. Above it hung a massive canvas capture of Chief Executive Rhitel.

Those eyes, always watching. They were present in every class-room, every store, so they didn't shock her now, even here. For some reason, the only place without his face was church, but maybe it was because, like the Holy Father, his presence was supposed to be felt, not seen.

"Know what this is?" he asked, holding the smoking stick be-tween his fingers, taking a pull.

"No."

"No, what?"

"No, sir."

"It's called tabacum. Illegal in this hemisphere because of the environment, but you can get some smuggled from the Southwest-ern, if you know the right people."

He put it to his mouth, inhaled again, deeper this time. As the thick smoke curled toward her, he parted her lips with his fingers and inserted the stick into her mouth. "Suck, but don't swallow."

She pulled on the stick, dense smoke filling her mouth before she accidentally brought it to her lungs, coughing so violently that her throat became raw.

All he did was smile, drop the stick onto the floor, and grind it into the white carpet with his boot.

"Take my clothes off."

Light-headed and nauseated from the tabacum, she knelt down on the bed behind him, struggling to tear his black jacket from his back. It was the same with his button-up and white undershirt; she had to use both hands to peel them from his rock-like flesh.

"On your knees now. In front of me."

This can't happen. This can't happen. This can't happen.

But she got off the bed, moved in front of him and, as he lay there, dropped to her knees.

"The pants."

She unbuckled his belt, used her dwindling strength to get his black pants over his bottom and down his thighs. Her intestines twisted themselves into unnatural shapes as she lowered her head, staring at the floor, figuring out what to do.

Seduce him, just how Red taught you. Convince him to give you a city pass without raising alarm. Save Sweetsmoke. Save Sweetsmoke. Save Sweetsmoke, even if you have to sacrifice yourself. Even if—

His knee crashed into her chin, the room shifting as her eyes rolled into her head. Back on the floor, the monster was on top of her, his hand a vice crushing her throat more, and more, and more.

"Never keep me waiting, girl. Or this will be the last night you—"

Commotion outside the door. Women screaming, footsteps growing louder. The room was going dark, but she moved her eyes toward the door and saw it fling open, Sanford pausing, then throwing his entire body into the monster, not knocking him over, but knocking him off balance, off of her.

Hemispheric Guard Associate Deputy Director Ribussce rose to his full height, in nothing but his underwear. If the circumstances were different, if she were watching this on the display, she'd laugh. But when he wrapped both hands around Sanford's throat, his feet kicking in the air as the monster lifted him, she knew it was life or death. For both of them.

"Stop," she said, her voice calm but also coarse now, rubbing his biceps. "Put him down. Maybe he's had one too many patches and thinks you're someone else."

He stared at Sanford a moment, his eyes wild, lips twitching, then dropped him before kicking his crawling body once, twice, thrice.

Sanford coughed, blood splattering the white carpet.

"Are you lost, boy? Is that it?" Hemispheric Guard Associate Deputy Director Ribussce asked. "Or do you have business here, with my vizzer?"

She knelt next to Sanford, her lips brushing his ear. "Don't worry," she whispered. "I got this." Then, louder, "Get up and go find whoever you were looking for! I'm not her."

Hand, foot, hand, foot. Sanford worked his way up, gripping his stomach. He looked at Glitter, then Ribussce. "My mistake, sir. I thought— I thought she was someone else. Please forgive the intrusion."

"You're lucky I'm in a good mood," Hemispheric Guard Associate Deputy Director Ribussce said. "You're leaving with your life."

"Thank you, sir," he replied, retreating, closing the door.

"Back down," he ordered.

She did as she was told, eyes focused on the ground, trying, fighting, to still find a way forward. All she saw was her silicone bag, the one Red had given her.

Ah! She remembered the small glass bottle she'd put in it, the one with the clear liquid and floating red drops Mr. Tenmase had given her. Could she use it? She had to try. She had made it this far, *so far*, and couldn't leave empty-handed.

"My underwear."

"Wait." She rose, got on top of him.

"What are you doing?"

"*Sh.*" She brought a finger to his thin lips, turned red from the light. "What's the rush? We should savor this, like a delicious meal." She was doing her best to imitate how Red spoke with Sanele, how she'd taught her to speak earlier that morning.

He leaned his head back, exhaled. "You're right. We're in for a long night."

Moving her hips now, she felt him get hard, placed her hands on his chest.

"Squeeze them," he said, his nipples between her glitter-covered fingers. She continued digging her hips into his own, and, when she pinched his nipples as hard as she could, his penis throbbed. Now was her chance.

"You know, Red told me you're a big hemispheric guard. Almost as big as Hemispheric Guard Director Curts."

He sat up and let out a sneering laugh, nearly knocking her off the bed. "Don't insult me. Curts is on his way out, even if he doesn't know it. You've heard of this vizzer Shanu?"

"Of course." She squeezed his nipples once more, wrapped her hand around his throat, forcing him onto his back again. Her new plan gave her power, but this, as hard as it was to admit, gave her pleasure.

"If it were me," he said, struggling to speak as she increased her grip. "I would have killed him already. All you have to do is take his parents"—she loosened her hand—"or his sister, and threaten to dismember them. Or actually do it, on the display for everyone to see, and I guarantee he'd ooze out of the shadows like the scum he is."

She brought her teeth to his ear, bit down as hard as she could, the metallic flavor of his blood on her tongue. "I'm sure he would . . . if you were in charge," she whispered. "You say he has parents?"

He sucked his bottom lip and nodded. "They live in Upcity."

So it's true. Our parents are big, rich Invisibles living perfect lives without us.

"Enough talking," he said. "Go into my pants and retrieve the green and purple patch with 'DS' on it."

Don't panic. I've trained for this.

She found the patch, began removing its protective layer. "What's the 'DS' for?"

"Deep sedation. Give me it."

"I got it. You relax."

He sat up, his huge hand raised, ready to clap her face. "Now."

Pain shot through her body, remembering how his knee cracked against her chin moments ago. Red had told her to make sure *she* put the patches on, to not feel the effects so strongly. But there was no way out. She handed it to him.

245

Gripping her by the hair, he wrenched her head back, slapped the patch against her neck, hard. Immediately, the pain streamed out of her, each anxiety and worry wiped away.

She felt a comfort she'd never experienced pulling at her. Every cell inside of her seemed to relax, and she went to the place she enjoyed most, where she floated, free and unbothered. But then she thought of Sweetsmoke, heard Hemispheric Guard Director Curts's words, "through death or rule," and pictured her brother hanging from a tree, swaying as his weight tested the wooden limb's strength.

Calling on the unknown ancestors that lived in her rumoya, she prayed for them to not let her fade away, to help her fight against the overpowering desire to give in to this patch, to escape. *Please.* But the darkness was spreading, the dizziness increasing. Then she felt it: the clawing. Her spirit extending itself wide inside of her, increasing alertness, movement, strength.

"I'd like to see their house," she said, voice shaky.

"Whose?"

"The Invisible's parents."

He lay on his back now, but from the way he hadn't sat up or struck her, she could tell she piqued his curiosity. "And why would a whore like you want to go to their house?"

She shuddered at the word. "Because," she said, giving her voice a childish quality, "I never get to have any fun. It's just forest, church, Minx. Forest, church, Minx. But this, going to the house of the murderer's parents and taking a capture, like a special piece of history, would make me *sooooo* happy. And if Glitter is happy"—she stroked the inside of his powerful thighs, making him convulse—"you'll be happy."

He raised his head toward her. "I can't do that. Impossible."

"Who says, Hemispheric Guard Director Curts?" Her fingers

moved ever so closer to his crotch. "Compared to you, he's such a skinny, weak man. My people laugh at him, but not you. We fear you."

"As you should," he spat. "Curts is no one. Nothing but an embarrassment to our race." She felt his pulse rising just at the mention of the man.

Glitter got back on top of him, slapped him as hard as she could, the *POP!* echoing throughout the room. "So do it, Director. No one will ever know, except the two of us. And the next time I see you will be even better than what we're about to do tonight."

In the second it took him to breathe, she didn't know if she'd overplayed her hand, if this was it. She still felt the effects of the patch, though lighter now, and had to struggle against the fatigue that fought to overtake her.

His penis was hard again. "Fine," he said. "But only for tomorrow. Then, afterward, you come straight back here and let me whip you until dawn. Tonight will just be the appetizer."

"Of course, Director. Tomorrow I'll come straight back here . . . like a good whore, and you can tear me to shreds."

"Glitter, yes?" His hand hovered in front of the wall, eager to finish this and get to it.

"No, program it for Candace. That's my real name."

A huge risk, but a necessary one. Plus, this man wouldn't remember her name. He was worse than dumb; he was confident. Confident to the point that he couldn't imagine a world where a woman, especially a woman like her, ever got the best of him.

Two swipes, combined with additional information on her end—tapped in without his watching—and it was done. He went to grab her, but she pushed his hands away and sank to her knees. Then she was back on top of him, the small glass bottle in her hand. "Open your mouth and lean your head back."

He narrowed his eyes at the bottle. "What is that?"

"It'll make this all better, trust me. You think your tabacum and fermented grains are good? Wait until you have this, *Director*."

He did as he was told, and she let one, two, three, four drops fall into his mouth. Mr. Tenmase had warned her that even one could be too much, but she couldn't take any chances, not with someone as sinister and sadistic as he was. Immediately, his body went cold, his breathing became deeper.

"Come, Glitter. Give me what I deserve," he said, his voice drifting away.

She placed her ear to his chest, sighed when she heard him breathing. Hate burned in her heart for him, but she wasn't a murderer, even if killing him would somehow save millions of her own people. Maybe one day she would be capable of that, but not today.

The sound of slow clapping came from the corner of the room. She looked up, but didn't see or smell anyone, or sense a rumoya. "Who's there?" They must have been watching her the entire time. "Abe?"

No response. She didn't know how long Hemispheric Guard Associate Deputy Director Ribussce would be out for, couldn't risk it to uncover the clapping's source. Moving backward, eyes on that corner of the room, she left without a sound. The dark hallway spit her back onto the blue-black floor. Red, and the other Rainbow Girls, stood by the bar.

"I was occupied myself," Red said, "but heard you had an unexpected visitor. The dippy from downstairs."

"I took care of him."

"Good. And did you get what you need?"

"I did."

"And look." She took Glitter's face in her hands. "You're still in one piece. I knew that big monster had nothing on my girl Glitter. Listen . . ." Her eyes were hard now. "Whatever you had to do in there, you did for Sweetsmoke, okay?"

"I know."

"Good. Now let's go home."

They crowded into the elevator, Anele joking with them the entire way down to the platform. Back in the forest, everyone said goodbye. Glitter hugged Red, thanking her for everything, then walked back to her cabin, dazed. Once in the outdoor shower, she felt the warm water pound her back, watched the paint and glitter, under the moon's radiant eye, swirl and slowly disappear down the drain. Hoping, praying, she would never have to be her again.

CHAPTER 27

WHO ARE YOU?" CURTS WHISPERED TO HIMSELF. THE SUNLIGHT fought through the wooden slats covering his study's bay window. He lay next to it, a pillow pressed into his face. He had been asking himself the same question all night, until night became early morning.

It was the same question he'd asked at the academy. His superiors saw that he had a way with the Invisibles whose forests he patrolled. He led with calculated kindness rather than haphazard aggression, gaining their trust by learning their language and treating them as people rather than problems. But his methods were met with ire from his fellow trainees and his less sympathetic higher-ups. They said he wasn't Hemispheric Guard material, that he should have been a reverend, doctor, or professor. A job for soft men with soft hands.

But when a "special" case came up, as his superiors called it, they gave him a shot. The assignment was to find an older Invisible man who had gone missing. Authorities assumed he had escaped to another region, but no one in his forest knew which one, and no amount of torture by Curts's commanding guards or peers yielded any results. He, too, had spoken with the man's relatives and neighbors, and even though he didn't have any solid leads, he did gain a fuller picture of who the man was.

Breaking protocol, Curts lived as that man for days, strange as it was—sleeping on his dusty mattress, eating and drinking as he did—and began to establish a trail that he followed all the way to the Rubber and Silicone Region. Section by section, he combed his way throughout that region, until one day, as he knew he would, he found the man hiding in a hole beneath someone's kitchen. The family that harbored him was spared, Curts had begged for it, but the man . . . Word of his gruesome, limb-by-limb execution spread like sweet vegetable jam on a fresh piece of toast. It was this ability to empathize with and track Invisibles, armed with nothing more than intuition and a kind disposition, that earned Curts the name "The Happy Grabber," uttered with more derision than admiration, as well as promotion after promotion, all the way to where he was now.

And where was he now? Lying on the second floor of his home, inspecting every detail he knew about Shanu and failing spectacularly, publicly. Yesterday's mission was a total embarrassment, for him and the Hemispheric Guard. When they attempted to retrace the collar hack, they discovered a convoluted hemisphere-crossing entanglement. It was impossible to know who, exactly, was responsible: Shanu, the Children of Slim, another hemisphere, anyone who wanted to take advantage of the Northwest's perceived weakness— his perceived weakness.

No other hemisphere had dared challenge them, no internal opposition had thrived for more than a heartbeat. Until now. The fall of his hemisphere, like the Romans and Russians he'd read about, would be historic. *Damn this Invisible.*

The truth was, when he attempted to inhabit the mind of Shanu, he only found an angry young man who would do everything he could to wreak as much destruction as possible. He could be thousands of kilometers outside of the hemisphere by now. But Curts wouldn't give up, he couldn't. Too much was on the line, and there was still time.

His earsphere vibrated across the room. He sat up, swiped the closest wall. It was HGADD Ribussce. "What?"

"Good morning to you, too, sir. How am I? I'm fine. Had a bit of a wild night at Minx. You know how these young vizzers are, doing things our women would never do. I had this fierce one on top of me, slapping, choking—"

"I don't care what you do on your own time, Ribussce," Curts said, gripping his forehead. "What is it? I'm busy."

"Funny. I'm busy, too. Except I can't imagine what you're doing, because here I am, at the Executive Estate, trying to find this vizzer. And there you are, at home, fiddling with your dick."

Curts split the blinds, peering through his window to see who, aside from his personal guards, was outside. No one new, so was one of his own men feeding Ribussce information?

"Are you spying on me?"

"I would never, sir. But it's a good thing you're home right now. Get comfortable and turn on the display. I'll see you soon." Then he hung up.

Curts brought up the NWN. There was Anna Franklin, standing on the Executive Estate's South Lawn, the same place she had been with Jolis the day before.

"At the request of former Chief Consort Rhitel, we polled a few million Northwesterners to see how they feel about the search for Shanu, the Invisible, and the results are in. An astonishing seventy-three percent say they have lost faith in Hemispheric Guard Director Curts. Anonymous comments include, and I'm quoting directly, 'If Curts doesn't find this Invisible, he should be fired.' 'How can one BLEEP make the most powerful hemisphere on the planet look like a joke?' 'Curts or this BLEEP, I don't care. Someone will hang soon.'

"Here with us," she continued, guards moving in every direction behind her, "is Hemispheric Guard Associate Deputy Director Ribussce, who will speak to this morning's poll and the search for Shanu." Ribussce entered the frame, all smiles, muscles, a crisp uniform.

"Bastard," Curts whispered.

"Hemispheric Guard Associate Deputy Director Ribussce," she said. "Can you please explain what's going on? People are more afraid than ever."

"It's all simple." There was a glint in his eye, as if this entropy aroused him. Curts sat and watched, limp. "Our Director isn't fit for the job. And this is something all of us in State, even The Chief Executive himself, may the Holy Father bless his soul, knew. Now you all know it, too. You see, Invisibles are like children. Babies, actually. If you allow them to run amok, they'll think that that's okay. But what they need"—he smashed his iron fist into his tight palm—"is a firm hand. Discipline. Harsh punishment.

"So I am not surprised that millions are against Curts. I am against Curts, and so is my dear aunt, Chief Consort Rhitel, who is devastated by the fact that her husband's murderer remains free. One day was atrocious, two was unspeakable, but three? What would explain Curts's inability to capture one little BLEEP other than he doesn't want to?"

Curts swiped off the display and stood there, in the center of his study, eyes on the polished hardwood floor. *Traitor.* He had to see Croger. There was a rumor he'd heard years ago that, if true, could make this all go away. The Great Inventor had severed relationships with everyone in State for years now, aside from Stephan, but he'd have to make an exception. And if he didn't comply—well, Curts had been fattening the file he had on him over the past year in case he ever needed to use it.

He grabbed his earsphere, called Lucretia.

"Sir," she said. "I swear I didn't know he was going to do that. He's trying to take both of our heads. This perverted—"

"I know, but it could only be expected, so don't let it distract us. We have two more days. What's the latest?"

"We've increased crackdowns in every Invisible section across the hemisphere, but no new leads. Just a lot of scared people, and even a few deaths, unfortunately."

"Make sure *no one* finds out about those. And call the Public Force. I'm on my way. In the meantime, pay Ribussce no mind. Once this all ends, and provided we're still here"—he shook his head—"he'll face the consequences of his actions."

"See you soon, sir."

Eva's unmistakable wailing ripped into the air from downstairs, followed by Della's shushing her. He ran down, found them curled in each other's arms on the couch, twin rivers running down their cheeks.

Seeing him, Eva jumped out of her mother's arms and threw herself against his chest. "I don't want you to die, Daddy! I don't want you to die," she screamed, snot and tears turning her face a mess. "Please don't go. Please, please, please don't go."

He knelt and held her as tightly as he could. "I'm not going to die, Small Potato. I promise. That man on the display was just playing a joke. It was all a joke."

Della wiped her own face. "No, you can't lie your way out of this, Leon. What we need for you is to find him, *now*. Not just for us, but for all those people who—who want you dead."

"I'm going to make this right, Del. I—"

"You what? You promise?" She was on her feet now, pacing back and forth across the living room floor. "Every day you lie to us, the hemisphere, and yourself. Where is he, Leon? Where are you?"

"You should get ready for work."

"Work?" She laughed. "I'm Secondary Arborist, Leon. All of the trees in the region will be fine for a few days, but none of it matters if the hemisphere is on fire."

"What about your research, I thought you were close to eradicating those phytoparasites in Forest Four?"

She didn't even dignify his diversion, no matter how genuine, with a response.

His daughter gripped his arms with more force, but he gently pried her off. "I have to go now." He stood up, dug into his pockets—shaky, desperate hands feeling around and finding nothing.

"Looking for one of these?" Della asked, retrieving something from her bra, then throwing a pack of patches in the air. Tiny white squares rained on them like the confetti they'd covered each other in for Eva's last birthday. "You think I couldn't tell? I mean, I know you're under a lot of pressure, but I thought you were done with all of this. My husband not only can't do his job, but he's a patcher. A patcher!"

"What's a patcher?" Eva asked.

Stuffing a handful into his pocket, he said, with forced calm, "I have to go. Please get Amahle to clean this up and make some lunch. You both need your strength, too."

"Amahle is gone."

"What do you mean 'gone'?"

"I let her go. We can't have you searching for an Invisible and keep one in our house. The neighbors were talking, Leon."

But Amahle was family to them. A sister to Della, aunt to Eva, saint to him. "Are you still paying her?"

"Of course, I'm not heartless."

He ran his hand over Eva's wheat-colored curls, turned to his wife. "Have I ever let you down before, Del?"

"No," she whispered.

"Please don't forget that."

Eva ran to her mother, and he opened the basement door that led to his private platform. He struggled with every step, fighting the urge to run back up the stairs, kiss his daughter, embrace his wife, and confess his deepest fear to her, that of his glaring personal and professional inadequacy. But he couldn't, not if he wanted them to live, and not if he wanted to be able to live with himself. He would protect his family, he would make them proud. And he would do whatever it took to prove to the hemisphere that he was anything but soft.

CHAPTER 28

THIRTY MINUTES. THAT'S ALL SWEETMINT WAS ABLE TO SLEEP BEfore getting up for Daily Prayer. *How do the others do it?* Her head pounded. On a normal day, when she'd go to Castle Tenmase, a headache was the last thing she could afford. But now, with the upcoming adventure to only the Holy Father knows where Abe was sending her, she couldn't even acknowledge it. Close to the end of the day before, he had given her herbs that made her temporarily sick, as promised. And before she went home, to meet Red and go to Minx, she'd asked Mr. Tenmase if she could take the day off. Seeing how ill she was, he said of course. Today, she had to power through; pain was a luxury few could afford.

She fetched some needle leaf, brewed it, and gulped down the hot, bitter liquid before she could think twice. Her veins widened, the headache ceased, and a tremor moved like a wave from her toes to the top of her head. The herb was working, but now she was jittery. Still, she'd rather be awake and jumpy than tired with a head full of hammers crushing tiny rocks to bits.

"Smells strong," Darksap said outside her door.

"It is. Come in."

"Ah," he said, his voice smiling. "There you are."

Hearing him happy made her happy, and after last night, a familiar face was exactly what she needed. "Here I am."

His footsteps grew louder, his thick, syrupy smell stronger as he approached her, his collar floating in front of her, below her own. Without warning, he grabbed her hand, placed his other around her waist, and pulled her close to him, until their chests were touching; two hearts beating as one.

"Wait," he said, letting her go, walking to the nearest wall, and tapping once, twice. Gentle piano music shyly trickled into the cabin. Darksap brought his body to hers again, and now, the surprise having subsided, she allowed her head to fall onto his shoulder as he lightly moved her across the wooden floor, her body somehow already knowing the steps without his having to tell her.

"I'm sorry," he whispered.

"For what?" she whispered back, careful not to ruin the moment.

"For how I acted yesterday. When I saw you with Red, and all that paint. It just threw me off, I guess. And I, uh . . ."

"You what?" she said, her head still on his shoulder. "It's okay. Be honest with me."

He exhaled into the damp curve of her neck. "I was worried you'd go to the clubs and do what the Rainbow Girls do. But it wasn't right for me to judge."

She raised her head, found his chin, and lifted it toward her. "I'm fighting right now, Dapp. Doing everything I can to fight against an entire hemisphere for my brother."

His fingers curled around her own. "I know, and I wish I could help, but what I promise is that you won't have to fight against me, too. You can count on me. Always."

They stood there, breathing as the music faded out. She couldn't name it, but that thing—once hard and inflexible—that had begun opening itself up to him, becoming soft and bending in his direction, continued to grow, and she was close, so very close, to finally allowing it to overcome her. Surrendering had never felt more urgent, more necessary, but he would need to continue being patient, if only for a little longer.

"Time to go?" she asked, though she meant it as a statement.

"Time to go."

They stepped outside into the humid forest, sunlight dripping through the canopy of leaves above them—something they'd done countless times before, but now felt new; thrilling, even. Neither of them spoke as they walked, slower than usual, prolonging the moment. They continued down Softstone Path, and at some point, after passing cabin after cabin, her hand found his, interlocking, the branches of two trees joining to receive the sun's light together, and in turn, sheltering others. She heard his sharp intake, felt the brief tensing of his body, and then, without a word, he relaxed, as if this were the most natural thing in the world.

Most of the pews inside the church were filled with floating collars and painted skin. Darksap found a seat next to his mother, Sweetmint grabbed one in the back. Without even realizing it, she sat next the Rainbow Girls, all with fresh coats of paint, as if last night never happened.

They turned to her and laughed, but this laughter wasn't the same as it had always been, swollen with ridicule. No, the low sound coming from their mouths was knowing, sympathetic, conspiratorial. Red must have told them some of what had happened. Now they seemed to have a new respect for her. The question of "Are we friends?" popped into her head again, but she'd have to wait and see.

She looked around. Something was wrong. Dozens of shibs stood along the walls, hands on the curled whips hanging off their belts, eyes hard and alert. Feet planted, ready.

The door slammed shut and Reverend Achte appeared behind

his pulpit, head tilted down, exposing his bald crown. "Welcome, my children," he whispered, so low that she knew the shibs couldn't hear him, but she and her forestfolk could.

"Good morning, Reverend," they responded with the same fervor as they did every day.

"'Walk in obedience to all that the Holy Father has commanded you,'" he began, still staring down at the wooden pulpit. "'So that you may live and prosper and prolong your days in the hemisphere that you inhabit.'" The reverend finally faced them, his wrinkled skin more pink than white. "Deuteronomy 5:33."

He lifted his glass tablet, displaying an illuminated crimson Bible, above his head. And said, with more vigor, "'Do not merely listen to the word, and so deceive yourselves. Do what it says.' James 1:22." His frail arm shook as he spoke, his face now red.

With a swiftness, he moved from behind the pulpit, stormed down the aisle, glass tablet still raised, and stopped right in front of where Sweetmint sat. His face, the same color as the illuminated Bible he held, twisted in what she saw as insanity, agony. When he spoke next, he showered her and Blue, to her immediate right, with frothy spit. "'Whoever heeds discipline shows the way to life!'" he shouted at the top of his lungs. "'But whoever ignores correction, especially if Invisible, leads others astray.' Proverbs 10:17. Get up!"

It looked like he was ordering *her* to get up, but why? Her feet were glued to the floor, her bottom and back to the wooden pew, but her mind, like the tiny white mushrooms on a peeling bark tree, sprouted with question after question after question. *Was the old man always this strong? If he is actually speaking to me, is it because I was late? I thought he didn't have didanlenses?*

She turned to the Rainbow Girls, their faces only returning shock. "*You*, Candace!" he yelled. "Up. Now!"

Like last night, she did as she was told, following him to the front of the church. But he wasn't some pathetic DP sitting at a bar waiting for a woman's affection. This man, their forest's protector, who was little more than translucent skin and bones that she could have snapped in two with less force than her foot on a twig, made her blood run cold.

"There." He pointed to the space to the left of his pulpit, in direct view of the congregation.

Of the visible faces she could see, she found wide eyes, covered mouths, and stoic masks of detachment. Excitement danced across the shibs' upturned lips as they aggressively stroked their whips, begging for the permission to pull them out.

"Have I not shielded you from harm your entire lives?" Reverend Achte asked, banging the pulpit with his hand. "Have I not made sure a day like today, with hemispheric guards flooding your forest, never came to pass before? You all truly have no notion of what transpires in other forests, other regions, and it is I who am to blame."

Over her shoulder, she saw Reverend Achte shake his head in pure disgust. "Yes, the fault rests with me. All we have ever asked is that you fulfill your duty and defend this great hemisphere whenever the call came. Yet *all* of you," he said, swinging his bony finger from one side of the church to the other, "do *nothing* when we're in need of you. When one of your own from this very forest has committed the highest sin. Well . . ." He paused. "The blessed days are over."

He turned to the nearest shib, who couldn't have been older than fifteen, and nodded. The boy walked over and stood behind Sweetmint.

"Bend down," the reverend ordered. She arched her back, placed her hands on her shaking knees.

It was like she was in the middle of the Northwestern Ocean, with a heavy weight tied to her feet, and she could no longer see the sunlight above the water's blue surface, enveloped by an inescapable darkness. Aside from Shanu, Rusty was the one who was always there to grab her hand and pull her to safety, but she not only failed to feel his rumoya emanating from some part of the church, she also believed, with a debilitating, spirit-slaughtering sense of doom, that he wasn't even there. Again.

"May what takes place today inspire you," Reverend Achte said.

The first crack of the boy's whip came fast and hard on her back, the sound not unlike Sweetsmoke's axe meeting a tree's stony exterior. Her scream, though, was in a league of its own.

"Where's Shanu?" Reverend Achte asked.

"I don't know, Reverend," she said, her eyes still on the church's wooden floor. "I promise you."

The whip sang a hymn as it sailed through the air, its tip like fire on her torn skin. A sound ripped across the church, and she, now on her knees, stuck fingers into her own ears to shut it out. Only when Reverend Achte slapped her mouth so hard that her teeth rattled did she realize that this screeching, this stomach-churning articulation of pain, was coming from her.

"Get off of her!" Darksap yelled. She heard him leap from his pew and rush toward her, but the shibs were already on him, a whip wrapped around his neck, dropping lower as the shibs kicked him to his knees and restrained his mother, who tried to reach him.

"Stop your screaming!" Reverend Achte commanded Sweetmint. Hands on the floor, her entire body in shock from the whip's second skin-splitting blow, she couldn't have raised her head to look at him even if she wanted. But she didn't have to, because now his lips were spraying spit into her ear.

"Where is he?" he whispered. "Tell us where he is, and this will end."

"I—" Two shibs, older than the wielder of the whip, jerked her to her feet. *The only way through it is to do it.* Words Sweetsmoke told

262

her often. Words she'd spoken to herself too many times to count. Words and nothing more? Maybe. Probably.

One of the shibs gripped her hair, snapped her head back so hard she saw stars burst across the church's ceiling. A whip was still wrapped around Darksap's neck, another around his mother's. This was all her fault.

"I haven't seen him in three years," she said through gritted teeth. "He left me! Didn't you hear? He. Left. *Me!*"

She didn't want to cry, but when the whip struck her back a third time, it was impossible to stop the tears. The congregation let out a collective gasp. A shib kicked her to the floor, and she lay there, reduced to a pile of leaves, a mound of dirt, a stack of stones—fallen, heaped, broken. But still breathing. All she could see were shiny black boots, not one speck of dirt on them.

How is it possible to feel so much hurt? The pain on her bloody back had unfurled itself through her body like water working its way into every crevice. What made her heart ache most, though, was the belief that none of this would be happening if Sweetsmoke had just stayed. If she could have made him stay.

"This will take place every day until Shanu is apprehended," Reverend Achte said, his tone neutral, his words coming out as fact. Gone was the shaking, the anger of biblical proportions. "It will happen to any of you. Perhaps all of you. 'When justice is done, it is a joy to the righteous, but terror to evildoers.' Proverbs 21:15. Glory, glory."

"Glory, glory," her forestfolk responded loudly, as if their lives depended on it.

She lay there, on the church floor, the shibs pushing everyone out.

With great effort, she rolled herself onto her stomach and managed to stand. Swaying like a patcher, she pressed her palm against the church's wall as she walked to the entrance. Outside, the sunlight slapped her with its intensity, but she didn't flinch.

The women quickly selling and buying vegetables and juice, the children hesitantly playing in the square, the men tensely standing around—they all stopped to watch her stumble out. Feet dragging lines in the dirt, collar shaking. Even the shibs, already shoving, screaming, and threatening to whip people at random, paused.

Darksap and his mother, Wetmoss, were outside the church's door, coughing and struggling to breathe. A strong wind blew through the square, carrying dust that stuck to everyone's skin and hair, revealing the torn, flayed skin on Darksap's and Wetmoss's swollen necks.

"I'm so sorry," Sweetmint said.

Darksap rose and, seeing her, shook his head. "No, I'm sorry. I wish I could have stopped them. But this?" He pointed to his neck, laughing. "This is nothing. I would have done it a hundred times again."

Stepping toward him, she grabbed his face, pressed her lips into his. Then, as he placed his hands against her cheeks, she felt his own lips pressing back. Her forestfolk didn't start dancing, the planet didn't stop spinning, and Drams Jams Ivy didn't suddenly appear, serenading them with a song about love. None of that. What she felt was a parting of earth, a seed being planted into soil, and something strong already taking root. They reluctantly separated, but their hands had only moved to the other's shoulders, still thirsty for touch.

"See you soon?" he asked, his voice casting sunshine in all directions.

"See you soon," she echoed, kissing his hand, suddenly hopeful that there would be happiness waiting for her on the other side of all this hurt.

Head held high, she moved carefully through the silent mass, feeling their eyes on her the entire time. CASTLE TENMASE appeared on the platform's thin glass display in white letters, as it did every other day, with 4 MINUTES beside it, just like Abe said it would. Whoever he was working with was skilled.

"Here," someone said behind her. The smell of green pine gave Freshpine, Rusty's wife, away. Sweetmint had almost wondered why she hadn't helped her, but she already knew. Freshpine had children, and their well-being would always come first. It would have been different for Rusty, though. In her heart, that wasn't up for debate.

"Can I rub some of this medicine onto your wounds? It'll heal them in no time."

Sweetmint nodded and soon felt the salve's burning, then soothing, on her skin.

"Mambonga," she said, still facing the platform. Her train was approaching.

"I'm sorry, Sweetmint," Freshpine whispered. "I wanted to help, but—"

She turned around, saw Freshpine's collar shaking, and hugged her. "It's okay. Really, it is. But where's Rusty?"

"Handling business," she replied through sniffling and tears that wet Sweetmint's chest. "You know he sometimes has dealings in the city, meetings every now and then with the dippies who manage the tree fellers. According to him, he can never say no. In truth, I don't ask too many questions."

"I get it, he's always made sure to separate the personal from the professional." Her train was approaching. "I have to go." She released Freshpine, but still held her hands. "Mambonga again for the medicine. It's already working."

Both outside and inside, the train looked and felt exactly like Mr. Tenmase's to the point that she didn't believe it wasn't. Her back still tender, she remained standing, one hand on a velvet chair for balance. By the time the train moved—not north, as Abe had said, but south, toward Castle Tenmase—she was convinced that this was one big joke. *But why would he go to these lengths to laugh at me?*

Maybe he didn't like the way she'd treated him, as if abandoning her and her forestfolk for Mr. Tenmase made him the worst kind of sellout, when people did it every day. Maybe—

Suddenly, the train jerked to the left, throwing her into the window, before coming to an abrupt stop. But the doors didn't open. The train, as if changing its mind, reversed direction, and when she finally stood, she saw, to her relief, that she was on another track—one leading her to a place unknown.

CHAPTER 29

THE TRAIN DEPOSITED HIM IN A HIDDEN PART OF THE EXECUTIVE Estate. From there, Curts followed twisting and turning dimly lit hallways to an elevator that brought him to the same small, airless room where he'd met Lucretia and the Public Force three days prior.

"Sir," they said, standing and, he assumed, saluting. Only one chair remained in its initial position.

"Sit," he ordered. "Either you're missing someone, or they decided I'm not worth standing up for."

"Lieutenant Imbuka, sir," Captain Kandolo said, referring to the stocky woman with the tight braids Curts had promised a life of ease after she completed her covert mission. "The Children of Slim must have discovered her true aims. We haven't received word from her in days, and her collar was deactivated. However, the last we heard was that they still hadn't made contact with Shanu, so they're not a top priority."

"Yet it was them, or someone, who deceived us with that collar trick yesterday. It was them, or someone, who blew up a room in this very building—the most protected in the entire hemisphere.

And after all of these years, we still don't know where the COS disappeared to. So tell me, Captain, if they're not a top priority, what is?"

His question was met with silence, every person in the room likely weighing their words against the rapidly expanding tension. Then, removing any hint of a tremor from his voice, Captain Kandolo said, "Continuing with the strategy we set forth when we last met. Using each operative to extract information from anyone who can lead to Shanu's capture."

Curts moved toward the space between Captain Kandolo's chair and the table, making himself larger. He peered down to where he believed the Invisible leader's face was, drilling into his eyes. "And," he said slowly. "What do you have so far?"

"N—"

"NOTHING!" Curts roared, slamming his fist onto the table instead of where he actually wanted to lay it—through the captain's burly chest.

"NOTHING!" He pounded again. "NOTHING!" Again. "AND MORE NOTHING!" He stood there, sweat pouring from his reddened face, his chest inflating and deflating until he caught his breath.

"A few things," he said, forcing composure. He smoothed his uniform and righted his cap. "If you haven't already noticed, your respective sections have lost their immunity. Hemispheric guards are treating your friends and family just like every other Invisible in the hemisphere: as a suspect. And if you think the harassment is bad now, just wait until what's coming. No more ration trains. Your homes destroyed. Gathering places obliterated.

"Why? Because we need results. My life, and my family's life, is on the line. And your life, and your families' lives, are in grave danger. If I go, Ribussce will murder any Invisible with privileged standing and information in a heartbeat. That means you all." He paused, letting that fact permeate the room's stale air and seep into their blood.

"But." He smiled, shaking a raised finger. "*I* have a solution. One that will both buy us time and turn the heat up, for lack of a better term."

Lucretia rubbed her collarbone, looking around the room, then at her superior. "What do you propose, sir?"

He swiped his hand across the wall, bringing up an illuminated map of the hemisphere with color-coded regions. "Which do you think is the most useless region?" he asked, waving his hand in front of the map. "I'll tell you: Clothing." His finger found the brown region in the southwest. "It's smallest in population and area, and the Invisibles have it pretty easy. They don't grow any crops there, nor do they have any major water or power systems."

"And?" Lucretia asked, her tone uneasy.

"Don't you see it?" He jabbed the illuminated region again. "It's a useless region full of useless people. And we're going to burn every tent town down. Tonight."

The chairs shifted, a few of the Invisibles coughed, tapped their fingers on the table.

"Sir," Lucretia said, touching his arm. "That will displace at least five hundred thousand Invisibles."

He swiped the map away. "No, it won't."

Silence, then understanding.

"What you're proposing," Captain Kandolo whispered, "is a massacre, sir. Sergeant Sipho here is from the Clothing Region."

"Sergeant Sipho, you have permission to evacuate your blood and *only* your blood."

"Thank you, sir."

"Sir—" Captain Kandolo began.

"What I'm ordering, Captain," Curts said. "Is a solution. The massacre of Forest Seventy-Eight was a symbol, and symbols don't have eyes, teeth, and skin; they only have meaning."

"This isn't who we are," Lucretia said, bewildered. "We can't do this."

"*We* aren't taking credit for it. That's the genius of the plan. The NWN will show burning tents, not the flaming or bullet-filled bodies of those who try to escape. The hemisphere will think it's an accident, because they'll have to, but they'll know it couldn't be. The Invisibles will be afraid, the DPs will only wonder about how they're going to buy their mesh dresses and perforated shirts. And this will buy us the time we need to find Shanu, possibly even provoking him to appear, before the upcoming election. We can't rely on Jolis, that cunning buffoon, to save us if it all goes to ruin. Even though," he said, grinning. "I did just anonymously supply Washington with a piece of damning intelligence, so maybe his chances of winning will increase, which would be good for us."

"And if this maneuver in the Clothing Region doesn't cause Shanu to show himself?" Captain Kandolo asked.

"Then none of it will matter, because we'll be dead, just like those Invisibles in the CR tonight. HGDD, make it happen."

"I won't," Lucretia said.

He closed his eyes, laughed to himself, air rushing out of his nose in spurts. "I want you to take a second to think about that, Lucretia. Think about how your rarefied position allowed your father, despite having a copper tinge to his skin, like you, to become Deputy Director of Production in the R&S. How your mother, who once managed a Rhitel Burger, is now a bona fide socialite; glitzy gatherings at the Regional Mansion, high herbs at that place she loves to frequent with Mrs. Breckenwood—what is it, some illicit den where they also buy smuggled diamonds and gems off the unseen market?" *Tsk-tsk*ing, he added, "We ought to look into that. As you know, these days, anyone can find themselves in His Executive's Prison, or managing a mine, like the one we went to, where the dust coats your lungs until you just can't get it out. And that divorced sister of yours, Patera, who somehow was never forced to join The Defiled. I mean—"

"Okay," she whispered, face to the floor. "I'll do it."

The Director looked around the room, every chair so still, he might have thought them empty. "Anyone else want to file a complaint?"

"No, sir," they each said, one after the other.

"Good. Let order prevail. And you," he said to Lucretia, "go with only a handful of your best and most discreet men. Bring Ribussce along. This is the type of operation he was made for."

"Yes, sir," she said, tears racing down her face.

CHAPTER 30

S WEETMINT OPENED A WINDOW, CLOSED HER EYES, AND LET THE air rush past her for what could have been twenty minutes or an hour, she couldn't tell, before the train slowed to a stop. Outside the car's front window was a wall of boulders blocking her path.

Holy Father.

A swift, static-filled mechanical whirring, then the train plunged into a deep, cavernous hole. Her stomach rose as she fell backward; her wounds from Daily Prayer smacked into the back of a cushioned seat, causing her to scream. Only when the train came to a smooth, noiseless rest did she realize she remained on a track. She believed her feet were still on the ground, but there, in nothing but the color of pure night, was a complete sensory breakdown of where her body began and ended.

The door slid open, and her feet brought her to the threshold, as if carried by the darkness. Once she exited—soles touching cold, hard rock—the door closed behind her, and the train left the same way it came.

Far down the platform, if it even made sense to call it that, was a light so dim that she didn't know if it was artificial or the sun breaking its way through the rock. She held her hand to the rough wall to guide her, walking as close to it as possible, in the direction of the light, which grew brighter. When she finally stood below it, she saw that it was only a bulb half the size of her fist—like the antiquated ones Mr. Tenmase had said people used to use as a light source—hanging in front of a rusted steel door without a handle.

Not knowing what else to do, she knocked. After a minute, she knocked again, and a voice that sounded close and faraway at the same time said, "Who is it?"

"Candace," she announced. "Abe sent me."

Silence, then, "Are you alone?"

"Yes."

"Aghe othile ast ngetu, bengit."

Vilongo? Yes, but what accent is that? They were telling her that if someone was with her, to say it. She hoped this person was Invisible, she hoped this wasn't a trap.

"I promise, no one came with me," she replied, opting for Northwestern. Just coming here was enough to have her imprisoned or killed; she didn't want to add to it by speaking her illegal language. "The train already left."

Heavy metal clicked behind the door from top to bottom. She closed her eyes as light flooded the dark tunnel. When she opened them, there was a small room with a rock floor and rock walls to match, but the smells, the pulsing rumoyas—there were too many to decipher.

"Welcome to Tintaba, Sweetmint."

"Abe?"

"Come in," he said. "We weren't sure if you were going to make it, but here you are. Cheer blood."

"Cheer blood," a group of others in the room, she didn't know how many, echoed.

The door shut behind her as soon as she stepped in.

"Follow us." It was the same voice with the same accent that first spoke to her from behind the door. A woman, she knew that much. But even though the room was bright enough to expose the different-colored layers of stone around them, she couldn't see any of the people in it. They were collarless, unpainted, mostly clean of dust, and none of them, she guessed there were five or six from the room's size, held any tools, weapons, or other items.

A door cut into the wall opposite her opened to a narrow hall-way with a thin strip of orange-yellow light running through it. Once she followed everyone out, the door to the rock room, just like the last one, immediately closed behind her. She wanted to ask questions, but patience also had its place.

The hallway was long, with no end in sight; rock, rock, and more rock. Somehow, they were *inside* of a mountain.

Distracted, she crashed into the soft back of the person in front of her who, along with the others, had stopped.

"Trust us," the woman with that strange accent said from the front of the line. "And we'll tell you everything you want to know." She opened a door, and when it was Sweetmint's turn to step through, she paused at the threshold, whispering, "What in the . . ."

A massive cave with a domed ceiling that must have been at least thirty meters high. Light strips, each glowing a warm blue, ran from the ground all the way up in rings around the cave's interior, only breaking for three dozen or so tunnel entrances, like the one she stood in now.

She focused on the scene in front of her, carts entering and exiting the numerous tunnels, men and women pushing them with dust-covered bodies and black hard hats atop their heads, as if they were working construction or digging through rock and earth. *What's in those carts?*

Some people carried long rolled-up pieces of canvas from one tunnel to another, nodding as they spoke to each other in hushed tones. The cave, like a cotton-stuffed cushion, seemed to absorb sound.

It was hard to keep track of the hundreds of people coming and going, attending to their various tasks with urgent focus. A squeal of laughter slashed through the air and Sweetmint's eyes darted to a round stage at the center of the room made of an unfamiliar polished black rock. In the cave's low blue light she saw a small girl, the particles clinging to her skin resembling star dust.

The girl danced around the stage's stone podium—a symbol of two linked fingers carved into its front. Then a man picked her up and threw her high into the air before catching her and doing it again. It was Abe. Laughter filled the enormous space.

"Sister Sweetmint," he called. "Come up here."

She walked toward the stage, ascended its stone steps, and stopped in front of him.

"This," he said, bouncing her in his arms, "is Daughter Blackstone. *My* daughter. Daughter Blackstone, meet my old friend, Sister Sweetmint. She comes from the same place I do."

"Forest Twenty-Six?" she asked.

He kissed the little girl's plump cheeks. "That's right, my sprout. Amazing memory."

"Daughter?" Sweetmint asked.

"My daughter, yes. I have a wife, too. You've already met her."

"Wife? Abe, haven't you been working with Mr. Tenmase for the past five years? How do you have a wife and a daughter? Daughter Blackstone must be at least five herself."

He laughed. "She's four. And, yes, I've been working for Mr. Tenmase for the past five years, that's right. But I've been coming here much, much longer. It's here that I met my wife, the woman who led us through the tunnel just now. That's Sister Blackstone. She's from the Southwestern Hemisphere."

Southwestern Hemisphere? But how?

He laughed again, which was unsettling. She hadn't seen this Abe, an Abe who laughed more than he bowed and played more than he cleaned, since before he'd left their forest. There was no way he was the same person who fetched herbs when Mr. Tenmase asked for them, who picked up tennis balls as they knocked them around behind the castle, who kept his eyes on the carpet so often that it was like he was always searching for something, his rumoya as flat as a battered nail. Yet now his rumoya was on fire, blazing with pride.

"We have the whole day together, and I'll answer as much as I can. But it'll depend, of course."

"On what?"

"On you. Be patient, though. We're almost ready to begin."

People streamed out of the tunnels, each with a wooden chair in their hands. They placed the chairs around the stage, in circles that grew wider and wider, like tree rings.

"You see that chair leaning against that tunnel?" he asked, pointing.

"Yes?"

"That's your chair. Please go and get it, and put it down here, next to the podium."

"But why?"

He set his daughter on her feet and whispered to her. She ran down the steps, disappeared into the swelling mass of Invisibles.

"Because we are all responsible for our own place here, Sister Sweetmint. There's also a small bucket of water near the stage's stairs. Please use it to wipe the dust from your skin before you come back up."

She walked down the stairs, doing her best not to knock into anyone, set the chair against the shiny stage, dipped her hand into the warm bucket of water and splashed it all over her body. It felt weird to clean herself in front of so many strangers, now seated in the chairs rippling away from where she stood, but she preferred this to being viewed as a piece of flesh by even one DP in Minx. When she looked up, she noticed few heads were even turned in her direction.

The air confused her, too. Despite being in a cave, it wasn't thick and wet; there had to be some ventilation, especially because of how quickly the water dried on her body. This place, whatever it was, utilized some kind of advanced technology—imagination paired with ability. *Invisible* imagination. *Invisible* ability. All away from the prying, oppressive eyes of the DPs. *How was this even possible?*

More people joined them onstage—their chairs formed into rows of two behind her own—as towering platters of food and pitchers of juice floated out of tunnels. The bearers of empty plates and cups, platters of roasted vegetables, and pitchers of juice shared them out to the hundreds of seated people, one by one, without rush. Every function performed with ease, pleasantries exchanged between the givers and the getters.

Once everyone in the ringed rows had a plate full of food and a cup full of drink, Sweetmint and her companions onstage were taken care of. Corn, potatoes, carrots, and mushrooms; beet juice filling her cup to the brim. An abundance. Of everything.

Her stomach thundered in hunger, the food's savory aromas reminded her that she hadn't eaten since lunch at Castle Tenmase the day before. *Maybe that Rhitel Burger Red suggested before Minx would have made sense.* But when she raised a lightly charred piece of potato to her mouth, Abe said, "Not yet, Sister Sweetmint. In a moment."

"Oh, I'm sorry."

A familiar smell, of burning bark, drifted through the air, but she wasn't sure what, or who, it was.

"It's okay," he added. "Just a few more minutes."

Abe's plate hovered, then rested on his chair; his steps *pat-pat-pattered* to the podium. "Children of Slim," he said, his tone beaming with bliss, causing the chattering to stop. "How are we?"

"STRONG!" the people replied in unison, as if the word were coming from one body, their voices matching the joyful pride of Abe's own.

"I said, 'Children of Slim. How are we?'"

"RIGHTEOUS!"

"Strong, yes. Righteous, of course. But what else?"

"HAPPY!"

"Cheer blood and may the rebellion stay happy. Today is a special day because we are birthing a new sibling, together in this space, as is the custom. But before getting down to business, I want you to observe your surroundings. Go on, look up, look down, look to the left, look to the right. Think about where you are, the ground your feet rest on, the miracle of our domed ceiling. What you're seeing"—he turned to Sweetmint—"is the inside of Tukhali Intaba—Hollow Mountain—*Tintaba* for short. Unmoving and resolute in its destiny. And though some of us have traveled far and wide to get here, I am sure no one, including myself, has ever seen a mountain made of rubies or diamonds. Because that which lasts is cut from the common stone, the everyday rock. We"—he clapped—"are that rock."

Sweetmint realized her mouth was open. Never had she heard Abe so articulate, so compelling.

"Regarding our latest movements," he said, his words booming throughout the cave, "let us honor Brother Firerock, who faced off against Curts the Patcher in the I&S."

A plate and cup floated upward, turned around the cave as the people applauded.

"The idea of replicating collars, beginning with Brother Firerock in a mine, was the ingenious plan of Sister Blackstone. It was only with this distraction that we were better equipped to pull off the bombing of the Executive Estate. Now we have more time to find The Illuminator. I'd also like to honor Sister Strongsalt, who went undercover as a working woman and made an attempt on Local Tormentor II Jolis's life, to kill the seed before it grows. She was unsuccessful, but she lived to tell the tale, which is cause for celebration."

Every person gave Sister Strongsalt the same outpouring of respect.

"Now, we have scoured the hemisphere in search of The Illuminator, and we have come up empty-handed. Our siblings in the other hemispheres continue to search for him as well. But today we have made progress in the form of this young woman sitting right here." He directed his voice to Sweetmint. "Sister Sweetmint, The Illuminator's sister."

Who?

Though she couldn't see them, she knew that hundreds of eyes, like tiny tendrils of moss on the side of a tree, latched on to her. Except she felt no hostility in their stares. Just an unexpected warmth, like the food in her lap.

"Do you feel that?" Abe said to her. "You must, Sister Sweetmint. Every single one of us is overjoyed that you made the decision to come here today. The only question"—he paused, her blood thrumming louder—"is will you join us?"

She looked out to the hundreds of seated people, then back toward the podium. "I'm sorry," she said, her voice cracking. She cleared her throat and started again. "I'm sorry, Abe, but what is all of this?"

Abe, a film of dust drifting from above and cloaking his skin like some biblical anointment, clasped his hands. "Of course. It would take a long time to explain everything, and, I promise, we will, but for now please excuse my brevity for the sake of our siblings who are here to both bear witness and lend us their energy in birthing you as a new member of our family. Also, if you don't mind, call me 'Brother Blackstone.' All state names are dropped inside these walls."

He extended his speckled hand outward, waved it across the ringed rows of people. "We are the Children of Slim. A resistance group founded over seven decades ago, after the Shipping, when Chief Enemy Rhitel seized power and began to persecute us. I took up the title of Brother Blackstone a decade ago, when the first Brother and Sister Blackstone died. Our mission is to combat the oppression of Factfolk, in every hemisphere, by their respective dippies. In this cave is only a handful of our family. Cheer blood?"

"CHEER BLOOD!" the people responded.

"We are professors," Sister Blackstone said, joining her partner at the podium. "Domestics, construction workers, tree fellers, blacksmiths, hairdressers—even some of the athletes and entertainers you see on the display. Our family has dealt devastating blows to our persecutors, though they rarely ever make the news, because the powers that be would rather you believe that they have everything—most of all, you—under control. They believe it, too, which is why they're so vulnerable."

"Let me ask," Abe—Brother Blackstone—continued. "What do you think were in those carts when you entered?"

Sweetmint was so busy listening and trying to understand how any of this was possible, if all of it was even real, that it took her a second to realize she was being asked a question. "Um, I don't know. Food?"

He laughed. "Sure, food. And weapons. Real weapons that we've stolen from the Train and Technology Region."

A handful of people clapped from one section of the cave.

"Those would be some of our most skilled *acquirers*, affectionately called the 'Contrabandits.' One part of Tintaba is dedicated to special training. Another is for our future: babies that are born or brought here. Others are for food production, which is how you have such a delicious meal sitting on your lap."

Another section of people let out a few shouts of jubilation.

"Yes, cheer blood for our preparers of food, the 'Hunger Killers.' With the help of dippy allies, we hacked into the Northwestern Display Network decades ago, and we've siphoned thousands of years' worth of hidden history. *History*, Sister Sweetmint. Like how we came to be. Slim? Oh, Father Slim was just the beginning. Our progenitor, born to a working woman in a place not too far from downcity Rhitelville, called 'Manhattan.'"

"Man-hat-tan," she whispered to herself. The word felt made-up.

Brother Blackstone closed his eyes and lifted his head toward the ceiling, the lights tinting his dusty skin pale blue. "He came out in a flash of white light, and as soon as he was born, he was taken from Great Mother Makeda, experimented on, then discarded, as were thousands of others. We are his children, and we will never forget. Cheer blood?"

"CHEER BLOOD!" the people responded.

This was all so much, too much, really, for her to take in. Sister Blackstone must have known that, because she said, "We will explain more later, sister. You are here because we need to get to Brother Sweetsmoke, The Illuminator, who will deliver us out of the darkness and into luminescence. Brother Blackstone tried to recruit him a long time ago, before he disappeared, but he didn't join us."

A chill ran from the top of her neck down the ridges of her spine.

"While those in your forest and across the hemisphere condemn him, we revere him. He acts, while the majority acquiesce."

"Now," Brother Blackstone interjected. "We need to combine our efforts with The Illuminator's and build upon the momentum we have. You know, just the other day, Brother Burningwood caught a spy named Imbuka. We don't know who she was with, but he took care of her."

Brother Burningwood. *That's* who the smell behind her was.

Cetewayo. The one who had accused her of endangering all of her forestfolk by teasing those DP children at the Annual Painting. The one who, at the Baz Buthani, interrogated her about Sweetsmoke and almost received the hack of Darksap's axe. He was working with the Children of Slim the whole time.

"Right now," Brother Blackstone said, "Factfolk in every region are being beaten down, imprisoned, and killed by dippies. Shibs *and* civilians. But we won't stand for this. We're taking matters into our own hands. If Local Tormentor II Jolis is elected the next Chief Enemy, well"—Brother Blackstone grinned—"he won't survive his acceptance speech. We'll make him disappear with a blink and a blast. Cheer blood?"

"CHEER BLOOD!" the people responded.

Shaken by all she'd heard, of collar crimes and attempted murders, Sweetmint said, "I—I don't know where he is. I can't help you." Her eyes were on the pile of food that lay beneath her, fallen without her noticing. "I'm sorry."

"We know you don't know where he is. But if you join us, you're swearing that if he contacts you, you will tell us. You are taking a solemn vow to fight the dippies alongside us."

These same words, but spoken by his brother. Why, she wondered, was Rusty not here? Would aligning herself with these people be a betrayal to the one who'd always protected her? And why do they call Invisibles "Factfolk"?

"In return," Brother Blackstone continued, "you'll receive access to all the knowledge we've amassed; answers to questions you've never asked. Like why you don't see any Factfolk as old as dippies around. What life is like for our siblings in other hemispheres. How your train moved through a mountain. So, so much, Sister Sweetmint. But most of all, you will gain a family that will embrace you for who and how you are. That will live and die for you. That will never leave you. Ever." He stopped speaking for a moment, his last words echoing inside her. Then, "Do you accept?"

Rusty was family, but where was he now, when she needed him most? Sweetsmoke had forced her to view family as a unit so tight that it became a dot. And Mr. Tenmase and Sanford—there was always an obstacle, always a test in order to access truth that should be a right more than a privilege; a lack of openness compared to what these Children of Slim were offering her for nothing more than a reciprocation of loyalty. These people in front of her were not a dot, or a circle, but many rings. They were vast, expansive, and committed to growth, not games. But above all, what pierced the core of her being most was that they weren't afraid; they were prepared. For anything.

She closed her eyes, inhaled the cool air, then raised her head. Not toward Brother and Sister Blackstone, but to the people. "I do."

One by one, they placed their food on the ground, stood, and linked their dust-covered index fingers, holding their arms toward the domed ceiling. She heard the sound of feet hitting the floor, and it grew and grew. The pounding, like the bass at Minx, penetrated her heart, but instead of dancing, she found Sister Blackstone's index finger and raised it above her head, allowing herself to be delivered into a new family, into the common rock surrounding her.

"Welcome home, Sister Sweetmint," Brother Blackstone whispered. "Welcome home."

CHAPTER 31

JOLIS SHOOK HANDS WITH HIS SUPPORTERS AS THEY ENTERED THE
Gallery of Rule. Yes, the chief executiveship was his; a new
world, created in his own image, imminent.

The last of the men entered, but he didn't follow. A guard turned
to him. "Coming in, sir?"

"Just a moment. Feel free to close the door."

He stood at the top of the marble steps, waiting. Anna Franklin
approached, her captureman right behind her.

"Sorry," she said, hurrying to set up the shot. "We had an unexpected interview with HGADD Ribussce earlier."

"I'm sorry to have missed it. Anything I need to know?"

"Just that Curts is done if he doesn't find Shanu."

Jolis laughed. "We'll see about that. Let's get this going, though.
I only have a few minutes before I hit Washington with another
Mandla-sized blow."

She gestured for him to join her at the bottom of the steps. "Our
first date, at the arena. Mandla versus—"

"Bheku." He grinned. "I'd never forget it. The match, and everything that came after."

Her jaw tightened, then loosened, as the rest of her face followed. "Washington doesn't get these impromptu interviews for a reason."

"I'm aware, Anna. You've always been there for me."

Her captureman raised his fingers, silently counted down from three, two—

"Good afternoon, Northwesterners," Anna began. "In a fortuitous turn of events, we have yet another interview for you today, this time with Local Manager II Jolis. Local Manager II Jolis"—she turned to him—"I know you have to head inside for your second-to-last debate with Local Manager IV Washington, so let's not waste any time. How are you feeling?"

He stared into the thick piece of capglass. Then, as if someone pressed a button on his back, he broke out into a smile fit for an Instafresco commercial. "To be honest, I couldn't be better. I know every single Northwesterner is waiting to see who the next Chief Executive will be, but you're already looking at him. Washington is a dangerous man who not only aims to set the hemisphere back three-quarters of a century, but who is sympathetic to murderous Invisible vigilantes like Shanu."

"I'm happy you brought up Invisible vigilantes, Local Manager II Jolis. You're right, the hemisphere is anxiously awaiting the outcome of the election, but they're more concerned about Shanu and whether Hemispheric Guard Director Curts will catch him. According to this morning's survey, seventy-three percent of Northwesterners have lost faith in him; some even went as far as suggesting he be hanged. What are your thoughts?"

The young local manager ran a hand through his hair. "The thought of Hemispheric Guard Director Curts—a good friend of mine, by the way—not capturing this Invisible never crossed my mind. One way or another, this great hemisphere will receive justice for the murder of Chief Executive Rhitel, may the Holy Father bless his soul, and the Director will be the one to do it."

"We'll be waiting. Thank you for your time, Local Manager II Jolis."

"The pleasure was mine, Ms. Franklin. May the Holy Father bless the Northwestern Hemisphere and provide safety, prosperity, and morality for us all."

Anna nodded to her captureman, who cut the live feed. "Don't forget about me when you win, Stephan."

He wrapped his arm around her bony shoulders. "Trust that when I'm elected, you'll get anything you want. More rhitellings, a formal appointment as Director of the NWN, a bigger home—"

"You?" She looked up at him, eyes unwavering.

Jolis held her in front of him. "Let's just take it day by day. In the meantime, do me a favor."

"Which is?"

"Go easy on Leon. He has the whole hemisphere on him, and we need to support one another instead of giving time to privileged crater mouths like Ribussce."

"Someone has to answer for a lack of results, Stephan. People are more afraid than ever."

He let her go and started walking up the steps. "I know, I know. But fear only grows when it's fed. In a few days, people will breathe easier. We'll have celebrations across the hemisphere. And in a couple of months, no one will even remember what happened."

After Jolis lightly knocked, the Gallery doors opened.

"More press, Local Manager II Jolis?" Grand Magistrate Royger asked from his bench.

"What can I say? The capglass loves me," he replied, rounding his podium. "It's not my fault the glass cracks whenever Washington steps in front of it."

An immature joke, but most of the men still laughed. Oh, Jolis was feeling *good*. He turned to Washington, hoping to see a flicker of embarrassment, but he found his opponent smiling back at him. Later on, he would remember the way Washington had looked at him, as if Jolis were a tree that had just received the final hack of the axe, unaware of its impending, inevitable fall.

CHAPTER 32

Brothers and sisters,

It will be hard to believe what I am about to write, but I assure you every word is true. Understand that I am doing my absolute best to not jump with unrestrained gaiety lest I sprain my pinkie toe like I did the last time I tried to— Never mind that.

Local Tormentor II Jolis entered the Gallery with his usual flair: jokes, winks, a repartee with Grand Magistrate Royger about giving yet another interview. Local Manager IV Washington is usually quiet during these vulgar exhibitions of machismo and faux dominance, as he was today, but there was also something else to the quality with which he remained behind his podium. It was if he stood a little straighter, smiled a little wider, his eyes glowing a bit brighter. It was then I knew, oh, brothers and sisters of Slim, I *knew* something was coming.

And I was right.

The day's guest of honor was none other than Reverend Achte, that robed deceiver of people who claims to be a vessel for the Holy Father, when we all know he is no more capable of carrying a holy word than a cracked herbcup is of holding water. The crumbling crony of Chief Enemy Rhitel spoke of the responsibility that all dippies have to live and lead not only for ourselves, but also for those to come. "A hemisphere," said he, "is not the sum of its past and present, but also of its future."

I begrudgingly admit that there was one thing he said that I appreciated. "To be chosen is never enough. It is what you do with it that matters most." Unbeknownst to him, he spoke directly to our happy rebellion, and it filled me with pride and satisfaction, especially because Jolis looked to be in mortal pain as the reverend spoke.

The topic of debate was education, and though we would all receive an education in the bristling hypocrisy of this "great" hemisphere, no one expected what happened next.

Washington walked to the magistrates' bench and asked if he could share something with the Gallery. We all leaned forward in our seats. Jolis, that vault of insecurity, was tense, beads of sweat, like morning dew clinging to blades of grass, sprouted from his forehead and neck. Forgive me, Sister Blackstone, but I'm feeling quite poetic this afternoon.

As if he were strolling along the coast, Washington took his time moving from the magistrates' bench back to his side of the Gallery. Every eye was on him as he swiped the wall and paused before the illuminated display.

He faced us and said, "Men, please believe that I didn't want to have to do this. But given what's at stake, and the fact that we need to have confidence that our leaders are who they say they are, I have no choice."

Tap. Tap. Tap. Oh, brothers and sisters. High above us, blue light appeared on the room's wood paneling. And with one last tap, an illumination for the ages. It was Jolis, in a bedroom, sweat pouring down his focused face, his eyes as hard as black diamonds. In front of his naked, thrusting body was an Invisible woman clenching a pillow so hard, and screaming in pleasure so loudly, that we didn't need the thermographic overlay to know she was there. This man, whose entire career and platform has been built on the hatred of Invisibles, was having sex with two—a small rope whip connecting with his shiny back, wielded by another woman behind him! The hero of the hemisphere was made see-through for all to witness.

Grand Magistrate Royger asked what Jolis had to say, but then the "BOO"s, "VIZZER LOVER"s, and "JELLYBACK"s began (a "jellyback," as you may or may not know, is a common dippy term for men lacking backbone). Within seconds, men on both sides of the Gallery hurled every insult at him—verbal knives sharp and cutting him down, down, down to the point that he didn't dare raise his head. He knew he was done, even if he was guilty of something that at least half of the men of rule are as well.

I know I'm not supposed to ask questions, and I won't attempt to spoil this day by seeking answers that aren't for me to know, but as I dictate this, I can't help but wonder if you, my dear brothers and sisters of Slim, did this. Jolis no doubt has enemies across the hemisphere and around the world, but this fortuitous deliverance from evil smells of Slim. No matter, let us celebrate, because we have killed the man without spilling a drop of blood; the most marvelous murder there is.

May the rebellion stay happy,
Brother Lesbod

CHAPTER 33

CASTLE TENMASE'S PROPERTY BECAME DARKER AS CURTS MOVED across the great lawn. But when he came to the top of the hill, he saw light falling through a handful of the castle's windows, torches blazing on its brick facade; the two towers, adorned with their Northwestern flags, crowned in halos of white light.

Left, right, left, right, left, right. He stood before the front doors, grabbed the heavy bronze ring, and knocked it three times, which reminded him of how the hemispheric church clock chimed throughout all of midcity. *Dooooong, dooooong, dooooong.* He expected the Invisible servant, Abraham, to materialize, but no one came. *Dooooong, dooooong, dooooong.* A window opened above him, and there was Croger, that childish mess of long black hair, like spindly vines, stretching toward him.

"Leon?"

"Croger," Curts said, trying to sound friendly, as if he stopped by this looming and utterly isolated castle often. "May I come in?"

"Of course. One second."

The door opened, and the Director peered down. "Apologies for the intrusion, Croger."

"Please," he said, stepping aside to let Curts in. "I'm overjoyed to see you, Leon. It's been a long time."

"It has. 'But what is time other than the counting of nothing?'" He entered, waited for Croger to close the door behind him.

"You remember your Saller," he said, moving past him, ascending the blue carpeted stairs. "Good. Follow me."

The drawing room was just as Curts remembered it. Antiques neatly organized on tables, shelves, and behind glass panes—sprinklers, a television, fingerless gloves; many of them he'd seen in the programs he enjoyed in the archives—all adhering to a sense of order fit for The Great Engineer. His desk was covered with creased papers, scuffed tools, smaller relics of the past, like a stick of plastic and metal they would use to gauge a person's temperature. But what caught Curts's attention was the old leather armchair, his favorite, with the same uncomfortable couch next to it and the small wooden table in front of them.

Nostalgia touched its worn fingers to the back of his neck, encouraging him to drop his guard, forget his mandate, and travel back, through some hidden doorway, into a previous version of himself. The version where order, or the idea of it, actually prevailed. Where his place in this world, his material existence, wasn't in question or peril. But he only took a breath and squared his shoulders to the older man.

"Please, sit," Croger said. "I'm sorry, Abe isn't here today, so we'll have to fend for ourselves. Herbs?"

"No, thank you," Curts replied, sinking into the armchair as Croger took the couch. "I don't want to impose any more than I already have. If I may ask"—he looked around the room—"where is Abraham?"

"It's his day off, so I'm not exactly sure. Is he in trouble?"

"No," Curts said, shaking his head. "But I do need your help, Croger. I assume you've been watching the news, and that you're aware of how . . ." His voice trailed off. "Dire the situation with this Invisible, Shanu, has become."

He nodded. "You know I don't get involved in matters of State, Leon. Besides, there's not much I can do to assist you. I'm afraid this great inventor is all out of tricks."

"The truth is." Curts removed his cap, ran his fingers over the golden hemispheric seal. "I've exhausted most of my options. If I don't find him, I'll hang, and"—flipping the cap over, staring at the capture of Della and Eva—"who knows what will happen to my family."

Croger took a sip of his herbs. "I understand your predicament, but that still doesn't change the fact that I can't help you, Leon." He shrugged. "I don't know what will happen to any of us, but it's in these times that I humble myself in the face of the unknown."

Curts surveyed him, so serene, as if this were just another day in the hemisphere and worlds weren't burning beyond the castle walls.

"Croger," he said, leaning closer. "I'm here because I once heard a rumor about a tracking device you'd invented that wasn't connected to collars. Something that can track any Invisible, anywhere in the world."

"And?"

"And I need it."

The Chief Architect found the Director's eyes—serenity falling from his face, little by little; biscuit crumbs drifting from a mouth. Suddenly, he jerked his head back and laughed, his whole body shaking like a struck bell. On any other night, Croger Tenmase's laughter would be contagious, just as it had been those many years ago when he'd regale Chief Executive Rhitel and the men of rule at the Executive Estate, or host historical parties in this very castle. But tonight, tonight it produced a foreign, murderous desire in Curts's heart.

"I'm sorry, Leon. I know this isn't a time for laughter, but the assertion is ridiculous. You know as well as I do that our hemispheric surveillance has blind spots, something Chief Executive Rhitel was never worried about. Though I did once recommend injecting Invisibles at birth with a tracking substance that would bind to their blood, but The Chief Executive said that collars would suffice, and if any of them got out of line . . . Well, we saw what happened in Forest Seventy-Eight, and of course there are countless other examples that never made the news."

The Director sat back in his favorite armchair. The thing about Curts that gave him an advantage over others, that helped him maneuver hundreds of sticky scenarios, was that he could always, always tell when someone was lying. And Croger *was* lying, which meant that he was slowly turning into his enemy, and Curts was an expert in dealing with his enemies. Yes, some called him "The Saint," others, before that, "The Happy Grabber." But to himself, he was the man with *spirals of files with files with files.*

"We've always been friendly, haven't we, Croger?"

"I'd say so," he responded, smiling.

"Yet you're forcing my hand here, when you, more than anyone else, understand the access that my position affords me. The nature by which I can unearth that which someone would rather remain hidden and bury it in my own plot of information until it's time to harvest."

Croger's face became puzzled. "I'm afraid I don't know what you mean."

"Okay," Curts said, crossing his legs, settling into the armchair even more, surprised by how relaxed he felt. "We both know how Chief Executive Rhitel, may the Holy Father bless his soul, came to power. And we both know that his opponent, Local Manager XII George Elmor, had a son. But what I discovered last year, following a bad case of curiosity, is that when Elmor and his wife were killed, their Invisible servant smuggled their son out of the Forest Region and into the Clothing Region, where he handed the child to a random young man and woman sitting in a park. Along with a note."

The Great Engineer shifted in his seat, brought his herbcup to his mouth, but set it back down before taking a sip. "A physical note?"

"That's right," Curts said, observing with pleasure the older man's discomfort. "The Invisible servant was intercepted on his return to the Forest Region and executed, but not before my predecessor got this story out of him. Despite this, Chief Executive Rhitel, may the Holy Father bless his soul, said no further investigation was necessary—that they had more pressing concerns."

Croger, as still as a sculpture, only moved his lips. "But what happened to the adoptive parents, the child?"

Curts's confidence was soaring now, his body ready to thrust itself out of the armchair and through the castle's roof. "I had the same question last year, and a bit of time to explore it. The man and woman had died, but a relative told me their son was, from a young age, skilled in all forms of machinery. So gifted that the Regional Head of Manufacturing took the boy under his tutelage, accelerating his growth. Then, at eighteen, the boy, upon receiving that note from his adoptive mother, written by the Invisible who'd smuggled him, disappeared. Never to be seen again."

"He's probably dead," Croger said, staring into his herbcup. "The world's a tough place for young men with ideas." His tone was mournful, his entire demeanor diminished, as if the internal light that shone throughout his every pore and orifice was snuffed out. This was all the proof Curts needed.

"Croger," Curts said, uncrossing his legs, leaning forward, and touching the older man's arm. "We know this young man isn't dead. We know he partnered with Chief Executive Rhitel, may the Holy Father bless his soul, eighteen years into his reign, wielding incredible influence through inventing new technology that would further subjugate Invisibles and turn this hemisphere into a worldwide force that others would fear. All the while, waiting, like an old-world animal, to strike."

"What," Croger said faintly, his eyes still on his herbcup, "are you saying, Leon?"

"I never understood why you requested that The Chief Executive give you this abandoned castle, the same home that Local Manager XII Elmor and his family had lived in." He now delivered his words softly, a bit of sorrow strewn across them. The feeling of triumph that was so close to exploding through his skin moments ago had dissipated, leaving him deflated. He knew what it was for someone to take advantage of your vulnerability, but he had to press on. Not just for himself, but for Della and Eva.

"You can imagine my surprise," Curts said, "when I began to put the pieces together last year. I was hoping that it would all lead to nothing, but my hunches almost always do. Your own blood sample, in the Hemispheric Hematic Directory, which you created, traces back to no one, as if you were born from nothing. All those years ago, guards never thought to take Elmor's blood sample. But if they had, you and I know it would match your own. And while I can't prove that you had a hand in The Chief Executive's murder, we both know you did, Croger. Anyone in your position would have done the same." He paused. "I'm sorry to have to bring all of this up, but, like I said, I need that tracking device."

The older man slowly moved the hair from his face, strand by strand, poured himself another cup of herbs, and took a sip. Then he did something so alarming that Curts flinched. He grinned, and said, "Who cares?"

Who . . . cares? The room dissolved, and Curts was still in that leather armchair, but now he was smaller. The world in front of and around him was black, but he could see almost half a dozen fingers pointed toward him. Fingers that were too easy for him to identify. One thick with black hair sprouting from its knuckles: his father's. Another long and pale with purple nail polish: his mother's. A third with the nail bitten down to the bloody flesh, a thin line of dirt caked underneath it: Cristoph, the boy who had bullied him for a decade. A fourth, so small that it was obviously Eva's. And finally, a fifth, unmistakably Della's. All of them attached to unseen bodies screaming a litany of his personal inadequacies at him before breaking out into a chorus of laughter.

He was dropped back into Croger's drawing room, the man known as The Chief Architect living up to his name—so poised, so calm, so unnervingly one step ahead. "Croger," Curts said softly, "when you stepped down as Director of Progress, all of your access to intelligence and State privileges were not only revoked, but you ceased to be a hemispheric asset. If I tell the men of rule and the magistrates the same story I told you, even with its cracks and gaps, they'll believe it. And you will die before the week is over. But"—he crossed his legs in pretend munificence—"this doesn't have to happen. Give me the tracking device, and we can move past this. Your secret safe with me, forever."

The upward curve of Croger's lips drove his cheekbones toward his eyes. "It's fascinating," he said, "how fear reveals the true nature of a man. And how it blinds him."

"Let's drop the riddles and rhymes. Either you give me what I need, *now*, or you'll exchange your lavish castle for a suffocating cell. If you think I'm someone you can—"

"You're looking in the wrong place, Leon." Croger paused, and Curts's mind began to zigzag. "Like you, I am a man who often comes down with a bad case of curiosity. And my own explorations have led to a most improbable, but entirely logical, conclusion."

"Which is?"

"Which is that Shanu is right there, in the Gallery of Rule, masquerading as a great crusader who plans to populate the hemisphere with flowers and free the Invisibles from their transparent chains."

"What?"

"Think, Leon. *Think.*"

He wet his lips, calculating and recalculating the odds, reimagining the impossible. No, as Croger just said, the *improbable*. "Washington?"

"In addition to their removal during the Shipping, Rhitel's decree against mixed relations put an end to these biological *aberrations*, if you will—these people of blended Invisible and Dominant ancestries who could flip, like an old-world switch, the presentation of their skin. Invisible one second, visible the next."

Washington. Yes, it did make perfect sense. He, more than anyone else, abhorred The Chief Executive and all he stood for. Given his position as a man of rule with considerable influence, he could have brought some of Curts's more sympathetic guards into his own fold, using them to gain entry into The Chief Executive's bedroom in order to smother him, and having them, or someone else, like the Children of Slim, cut that area of the Executive Estate's surveillance. Or, he could have requested a special meeting with two of the guards watching the bedroom, then, using red drops, got in and out undetected, becoming visible again in another part of the Estate. The opportunities to commit a crime of this specificity, and get away with it, increased if you could be two people at once. No wonder he couldn't find the Invisible. Because it wasn't an Invisible who committed this crime.

"Now you see," Croger said, grabbing his arm. "Don't you? How much sense it makes? If you look in the Hemispheric Hematic Directory, *Washington's* record is nonexistent. All claims of his upbringing have been falsified, his moral superiority an act, but his true allegiance, to Invisibles, brazenly out in the open. And—"

There was frantic knocking at the front door; the bronze ring crashed into the wood with the force of an axe. Both men moved to the window, but when Curts looked down, no one was there. The drawing room's door flung open, and standing in the frame was Stephan Jolis, swaying from side to side—hair a mess, suit wrinkled, even the laces of his shoes undone. But what made the Director's mouth salivate were the patches on both sides of the local manager's neck: one brown and pink, the other green and purple. Mixing an "unrestrained elation" with a "deep sedation" was a horrible combination. He knew because he'd once done it himself.

"Oh, a parrrty?" Stephan asked, words slurring. "Perrrfect. Jusss the men I needta see."

CHAPTER 34

AVE DUST BLANKETED SISTER SWEETMINT'S SKIN, AS WELL AS THE skin of the other Children surrounding her, turning them all into shimmering, wondrous beings. A smiling woman's hand on her shoulder, a little girl's palm pressed to her stomach, a boy's hand enmeshed in her own—excitement and exclamations whirled around and stunned her into a state of enchantment. Yes, she already felt that she was home, that these people were her siblings.

Sister Blackstone approached. "Get back to your tasks, Children," she said, breaking up the reverie. Then, to Sister Sweetmint, "Ready?"

"I don't think so."

Sister Blackstone raised her chin toward her. "First lesson? You're capable of far more than you believe you are. Follow me."

She led Sister Sweetmint through a tunnel on the west side of the cave into an empty room with rough rock walls and a smooth floor.

"What's this for?" Sister Sweetmint asked.

The older woman found a rock that looked like all the others, but when she ran her finger over it, three walls slid open, revealing something Sister Sweetmint didn't understand. Golden weapons were being taken apart, polished with cloth and oil, then floated to the hands of other people, who reassembled and placed them in their wooden slots. Smaller weapons, that fit in the palm of your hand, were spread out on a table, along with spheres of various sizes and colors. Sister Sweetmint picked up one of the spheres, and the movement in the room stopped.

"Careful with that," Sister Blackstone warned. Everyone held their breath.

"What is it?" Sister Sweetmint asked, rotating the sphere.

"A highly effective explosive. We used the smaller version on the Executive Estate. And that one you're holding between your finger and thumb has the ability to level half of your forest."

She went stiff and carefully placed it back onto the table. "How— How do you have all of this?"

"Some were stolen, but most were replicated or invented here. We have a testing ground through a tunnel on the north side of Tintaba, where we can better contain our experiments, and a shooting range through a tunnel on the east side, for training. But come."

Sister Blackstone led her back through the tunnel, then looped into one that ran parallel to it. At its terminus was a circular room full of physical books. Sister Sweetmint spun around and around, speechless. A large machine in the room's rear noisily fed blank pieces of paper—paper!—into itself before spitting word-inked pages out.

"Our library and printing press," Sister Blackstone said proudly.

"But . . ." Sister Sweetmint shook her head. "Why?"

Sister Blackstone grabbed a book from a shelf, dusted off its cover to reveal the words *The Autobiography of Malcolm X*, and handed it to her. "This book"—Sister Blackstone tapped its cover—"is almost six hundred years old."

Sister Sweetmint cracked the cover, flipped the pages and brought them to her nose, inhaling the old words' synthetic odors.

"You've never held a physical book before, have you?"

"I have, actually."

"Of course," Sister Blackstone said. "Mr. Tenmase is also a fan of the illicit."

"But again . . ." She peeled her eyes from the pages and looked over at her. "Why?"

"Nothing we're experiencing now is new, Sister Sweetmint. Nothing at all. The world, life itself, is cyclical, and all that is happening now has happened before; all that will happen has already happened. We know that physical books went out of use because of environmental concerns, and illuminated pages are both easier to access and take up no space, but they're also used because they can be monitored. These texts"—she tapped the book's cover—"millions of them, even before Rhitel took power, were outlawed because they contain truths that the State doesn't want you to know. Strategies that would bring down this hemisphere in a year."

"And you're making more of them, for what?"

"For those who come here to read and learn. We'd like to be able to share them throughout the hemisphere, but it's too risky. When people first come to Tintaba, they're encouraged to read as much as they can. But at their own pace. Sometimes too much too fast scares people away."

She understood, because being here, in this room full of so much information, history, and solutions to their present problems, made her afraid. Afraid of what it would mean to learn and unlearn everything, from the beginning. Afraid of what she'd discover, about herself, her people, her world. Afraid because, once you obtained knowledge, you were forced to make a choice—act with courage or remain a coward—and no one wanted to view themselves as a coward, including her.

Sister Sweetmint circled the room, picking up *The Invisible Guide to Survival*, *We Are the New Animals*, collections of poetry, books full of hand-drawn illustrations. "What's this?" she asked, holding up a book that resembled Reverend Achte's illumination of The Chief Executive Bible.

"That," Sister Blackstone said, taking it from her hands and putting it back, "is for another day. There's more, much more, to show you."

On the northeast side of the cave, they reached a room with a smooth rock wall and rows of empty chairs. Sister Blackstone motioned for her to sit. Then, a capture appeared: a mustached man with skin the hue of dark tree bark linked arm in arm with other men and women, all dressed in clothing, like DPs.

"But they're . . ."

"You think non-Factfolk are only pink-white? In this and the Southeastern Hemisphere, yes. But in my hemisphere, they're closer to the color of wet sand. In the Northeastern, they're a lighter brown, with their own distinct features, and their own methods of oppression. These people you see here"—she pointed a dusty finger at the illumination—"were marching for freedom, from their own oppressors, who believed *they* were the 'Dominant Population.'"

"I don't understand," she said, feeling as though her ignorance had formed into two fists beating upon her head. "These people are visible. Why would visible people oppress other visible people?"

"Human beings will always find a way to differentiate and subjugate, Sister Sweetmint. Especially when they closely resemble one another."

The capture flipped to an empty battlefield, long flat knives with wooden handles strewn all over the ground like silver blades of grass, smoke rising off in the distance.

"Next to each of these weapons is a Factfolk soldier. Dead. Used by non-Factfolks in wars against other non-Factfolks, or non-Factfolks against Factfolks. This capture is from 2149, a war fought in what was back then called the 'Southern Quadrant' in 'Africa,' which is what much of the Southeastern Hemisphere was referred to for over half a millennium. This hemisphere, even more than the Northwestern, is where our kin is persecuted to unbelievable degrees, which is why once we succeed here, in your hemisphere, we will move there."

"Why?" she whispered, a sorrow she hadn't known pulling her apart. "Why are you showing me all of this?"

"To show you that we are not alone, that this world is bigger than you can even imagine, and that we are but small actors on the vast stage of history, doing what we can, how we can, when we can to build a better world. We call this seismic shift toward a new society the 'Fundamental Flip,' which is what we, and now you, are working toward."

"And what do you plan to do with the dippies?"

"We will not treat them as they've treated us. We will not torture or enslave them. But they will no longer be allowed to nurture their baser natures. We will give every Factfolk the choice of where to live and how to live, creating new industries with our people in mind, freeing them from the shackles of the rhitelling, of bonds visible and hidden. It will take place in phases, starting with a period of improving the image they have of themselves, and of our people, but then we will thrive. Especially because of the food."

"The food?"

"The food that they feed us stunts our growth, limits our life spans, and curbs our women's potential to have children, in order to keep our population in check."

Holy Father. Mr. Tenmase was right about Rhitel Burger. Sweetsmoke was right about the ration trains. Suddenly, she was short of breath, heat spreading from her chest toward her now sweaty face. She closed her eyes, inhaled, exhaled, and waited for a wave of nausea to pass.

"Breathe, Sister Sweetmint," Sister Blackstone said, a hand on her shoulder. "What you're feeling is completely normal. Just breathe."

When she recovered, she said, "So, if we're doing all of this, what will the dippies be doing?"

"Likely throwing a tantrum, as if they were a child torn from their mother's nipple. There will be blood. There will be death. There will be battles from here to the Waste Renewal Region to the Farming Region to the Train and Technology Region. Everywhere. And then, when we've won, when they have been made to be self-reliant, they will come crawling back to us. Finally, peace will be possible here, just as it exists in my own hemisphere."

"And how long will that last, if, as you say, life just repeats itself?"

Sister Blackstone was quiet then. Sister Sweetmint felt a change in her new mentor's rumoya—doubt began to douse the bristling confidence. Then, "I don't know. But you're right. Peace is only appreciated because it ends. The way of my hemisphere will end. The world after the Fundamental Flip will end. There may even come a time when we, who believe ourselves to be noble, oppress others in the name of our nobility. Yet"—she raised her head toward the ceiling—"that doesn't mean we can't try to be better, do better, today, and have faith that century by century, millennium by millennium, we become less violent, less selfish. If see-through skin can come about out of nowhere, so can a new kind of human. One with more humanity than all who walked before."

In some ways, her life had never felt smaller, more insignificant. But now she also felt something larger sweeping her up, giving her existence meaning and purpose beyond the individual aims she'd previously held. The fear of not having enough courage to press on was still there, though, as was the feeling of being pummeled by brutal fists of ignorance. "I have so much to learn," she said, her voice hollow.

Sister Blackstone wrapped her arm around Sister Sweetmint's waist, guiding her out of the room, back through the tunnel. "That's good, sister. Very good. Because I have so much to teach."

CHAPTER 35

"GRAB HIM BEFORE HE FALLS FLAT ON HIS FACE," CROGER SAID. HE and Curts each took one of Stephan's arms and led him to the couch, on which he immediately stretched out.

The Chief Architect pointed to his protégé's neck. "You remove the patches, and I'll replace them with two QFs."

Two? One "quick flush" alone was enough to make a man puke his brains out; two could make Stephan defecate himself.

"Get that trash can," Croger instructed. "Next to my desk."

The local manager tossed his head back and forth, his bottom lip shaking. "Isss all ova. Em goin' backta no-thing. Backta a world whur em—"

A patch in each hand, protective layers already removed, Croger slapped them onto Stephan's neck, cutting him off before he could complete whatever nonsense he was trying to articulate. Then he threw up into the golden receptacle as Croger rubbed his back.

"That's it," Croger said. The local manager leaned back on the couch, wincing in pain, then, like a self-cleaning window wiping off a layer of grime, was rid of his intoxication; no more sweating, his skin's greenish tint gone. When he opened his eyes, they flashed with brilliant life.

He sat up, smoothed his suit, and flattened his hair so that it no longer resembled a wild bush. "Ah, Croger." Stephan grinned, gripping the older man's arm. "You brought me back to life, my friend. And you, Leon. What a nice surprise. What are you doing here?"

"Just paying Croger an overdue visit." The Director finished wiping his boots of stray vomit and returned to the armchair. His eyes focused on the spent patches they'd removed from Stephan's neck, including one hidden in the back—all black, a large white *O* printed on it. "Oblivion."

"It seems like we're both down-and-out," Stephan said, snapping Curts back to attention. "After today's session"—he turned to Croger—"everything we've worked for is done. Those hypocrites. So what if I have sex with an Invisible woman every now and then? Who doesn't like a little forbidden variety? These men are at Minx every night, making these Invisible whores rich with all the rhitellings they give them. But now I'm being sacrificed so they can sleep at night thinking they're upstanding hemispherians."

Now on his feet, he paced behind the couch. "And you, Leon," he said, a hand outstretched toward him. "Look at how the hemisphere treats a man who has done nothing but serve them with all he has. Even though you and I have our differences, you've kept order for years, in your own way. I heard about the survey—Ribussce, that entitled traitor. What a world we live in where a DP is treated worse than an Invisible by his own people."

Curts sat there, hearing Stephan's words, but wondering if it was all an act. Over the years, he'd watched him hone a level of showmanship unparalleled when it came to politicians: not just speaking the right words at the right time, but knowing how, and when, to increase the heat, an almost unnatural sense of an audience's temperature. He'd often ridiculed Stephan's intelligence and unbridled ego, but he, like Curts, was a master in the art of adaptation. Still, the local manager thought he was the hardest thing since stone, and Curts was ecstatic over his recent humbling, which he'd had a hand in.

"Okay," Croger said. "Let the lamentations cease. You sound like Ramina on *Hemispheric Housewives*. Neither of you is finished."

Nodding in Stephan's direction, Curts asked, "Does he know?"

"Do I know what?" Stephan said.

"Croger here has a theory that Washington is Shanu."

Stephan paused, turning to Croger, and Curts saw his jaw clenching. "No," he said slowly, "I've never heard this theory. And why is that, Croger?"

"Because," the older man replied, swatting his hand in the air, "it's just a theory, and a very hard one to prove. I told Leon here so that he could investigate. And I kept it from you because it would only be a distraction."

"But . . ." The local manager closed his eyes, as if he had a headache. "An Invisible becoming a DP? That's impossible."

"It's not," Curts said. "However, it is rare. I've never come across a case like this myself, but there are records of them before the Rebirth. And it also tracks with our inability to capture him. He's taken advantage of our"—he paused, anger and shame swelling inside of him—"*my* understanding of law and order, by becoming lawless and not adhering to the natural order. It almost makes you want to skip the magistrates and dispense your own sense of justice."

"But *Washington*?"

"Think about it," Croger said. "How radical he is in trying to uplift Invisibles and improve relations with the other hemispheres. His record in the Hemispheric Hematic Directory is missing because it already belongs to Shanu. I mean . . ." He stood, swiped the nearest wall, and brought up the Invisible's capture from three years ago. "He even looks like Shanu!"

Stephan laughed. "For that matter, so do I. People sometimes think Washington and I are brothers. An unfortunate coincidence."

"You?" Curts suppressed a chuckle rumbling in his chest. "You hate Invisibles so much that, if you were one, you would kill yourself."

"Oh, in a heartbeat, my friend. So then, what do we do about Washington?"

"*You*," Croger said, "do nothing. Leon will investigate. But in the meantime, might we broker a truce here?"

"What kind of truce?" Curts asked.

"First, you share whatever incriminating evidence you have on Washington in that file you've been building."

"File?" Stephan swung his face toward Curts. "You've been building a file on my opponent and never shared it with me?"

The Director's eyes burned into Stephan's. "Why would I? I wanted Washington to win, until now."

"If The Chief Executive were alive to hear that, he'd stab your eyes out, cut your tongue, and—"

Curts leapt up and rushed toward Stephan, his skinny chest pressed against the local manager's powerful frame. "Well, he isn't here, and now you're about to lose it all and have to retreat back into whatever hole you crawled out of like the worthless—"

"Worthless?" Stephan threw his head back. "You've redefined the word, Leon. Crying about a harmless joke I made months ago and asking me to apologize, as if we're children in a schoolyard."

"So you *do* remember! You lying commoner impersonating a politician. What's harmless to you is harmful to many others! But you're made of metal, yes? Stephan Jolis, so hard, so masculine, so unshakable. Yet here you are, with what should have been an easy win turning to dust right in front of you, ha!"

Stephan raised his fist, but Curts didn't flinch. He raised his own. Croger, that tiny but nimble man, jumped between them. "As you two fools get ready to batter each other into extinction, Washington is out there, laughing. At you"—he poked Stephan's chest—"and you"—he did the same to Curts's. "Now, are we going to come together so that an Invisible doesn't ascend to the highest seat of our hemisphere, or should I just go make another pot of herbs and watch as you two act as if we're in Rhitel Arena?"

Croger continued staring up at them, then Stephan lowered his fist, and Curts did the same. "If you, Leon, give Stephan any evidence with a bit of weight, it will be enough to sway the men of rule. They're only persecuting him because they believe they have to. And if you, Stephan, triumph over Washington, then you have to ensure that nothing happens to Leon, or his family, even if he can't prove Washington is Shanu and The Chief Executive's murderer walks free."

The Great Engineer was right. Washington abhorred Curts and anyone who had been in The Chief Executive's favor. If elected, he would gladly wrap the rope around Curts's throat before dropping him from the Eternal Elm—broadcasting his execution throughout the hemisphere to declare his rule. A rule that called for all fingers of the previous Chief Executive's hand to be amputated, one by one. Della and Eva would be spared, Washington wasn't inhumane, but his wife *would* be compelled to join The Defiled, thus making his daughter, his little girl with the golden curls, an orphan. No.

"*Do* you have something?" Stephan asked.

Curts closed his eyes, flipped through a file of a file of a file, and saw it. "Yes," he said. "A piece of information that The Chief Executive, may the Holy Father bless his soul, was sitting on, still deciding what to do with it, before his murder. I can't guarantee it'll be enough, though."

"Let me worry about that," Stephan said. "So"—he extended a hand—"deal?"

"But what if you don't win?"

"I will. Washington already played his strongest hand. Now it's my turn."

Curts looked down at Stephan's hand—his stomach churning with sudden hunches and unfulfilled urges—then lifted his own, formed it into a fist, and rammed it into the local manager's nose. *CRACK!* A syrupy glaze of blood dribbled down his lips and chin.

The Director didn't retract his fist, but held it there, the cuff of his uniform becoming soaked with red. Only then did he pull it back. "That was for your 'harmless' joke."

None of the men screamed. There wasn't any grabbing of lapels, shuffling of feet, or labored breathing. Just silence as Stephan brought his fingers to his nose, the blood continuing to flow. Then he offered his hand, just as he had before, but now glistening crimson.

This time, Curts took it. "Now we have a deal."

The display, without any prompting, flickered on, and the three of them turned, shock spreading across their faces.

CHAPTER 36

EVERYTHING HAD WORKED ACCORDING TO PLAN. WHEN CANDACE left Tintaba, vibrating with excitement, she returned to Forest Twenty-Six. After waiting on the platform for a minute, the public train appeared. She confirmed that her city pass was still active, and joined the people headed for their night jobs. Janitors whose work could only be done when DPs weren't present, evening construction crews ensuring buildings went up as quickly as possible, domestics who didn't live with their employers but accommodated their schedules nonetheless.

Though she knew them each by name, they kept their distance from her, choosing, instead, to act like she wasn't there, standing in the middle of the train for all of them to gawk at—their rumoyas emanating exhausted anger. To them, she was worse than an outsider. She was the source of their present troubles made manifest. It ached.

But this feeling wouldn't last. Not with the Children of Slim now beside her; Sister Blackstone's guiding hand to her back. Just the thought of her new family at Tintaba buoyed her as she exited the train at Progress Park. She paused at the bottom of the station's stairs by the exit, the other people passing her without a second look, and waved her hand in front of a large glass display. A pulsing red dot appeared, representing the station, and then a blinking blue one, her parents' home. A white path between the two dots weaved throughout the park, bringing her to Honor Avenue, a long street that ran along the park's west side before ending at her destination: Eminent Estates. Once she had memorized the route, she set off up the stairs.

She had expected to see DPs everywhere, but when she got to the park's center, it was empty. Bringing her hand to the small cloth bag tied to her bicep, she felt the compass that Rusty had given her before her interview with Mr. Tenmase forever ago, the one that always pointed to Forest Twenty-Six. *The only way through it is to do it.*

But then she looked up at a statue, of The Chief Executive holding a boy's and girl's arms up in victory, as if they'd just won something, and it knocked her back a decade, to the night when Sweetsmoke, eighteen then, returned from a boxing match in Rhitel Arena. He'd entered the cabin without a word, covered in red paint, his color of choice for match day. What struck her fourteen-year-old self as odd, though, was that his paint and face were largely intact—no gash-like streaks, no swelling around the eyes, no busted lips.

"Did you fight?" she asked, taking his bag from him.

"I did."

"Did you win?"

"I did."

"So then why do you seem upset, and why is your paint still so perfect?"

He walked past her, filled a glass with water, then sat on their couch. "I wasn't supposed to win."

She joined him on the couch, eyes narrowed. "What do you mean?"

"You know I was fighting a dippy tonight, right?"

"Yeah," she replied. She always knew the details of his fights.

"The Association thought it would be a good way to generate more rhitellings. They never told me *who* the dippy was, though. It was some relative of The Chief Executive, a kid from the Train and Technology Region trying to make his name by defeating the number one Invisible under twenty-one."

"So what was the problem? He lost, and that's that."

"The head of the Association told me to lose, Little Me. That there was no way I could beat *this* dippy, in midcity Rhitelville, in front of The Chief Executive. But when I got in the ring and saw how unprepared he was, something lit up inside of me. I couldn't do it—I couldn't just give up. So I beat him, badly, to the point where he couldn't even touch me. Rusty didn't talk to me the entire ride back."

When Rusty showed up at their cabin later that night, he pulled a chair from the kitchen to the living room, sat down facing them on the couch, and finally said, "I'm not mad."

"And I'm not sorry," Sweetsmoke replied.

"Good. I didn't expect you to throw it, and, I'll be honest, I wouldn't have respected you if you had, but I would have understood it. The head of the Association is upset, of course, and said that the only reason you're not going to be killed or sent to some mine in the I&S or a basement processing plant in WR is because it would only validate what happened tonight."

Sweetsmoke sat up, shook his head. "But they have to do something, right? They wouldn't just let me off without any punishment. Not for this."

Rusty, painted the same red as Sweetsmoke, nodded. "Tonight was your last fight. The Association has barred you from ever boxing again." He steadied his breath. "The story is that you had a patch stuck between your cheeks; one that gave you an advantage over the kid."

Her older brother sat back and laughed, and laughed, and laughed. She had never seen his mouth crack open like that, his body convulsing as he doubled over, fell to the floor, and slammed his open palm onto the hardwood again, and again, and again. He was still laughing when Rusty left. She could only kneel, place her hand on his back, and hold it there until his laughter faded into silence, until he stilled and slept through the night, there on the wooden floor.

After that, he became even more radical. It was as if the fire he'd always had—speaking up at the Baz Buthani, disrupting Daily Prayer, being gruff to just about anyone who wasn't her, Rusty, or Freshpine—turned inward. He would only share his thoughts with the three of them. Boxing had stopped, but he'd begun to increase his output as a tree feller, growing bigger, stronger, and more bitter, like the tree bark they sometimes ate. Still, he'd always manage to smile at her, hold her when she needed to be held, and make room for her to be soft with him, so long as she continued to be hard with others.

Maybe, she now thought for the first time, staring up at the statue in Progress Park, *he did kill The Chief Executive*. But even if it was true, it wouldn't matter. Not to her. Her brother would always be her brother, and no one deserved to be defined by the worst thing they'd ever done.

Rounding the statue, she continued straight, picking up the pace, then turned onto a wide, tree-lined walkway. When she reached the intersection where she was meant to turn left, her blood knocked against her temples. She heard a whistle to her right, and stopped. She heard another, in front of her. Then another, to the left. Then another, closer than the others, behind her.

Before she could understand what was happening, a DP woman emerged from a bush onto the path a couple of meters in front of her. Candace turned, saw another woman coming from the left, a man striding toward her from the right, and a man dressed in black behind her.

"We got one!" the woman in front of her said, clapping.

"Oh, yes, we did," the man behind her confirmed.

"*Holy Father*. This is a big vizzer," the woman closing in on the left announced with unmistakable delight. "It's true what they say—no one starves in our hemisphere, not even Invisibles."

"The bigger the better. And unpainted? Who does she think she is?" the man on the right asked.

Once they'd all surrounded her, laughing to one another as if they were about to feast, she said, "I have a pass. I'm just on my way to work."

The woman in front of her, tall, with long black hair to match her slender, hate-filled face, said, "We don't care about a pass, vizzer. You have DPs scared for their lives and think you can just walk through one of our parks as if nothing is wrong?"

"I—"

"Look at her," the man behind her said. "Not even a drop of paint on her. She's asking for a beating, or"—he grinned at his companions—"how about we have some fun with her first? See if she likes how we all taste?"

The knee of the woman in front of her jerked forward, her chest rushing toward the ground. Candace spun around, saw the woman to the left bounce backward, her wavy brown hair yanked straight, as if someone were pulling on it, until her head met the cobblestones.

"*What?*" The man behind her raised his fists, threw punches at the air. The second man, to her right, eyes wide with alarm, took off down the path he'd come from, until his neck collided with something thick and concrete that crumpled him.

Still punching wildly, the man behind her said, "Show yourself, you coward."

Suddenly, his head jolted upward and his feet lifted from the ground. One . . . two . . . three. His eyes began rolling inside his skull.

"Go," a voice said.

She took off for Honor Avenue, her footsteps smacking against the gray cobblestones like water hitting concrete, the DPs' moaning and groaning fading as she approached the avenue. She turned around, and no one was behind her.

Her chest burned. *Who was that?* She couldn't smell them or sense their rumoya. It had to be someone from the Children of Slim, watching out for her. She took only a second to catch her breath, then continued up the avenue, north. Head down, feet quick, she focused on the dimly lit sidewalk that bordered the park's black iron fence. She should have smelled and heard those DPs before they appeared, but the park, the lights, the emptiness—all of it distracted her.

She looked up and saw a building that stopped her mid-stride. Five or six stories, it was the tallest building she'd ever seen. The exterior was completely glass, but she smelled the timber used for the main structure, as well as the adhesive that allowed the timber to be pressed so tightly that it was stronger than metal. Maybe Sweetsmoke and Rusty had cut some of the trees that went into it.

From where she stood, it seemed that every story had two large apartments on either side, balconies poking out, allowing their owners to hover above pedestrians like her. She marveled at how each apartment's glass windows stretched from their floors to their ceilings, and while most were opaquely colored for privacy—hazy blues, smoky reds, mist-filled yellows—there was one, on the middle floor, that was see-through.

Inside, she saw what looked like a living room. Two DP children, a boy and a girl, sat on a couch. The light of what she assumed was a large display flashed across their tiny faces as they gripped fistfuls of blue popped corn and stuffed their mouths, only pausing to laugh or turn toward the kitchen. An older woman, meticulously cut brown hair resting atop her shoulders, red lip paint coloring her lips, a tender light shining from her eyes, made space between the children and sat. A man, who could've been her twin, sat on the other side of the girl, closest to the window, and plunged his hand into the bowl before tossing the blue popped corn into his own smiling mouth.

He turned toward the kitchen, called for someone. A half second later, an Invisible woman, painted white from her braided hair to her bare toes, came in with four glasses of juice resting on a tray. The mother and father paid her no mind, the young boy grabbed his drink with two hands, laughing at whatever they were watching, and the girl, with a child's carelessness, knocked her glass over, spilling the orange-red liquid onto their white carpet. On cue, the Invisible woman left, then returned with some cleaning product. *Probably that Mooncurl Drams Jams Ivy is always singing about.*

The woman got down on her knees and dabbed, dabbed, and dabbed, doing her best to avoid the parents' long legs and the children's kicking feet, which landed on her back, and, once, her head. When she made it to the end of the carpet, directly in front of the window, she looked up and, probably noticing Candace's tiny bag and collar floating in the air, their eyes connected. She stood, staring at Candace now, a towel in one hand, and raised two fingers, wiggling them. Candace wiggled hers back, then the woman turned, nodded at the family, and went back to wherever she stayed to remain out of sight. There had been pain on her face, but also a hardened dignity. At least she hadn't lost that.

Then she heard them. Two shibs emerged from the park a distance in front of her and, upon seeing her, darted in her direction. She turned around, the stretch of Honor Avenue she'd just walked vanishing to a point she couldn't see. Running would only make it worse. She stood firm.

When they were in front of her, she saw a man, every part of his face—lips, nose, ears—long and sharp; the other, to her surprise, was a woman. Strands of black hair escaped her moss-colored cap, and her round cheeks and thick lips made Candace think that she might have had some non-Northwestern ancestor whose features refused to be erased.

"What are you doing?" the woman asked, the words barely slipping past her grimace.

"Heading to work," Candace replied, as solid as the concrete beneath her.

The man got close to her face, so close that his raw onion smell became inescapable, especially when he opened his mouth and laughed. "Work? Minx and the other clubs are in that direction." He pointed behind her. "And a train ride away. What type of work are you doing here?"

"And without paint," the woman said, inspecting Candace as she rounded her. "Are you an enemy of this great hemisphere?"

"No."

A heavy hand connected with the back of her head, knocking involuntary tears out. "No, *ma'am*," the man commanded.

"No, ma'am," she said, the pain in the back of her head spreading down her neck.

The woman stabbed her hand into Candace's stomach, and she instantly collapsed to the concrete, clutching herself, while doing her best not to throw up.

"They're so bold," the man said. "Walking on Honor Avenue like one of them didn't kill the man who allowed them to breathe Northwestern air."

"Once the Director finds that one— What's his name?"

"Shanu," the man said, thick spit showering Candace's face as he spoke. "Maybe she knows him." He poked her back with the sharp toe of his boot. "Do you know him, girl?"

"Once they find him," the woman continued, her words coated in an excitement that seemed sexual, "and chop his head off—or take a knife and unzip him like a jacket, or drown him in the park, for all of the hemisphere to see—that's when they'll learn." She paused. Then, "Let's bring her in."

Candace rolled onto her back, still gripping her stomach. "Ribussce . . . I have a pass from Hemispheric Guard Associate Deputy Director Ribussce," she said, followed by a burst of coughing so severe she thought she'd soon spit up a piece of her heart.

"Ribussce?" the woman asked, turning to her fellow guard.

"She's lying," he said. "What would she be doing with a pass from Ribussce?"

"He—" She tried to suppress her coughing. "He knows the family I work for, and gave me a special pass, since it's so dangerous out here. Check . . . Check for yourself."

The man knelt, removed a glass tablet from an inner pocket. "If she's lying, she's going to wish that His Executive's Prison was the worst she'd get." He held it above her face. It beeped. After checking it himself, he showed it to his partner.

"Eminent Estates," the woman said, sounding surprised.

"Who knows, but it checks out," he said, rising to his feet. He dusted himself off, the particles falling onto Candace's face. "Don't let us catch you here again. Understood?"

"Yes, sir."

The woman's boot floated past her eyes as she stepped over her. Lying there on the warm ground of Honor Avenue, she felt crushed, as if a boulder had been released directly above her and she was specially selected—"a model Invisible," as Reverend Achte had called her—to absorb its full, pulverizing weight. It would have been far easier, and probably far wiser, to just stay there, accepting her place in the world as something, not even someone, to be trod upon. *Come on, Sweetmint. No point feeling sorry for yourself now. Come on.*

Just as she had done at Daily Prayer that morning, she propped herself up and, bit by bit, worked her way onto her feet. Humming a hymn for safety—*I see the mountains, I see the stars. In every natural wonder, you're never too far*—she reached the golden gates of Eminent Estates, where two shibs stood guard. After displaying her pass, they let her in, showed her where the house was on a map, and told her to tell the Rawdens they said hello.

The Rawdens?

CHAPTER 37

A REGIONAL REPORTER FOR THE NWN, FROM THE CLOTHING REGION, appeared on the display as fires raged in the distance behind him. "We don't know what caused this," he said, a lack of concern on his face. "But every tent town in the region from the south to the north has gone up in flames. Initial reports put the estimated deaths at three hundred thousand Invisibles, zero members of the Dominant Population. On the ground with us we have Hemispheric Guard Deputy Director Mund." Lucretia, blank-faced, entered the frame.

"Hemispheric Guard Deputy Director Mund," the reporter said. "Please tell us what you know so far."

Her eyes slashed into the capglass, making Curts think she was staring directly at him; all the anger she felt ripping through the display, reaching what parts of his heart still existed. "After speaking with a handful of guards stationed throughout the region's various tent towns, we've concluded that these fires were started by a handful of Invisibles, all now deceased. These Invisible arsonists were instructed by Shanu himself in order to have the hemisphere believe that DPs did this in retaliation for his actions, stoking embers of division."

"So," the reporter said, "Shanu is not only to blame for the murder of Chief Executive Rhitel, may the Holy Father bless his soul, but also for the extermination of hundreds of thousands of his own people?"

"That's correct. Every mass grave in this region, where the bodies are see-through, but the smell of burnt flesh has flooded the air—all of that, if you're watching, is on *you*," she said, monotone, continuing to stare into the glass.

Croger shut the display off and turned to Curts. "What do you know about this, Leon?"

"It's news to me." He patted his uniform all over. "I must have left my earsphere on the train. But as Lucretia said, this is all the doing of Shanu, and someone will have to pay."

The older man stared at him for longer than expected. Stephan, who always had a word waiting on the tip of his tongue, was quiet. Hundreds of thousands of Invisibles were dead, not by accident or holy intervention, but because of one man. And, as far as anyone knew or would ever know, that man was Shanu. If the Invisible had a conscience at all, this would make him appear, but Curts was no longer waiting. From his meeting with Croger and Stephan, he had received plenty to investigate, and now, with the Clothing Region's tent towns on fire, he had more room to do so.

Curts stared at the wall where the display had just been, Lucretia's unmoving eyes still there as if they had, through some strange science, become ingrained in the wall itself. Adrenaline pumping through his veins, he thought back to a piece of advice Rhitel had given him when he was appointed Hemispheric Guard Director: *Be careful of what you commit to, because you'll be forced to change in order to achieve it.*

The simple fact was this: hundreds of thousands of Invisibles were now dead, and history would never remember their names. But the act, the act itself would serve as a necessary distraction from Curts's failures today and live forever tomorrow. And that was the point.

CHAPTER 38

E MINENT ESTATES WAS EVEN QUIETER THAN PROGRESS PARK AND Honor Avenue.

Whereas most of her forestfolk wanted to be close to one another, the DPs in this part of the city seemed to want as much space as possible from their neighbors. Candace wondered, continuing up the block and crossing an intersection with a stone-faced statue of a seated Chief Executive, Chief Consort, and Chief Daughter Rhitel in its center, if these people felt connected to one another in any way, or if they simply coexisted. Yes, she, too, liked distance from the hustle and bustle of the main square, but she knew that if she needed help, it would be there. *At least that's how it was in the past*, she corrected herself.

Where was their Baz Buthani? There were no fields in sight, no women selling vegetables on these paved rainbow-colored corners, so how did they get their food? As Mr. Tenmase had said would be the case a few days ago, she hadn't seen one Rhitel Burger since leaving Progress Park Station. Only sidewalks illuminated by light strips; two-story homes standing behind great lawns, no blade out of place, trees shaped to perfection. All the homes were made of stone, as if to say, *We're not going anywhere anytime soon.*

What was most disorienting, though, were the ocean sounds coming from the ground. Aside from the Heroic River to the west and the Rhitel River to the east, there was no large body of water nearby—she would have smelled the salt and other minerals—yet the crashing of towering waves surrounded her. These sounds, she figured, were being artificially played through hidden holes to make the DPs here feel better about living so far removed from the real nature that she and her forestfolk inhabited.

After a few more minutes, she arrived at her parents' home. It was similar to the others with the exception of a roof that spread and sloped at different angles, resembling the top of Forest Twenty-Six's church. A church that she would have never known had her parents not disowned her. That journey from the orphanage she would have never made, along with the aching in her four-year-old feet that, decades later, remained. The even deeper, more visceral pain of not being wanted by the very people who were supposed to more than want you. So much and too much that should have been avoided.

What would it have been like to grow up here?

The reality of the moment slapped her in the face. She was an Invisible woman whose parents were also Invisible and lived here, yes, but she didn't belong. Candace smacked her lips together, her mouth so dry that she couldn't even gather spit, and she stepped onto the white cobblestone path that stretched from the street to the front door.

As she approached, she knew there were at least two people inside; she could hear and smell them. One had a bitter aroma, like the fermented grains at Minx. The other had a light, sweet scent, which reminded her of a drink she enjoyed, made of watered-down sap, crushed mint, and squash.

Rubbing Rusty's compass through the pouch tied to her arm, she knocked on the glass door, which was programmed to a cloudy pale yellow, making it impossible to see inside. The voices paused, then continued. *Knock, knock, knock.* Harder this time. The sound of footsteps became louder and stopped when a silhouette appeared behind the door. She assumed they were painted, or maybe it was a DP friend of their parents.

"Who is it?" A man.

"I'd like to speak with Mr. Rawden."

"Yes, but who are you?"

"My name is Candace. I know Mr. Rawden."

He paused, then said, "We don't know any Candaces, especially any Invisible ones. Please go away before we call the guards."

What did I expect, just to be let inside? She took a breath, her hand latching on to her stomach where the shib had struck her, and, forcing herself to breathe through the pain, said, "I'm here about Shanu. Mr. Rawden will know who that is. I'm his sister."

She waited for a response. If the guards came, she decided she'd finally give up. Sweetsmoke, seeing all she'd done, wouldn't blame her. He couldn't. Look at where she was, where she had been. If this was the end of the path, then—

A lock turned. The door swung backward with a tiny *click*. Standing in front of her wasn't a painted Invisible, but a DP: tall, a chest that puffed out, and a pair of dark brown eyes that were jumping all over her body. At first, she assumed he was a friend of the Rawdens, or that, after everything, she'd ended up at the wrong house. But when she saw the carved straight line of his jaw, the original wood Sweetsmoke's own was cut from, her rumoya knew.

But how?

"Is it really you?" His eyes moved across her, as though they couldn't decide where to settle.

"If you mean, am I who I say I am, then, yes. It's me. But who are you?"

He moved to touch her. She backed away. He dropped his hand, nodded. "Come in, quick. Before someone sees you."

She entered and stood in what Mr. Tenmase called a *foyer*. Two wooden staircases decorated with crimson carpet, curved, like parentheses, from where she stood up to the second floor. The door clicked closed behind her, just as a woman emerged from a hallway in front of her, then abruptly stopped.

"An-drew," she said, breaking the name into two. Brown-blond hair fell in curls tighter than a typical DP woman's. A nose, short and bulbous, lay between two copper-colored eyes. The eyes weren't familiar to Candace, but the nose was the same nose that greeted her in the mirror whenever she painted herself.

No one had to tell her who this woman was.

Had she thought about this moment before? Thousands of times. Lying on her mattress, staring up at her cabin's ceiling; at Daily Prayer, watching mothers smile at their children or scold them for not paying attention; around the fire, at the Baz Buthani, as flames cracked in the air, spitting harmless embers. In every place, she had tried to insert her own parents. She had tried to envision their smells, the sound of their voices, the way their palms would feel against the back of her neck as they brought her close to their chests. And here they were, not a figment of her imagination, but also nowhere close to the reality she'd pictured. *How were they DPs?*

"What's this thing doing here?" the woman asked.

"Audrey," the man said, laughing. "This isn't a *thing*." He walked and stood between them, extended his arm in Candace's direction. "This is our daughter. And her name is *Candace*. She's here about Wash."

The woman tilted her head, blinked multiple times, like Candace was something in her eye to get rid of. "Daughter? Andrew, did you hit your head? We don't have a daughter. As for the boy, we already did enough when Hemispheric Guard Director Curts came knocking, so I hardly think it's necessary for us to have this thing dirtying our floor."

"Call me a thing one more time," Candace said, stepping toward her, "and I'll dirty your floor with your face, *dippy*."

Audrey swiped the wall nearest to her. "I'm calling the guards."

Andrew rushed to her side, gently pulled her hand away from the wall. "Stop, please. Let's just see what this is all about."

Breathe in through your nose, then out through your mouth. Once again. "I'm not staying long," Candace said. "I just want to know what you said to Hemispheric Guard Director Curts, and if you know anything that can help me find my brother."

Andrew lifted his eyes to the ceiling. "We told him a partial truth. That we haven't seen him since we dropped you both off at Clasped Hands Orphanage. We used to live downcity, and then—"

"Enough!" Audrey shouted, stomping her slippered foot on the ground, her voice echoing off the bare walls. "For the love of the Holy Father, leave the past in the past, Andrew!"

"It's always been easier for you," he said, facing his wife's back. "These are your *children*. Your son and daughter. Maybe if we would have done it differently, moved somewhere safer— Holy Father." His voice fell to a whisper. "Please forgive us, Candace. I don't know how, but please forgive us."

"For what?" she asked.

"Go on, Andrew," Audrey said, spinning around, an open hand thrust toward him. "You want to absolve yourself of your sins so badly, do it. Tell her everything. Tell her how I gave birth to the most beautiful, sweet boy a mother could ever want. A boy who never cried, whose laughter drowned a room with joy. A boy who, at three years old, began to flicker."

"Flicker?" Candace asked.

"That's right. Flicker. When the boy turned three, he disappeared right in front of our eyes. We couldn't see him, but we could touch him. He wasn't sick, he wasn't hurt, but he was as see-through as the rest of you. Then, at random, he would flicker back to his normal visible self, still laughing his big laugh, but"—she closed her eyes, as if she could hear it now—"it never sounded the same."

Flicker. She'd never heard of a child being born DP, then becoming Invisible. You were either one or the other. No in-between. Ever.

Andrew walked over to the staircase and sat, his head between his hands. "We don't know how it happened. We'd never known such a thing to be possible, but then Audrey said—"

"It's my fault," she cut in, one hand on the staircase's curved railing. "My mother's grandfather was a vizzer, who married a normal person when it was legal, but I didn't tell Andrew. I thought everything would be fine, because my mother's father came out normal, and so did she, and then I did, but then . . ." Her grip tightened on the hardwood. "The blood, even after three generations, was still spoiled."

"We thought it was just a phase," Andrew said. "And we decided to have another. But—"

"But I came out Invisible," Candace said. "While Shanu kept flickering."

Black eye paint and tears streaked down Audrey's face. "No. He stopped. And when he did, he was just like you." Now she pointed at her husband. "*He* wanted to keep you both. To break the law. To move somewhere far away, where hemispheric guards would never find you, and we'd live as one family, happily ever after. But I wouldn't let him do that. You both— You're not my children." The words hung in the air for a moment. "I didn't even waste my time naming you. And look at all we have now. We wouldn't be in this home, with everything we've ever wanted, if we allowed you to ruin it."

"Not everything," Andrew whispered. He lifted his wet face, looked at his daughter.

She heard the river rushing, the last crack of a tree before falling, sons laughing as they jumped into their mother's arms, fathers humming as they held their daughters on their shoulders, her own tiny footsteps *pitter-patter-pitter-patter-pitter-patter*ing over all those kilometers between Clasped Hands and Forest Twenty-Six. She felt Freshpine's hot corn porridge in her stomach, Rusty's rough hand tousling her hair, the way the floor would creak as he taught her brother how to shuffle, duck, and throw a punch. She remembered the acidic taste of never being accepted, the distinct flavor of being forgotten by her parents, but always having Sweetsmoke. Always, until she didn't.

Her mind had betrayed her. It had made her believe that by working with Mr. Tenmase, she would go on to be a hemispheric hero, a renowned Invisible inventor, the first of her kind, catapulting her to a place where her parents would see her, realize their colossal error, and do everything in their power to get her back—on their knees with open arms, begging for her to embrace them, to grace them with an opportunity to start over. But no. None of that. Standing there, she felt like that little girl wandering through open fields and forests with her brother, confused by why no place in the world could ever feel like home.

She straightened her back, met Andrew's eyes. "You said you used to live downcity. Can I have the address?"

"Stop whatever you're doing, Candace," he said. "Stop now, while you can. An Invisible girl is no match for a hemisphere full of hate."

"Then it's a good thing I'm not a girl. Just give me the address and you'll never see me again."

He shook his head. Audrey went back into the hallway, then returned, holding up a glass tablet with the address. Candace quickly memorized it. They were the same height, and she couldn't help but wonder . . . if she were born DP, would her hair be the same brown-blond? She hadn't inherited her curls, her and Sweetsmoke's hair was straight, like the man's, but what else was passed on? Andrew and Audrey were DP, but their essence, and the essence of their ancestors, flowed through her rumoya, manifesting in a myriad of ways she would never know. Then, just like that, none of it mattered. The Big Reset Mr. Tenmase spoke of, the Fundamental Flip that Sister Blackstone obsessed over, was happening to her now, in her own life.

She turned around, opened the door, and stepped back into the night. But before she was halfway down the cobblestone path, the door opened, a rush of footsteps behind her.

"Please," Andrew said, grabbing her hand, turning her around. "I haven't stopped thinking about you and Wash since we left you. You're in my dreams, I see you during the day, I even imagine hearing your voices."

"Wash," she said, the word *whoosh*ing past her lips. "Was that what you named him?"

He looked down, his tears slapping against the cobblestones, then laughed. "No. He was named Andrew Junior. Clasped Hands must have renamed him Shanu. But we liked to call him 'Wash.'"

"Why?"

"He loved to watch this program, *Mr. Washington*, about a baby who ruled the hemisphere. It always made his face light up with bright eyes and that smile that just melted you. One day, we started calling him 'Wash,' and that was it. Well, no." He paused. "Not exactly."

"What do you mean?"

A struggle ensued across his face, then he looked down at the the path they stood on. "You can't repeat what I'm going to tell you to anyone. Anyone at all."

"What is it?"

He raised his head to her, inhaled, exhaled, then, "Do you know who Williams Washington is?"

"I do. We Invisibles aren't complete idiots."

"No, I— Anyway. Audrey and I believe *he* is your brother. I mean, if you look at his capture, the similarity is striking, and then there's the name, which can't be a coincidence. It seems he's two people at once: this politician during the day, then some Chief Executive–murdering Invisible at night."

Local Manager IV Washington? His face, which she'd only seen once or twice on the display, came to her. Strong and defined, with hair the same brown as the man standing in front of her. Tall and clean-shaven, bearing powerful arms like someone who had spent time boxing . . . or felling trees. All of this, paired with the fact that she hadn't seen her brother in years, and even before then, hadn't seen him without a beard and shaved head since he was a child, made it more and more possible. Plus, Sweetsmoke was only ever painted and physically visible to her an infinitesimal amount of times compared to when he wasn't, to the point that she didn't even know if she'd recognize her brother, visible skin, eyes, *and* wearing clothing, if he'd sat right next to her. It would be too bizarre. She, like all other Invisibles, was far more used to identifying her people based on specific combinations of scentprints, rumoyas, and voices.

She tried to float, to retrieve every piece of information she had about Local Manager IV Washington, but there wasn't much; Invisibles were only shown what DPs wanted them to see on the display, and the prevailing narrative was that Local Manager II Jolis was *good* and Local Manager IV Washington was *bad*. But, then, why *was* he bad? If he was bad, it was because he didn't want to uphold the status quo, and if he didn't want to uphold the status quo, then he must have been an ally to her people, or something like that. And if he was an ally to her people . . . *Yes, it makes sense.* The

Children of Slim spoke about her brother being The Illuminator, "who will deliver us out of the darkness and into luminescence." Who better to deliver us than the next Chief Executive of the Northwestern Hemisphere?

"When Hemispheric Guard Director Curts came . . . why didn't you tell him?" she asked Andrew.

"Audrey tried to, but I managed to stop her. It was the least we could do, after everything. So we left that out." Something like pride flashed across his face now. "My son, The Chief Executive of the entire hemisphere," he said, shaking his head.

"Except he's not your son. And your wife was right: I'm not your daughter." She turned to leave, but he found her hand again, forcing her to face him.

"When I saw that capture of him from three years ago on the display . . . I know all of this is our fault, but Audrey's wrong, and she knows it." He threw his hand toward the mini castle behind him. "We *are* empty. Our lives mean nothing. But if you finally forgive us, maybe we can heal. Together."

She wanted to believe that this man, crying and shaking in front of her, wasn't a bad man. She didn't know how he made his money, whether he treated Invisibles like people or see-through servants, if he frequented Minx or one of the other clubs. If *vizzer* ever sizzled on his tongue. But she owed him nothing.

"Forgive you?" She pulled her hand out of his. "Sir, I don't even *know* you." Head up, back straight, she walked down the rainbow-colored street, through the gate of Eminent Estates, down Honor Avenue, across Progress Park, and, after waiting a few minutes, got on a train that took her straight to Forest Twenty-Six.

Home.

By the time she arrived at her cabin, she was already strategizing how to get to Andrew and Audrey's old home in downcity Rhitelville to see if she could find any traces of Sweetsmoke. But when she got to her door, she noticed strange markings in the dirt, illuminated by the moonlight. Kneeling down, she realized it was a note.

Little Me, it began. Even though it was written with a twig, the handwriting—*e*'s that curved like *u*'s; *r*'s that resembled right angles; *t*'s with the horizontal stroke *slightly* higher than expected, turning them into crosses—was so familiar that she'd know it anywhere. *Meet me here, tomorrow night, when the Three Teachers emerge.*

CHAPTER 39

IT WAS A DREAMLESS NIGHT. NO RUNNING FROM FACELESS ATTACK-ers. No hiking up a mountain that grew larger with each step. No falling from indecipherable heights, or crashing into the concrete surface of water. Finally, Sweetmint felt good. Damn good.

The morning sun's light seeped through the window, spreading over her face, and she stretched her fists back to meet it before turning toward Sweetsmoke's empty mattress. *Would he sleep on it?* She hoped so. The last time he was here, he hadn't even stayed the night.

Memory flipped her and her mattress upright, pushing her into the scene of that fateful evening. She'd arrived at Forest Twenty-Six after a long day of geometry, physics, and complex algebra at Forestaeum Minor, but even before she reached home, she knew, from the lack of dinner smells wafting toward her through her cabin's door, that something was seriously wrong.

She thrust the door open and found Sweetsmoke, heard the sounds of his big feet hitting the hardwood as he paced in front of the mattresses, whispering, "It's back. It's back. It's back."

"What's back?" she asked.

He stopped moving. Without a word, the steel trunk opened, a knife and hammer floated before dropping into his green canvas bag. Her brother rushed into the kitchen, threw some food into the same bag.

"I need you to transfer me most of the rhitellings in your account."

Sweetsmoke had never asked her for money before. They didn't have much, but what he made from felling trees with Rusty was enough for vegetables from the women in the square—he was adamant about refusing the food that came from the ration train and thought the grow tax was ridiculous—so he allowed her to save her educational stipend in case of emergencies. They never ate at Rhitel Burger, and though she'd sometimes let her eyes linger for a second on the Northwestern Boutique's display window, she never bought anything because, number one, she wouldn't be able to afford it; number two, Sweetsmoke would never permit it; and number three, she didn't think she could pull off jewelry or any bag other than one made of canvas or straw.

"Sweetsmoke." She stepped from the front door past the kitchen table to the living room, where he lifted his mattress and picked up a shirt and pair of pants before stuffing them into his swollen bag.

"Sweetsmoke," she repeated. "*Where* did you get those from?"

"It's just for fun, Sweetmint. Don't worry."

"Fun? You're scaring me." She grabbed his bicep, turning him around, then found his hands. "What's going on?"

"Nothing." He faced away from her. "You wouldn't understand, Little Me. Please transfer me all that you can, and just keep enough for food. I have to go away for a while, but not for forever. I promise."

"Go away? Where? What— What is this? Are you in trouble? You can tell me. *Please* tell me."

"The rhitellings, Candace." The firmness of his voice knocked her off balance. "Now."

She went to the wall next to the window and, in a few swipes, sent him fifty rhitellings, praying that if she did what he told her, he'd explain everything, because nothing, absolutely nothing, was making sense. This was scarier than a bad dream. There was nothing to wake up from.

"Thank you," he said, softer. "I have to go now, Little Me. You'll be okay. I know it."

He moved toward the kitchen, but she caught his hand. She never needed to see him to know where he was in relation to her—the swing of his arm, the direction of his eye, the placement of his foot—it was like she was a magnet of one charge and he another, the two of them forever connected. Until now.

"You can't leave me, Big Brother." Her voice cracked the sentence in half, her eyes already full of tears. "I don't know what's happening, but I know that you need me. And I need you. You're all that I have. What—" She broke down even more, still holding on to his calloused hand. "Please," she said, digging her feet into the floor as she tried to pull him back into the living room. "Whatever this is, we can get through it together. Just like always."

His body shook for a moment, then stilled. He tugged his hand from hers, but when she didn't let go, he snatched it away, hurting her wrists. She lunged for his bag, and they wrestled for it until he finally yelled, "STOP!" and ripped it from her hands.

"Listen. I'll be back once I do what I need to do, okay? Remember how I always said the time would come for me to change the world? I've just got my chance, and nothing is going to get in my way."

"But," she whispered, "I always thought we'd do it together."

"We will, one day. I'll come back. But in the meantime, just be brave, Little Me. Remember everything I taught you: the only way through it is to do it. And no matter what happens, no matter *what*, don't try to find me. I don't want you to get hurt."

She laughed, tears striking the cabin floor. "What do you think is happening now? All I feel is hurt."

His hands held her cheeks, thick thumbs wiping the tears away, just as they'd done hundreds of times before. "You're stronger than you think." He grabbed her hand, brought it to his lips, and kissed it before letting go and walking out into the night, headed for an unknown destination. Without her.

The present propelled her back onto the mattress, the painful memory no longer holding the same power because she was finally going to see her brother again, tonight. But what the memory did contain was information. The "it" that he spoke of was probably the flickering that Andrew and Audrey had told her about—see-through one moment, visible the next. *A glitch in the blood*, she thought, just as Mr. Tenmase had taught her that there were sometimes glitches in a system.

The more she ran with this theory, the more she realized. She'd seen this happen in her own forest. One tree's powder would ride the wind to another of a different species, then, a few months later, you'd see a sapling that shared the traits of both. If you went back to that same spot a while later, the young tree would have either grown to be a stronger combination of its two parents or died as something weaker that wasn't meant to survive. If this is what happened to Sweetsmoke, there was no doubt that he was stronger than Andrew and Audrey, because *she* was.

Rusty. It was late when she returned last night, so she didn't stop by, but she had to tell him the good news, provided he was actually there. Abe would find out later, at Castle Tenmase; a twin promise to twins kept. She rolled off the mattress, chugged a glass of water, and stepped outside to a world that had never felt brighter.

He was already outside, tinkering with some of his tools, when she approached his cabin.

"Sawukhoob, Sweetmint. Chunjani?" he asked, as if everything were fine, immediately destroying her mood.

"How am I? Rusty," she said, her tone as sharp as one of his axes, "where have you been?"

Tools floated through the air and rested on a small table set between two rocking chairs on his porch. He sat in the one on the left, which tipped back and forth under his weight, waiting for her to join him—their ritual whenever he wanted to deliver one of his "Rusty Lectures," as she called them.

"I'm sorry, Sweetmint," he said after she sat. "I know I've been gone, but . . ." His voice faded. "I've been needed elsewhere."

"Your tree feller meetings can wait, Rusty. You've been needed here, too," she said, rocking back and forth in her chair, working to contain an expanding rage. "Yesterday, it—"

His rugged hands covered hers. "Freshpine told me. Reverend Achte will pay, don't worry about that. I just thought . . . I thought I could protect us, that the things I was doing would prevent all the terror, fear, and pain we're experiencing now, but I was wrong. And"—his chair stilled—"it feels like I've been wrong most of my life. That trying to be two people with one body was always going to end in disaster."

Two people, one body. Did Rusty flicker, like Sweetsmoke? No, impossible; she would have known. Were the two people he spoke of himself and Abe, brothers somehow sitting on two sides of a spectrum? No, they hadn't spoken since Abe left to work for Mr. Tenmase five years ago. No new insight was forthcoming, and she didn't know where he'd been, but the regret in his voice caused the anger and abandonment she'd felt to disappear. He was her Rusty, there since she and Sweetsmoke first set foot in Forest Twenty-Six, and he always would be, no matter what.

"It's okay." She held on to his hands tighter. "You've always protected us. Especially me. So if you had to be away, there must be a good reason for it."

The moment stretched out in front of them, then, rocking again, he whispered, "Mambonga."

She couldn't hold it in any longer. "I have something to tell you. Something amazing."

"What's that?"

"Sweetsmoke, he's coming back!"

"What? And not so loud."

"Muxolo." She dropped her volume. "Sorry. Last night, I came back to a message from him. He'll be here, at my cabin, once the Three Teachers appear. But," she said, unable to suppress her smile, "I don't want to overwhelm him, so maybe come by a little later? Or I'll bring him to you. I'm sure he wants to see you."

Rusty leaned back, the bladelike tips of his chair pointed toward the sky. He was so quiet for so long that she thought she'd made a mistake, but then he rested the chair back on the porch, brought his hand to her shoulder, and said, "This *is* great news, Sweetmint. The best news indeed. Be sure to keep him there, okay? As you said, it'll be a lot for him, but one or two more familiar faces will do him some good. I'll give you both some sibling time and join you after. What do you think?"

She flung her arms around his neck, his locs tickling her cheeks. "I think that sounds perfect. Really, really perfect. I can't wait."

"Me neither," he said, laughing. "Me neither."

They, along with Freshpine and the children, headed to Daily Prayer and sat together in the middle row. Darksap was right in front of her, and she gave him a peck on the cheek. The fewer people who knew about Sweetsmoke the better, and she figured he'd understand when she told him tomorrow.

As promised, Reverend Achte selected someone else, a boy— whose mother painted DP women's nails and whose father installed pipes—and beat him in front of everyone while reciting verses from his Chief Executive Rhitel Bible. After the first blow, the boy's yellow-painted father leapt up and charged the reverend. But the shibs knocked him down, cracked his head against the wooden floor so hard and so loud that both his skull and the church's planks must have splintered. Rusty tried to stand, but Freshpine kept him pinned to the pew.

This will soon end, Sweetmint thought on the train ride to Mr. Tenmase's. Hemispheric Guard Director Curts wouldn't find Sweetsmoke—he couldn't, not with Rusty helping him escape. And especially not if Audrey and Andrew were right about who, and what, he was now. A new Chief Executive would be elected, and if it was the more dangerous one, Brother Blackstone and the Children of Slim would make good on their promise. If it was her brother, he would finally be free. Hope, that fleeting friend, stretched its hand toward her. In the past, she would have just stared at it, said, "No, thank you," and kept her head down. But now Sweetmint grasped it, and she grasped it firmly, smiling.

She only had to make it through the day.

CHAPTER 40

URTS STAINED A PIECE OF GLASS WITH BLOOD AND INSERTED IT
into his glass tablet. The results from the Hemispheric Hematic
Directory came back instantly, and he had his answer. Finally,
he had Shanu in his sights, thanks to his visit to Croger's castle. He
decided, then and there, that he would deal with this pompous im-
postor in his own way, not the State's, and he would do it alone. No
one, no one at all, could be trusted. But before he could fully process
the irrefutable evidence in his hands and plan the next steps, someone knocked on his office door.

He cleared the results, pocketed his glass tablet. "Come in."

"Sir," Lucretia said, stepping inside, closing the door, and saluting him.

He saluted back, gestured to one of the two seats in front of his
desk.

"I'll stand, thank you."

"That's fine. We didn't get a chance to speak last night, but I saw
you on the news. Good work, Deputy."

She stood there, as expressionless as she was on the display the
night before, staring through him.

"How may I help you, Lucretia?"

"How can you sit there?"

"Excuse me?"

"How can you sit there"—she hurled her hand toward him—"as if we didn't just exterminate hundreds of thousands of innocent people. Not criminals, but people. As if *you* didn't sentence them to death for no reason other than manipulating the hemisphere to buy *you* time to find someone who obviously won't ever be found to spare *you* and your family."

He stood, dragged his fingers across his desk as he rounded it, and planted his feet directly in front of her. "What's a few hundred thousand for the sake of one hundred fifty million?"

"This isn't one of your calculations that you use to pass the time. These were people, people with pasts and presents, but no futures. Because of you."

Curts sighed directly into her face. "Why does this bother you so much, Lucretia? Do you think we're better than all of the men and women of millennia past who did what they had to do for the sake of survival? I'm sorry to tell you, but we're not."

"How can you say that? There's what is right and what is wrong. You used to know where the line was, but now—"

"Grow up, Deputy. 'Right' is man-made, just like 'wrong.' There is no morality in nature; no sense of good and evil in the soft, fatty marrow of our bones. What is right for us is wrong for others, within our hemisphere and beyond. The opposite also holds true. *Open your eyes.*"

Her face finally broke, eyes narrowing, mouth hanging half open as her chest shook. "You are not the man I chose to follow. The man who was dedicated to law and order. To morality."

Curts threw up his hands and laughed. "After all of this, can't you see? *We* define order. *We* define law. *We* define what is moral. And until the world changes, that is how it'll be. So it was Shanu and his co-conspirators who set every tent town in the Clothing Region on fire. It's Shanu who's responsible for the deaths of hundreds of thousands of his own people. And it's Shanu who will be held to account for them *and* the murder of Chief Executive Rhitel, may the Holy Father bless his soul."

She shook her head, a gray pallor to her skin, as if she were about to vomit. "I won't follow you anymore."

"You will!" he shouted, slamming his fist into his hand. "Because if you don't, then you're my enemy. And if you're my enemy . . ."

Before he could continue, his earsphere vibrated on his desk. Instead of picking it up, he swiped the nearest wall, saw it was Captain Kandolo, and activated the call from there so Lucretia could hear.

"Captain Kandolo."

"Sir," he said, excited. "Good news."

Lucretia looked at him, curiosity softening her eyes, loosening her clenched jaw.

"Go on."

"Shanu. He left a message for his sister that he'll visit her cabin tonight, once the Three Teachers emerge."

"Three Teachers?"

"Rhitel's Belt, sir. The conste—"

Momentarily embarrassed, he said, "Yes, the constellation. I just forgot what you all call it. That's good news, Captain. The best news," he said, trying to sound elated. "What have you told her?"

"That I'll leave them alone in the cabin for a while, to get comfortable. Then she'll bring him to mine so I can say hello. We don't want to scare him off or alert him to our presence until the moment of capture."

"Understood," Curts said. "Hemispheric Guard Deputy Director Mund and I will take a dozen guards to Forest Twenty-Six, making it impossible for him to escape. Once the Three Teachers come out, we'll head straight to the cabin and apprehend him, then escort him directly to His Executive's Prison to await his trial. Make sense?"

"A perfect plan, sir."

"Good work, Captain. I . . ." Part of Curts wanted to apologize for cracking down on his forest and using Reverend Achte to further harass them, but tough times required tough actions, and that was nothing to apologize for.

"Once this is all over," Curts continued, "we'll remove the extra guards and Reverend Achte will cease the beatings."

"Thank you, sir. I do have one request, if possible."

"Make it quick."

"Please make sure that no matter what happens, his sister, Candace, isn't harmed. She hasn't done anything wrong."

"No promises, but I'll do my best."

Curts swiped the call away and faced Lucretia, but her head was pointing to the floor. "Results, Lucretia. They are the only thing that matters. Once this is all over, I promise that things will go back to how they were before. We will do so much good for the hemisphere that any losses we've incurred will not be wasted."

She remained motionless.

"Will you help me finish this?"

Finally raising her head, she said, "I will. But only because, despite everything, I still have faith that you can find your way back to the better parts of yourself."

"Good. Round up your most trusted golden guards, tell them the plan, and make sure Ribussce knows nothing. I have to go ensure that this all goes smoothly, as well as secure a backup plan in case Shanu doesn't actually show."

"Where are you going?"

"Home, then I'll return here, and we'll make a stop before going to Forest Twenty-Six."

Without wasting any more time, he entered the closet elevator and boarded his private train home.

When he arrived, he walked up the steps from his basement, and only when he opened the door did he realize he hadn't used a patch in over twenty-four hours—and that he had no plans to. He felt as though he were flying with his feet on the ground.

Eva sat in front of the display, her cheeks covered in orange dust, laughter spilling from her mouth.

"Hi, Small Potato."

His daughter snapped out of her trance. After regarding him with confusion, she screamed, "DADDY!" and ran to him.

"Where's Mommy?"

She pointed an orange-stained finger. "Upstairs."

"Okay, give me one minute." Of course he wanted to join her on the couch, but he knew it was his wife who needed tending to right now. Later, when it was all over, they'd go on a trip together, across the hemisphere, to somewhere new and exciting; he wasn't sure where, but he'd figure it out.

Like Eva, Del was lost in a task when he came upon her. He'd stood at the threshold of their bedroom door, and it was only when he coughed that she turned around, a long black sock in her hands. A live illumination of little Eva, still sitting on the couch downstairs, was on the wall behind her.

"*You're* doing laundry? I never thought I'd see the day."

She returned to the pile of clothes on their bed, searching with abnormal focus for the black sock's companion, eventually plucking it, balling them up, and tossing the pair onto the mountain of socks near their pillows.

"You're not wondering why I'm home?"

Her silence scared him, but he also understood it—one can only take so much worrying until nerves fray and give way to a protective numbness. But now he walked to her, wrapped his arms around her chest from behind, and placed his hands over hers, balling up another pair of socks before dropping it and kissing her neck.

"Leon."

"What?"

"Now's hardly the time."

"I disagree." He swayed, trying to get her to do the same, but her body was stiff, her feet stuck to their bedroom's white carpet. "Don't you want to know why I'm here, instead of at the Executive Estate?"

Her ribs expanded as she tried to fill her lungs with air, but his hold was too tight. She broke out of his grasp and turned to him.

"This cheery mood, when there's nothing but tragedy around us, makes me wonder if you're on a patch. And if you are, I want you to leave. Now."

"I'm not, Del," he said, raising his hands. "I promise. I'm done with those. I have good news, love. In fact, the news we've been waiting for."

She continued to stare up at him, her face an empty square of canvas.

"We've got him," he said, clapping his hands together. "He's visiting his sister tonight, and when he does, he's ours. This will all be over in a handful of hours."

"But are you sure?"

"Sure enough. Our intel is solid. I'm not trying to celebrate before we've earned it, but I had to come here, to tell you in person and see Eva."

Her hands found his face—her eyes searched his own, for what, he wasn't sure—then, finally, she smiled. "That is good news, honey. Everything will go back to normal, and even Amahle will come back."

"That's right." He took off his cap, brought her face to his own, and kissed her so hard that their teeth knocked, causing them to laugh. She lifted her arms in the air, and he slowly pulled her white blouse over her head, kissing her breasts as he bent to unzip her skirt, which fell to the floor.

There she was, radiant in only her underwear, taking her time to unbutton the cuffs of his shirt, sliding shirt then undershirt off, and kneeling to tug his pant legs away. Their history rushed back to him, the love they shared for each other only second to the love they had for their daughter.

"Come here." He took her hand, lifted her up, and lay her on the bed. Slowly, as if time had stopped and the world, with all of its worries and concerns, had faded, he rolled down her underwear, then his own. Sober and still, Curts disappeared into Della, and Della disappeared into him, affirming the foolhardy human belief that one moment of right can erase every wrong.

CHAPTER 41

CASTLE TENMASE, FOR THE MOST PART, HADN'T CHANGED SINCE Candace had been there two days ago. There were more shibs, but they didn't harass her. Sanford picked her up at the gate. He tried to apologize again, for not making her a pass, and he attempted to ask about the other night at Minx, but she stopped him at the top of the hill, the back of her slender hand on his cheek, and said, "I'm just happy we both made it out alive. Let's never talk about it again, okay?"

"Did Ribussce . . ." He paused, but maintained eye contact. "Did he hurt you?"

"What did I just ask you, Sanford? Leave it alone."

She moved to walk down the hill, but he pulled her hand back. "I can't. If you help me help you, everything will be easier. I promise."

"Help you help me?" Candace jerked her hand out of his and rubbed it, as if it burned. "What makes you think I need your help, Sanford? That anything I do has anything to do with you?"

"Because I *care* about you, Candace! I know you're this genius-level, prodigious inventor-in-training, but there's so much—"

"Sanford."

"There's something inside of you that thinks you don't deserve this. That you don't deserve us. I know the feeling. Growing up alone, so alone, and—"

"Sanford."

"But we're here, together, and nothing can stop us, except us, so I just really think you need to—"

"Sanford, STOP!"

His lips slowed, his voice trailed. Then, looking at her, as if caught completely off guard: "What?"

"Sanford, I appreciate how much you care, but the truth is, I just don't feel the same feelings you feel. I thought I did, or that I could, but I don't, and I can't."

He cast his eyes to the sky, then back to her. "I understand, Candy," he said softly. "Growing up in an orphanage like we did makes it almost impossible to accept love, to believe that every person who claims to be there for us won't abandon us. But this"—he reached for her hand, which she now pinned to her side—"is real. *I am real.*"

Despite everything he said, was saying, she knew that none of it was actually real. That from day one, they—he an actor and she a spectator invited onstage—had constructed an artificial world around them that she, in the *actual* real world, didn't have the privilege of inhabiting. Yet he still thought, with every fiber of his being, that they could trade fact for fiction, reality for fantasy. It was frustrating, but also sad.

"Can't you see it?" she said. "Our traumatic pasts aren't strong enough to bond us. And even if they were, I wouldn't want them to. I'm finally and completely focused on the future, and that's where I want to live."

"We can live there together," he said, his voice desperate. "I can see you when others can't, remember? All of you."

"You think you can, but you could never. Not really. You're an orphan like me. Had horrible things happen to you. But your visibility makes it so that you can never truly understand what it is to be me, what it means to be seen through more often than seen whole."

He was finally quiet, and turned his gaze toward the castle below them. The entire exchange, while necessary, had exhausted her, but she was done capitulating for the comfort of others; she was done shrinking.

Sanford gathered the salty air into his lungs, exhaled, and extended a hand toward her. "Friends, then?"

"Friends," she said, smiling with relief.

Abe, white paint and all, greeted her and Sanford when they entered the castle. His voice, the bowing—it was jarring to see him this way after she'd met Brother Blackstone at Tintaba the day before. But life among the DPs was one big act.

"See you later," Sanford said.

She waited for him to disappear, then turned to Abe. "He's coming," she whispered.

He looked over his shoulders. "Sweetsmoke?"

"Yes, at—"

Mr. Tenmase appeared on the landing. "Good morning, Candace."

"Good morning, Mr. Tenmase." She had to force a measure of cheer into her voice. Brother and Sister Blackstone had opened her eyes to too much, and she now regarded her mentor with the same healthy apprehension she had when they first met.

"Abe," Mr. Tenmase said, descending the stairs, "we're skipping herbs and breakfast today." Then he walked out the door.

"Where are we going?" she asked, after catching up to him.

Without stopping, he said, "The observatory."

"For?"

"What are observatories used for, Candace?"

"I understand what they're used for, Mr. Tenmase. I just don't know why we're doing this now. I thought we were continuing with our investigation of past technologies to help build the future. The Big Reset, and all."

The older man laughed. "Fingers reach for the future like trees for the sun, a race against time that can never be won."

Her lack of a response spoke for itself.

They arrived at the unpainted concrete tower. She craned her head back to take in the domed white roof of a building she'd never been in.

"Careful on the stairs," he said as they entered through a creaking gray-green door.

Looking up, she saw a spiral staircase, then ascended one step at a time. By the time she reached the top, she was so dizzy that she had to hold on to the wall.

"Easy now."

"I'm okay." She regained her balance, stood firm on the raw concrete.

The small room was dark, faintly illuminated by the light that coiled its way up from the entrance. But in its center, she could see a telescope—large enough to be terrifying—bolted into the concrete. Her professors at Forestaeum Minor had shown the students designs of telescopes, but never had she seen one in person.

"Close your eyes," Mr. Tenmase said.

"What?"

He pressed a button, a length of the dome's metal panels parted, and white nothingness exploded into the room.

"Excuse me," he said.

She moved aside, and he walked up a step stool to reach the telescope. He angled it, then said, "Ah, there you are."

"What is it?"

"Come and see for yourself."

Not needing the stool, she stooped to bring her eye to the lens and saw the full red-orange dot of Mars. It wasn't her first time viewing the red planet, but to be able to see it during the daytime was thrilling. The white craters, a black slash across its center, as if it were burned; the lighter orange hue of its bottom third. Evidence of a greater hand guiding the universe. Proof that perhaps everything was part of a grander plan.

"The Iron Orb is truly something, isn't it? Supposedly, there's an Invisible colony up there."

"Mars?" She kept her eye on it, imagining people, *her* people, living fully and freely. "Really?"

"Rumor is they made a great exodus when Chief Executive Rhitel came to power and carried out—"

"The Shipping?"

He winced at the sound of it. "Exactly. Some allegedly, avoiding relocation, obtained a ship, when ships still existed, launched into space, and never looked back. I'd actually discussed it with The Chief Executive once, and all he said was 'Good riddance.'"

She wondered if Brother and Sister Blackstone knew about this. *They must.* She'd ask them when she returned to Tintaba. Maybe, she thought, that's where Sweetsmoke had gone, and now he'd somehow found his way back to her, all the way from that tiny dot in the sky, which reminded her . . .

"Mr. Tenmase," she said, pulling away from the telescope, facing him. "I have a question."

"Coincidentally, I have many for you. Go ahead."

"Have you ever heard of someone flickering? Like being a DP and turning see-through, or the opposite?"

He closed his eyes, rocked his head side to side, then opened them. "I haven't, but it's certainly possible. Genetic anomalies are observed in nature all the time and there must always be a first."

This confirmation of her own theory, of Sweetsmoke's being

special, chosen, made her even more impatient to speak with him. To learn about how it felt, what he used it for, if he'd met anyone else in his travels like him. And—

"Which language do we speak, Candace?"

"What do you mean?" The question caught her off guard, but that was part of his game.

"I mean what I asked. Which language do we speak?"

"Northwestern."

"Did we always speak Northwestern?"

"No, of course not. Language changes over time," she replied, annoyed by the question's simplicity.

"True. Except Northwestern is exactly what many people in this part of the world, and others, spoke five hundred years ago. Before Vikench or Vilongo, except it wasn't called 'Northwestern.'"

Okay, now he had her. "What was it called?"

"It doesn't matter. Here's another: Have you ever wondered why you're not allowed to travel freely to other forests or regions?"

She hadn't, and she felt embarrassed. Aside from Castle Tenmase and this week's illegal journeys, the only time she'd ever left Forest Twenty-Six was to go to Forestaeum Minor for a few hours and then return after her classes. For the majority of her life, it had never occurred to her to even *want* to go anywhere else. She shook her head.

"Well, that's by design," he said, walking across the circular floor and leaning against the dome's wall. "There's a reason why things are the way they are. Why you and most Invisibles live in forests and other isolated locales, away from DPs. Why there are only a handful of Invisibles you can look to as hemispheric heroes—Drams Jams Ivy, Stella Irons, Slick Rivers, Mandla. Why every Invisible locale has a reverend and mandated Daily Prayer, yet DPs aren't made to pray. Why the ration trains always have a *bit* less than you actually need. Why—"

"Mr. Tenmase," she said, her mouth dry with fear. "Are you okay?"

"Why you don't know any real history. Why Invisibles are, overall, so much shorter than DPs. Why Invisibles paint themselves." He pushed himself off the curved wall and slowly moved toward her, forcing her to back up. "Why the news you receive is different from ours. Why the world is broken into four different hemispheres. Why—"

His hair fell in sweaty clumps over his forehead. The veins in his neck bulged, his eyes popped out of his skull. He couldn't stop talking, couldn't stop listing off all the questions she'd never asked herself, because before this week, she had done what most people she knew did, what was always easiest: accepted the world as it was.

"I'm scared," she said, barely audible. "Mr. Tenmase, *please*." She was shaking. "Please stop." Candace was taller than he was, yes, but he was physically stronger. His face was red and wet. She'd never seen him sweat before. *Is he on a patch? He must be.*

When he was in front of her and her back was up against the wall, leaving her nowhere else to go, he paused. "Why don't the seasons change, Candace? Centuries ago, you'd walk through a forest and hear beautiful music: chirping, buzzing, scratching, whistling. The true sounds of nature. An organic orchestra."

Chirping, buzzing, scratching, whistling—from what? And what are seasons?

She raised her quivering fists in front of her face, as Rusty had taught Sweetsmoke and Sweetsmoke had taught her. She hadn't come this far for a man to wipe her from the face of the Earth like dust from a table.

"There is a reason why you've never asked these questions. Or, if you did, why you would never find the answers."

He crossed the floor, rested his back against the opposite wall again. "A desperate man is the most dangerous type of man you'll ever meet, Candace. And please listen to me when I say that the men of this hemisphere are more desperate than they've ever been, which is why you need to get as far away from the Forest Region as possible. *Today.*"

"What— What are you talking about?"

Sorrow cast a shadow across his face. "Something that was supposed to happen today didn't. And now I fear your life is in more danger than before."

There was no way she'd leave, not with Sweetsmoke coming tonight. She didn't know what was going on with Mr. Tenmase, or if he knew what she'd been up to, but before she could ask, he wiped his face, smoothed his hair, tucked his white mesh button-up into his pants, and smiled.

"Tennis?"

CHAPTER 42

JOLIS WAS GREETED BY A SEA OF STUNNED FACES IN THE GALLERY
of Rule. He let them take him in—head up, back straight, on his
own two feet. In an instant, their wrinkled brows, opened mouths,
and turned heads narrowed, snarled, and tilted in disgust.

I pity the common man.

He continued to his podium, caught Washington looking at
him with a confused smirk. Grand Magistrate Royger paused, mid-
conversation, and raised his eyebrows.

"What?" Local Manager II Jolis said, underlining his question
with slow, satisfied laughter. "Did you all not think I'd show?"

The men whispered among themselves. Washington said, "It
would have been more noble for you to have not. But then again,
noble has never been a word to describe you, Local Manager II Jolis."

Funny.

Grand Magistrate Royger's eyebrows settled down. "Yes, no one
would blame you for abstaining, Local Manager II Jolis, but I ap-
plaud you for continuing to give it the good fight. Now, since it's our
last day of debates, we will forgo the festivities and appearances
from esteemed guests. Today's topic is culture. A wide-ranging

matter, of course, so I leave it to each of our candidates to state their positions and debate accordingly." He looked from Washington to Jolis. "In a civil manner, of course."

Washington, in a green and yellow pinstripe suit with a disrespectfully loud magenta tie, grinned as he looked down at his podium's display. This poor picture of a man really thought he'd already won—that Jolis, who had worked so hard to get here, would give it all up, just like that.

Blood bolted through the young local manager's veins. His penis was getting harder, but it softened when he remembered that he needed to focus; the more blood in his brain, the better. It *had* to be him. No one else.

"Grand Magistrate Royger," Jolis said. "If I may."

The Grand Magistrate sighed, his old body pushed beyond its limit these past few days. "Yes, Local Manager II Jolis?"

"I understand today's topic is culture, which I promise to touch on. But first, I'd like to share something with the Gallery."

"The Gallery can't afford any more mischief, Local Manager. Please adhere to the topic. It's your turn to begin."

"Grand Magistrate Royger, please," he said, his words firm. "Local Manager IV Washington was given the opportunity yesterday, so it's only right that I receive the same. What is justice if not fairness for all people?"

The old man shook his head, his white wig trembling. "Keep it short."

CHAPTER 43

Brothers and sisters,

   It is said that many, many years ago, before the invention and application of tectonic stabilizers, the
Earth used to experience violent and catastrophic rup-
tures resulting in the deaths of millions, natural dev-
astation, and irreversible shifts in terrain. This is
what occurred in the Gallery today. A true and total
shock wave.

   Like Washington, Local Tormentor II Jolis asked to
share something with the Gallery. Before doing so, he
affirmed the veracity of the illuminations shown the day
prior, and said that he promises to cease his late-
night rendezvous for the good of the hemisphere. I'm
paraphrasing, but his words were to the effect of: "A
man's nether regions have a mind of their own."

   Then, with a quick swipe, he brought up an illumination for all to see. The men immediately shouted their
disbelief and accusations of treason. The illumination

was of Local Manager IV Washington standing with Supreme Advocate Cadorno, Chief Enemy Rhitel's foe in the Southwestern Hemisphere. Jolis went on to twist the knife by describing how Cadorno is "a man who lets his Invisibles run around as though they're of the Dominant Population. They don't even separate their Invisibles from DPs over there, everyone is just 'Southwestern,'" he said, articulating the word with disgust and mocking quotes in the air. The men became further enraged when Jolis said this illicit meeting took place in the Southwestern Hemisphere itself.

Washington, lowered head and sweat dripping down his nose, gripped his podium with both hands. The man was already broken; the men on Jolis's side, and even many on Washington's, looked to be on the verge of walking down their respective aisles and strangling Local Manager IV Washington. I tell you, we DPs are addicted to chaos like a child to candy.

And Jolis, being the man he is, didn't stop. He reveled as he showed another illumination, of Washington with Head Rector Yaima, in a Northeastern cornfield. Another, of Washington and Key Defender Laanm, bathing together in some Southeastern ocean, surrounded by charming green mountains.

A coup, Jolis called it. Years in the making, though he didn't accuse Washington of killing the Chief Enemy, because "murder is for men." His opponent, words drenched in pain, pleaded for a chance to explain. He didn't deny the illuminations, and before he could speak another word, the mob of faceless men began screaming, "HANG HIM! HANG HIM! HANG HIM!"

Fighting to be heard above the noise, Washington

cried, "I just did what I thought was best for the hemisphere! Making plans for trade. Opening our economy so that we can flourish to our full capacity." He said that he'd planned to send a memo to Chief Enemy Rhitel, but first wanted to have everything in order.

Grand Magistrate Royger banged his mallet three times, concluded the debate, and instructed the men to be ready to cast their ballots tomorrow. Jolis, his victory all but assured, told the men of rule that "Hemispheric Guard Director Curts will bring our Invisible perpetrator to justice before the day is up, and I will be there, right with him, when he does!"

Brothers and sisters, I know I am not privy to all your plans, but I pray you've prepared for this. Come tomorrow, our hemisphere will be in the hands of a man who is cunning, calculated, and, most dangerous of all, creative. A vicious visionary determined to make history, whose unwavering focus is the accumulation of power and the decimation of all dignity.

I fear for what's to come.

May the rebellion stay happy,
Brother Lesbod

CHAPTER 44

"ROGER," CURTS SAID, STANDING AT THE THRESHOLD OF THE older man's drawing room.

The Great Engineer remained seated on the couch. Loose strands of black hair draped his face, which he cradled with one hand. "To what do I owe this pleasure, Leon?" he asked, fingers muffling his voice.

Curts scanned the room. Once he confirmed they were alone, he moved toward Croger and sat in his armchair. "Where's your help?"

"A good question. Abe's gone. Where to, I'm not sure. But he did find it fitting to leave me with this." He raised his head, hair parting to reveal a red welt still growing on the side of his forehead, crusted blood bordering his bottom lip.

"*Abraham* did this? I'll alert the men outside and make sure they locate him before he goes too far." The Director dug his hand into his pocket, finding his earsphere, but Croger waved him away.

"No bother, Leon. He won't be coming back, of that I'm sure."

Croger heaved himself off the couch and walked across the room. When he returned, he held a small white silicone instrument, a single ball bearing inserted into the tip, reflecting a distorted image of the room as he sat down.

"I've never seen a white celgen," Curts said.

"An early model." Croger moved his thumb along the bottom, then placed the tip to his wound. "But it works just as well as the black ones the State has. If you can believe it, the only difference is the color. Chief Executive Rhitel, always preoccupied with design details, requested the change. A real showman."

"I heard Jolis was successful today," Curts said, picking a few pieces of dust from his pants.

The Great Inventor, who seemed to have aged in the twenty-four hours since Curts had last seen him, removed the celgen from his forehead, his skin now as new and untouched as it had been before whatever scuffle happened with his servant. He set the device down and then looked at the Director. "All thanks to you." Croger shook Curts's knee. "Not having you as an ally would have killed him."

"All's well that ends well, as the saying goes."

The older man laughed. "At the end of time, all man will have is a pile of dirt and a pocketful of clichés."

"Maybe so," Curts said, nodding. "Except..." He stared at Croger, took a deep breath in, held it, then let it out. "I can't get rid of a question that has been eating me from the inside out."

Croger poured a cup of yellow herbs and handed it to Curts before doing the same for himself. "Those are the only questions that are ever truly worth it. But what's this one, if I may ask?"

Curts felt the lukewarm cup and set it down without taking a sip. "Even if you won't admit it, and even if I can't fully grasp it, we both know you played a significant role in everything that's happened. So my question is: Why do *you*, of all people, get to walk away unscathed?"

"I'd hardly call this unscathed." The Chief Architect leaned back, lips arcing upward, until he winced in pain. He brought the celgen to his lips. After a minute, they were as good as new. Then, "I've been honest with you from the start, Leon."

The fact that Croger was still treating him as some simpleton enraged Curts, but he had to remain calm. If he lost his nerve now, he would lose all of the momentum he'd gained. "I disagree," he said. "For one, that tracking device I brought up yesterday . . . it was more than a rumor, wasn't it?"

"What makes you think that?"

"Call it a hunch. It's just hard for me to believe that you can create *that*"—he pointed to the celgen—"the earsphere in my pocket, trains that cover hundreds of kilometers in minutes, the patches that intoxicate but never kill, and a heaping number of other inventions by which this great hemisphere functions, but not a way to track Invisibles unless they're wearing a piece of metal around their necks."

"It's funny. For some reason, Abe thought the same thing. Hence that lump. He swore, like you, that I had a way to track people like him, and he wanted me to find your Shanu. To tell the truth, the betrayal, after all these years with him, stung. But"—he looked up at the ceiling, shrugged—"tensions are high. And, as Shrift tells us, 'Only a taut string makes music.'"

Curts leaned toward him, gripping the chair's arm even tighter. "Do you take me for an idiot, Croger?"

"I take a man for the man he is, Leon. No more, no less."

"Then we're on the same page. You sit here," he said, waving his hand in front of Croger, "in your castle and believe you're conduct-ing an orchestra of fools. But I've snatched the baton now, and you're alone, in a theater of one."

High-pitched laughter flew out of Croger's mouth, pounding Curts in the face. "Quite poetic, Leon. Quite poetic indeed! But for all you think you know, you don't know much. The music you believe I'm creating has been playing before either of us was alive, and it will continue long after we're gone. Neither of us could stop it, even if we wanted to, but we *can* harness it for a while," he said, eyes aflame with passion. "When you understand that, you'll finally be free of everything that plagues you, of all that tells you you're not enough."

Enough of the verbal acrobatics. Curts had him beat, and he knew it. The Director grabbed his earsphere, inserted it into his ear, and said, "It's time. Second-floor drawing room."

"Why didn't you arrest Washington?" Croger asked. "You're just going to let Shanu get away?"

Curts, done with the back-and-forth, only stood there as four guards arrived. Without a word, Croger sighed and followed them out of the castle.

Night was fanning out all around them, but the sky still held a purple-blue hue. Once Croger was inside the train that awaited them, Curts entered and closed the door, leaving the guards in front of the gate.

"Hemispheric Guard Deputy Director," Croger said, finding Lucretia's face at the opposite end of the train.

"Director of Progress," she replied.

He bowed toward her. "I gave up that title years ago, but thank you."

Curts swiped, tapped a wall twice, then the sounds of a serene, old-world string symphony filled the train. Grinning at Croger, he said, "Strip."

"Strip?"

"Please help him, Captain," Curts said.

Captain Kandolo, his presence only known through his footsteps, jerked Croger's arms back, tore off his shirt, then yanked off his pants and underwear, leaving him with only his wire-frame glasses. His eyes shifted frantically behind them. Finally, something was beginning to break in The Great Engineer. A man, like so many others, who needed to learn who Curts was.

"You have me, Leon. Is this all necessary? I mean, what are you—"

"The special uniform, Captain," Curts said, "for this special person."

A compartment on the far end of the train opened up, then a cloak made of heavy metal mesh floated toward them before dropping to the floor with a clanking *thud.* "Put this on," Curts instructed Croger.

"I won't. This is medieval and entirely uncalled for."

"Captain."

Captain Kandolo grunted as he picked up the cloak, raising it high, as if it were a sheet, then, with one final effort, heaved it onto Croger, wrenched his head through the opening, and draped the bulky hood over his dome. The Chief Architect, the man who thought he was the smartest person to ever exist, collapsed onto all fours, trying, and failing, to raise his head.

"Look at me," Curts commanded, but the older man physically couldn't. Captain Kandolo gripped his crown, cupped his chin, and snapped his whole head upward.

"I want you to remember this for the rest of your life, Croger," Curts said. "How it feels to be looking up instead of down. All of that weight upon your body. The inescapable helplessness."

He continued staring down into Croger's unmoving eyes a moment longer, then nodded to Lucretia and moved toward the door. But before he walked out, he swiped the wall, tapped once, twice, and only then did the music stop; the sound of those sweet, peace-inducing instruments replaced with the strained, staccato breathing of a man, and nothing more.

CHAPTER 45

SWEETMINT DID A QUICK INSPECTION OF THE CABIN. NO DIRT ON the wooden floor. No dust on the mattresses, couch, or trunk. Her few plates, knives, forks, spoons, bowls, and cups were neatly stacked to the right of the sink. No grime on the windows on the far wall, above the sink, or above the couch. "Clean enough," she declared to herself. Time to get to work.

After three swipes and two taps, she selected a music program that played hemisphere-sanctioned musicians. Stella Irons was on, singing a tribute to Chief Executive Rhitel. She was tempted to turn it off, but knew it wouldn't last much longer.

Knock knock.

Already smelling Darksap, she didn't get her hopes up for Sweetsmoke. But when she opened the door, her pulse jumped all the same.

"Hello," she said, smiling.

"Hello," he replied, also smiling.

They stood there, unsure of what to do, but then he leaned forward, she leaned forward, and they kissed. Something still new for the both of them, yes, but also something, at least for her, that felt as if it never could, or would, get old.

"I could get used to that," he said, still standing in the doorway, but already holding her hand. "Cooking dinner?"

"Yes." She badly wanted to pull him over the threshold, sit him down, and tell him about her day and her brother's upcoming visit, pausing every few moments to find his left cheek with her lips, then his right, then his forehead, then his chin. But she couldn't. At least, not yet. Still, she didn't want to hurt his feelings. "But I'm actually not feeling too well."

"Oh." He placed his palm on her forehead, pressed it to her neck. "You're not too warm, but what can I do?"

"Nothing," she said, covering his hand with hers, then kissing it. "I just want to make some food and rest."

"Okay." His lips found hers again, and he held them there, soft skin on soft skin. Then, "Oh. I have something for you, though. Something that might make you feel better. Do you want it now?"

She had to get back to cooking, but what was another minute? "*Okay*. Fine."

"Mintsap."

"Mintsap?"

"Mintsap."

"And what's that?"

"The name I'm proposing for our garden. But only if you like it." She felt his hand moisten. "What do you think? Of course, if it's too much, and—"

"I think," she said, interjecting, "that it couldn't be more perfect, Dapp. Seriously. Mintsap Garden. The place where delicious goes to grow."

He laughed. "If you're feeling better tomorrow, I'll be there, before Daily Prayer, tending to the vegetables. Meet me?"

"I'll be there."

He held on to her, not wanting to let go. His rumoya throbbed with a joy that could only rival her own. But then he kissed her once more, and left before everything they were feeling made it impossible.

Okay, time to focus. Back at the sink, she inspected the vegetables Freshpine had given her. She rustled in a drawer until she found the peeler, then gently removed their rough exteriors. Sweetsmoke, the chef that he was, would've scolded her for doing so. "The richness is in the skin," he'd often say. But that'd make it harder to cook, and she wasn't sure how much time she had.

She grabbed her sole pot from beneath the sink, filled it with water, placed it on the rarely used two-burner stove, and ignited the biogas. A sprinkle of salt in the boiling pot.

Carefully, she removed her one sharp knife, wrapped in white canvas, from the drawer. Sweetsmoke *loved* this knife. He'd laugh and kiss it, cautioning her against ever using it unless she absolutely needed to, "because it's sharper than any of those State-issued saws and axes the dippies make in the I&S." And it was true. She'd seen him go behind the cabin and spend hours, with only a flat pitrock on top of a stump, dragging that knife back and forth with a hypnotic rhythm.

She sunk it into the hard flesh of the squash, the skin easily splitting apart. Then she turned her attention to the carrots, potatoes, and beets. She dropped them all into the pot with the beans. A new song was on, one by Stella Irons she hadn't heard before, but she quickly found the flow, humming along. Life was hard, yes, but it could also be good. So, so good.

As the vegetables boiled, she crushed cloves of garlic and diced two onions before tossing them into the pan she'd placed on the second burner, already hot with pumpkin seed oil. The music, paired with the smell of home cooking, made the cabin feel like it always had when Sweetsmoke was there, and it pulled her toward an earlier time, but she resisted, plunging herself back into the present. Why do we race to be anywhere but here?

She dropped a fistful of peppercorns into a mortar made of white fingerwood, a gift from Rusty, and, with a matching pestle, ground them into a fine powder that she then spread over the plates of steaming food. Finally, she filled two glasses with mixed juice Freshpine had given her, placed everything on the table, and took a step back. Hands on her hips, she was proud of what she'd made.

Oh. She went to the trunk, took out a round piece of hardsplit wood, and held it up to the light. On it was a portrait, carved by her brother, of the two of them together. When he'd given it to her four years ago, she instantly knew it was the truest depiction of them that there ever was, even though their physical features were only loose approximations. But their shared essence was there. He, more than anyone else, saw her. And she, more than anyone else, saw him. She placed it at the center of the table, and then, yes then, everything was perfect.

The Three Teachers must have been out for some time now. She gripped the doorknob to go out and check. But before she could pull it, there was a soft hand over her mouth—a warm, naked chest against her back.

"Don't scream." *A man.*

She didn't. But she did extend her lower jaw as widely as possible, and bit down on his index finger. There was no yelling. No cursing. Just the immediate snapping back of her neck as he grabbed a fistful of her hair, the roots threatening to tear if he pulled any harder.

"It's me," he said, his bare chest still pressed to her back, a heart *thump-thump*ing so strongly she couldn't tell whether it was hers or his.

Me who? Definitely not Sweetsmoke.

"Let me go!"

"Not until you calm down."

"Why can't I smell you?" she said, clawing at his grip. "Why are your hands so soft? Why were you hiding? Why can't I feel your rumoya? *Who are you?*"

He released her, and her head fell forward so fast that she almost banged it against the sink. Massaging the pain out of her neck, she turned around and sniffed, still smelling nothing. The voice *did* sound like Sweetsmoke. But everything else? Everything else was strange and conflicting.

The illuminated display appeared on the wall near the window in front of her. He tapped twice, and the music was off.

"None of that matters. But it is me, Little Me."

Those two words.

"Is it really you?"

"Who else would it be?"

She threw her arms around his neck, which wasn't as firm and powerful as she remembered. Her head against his chest, his heart slowed to a less frantic rhythm, and she allowed herself to lie there for a second. But she couldn't ignore the fact that his arms, instead of lifting and curling themselves around her, remained stuck to his sides.

Then, as if he had reached a time limit in his head, he removed her arms, his movements as stiff as a tree branch, and held her in front of him. "That's enough."

"Enough?" She laughed. "Sweetsmoke, it's been years. Sit. I made you dinner. And Freshpine gave me juice. It's all here, for you."

"I watched you cook. The music—you would have heard me if it hadn't been so loud. And Darksap." His voice grew even colder. "I'm disappointed by your lack of focus."

"Let's sit and eat. Then you can tell me about where you've been, and I can tell you everything I've been up to."

"I don't care to know. And I'm not staying long. I just came to see you one last time."

No. No, no, no, no. None of this was going as planned. This was her brother, but also not her brother. Three years wasn't a day, but it also wasn't a decade. *What had happened to him?*

"I spoke to Audrey and Andrew," she said, not knowing what else to do. "They told me about the flickering . . . Is that why you left? It came back?"

"None of that matters."

"Sweetsmoke," she whispered, stepping toward him. "Are you Williams Washington, the politician? Andrew told me about your nickname, and—" But she stopped when she realized how silent, how completely still he was.

"That's also not your concern, Little Me. At all. I'm here because everything as you know it—this forest, this region, this hemisphere, this world—is all going to change, and there's no going back. I came to make sure you're ready. But based on what I've just seen, you obviously aren't."

Numbness consumed her. Whole. One second she was leaning on a wooden chair for support, feeling like someone was ramming their palm into her forehead, then she'd fallen into the chair without even realizing it. Fully present one moment, startlingly absent the next.

"I've done so much to find and save you." Her eyes were focused on her hands, flat on the table. "I tried to get help from Mr. Tenmase, my employer. I went to Minx." She winced, remembering Ribussce—his hands on her, his breath, the damp rotting smell of tabacum and fermented grains twisting her stomach into itself. "I went to upcity Rhitelville, almost got brutalized by a group of dippies." She looked up at him, his rumoya as nonexistent as his smell. "I did all of this. For you. And now, after all these years, here you are, but . . ." Her voice became small. "Here you aren't."

Silence. The only sign that he was still there was the long intake of air before an equally long and slow release. "That was all pretty stupid, Little Me. Still, it shows you're strong. You'll need that for what comes next."

"I need you," she whispered, feeling like the little girl stumbling with her brother in the dark. But at least they had been stumbling together.

"I finally have power," he said, walking around the living room. "*Real* power. And I'm going to use it to change the world. It will be hard for everyone at first. But it will be worth it."

He spoke as if she weren't even there. Her brother had been hollowed out, like a tree trunk. He'd always told her not to be soft with sharp people. But now, she realized, *he* was one of those sharp people.

"Can we please just eat? I promise I won't ask you any more questions. You don't have to explain anything. All I want is to share a meal with you, even if it's for the last time. Even if we just sit here, in silence. It's been so—"

"*Sh.*"

"What?"

"You don't hear that?"

She listened for a moment, but heard nothing beyond light wind passing through the trees. "No, what is it?"

"Your senses have dulled," he said, his displeasure plain. "The station. A train has just pulled in, and men, many of them, are walking down the steps."

"So? That's what happens at a station. People come and go."

"Yes, but these men are headed here."

"*Here?*" She stood, opened the door, and listened. Faint footsteps, twigs snapping beneath boots, the sounds getting louder with each second. "Who are they? And why are they coming here?"

"For me. Be strong, Little Me. And trust no one."

His arm grazed her shoulder as he left into the night, and she stood there, peering into the dark forest in front of her, wondering if he had ever been there at all or if she'd only imagined it.

Back inside, she stared at the vegetables, their combined aroma already spread throughout the cabin, and pictured her hands latching on to the sides of the plate, raising it above her head, like Mandla holding his golden championship trophy to an crowd's unrelenting applause, and bringing it down onto the table with all her strength.

But she wouldn't throw the plate. She wouldn't cry. She wouldn't scream. Sitting there, she felt nothing. Now she was hollow, too.

The sound of boots and broken twigs grew louder. The smell of men, their bodies thick with sweat and excitement, became denser. Then they were at her door, knocking hard enough to shake the entire cabin.

"We know he's in there, Candace," a man said. The same man who, only days prior, had condemned her brother to death—who, on an empty train, spoke to her in her people's forbidden tongue. Hemispheric Guard Director Curts.

"Come out with your hands up and this will be over before it starts. There's no need for anyone to get hurt."

No need for anyone to get hurt? That almost jolted her from her numbed state. It almost made her laugh. *Hurt?* There was never a time that she lived without it.

"Come in," she said.

"If either of you attacks us," Hemispheric Guard Director Curts said. "We'll be forced to shoot."

"I won't."

The knob turned, the door swung open, and standing there were two shibs dressed in thick red and black uniforms she'd never seen before, with black helmets and visors, gold weapons of steel in their hands pointed at her.

"There's only the girl," one of them said.

"Is she armed?" Hemispheric Guard Director Curts asked them from behind.

"No," the other replied.

They didn't lower their weapons, but they did part, bringing Hemispheric Guard Director Curts into view. His sunken eyes and protruding cheekbones made him look more worn down than the last time she'd seen him. He entered the cabin, removed his cap, and swung his head left and right and left and right, a dried leaf *just* before it falls from a branch.

"He's not here," she said.

"Where is he?" he asked, eyes as hard as stone.

"I don't know."

He waved more men inside, four total, all dressed alike and holding weapons. They searched the cabin in a matter of seconds, finding nothing. "Tell the others to continue scanning the perimeter," he ordered. "He can't be too far."

Hemispheric Guard Director Curts looked at the food, the juice, her. "All of this goes away if you tell us where he is, Candace. Everything will go back to normal. I promise."

"Can't you see?" she said, eyes on the plate below her. "There is no going back. And nothing is normal."

He sat down next to her. "None of this food has been touched, but I know he was here. Perhaps it wasn't the reunion you'd anticipated." He paused, waiting for her to speak, but she didn't.

"He abandoned you, Candace. Left you, a girl who was already without parents, without a big brother. You've had to work hard to make something of yourself, which you have, despite the odds. That is a miracle, an umjzeh. Do the right thing, not only for the hemisphere, but also for your forest, for yourself."

A shib entered. "He's nowhere to be found, sir. But both Anna Franklin and Local Manager II Jolis are outside, waiting."

Though his hands were flat on the table, his leg was springing up and down, shaking the plates, glasses, and wooden portrait of her and Sweetsmoke.

"What do you want me to tell them, sir?" the shib asked.

"Leave," he ordered. "Everyone out. And close the door."

The shibs did as they were told, leaving only the two of them inside. She knew that anything was possible, but she wasn't afraid. What was the worst he could do? Threaten her? Bring his fist to her face? He was going to walk away empty-handed, and that was that.

She watched him grab the portrait from the table, feeling nothing. He rubbed his thin, twig-like fingers across their faces, the cogs obviously turning in his head.

"It didn't have to be this way," he said. "You were meant for more. An Invisible who had a way out and would serve as an example for others. But now it's too late."

Finally, we agree on something.

He set the portrait down and turned to her. "Get up."

She stood, ready for anything. He grabbed her arm, pushed her toward the door, and they crossed the threshold. Anna Franklin was outside, and her captureman held a piece of capglass toward her, a blinding light positioned above it. The reporter was smaller in person than Sweetmint had imagined, but just as fierce and focused as she seemed on the display. Sweetmint looked away and noticed that clean-shaven politician, whom the Children of Slim called "Local Tormentor II Jolis," smirking. A dozen or so shibs, all with those same gold weapons, stood in the background, a cluster of menacing trees.

"Stephan," Hemispheric Guard Director Curts said. She felt him tense, his pulse rising. Something about this man triggered him, but she couldn't tell what it was.

The politician grabbed Hemispheric Guard Director Curts's free hand. "Leon. I'd told everyone in the Gallery that justice would be served, and when Anna alerted me to where she was heading, I immediately hopped on a train. There was no way I could miss the opportunity to witness it firsthand. I hope you don't mind."

"No, of course not. But you really shouldn't be traveling without guards." His body relaxed a bit. "You're the most sought-after man in the hemisphere, after all."

The politician winked. "It won't happen again, Director."

Despite the smiling and winking, the politician's unyielding menace was clear to her—that he would do whatever it took to ensure her people were subjugated to a historic degree. If her brother, disguised as Washington, didn't win, the Children of Slim would take care of him. *So let him smile for now, while he still can.*

Hemispheric Guard Director Curts gripped her arm tighter and faced the capglass. "Live?"

"Live," Anna Franklin confirmed.

"My dear Northwesterners," Hemispheric Guard Director Curts began, "after a painstaking and thorough search, it is my honor to tell you that justice has been served. I won't stand here and say we've captured Shanu, the Invisible, because we haven't. Our intelligence tells us that he is in another hemisphere that we're still negotiating a hemispheric extradition with. But what I have here"—he yanked her forward, bringing her closer to the capglass—"is his younger sister and accomplice, Candace."

What?

"This young woman," Hemispheric Guard Director Curts continued, "not only confessed to serving as the actual mastermind of the plot to murder Chief Executive Rhitel, may the Holy Father bless his soul, but also to gaining the confidence of former Director of Progress Croger Tenmase by way of an apprenticeship, to throw us off her brother's trail. It saddens me to admit this," he said, looking at the ground, "but she even persuaded The Great Inventor to aid her, turning him into an enemy of this great hemisphere. He's currently being held at His Executive's Prison."

The regional reporter shook her head in what looked like shame. Local Manager II Jolis's overjoyed expression disappeared. There was no point in fighting any of this. Sweetmint's word was the word of one—an Invisible woman's, at that. Millions of North-westerners needed Invisible blood to wash themselves of the world they created. Yes, she saw that now, but what did sight matter in a world that was committed to remaining blind?

Local Manager II Jolis, his smile back, grabbed her other arm—something intimate about the softness of his hand, the way it curved around her bicep—as he joined her and Hemispheric Guard Director Curts in front of the capglass. "Our hemisphere has been harmed, but now is the time for healing. Hemispheric Guard Direc-tor Curts," the politician said, angling his face toward him. "I be-lieved in you from the beginning. You, who have always been a steadfast protector of law and order, of honesty and integrity, have proven to everyone today that we are far stronger than any tragedy, and that safety, prosperity, and morality will always reign supreme. Thank you for restoring the balance."

A lie is not a thing that survives on its own. Like a sapling, it needs to be sustained and cultivated, and these two men, with a true understanding of how the world works, weren't shaping real-ity, but creating it right in front of her eyes. One word at a time. She was surprised to find part of herself jealous of them, of their capac-ity for creation, for incredible invention.

"Thank you, Local Manager II Jolis," Hemispheric Guard Direc-tor Curts said, meeting his gaze. He faced the capglass again. "And thank you, my fellow Northwesterners. But our work isn't done. We are going to prosecute this woman to the full extent of the law. To-night. Let order prevail."

Everyone parted. Hemispheric Guard Director Curts and the politician escorted Sweetmint down the damp dark path—away from her home and all the bright possibility it'd held only hours ago. She turned around, in the direction of Mintsap Garden, and—

Heavy footsteps, a shout, a piece of metal slicing through skin and bone, agony made audible, then—*BANG!, BANG!, BANG!*—a burst of light, like the beginning of a new day—and finally, a body thudding to the ground.

Shibs surrounded her, Hemispheric Guard Director Curts, and Local Manager II Jolis. "All clear?" Hemispheric Guard Director Curts asked.

"Clear, sir," a shib in front of them replied, his fellow shib screaming. "But this vizzer sunk an axe in Milford."

"Apply a celgen and get on with it. Let's keep moving."

When they came to the dirt-covered body, she escaped from the men's hands and threw herself on Darksap. She felt two large holes in his chest, one in his forehead, trying to make sense of the impossible. A bloody axe still rested in his hand. She lay there on top of him, unable to breathe, unable to cry, unable to scream. *How?* If she didn't move, maybe time would freeze and rewind, all the way back to before she ever existed, before people walked the Earth. Anything before now, before this. She could still feel his lips pressed against hers, hear his laughter bouncing in her ear, smell his syrupy, woodsy smell—sense his hunger for her, all of her, and hers for him, all of him. A longing she had finally, after everything, embraced, because he saw her the way she wanted to see herself. Because he taught her that it was okay to just be. Because he loved her. *Why?*

It all rushed toward her then. The men shouting. Darksap's family screaming for him as shibs held them back. Two shibs pulled her up, dragging her by her arms as her feet drew lines in the soft dirt, no sound escaping her throat, her eyes opened, unblinking.

Once there was more distance between her and the smell of fire, sulfur, and freshly burnt skin, she smelled Rusty close to the path—prayed he wouldn't face the same fate as Darksap. But when Hemispheric Guard Director Curts, now walking alongside the shibs that held her, stopped and said, "Good work, Captain Kandolo," she dropped to the ground. Somehow, someway, Rusty had assisted this man in her capture, which meant he'd also betrayed Sweetsmoke— the one he had called a son for so long, whom he swore to protect at all costs. This, finally, forced the pain up and out of her body.

"Rusty!" she wailed, the shibs trying, and failing, to get a grip on her writhing body. The sound, as if her very heart were being cut out, was coming from her mouth, but she didn't recognize it.

"Rusty!" she shouted again. Freshpine, the children, and others with cabins along Softstone Path emerged from their homes, choosing curiosity over safety. Their scents flooded her nose as a feeling without a name consumed her.

"Rusty!"

"Grab her by her ankles and wrists," Hemispheric Guard Director Curts ordered. The bright light of Anna Franklin's captureman's capglass was back on her. Her body, as if it were a heavy sack of onions, was carried by four struggling shibs toward the main square.

She screamed, and screamed, and screamed until her throat was torn up and her face was soaked with sweat and tears. A crowd poured into the square from its two main paths, fighting to see what in the Holy Father's hemisphere was happening. And as the shibs brought her now-limp body up the platform and through the open door of the waiting train, she could only whisper the same question over, and over, and over again:

"Rusty . . . Rusty, how could you?"

CHAPTER 46

THE GUARDS HAD SAT HER IN THE CENTER OF THE TRAIN, BUT THE girl asked if she could sit in the back. There was nowhere to run, so Curts said yes and watched her make her way to the rear, one hand on a seat back the whole way, as if she'd crumple without the support.

Fifteen minutes to the Gallery of Rule. He was tempted to close his eyes, rest his head against the soft cushion, maybe even permit himself a few minutes of sleep, but his earsphere vibrated. A message from Del congratulating him, saying she knew he would do it all along.

He was safe. His family was safe. But his soul, if it even existed, was another matter. He'd made a choice, and there was no turning back; he'd traded an innocent young woman's life for his own, as well as for the exacting of revenge. Because regardless of what he'd just said on the news, no one would ever find Shanu after he dealt with him, and the hemisphere only needed to be sated and distracted. In time, they would move on, as they always did, selectively choosing to disregard the history that didn't serve, entertain, or soothe them. Still, he felt something somber pulling at him, tried his best to calculate the sum of a man beyond his actions, but he failed.

"Sir?" a guard said.

He looked up, met the young man's eyes. "Yes?"

"I said we're almost there, sir. What are our orders?"

The Director stretched his neck to the side to make sure that Candace was still there. The colors of her dirt-covered head registered orange-yellow through his didanlenses as she continued to face the darkness outside the window. Her coolness disturbed him, but it was better than the bloodcurdling raving she had done from the forest to the train. Just the thought of that sound—like a child was being ripped from her stomach—made chills run up and down his spine. He shouldn't have acknowledged Captain Kandolo.

"Secure the perimeter," he instructed the guard. "I'll bring her through the Sambrick Corridor. Two of you walk in front of us, two trail. Understood?"

"Yes, sir."

The trained pulled into Gallery Station, the private platform reserved for men of rule who wanted to avoid public appearances at all costs. With a nod to the guard he'd just spoken to, the girl was brought to him. Two armed guards led them through the Sambrick Corridor—a hidden series of well-lit hallways with locked doors at every turn, ensuring that if the wrong person got inside, they couldn't escape—and two guards followed.

She didn't make a fuss. No sounds, no stares, no slow-footed attempts to stall her fate. Her back, like one of the torture hooks guards had liked to use before Curts outlawed them, remained curved for the duration of the short journey to the antechamber.

"Leave us here," he ordered the guards when they arrived in the darkened room. The only light came from a faint white strip above the door in front of them and one at the other end of the antechamber.

The young guard from the train looked to the others, then at Curts, shaking his head. "I don't think that's a good idea, sir. If she tries to run, or, worse, attempts to—" He stopped speaking when he noticed the Director's blank stare, and then he left with the others; the hard soles of their boots hammering against the hardwood. It was now just Curts and Candace.

He wasn't sure what to say. His impulse was to give her some words of hope. But that would be cruel. He wanted to justify himself to her, to justify himself to himself. But maybe that, too, would be more bruise than balm. This seemed to take a courage that he didn't have—it was far easier to slaughter a faceless mass than murder an individual looking you in the eye.

Blame your brother. He's the reason you're here.

"Do you believe in the Holy Father, Hemispheric Guard Director Curts?" she asked, her back to him as she stood in front of the door to the Gallery.

"Why?"

"It's just a question."

It caught him off guard. He realized, then, that he hadn't asked himself that question in years. At least, not in a meaningful way. After all that had happened, Curts prayed that he wasn't real. An endless nothingness was preferable to anyone or anything that would hold him accountable for what he had done and was about to do.

"I don't know," he said, his voice thin.

"Me neither. At least, not anymore." She paused. "So what happens when we die?"

"I don't know that, either."

"You sure don't know a lot for a man who just killed me."

"I—"

She faced him. He knew she had nothing to lose, and that terrified him most.

"Do you have children, Hemispheric Guard Director Curts?"

"One. A daughter."

"After tonight, you'll see my face in hers. This moment will replay in your mind like a song you can't get rid of." She moved closer to him, their noses touching, a sweet smell rising into his nostrils. "I see you, wandering this world in search of purpose. Lashing out, like a child, because you haven't found it. Violence disguised as law, evil posing as religion, obscenity dressed up as order. After all these years, I finally see it."

"I'm—I'm sorry, Candace."

He swore she smiled then, which made him shudder. "Me too. Because sometimes the sins of the family become our own, the consequences unseen until it's too late." She turned her back to him. "I'm ready."

He joined her at the door, filled his lungs with air, then pushed it open. Light penetrated the antechamber, sound waged a total assault.

Curts lowered his forearm, turned to Candace, and saw her staring ahead, emotionless. She stepped forward. He followed. Grand Magistrate Royger and his twelve auxiliary magistrates sat on the elevated bench at the front of the room. The crowd of Northwesterners a shifting nonhuman organism made of hundreds of heads, hands, and legs.

Why are civilians here?

The plan was for Anna Franklin and her captureman, who stood to the left below the magistrates' bench, to broadcast the proceedings across the NWN, both restricted and unrestricted. But not for regular Northwesterners to be present. He hadn't approved this.

The girl continued to the center of the floor, stopping behind a wooden podium on the left, as the sounds of the room threatened to swallow them both.

He swung his head and settled his eyes on the ninety-nine local managers and directors in the ascending rows behind where he and

Candace stood. They screamed as violently as the crowd, tendons bulging at their necks, faces bloody sunsets, foamy spit gathered at the corners of their mouths. Curts looked to Candace again, and there she stood, unfazed, except now her back was as straight as the pillars outside of the Gallery, head held high.

"Enough!" Grand Magistrate Royger shouted, banging his heavy mallet once, twice, three times, silencing the hysterical horde. "At the ever-emphatic request of Local Manager II Jolis, and in the spirit of transparency and hemispheric healing, I have allowed you"—the Grand Magistrate pointed his mallet in the direction of the civilians, who were dressed casually as if going for a walk in Rhitel Park—"to bear witness to the delivery of justice this evening, but I will not permit a riot.

"We are here tonight to give due process to this young woman"—he looked down at Candace—"who is accused of aiding her brother, Shanu, in the murder of Chief Executive Rhitel, may the Holy Father bless his soul. As we all know, Hemispheric Guard Director Curts recently obtained a confession from her, but I see fit to adjudicate on behalf of the hemisphere's highest court, ensuring that she, like any other Northwesterner, receives a fair trial, and thus, a fair sentencing."

For a second, Curts permitted himself to believe those words— that the girl's death wasn't certain; that she, like any Dominant man or woman, would receive a fair trial. But when he looked around the room, he knew. As with all things in this great hemisphere, delusion was the most dominant denomination.

"Now," Grand Magistrate Royger said. "Candace, my aim is to give you a chance to speak for yourself so that we can better understand the claims brought against you by the hemisphere and the circumstances that have placed you here this evening. Do you understand?"

"Yes."

"Yes, *Grand Magistrate*."

"Yes, Grand Magistrate," she repeated.

"Good. To begin, how do you plead to the charge of gaining access to Croger Tenmase, by way of an apprenticeship, in order to hinder Hemispheric Guard Director Curts's pursuit of your brother?"

The entire room was silent. Curts, realizing he was holding his breath, assumed everyone else was doing the same.

Candace, in a clear, resonant voice, said, "Guilty."

A collective gasp.

The Grand Magistrate nodded. "And how do you plead to the charge of helping your brother flee the hemisphere?"

"Guilty."

Curts scanned the room, saw shock give way to that same compulsion to kill that the people had moments ago.

"And finally," Grand Magistrate Royger said, no discernable change in his even tone. "How do you plead to the charge of assisting in the murder of Chief Executive Rhitel, may the Holy Father bless his soul?"

Why was she doing this? It's as if she wants to die. Curts, in that moment, never hated himself more. Tears worked their way out of his eyes, and he quickly wiped them away so no one could ever accuse him of being a sympathizer. Shanu, that callous subhuman, would soon pay. And it was Curts who was set to collect.

Someone coughed, breaking up the deadening silence.

Candace looked away from where the magistrates sat and faced the men behind her. Slowly, she turned to the crowd on the left side of the Gallery. Just that one look from her set them ablaze. Guards rushed to make sure that none of these upstanding hemispherians mobbed her. But she didn't avert her eyes as she said, "Guil-ty."

A waterfall of sweaty and suited men streamed down their wooden rows toward her. In the surge, Curts saw Jolis staring down onto the scene with a serene expression, stirring his own yearning for violence.

"TEAR HER TO BITS!" a man shouted.

"KILL THE VIZZER!" a woman called.

"CHOP HER HEAD OFF!" a child screamed.

The guards, working to maintain order with nothing more than rope whips and the authority of the hemisphere, were about to be overcome. Curts just stood there. Someone, maybe Lucretia, ordered the golden guards onto the floor, and only when the crowd saw their high-grade ballistic weapons encased in gold and steel did they calm down. He knew they'd never seen real weapons before, most people hadn't.

Grand Magistrate Royger removed his rimless glasses, wiped sweat from his forehead, and returned them to his face. "Please don't think that those weapons are just for show," he said. "This is the last time I will call for order"—his eyes moved from the crowd to the men of rule in the back—"from *everyone*."

The men of rule sat back down and the crowd moved toward the wall they'd stood in front of. A line of guards acted as a barrier.

"Thank you. Candace, given that you've already done a service to the hemisphere by making these proceedings as honest and easy as possible, I will bestow upon you the opportunity to explain and repent, after which I'll deliver the sentencing. Proceed."

She dropped her head, let it rest on her chest as she stared at the wooden podium. Silence setting the room on edge again. After a quick breath, she looked up.

"As you all probably know by now," she calmly began. "I am from Forest Twenty-Six. North of where we stand tonight. It's the only place I've ever called home, and while I don't know what other forests in our region look like, I know that there's no place more beautiful."

A small smile appeared on her face, then vanished.

"For a while, I thought much like I assume you do, that the simple lives we live aren't to be envied. Maybe you pity us, maybe you scorn us, or, more likely, maybe you never think of us more than you need to. Instead of people, you see domestics, tunnel diggers, janitors, and other hired hands. That used to anger me, how you treated us as see-through as our skin. But I've learned.

"I've learned that despite not having parents, I had a community to raise me. That my brother, the one you all cast as a murderer more than a man, was troubled, but also braver, even as a boy, than any of you could ever be. As Hemispheric Guard Director Curts claims, I did seek to assist my brother. I attempted to get help from Mr. Tenmase and his nephew, but they told me"—she looked at Curts, who couldn't meet her face—"just like you did, to know my place. Still, I persisted. I went to Minx, one of the most honest places in our hemisphere. A club where DP men, like the ones behind me, go to engage in acts with Invisible women they wouldn't dare do with their own women. The irony is that it's the Invisible women who hold all the power there. And it was there where I poisoned a man, a high-ranking hemispheric guard, to gain access to Eminent Estates."

People brought their hands to their mouths. Some of them covered their children's ears. When Curts surveyed the men of rule, they were all leaning on the edge of their seats, gripping the wooden rails, their faces empty and open. These men, like the civilians, like Grand Magistrate Royger and his fellow magistrates, and like Curts, were all doing what they hadn't done from the moment Candace had walked onto the floor. They were listening.

"Maybe some of you live there," she said. "I went, and I met with two people I thought would lead me to my brother, but they were of little help. My brother, as Hemispheric Guard Director Curts said, is gone." She looked to the ceiling, the hemisphere's flag carved into the large squares of dark mahogany that stretched across it. "And I now know that he was long gone before he ever disappeared from our cabin.

"What has all of this taught me? I keep saying 'I've learned,' but what did I really learn?" She leveled her head at the magistrates' bench, turned around the room in a complete circle, touching every single person with her gaze. "I've learned that if I am guilty of anything, it's of believing that by doing all the right things, by following the rules written by the men in here, I would be safe. But safety is only an illusion in this world. And freedom comes from taking real risks.

"The true guilty ones," she said, her voice rising, "are *you*. You are convinced that this world exists for your pleasure. You believe that you are in power. You do what you do behind closed doors and never expect anyone to find out, even though your transgressions are written on your faces, etched into the way you walk, the way you talk, the way you laugh, the way you smile, the way you cry, the way you lie, the way you lie, the way you lie, the way you lie.

"It's funny." She laughed. "You call us 'Invisible,' because our skin is see-through, but we see each other as clearly as we do a bright, brilliant morning, which is why I am not here to convince you of our humanity. Understand that this is not a plea—this is a warning. One day, very soon, you'll see just how cursed you are. May the Holy Father bless the Northwestern Hemisphere, because none of you are safe. Not anymore. Not ever again."

Curts only heard the rush of blood in his ears. He fell forward, his elbow pushing Candace to the side as he grabbed on to the podium to steady himself.

Grand Magistrate Royger cleared his throat. His ordinarily joyful face, marked by years of service to the hemisphere, was taut. His mouth a line as straight as the world's horizon. His eyes concrete. It was as if the Earth itself had stopped spinning, disrupting the great celestial order.

"Someone," the Grand Magistrate eventually said, "please call Drams Jams Ivy and tell him he's out of a job. This young woman can act and perform better than any Invisible I have ever seen!"

The crowd laughed so hard that the floor quaked. Children imitated their parents, shaking one another as their faces cracked open and sound shot out of their tiny mouths. Men grabbed their stomachs, stomped their feet. Perhaps there were a few who weren't laughing, but Curts couldn't see them. He just knew that *he* wasn't laughing.

Grand Magistrate Royger, finally composing himself, blew his long nose into a crimson handkerchief. "On behalf of the highest court in this great hemisphere, I sentence you, Candace of Forest Twenty-Six, to death by hanging."

As the Gallery cheered and applauded the decision, Curts looked to her, thinking that she'd finally break down and beg for mercy. But what he found on her face was something far stranger, something he himself would never be able to experience again.

Relief.

CHAPTER 47

BROTHER BLACKSTONE WATCHED HIS WIFE, A BULLET SHOOTING beneath the water, complete another lap in the pool. Blue light glowed throughout the room. When she surfaced, he was already there, towel in hand.

"Thank you," she said, patting her face.

"Run me through it again."

"Again?"

"Again."

She sat on the smooth rock bench near the pool's edge, and he joined her.

"Seven Children out in the open, that's it. All in their undercover roles. Executive Estate servants in the crowd, landscapers on the edge of the lawn, a mechanic who thought his supervisor said he needed assistance. The servants will have handheld ballistics taped beneath their trays, the landscapers hiding weapons in their supply carts, the mechanic with explosive spheres in his tool belt. If Local Tormentor II Jolis is elected and walks onto that balcony, whoever has the clearest shot takes it. Regardless, five other Children, led by Brother Burningwood, will handle the train and Sister Sweetmint's rescue."

"But what if what I heard Tenmase tell Curts and Jolis is right?"

"If Washington *is* Shanu, as Tenmase believes, then he'll be fine. With Jolis gone, his status as the next Chief Executive is secured. Having him in power, so long as he's working with us, will make the Fundamental Flip imminent. And if Washington isn't Shanu, then we'll continue our search until The Illuminator is found."

Brother Blackstone took a breath, looked out at the clear pool surrounded by rock, his ambitious, determined wife by his side. If this were any other day, it would be the picture of perfection, but now he couldn't shake the bad feeling that had taken root in his heart.

She brought both hands to his face. "You worry too much. This is a happy rebellion, remember? You are strong, you are righteous, and you are, on most days, happy. So please don't waver now, not when we all need you—when I need you."

"Okay," he said, kissing her. "The movement needs to be tight and quick. Sister Sweetmint . . . She's—"

"She's being tested. That's all. And from what you've told me, our little sister hasn't failed a single test yet."

CHAPTER 48

"ANDACE."

She woke with a start, her body moving from a line to a right angle in an instant. Her eyes touched each of the four cloudy glass walls that surrounded her. The floor was also made of glass, the room full of bright white light, giving her the sensation that she was in a box, on display, like jewelry at the Northwestern Boutique. But if she was being monitored, she couldn't tell.

What was the last thing she remembered? Shibs, including Hemispheric Guard Director Curts, escorting her out of the Gallery of Rule, back through the maze of hallways, and into a waiting train. One threw a black cloth over her head and told her, with satisfaction, that she was headed for His Executive's Prison. Yes, she'd heard of the airtight chambers of doom, located on a lower level of the Executive Estate. She knew, from her forestfolk's whispers, that no one ever returned. "The Final Destination," some called it.

If Hemispheric Guard Director Curts had anything to say to her, he hadn't shared. She had seen him looking down at his shiny boots—she'd inhaled his unmistakable odor of shame and fear, hoping he'd carry that scent with him for the rest of his life. But circumstance had turned her into a realist. Hemispheric Guard Director Curts, like every other DP, would join in a collective forgetting that would save them from themselves. But not from the Children of Slim.

"Candace," the voice repeated, the room so small that it was hard to tell where the sound came from. She'd thought it was in her head, an inner voice waking her out of the deepest, sweetest slumber she'd had in a long, long time. But when she heard it again, she knew it was real. Maybe the shibs wanted to torture her, just for fun, before her execution.

"Candace, it's me."

The third time confirmed the voice's owner.

She stood up. "What are you doing here, Mr. Tenmase?"

"I warned you to run away, but you didn't listen. Why didn't you listen?"

"Can anyone hear us?"

"Do you think I'm an amateur? I designed this prison."

"Of course you did. But what does that mean?"

"It means I overrode the system so that you and I could speak. There's also a loop on their displays of us still sleeping. We don't have long until the guards come to wake us."

What was the point? This was the end. Certainly for her, but maybe not for him. She was curious about how he'd ended up here, but it didn't really matter.

"I'm sorry you're here," he said. "But I'll get you out, don't worry."

"I'm not worried."

"Good. There are some things I want to tell you. They may not make any difference now, but maybe you'll be able to live with less regret, knowing that this was all out of your hands from before the beginning." He paused, then, "Remember when I said I was working on the invention of a lifetime?"

She did. It was only a few days ago when he'd brought it up

again, before they'd worked to take apart the cell phone, but it felt like it'd been years. "You said I was going to help you create it. That we would trigger the Big Reset together. And—" The seed of a realization interrupted her. "What did you do, Mr. Tenmase?"

"What I had to. And perhaps things I didn't. I admit it's hard to know where to start, and we don't have much time."

"Just start at the beginning," she said, sitting back down.

Mr. Tenmase told her how Chief Executive Rhitel had murdered many people for his position. He smothered the previous Chief Executive. Killed his main opponent, Local Manager XII George Elmor, and his wife. But not his son.

"This boy traveled great distances to become Chief Executive Rhitel's partner in persecution, patiently waiting until the day when he would be able to—"

"To what?" Candace asked, pushing him to fill in the blanks.

"To murder him. And that moment eventually came when the boy, now much older, met your brother, Shanu."

"Shanu?"

"Yes," he said, his voice far away and empty. "He met your brother, even if he didn't know he was your brother at first."

"But where did they meet?"

"It's not important. What you need to know is that he believed, with the help of Shanu, that they would forever change the world. Then, for the poetry of it all, he enlisted the help of his nephew to suffocate The Chief Executive in his sleep—and blamed it on Shanu."

"Why? Why would he turn on my brother?"

"Because the hemisphere needed someone formidable to hate. Someone who had already eluded the authorities for years. This would allow a new Rhitel-like figure, Jolis, to rise. A man who is the key to our advancement."

"And you are the son of Local Manager XII Elmor, who invented all of this," she said, unsurprised, yet still disappointed in herself.

She should have seen it from the beginning; someone more aware of their hemisphere's realities, like Red, would have. Even despite her initial reservations, Candace was too trustful, too hopeful, too eager to run from her past toward the future.

"Yes," he replied.

"But how did Sanford murder The Chief Executive with all of his guards?"

"It was simple, really. Hacking the Executive Estate surveillance. A golden guard's uniform and appropriate credentials. Utilizing particle displacement technology so that he could move through walls undetected. And a few swipes to erase our train's journey to a secret part of the Executive Estate. You'd be surprised by how easy it is to do something when people are so confident that no one would ever dare do it."

Sanford was a murderer. No, he was *the* murderer people so badly wanted Shanu to be. And he was never even a suspect. An actor, just as she'd assumed, playing a role, playing her, playing everyone.

"But why me?" she asked. "Why did you choose me for the apprenticeship?"

"I wanted to use you, to dangle you in front of Shanu as a test to ensure that he was committed to go as far as he would need to, irrespective of the personal cost. He wasn't aware that Sanford and I murdered Rhitel and blamed him, but he did use that moment to become the person he'd always wanted to be."

Time was running out, and despite all of the immeasurable betrayal and heartbreak she was feeling, she still had so many questions. "Shanu and Jolis are working together?"

Silence.

"Mr. Tenmase?"

"You could say that," he finally replied.

"Aren't they on opposite sides, though? Jolis and Washington?"

"What do you mean?"

"We don't need to keep up the games. I know my brother is Washington. And even if he loses the election, he wins, because he's fooled all of you. He humiliates you every time someone shakes his hand, pays attention to what he has to say, belittles themselves to get into his good graces. The graces of an *Invisible*."

"Candace—"

"Yet," she continued, the momentary flash of pride turning to uncontrollable rage. "I'm the only one who loses everything. Darksap, who loved me, is dead. Kandolo, who I thought loved me, is working with Hemispheric Guard Director Curts. Sanford never cared about me. You . . . I trusted you. I admired you. I wanted to *be* you. But you were manipulating me from the beginning. And here I was, naive enough to believe that I could somehow win against all of this."

"If I could have done it differently, I would have, but—"

"You know," she said, "you are rotten to your core, just like the rest of your kind. But I can't even blame you. Exploitation is in your genetic coding. It's the only explanation for all you've done, all you're doing, and all you'll no doubt do. Again, and again, and again."

"Maybe so." He paused. "Candace, what do you really know about the Shipping?"

"I know what I was taught. When Chief Executive Rhitel came to power, our elders were relocated to a hidden part of the hemisphere, never to be seen again. I'm sure it was all a lie, though. Carefully crafted by none other than you. The Great Liar. The Chief Falsifier. The Director of Deceit."

She could hear him taking a breath. Had she hurt him? She hoped so. It was time he finally understood what the word *hurt* really meant. How to dispense it was one thing, but to receive it another matter entirely.

"Growing up in the Clothing Region," he began, his tone subdued, "I saw Invisibles, all over the age of five, marched through the streets and forced onto trains. Heard murmurings that this was taking place across the hemisphere, along with weekly uprisings. Only later did Rhitel privately confirm to me what the Shipping was: genocide. See-through bodies dumped into the ocean, floating on waves until they became waterlogged and sank. The attempted annihilation of an entire culture, language, and history. Death for all DPs who assisted in resistance. Men will do despicable things in the name of progress. But my way," he said, his voice shaking, "was different. Exert control and dominance through less physical means. At least give Invisibles a life they could be happy with, despite the limitations. Look around your forest, how happy people are—"

"Happily ignorant," she spat. "If they knew the truth about this hemisphere, the truth about how manipulative and malicious you all are, I'd bet most of them would rather be dead. No, I'm sure of it."

"People can live under extraordinary circumstances, Candace. But this was the essence of the Big Reset—to flip the switch on the world again, creating chaos that would then lead to a better world for all of us."

"So why not just do *that* when you first met Rhitel? You could have killed him and been done with it."

"No." She imagined him condescendingly shaking his head. "It wouldn't have worked. I had to gain his trust, work with him to change the landscape, where bloodshed was no longer commonplace."

"So much for what happened in Forest Seventy-Eight."

"Without me, massacres of that magnitude, and what happened in the Clothing Region two nights ago, would be a daily occurrence, as they once were. Despite how it seems now, the world of tomorrow will be worth it, I promise. Inot Droffow says, 'The future forever echoes the past, growing distant from its source, but never without it.' What has happened won't be forgotten. And you *will* be here to not only witness what comes next, our second genesis, but also to help create it."

She closed her eyes, rubbed her fists against her forehead, try-ing to still the unrest in her mind. The explanations, justifications—all of it clay for men like him to shape as they see fit.

"Do you ever wonder what all of this striving is for?" she asked.

"How so?"

"I mean, I'm just so tired, Mr. Tenmase. So, so tired. And if this has already happened before, to someone else, in a similar way, and it will happen again, to someone else, in a similar way . . ." She filled her lungs to the brim, emptied them. "Why try?"

Silence. Again. She was ready to lie down and return to sleep, resting before whatever came next. But then he whispered, "Love."

Her eyes snapped open. "Love?"

"Love. We are all loved, and we're all born with love inside of us, if only because someone *chose* to bring us into existence. When we learn how dark and destructive the world can be, it's too late; we already have something to live for. Love is why we try. Why we've always tried and will keep trying, until the very end of time, no matter how predictable the eventual outcome."

She thrust her hand toward the door. "And what do you know of love? You have no wife, no children, no kin."

His silence made her think that whatever connection he'd cre-ated to make communication possible was finally severed. But then, "Sometimes its absence teaches you more than its presence."

The glass must have been soundproofed because she didn't hear any footsteps—she only saw the black silhouette beyond the cloudy glass door before it slid open. Standing there was Local Manager II Jolis. By the way he shuffled his feet and extended his hands, comedian-like, she knew he had just won the election.

"Good morning," he said, as if it were any other day.

"Good morning," she mimicked. What soon awaited him when he stepped onto that inaugural stage gave her an ocean-deep sense of bliss.

"Did you sleep well?"

"Surprisingly, yes."

He walked inside, the door sliding closed behind him. "May I sit?" She moved over and he joined her.

"It's Chief Executive Jolis now." He swiveled his head around the room, settled on the glass ceiling, and smiled. "That's going to take some getting used to."

She'd seen him the night before, but he had been a blur. Now she saw that he was as big and broad-shouldered as he looked on the display. His artificial aroma of sawdust and steel, probably an attempt to come off as more rugged and common, filled her nostrils. Still, beneath it all, something more natural escaped through his pores: a hint of smoke.

The Chief Executive faced her, his eyes startling Candace by how blue they burned, the hottest part of a flame. "I'm here because I was impressed with your performance last night. Instead of hanging your head, you raised it high and told the entire hemisphere what you thought and how you felt, all without fear. It was . . . inspiring."

"Glad I could be of use," she said, her tone flat as she stared at the wall.

"You *have* been of use, Candace. In more ways than you'll ever know." He cupped her chin, forced her to look at him. "I'm sure Shanu, wherever he is, is proud of you."

She cringed at hearing her brother's name come from this man's mouth. But curiosity, that insatiable foe, betrayed her once again.

"Is it true that you know my brother?"

"I do," he said, holding her gaze. "And despite how it all seems, we want the same thing: to forever change the world."

"How could you and Shanu want the same thing? You hate Invisibles."

"Hate you?" His eyebrows came together as he shook his head.

"I don't hate you. Shanu thought that he would free you all, but when he learned more about how this hemisphere works, *really* works, he realized that everyone, including the Dominant Population, was imprisoned in cells of their own devising—that *everyone* needed freeing. And what Northwesterners need most is a man who can rule with a fist of iron and steel. The hemisphere of tomorrow will be a hemisphere where the hard survive and the soft subside. Just imagine how unstoppable we will be." He nodded at her. "You would have done well in it."

"Then why do I need to die?"

"This great hemisphere requires your sacrifice to move on. The DPs need blood. The Invisibles need a martyr. Unfortunately, it's your destiny to be both, because peace isn't on the horizon, Candace. Not yet. Peace can only be earned through conflict."

"Sacrifice," she whispered, shutting her eyes. "Why does everyone always expect someone like me to sacrifice everything for them?"

He stood, prompting her to open her eyes, and looked down at her. "'Place me like a seal over your heart, like a seal on your arm; for love is as strong as death, its jealousy unyielding as the grave. It burns like a blazing fire, like a mighty flame.' Song of Songs 8:6. But you already knew that."

The Chief Executive turned from her and pressed his hand to the door, which slid open. With his back to her, he said, "Enjoy the show, Little Me," and stepped out. The cell door closed with a *swoosh*.

She sat frozen. When the words reached her brain, she jumped to her feet, pounded on the glass door, screaming, "Sweetsmoke! Sweetsmoke, wait! Sweetsmoke, come back!" Her fists slammed against the door again, and again, and again, doing all she could to get the attention of the guards.

"Mr. Tenmase!" she called, her back to the door now as she yelled his name, hoping he could hear her. "Mr. Tenmase! It's Shanu! He's Shanu! Please, we have to stop him!"

CHAPTER 49

I

Curts, huffing, reached the place on the hill he'd marked. A dense row of trees stretched to his left and right. He got down, his clothing the same brown as the dirt below him and the tree trunks beside him, ensuring that no one would spot him. Stomach flat, he attached the long-distance scope to his weapon, planted its bipod in the soft ground. One eye to the lens, he took in the scene at the Executive Estate: so many happy people on the lawn, two sets of white stairs curving up to the balcony, where the wooden podium stood; reverends, local managers, and directors from the Legacy Coalition gathered, waiting for the man of the hour. Powerless guards standing vigilant.

There was no need to slow down his pulse, to breathe deeply and fully. After Curts had struck Stephan at Castle Tenmase, he'd removed some of the local manager's blood from his cuff and tested it. Once he saw the result, he knew this is how it would end. The realization that Stephan was the man he'd been looking for the entire time, making a mockery out of him, the hemisphere, and everyone else, didn't stun him. It made sense. But it also scared him, because no one was safe as long as this man was alive.

Chief Executive Jolis appeared, whipping the adoring crowd into an even wilder frenzy as he walked up the stairs. He stopped at the top as the sun shined in his face. With his fists in the air, the roar below him grew louder.

"May the Holy Father bless your soul," Curts whispered.

Jolis dropped his arms.

Curts pulled the trigger.

The sky clapped once, and once was enough.

I I

The seven Children, each painted in thin stripes of the Hemisphere's red, black, and white, took up their positions. Four servers, after fulfilling final requests for juice, herbs, and biscuits, slipped into the background of the balcony, behind the Chief Enemy's supporters. The mechanic—brown tool belt slung around his waist—was off to the side of the crowd, inspecting one of the automated sprinklers. Two landscapers pushed their supply carts around a bend along the rear area of the South Lawn.

As Chief Enemy Jolis appeared, his smiling face a mask of evil, their other brothers and sisters were ready to infiltrate the Executive Estate's lower level, preparing their escape and completing the rescue. The shot was the signal.

The crowd cheered for their savior, a man who they believed was the future of the hemisphere, the key to their comfortable lives staying comfortable. A mirror that hid the blemishes, erased the ugly.

With each step he took up the stairs, the praise increased, people tearing their throats, faces soaked. The orgiastic joy was so unseemly, so perverse.

Finally reaching the balcony, he looked back at his supporters, then up into the sun's light. When he raised his hands to the sky, each of the seven Children poised their weapons.

But before any of them could take the shot, thunder struck.

III

A display appeared on the glass wall to the right of her, a live illumination of the Executive Estate. Chief Executive Jolis walked up the stairs, waving to the clapping and cheering crowd as he slowly ascended, savoring the moment. When he reached the top, he held his fists in the air, just as she had seen her brother do in the woods behind their cabin countless times, recounting how he'd beaten an opponent, or showing her how he'd celebrate upon being crowned the best boxer in the hemisphere. Her entire body shook as she remembered those simpler days. An inconceivable wave of grief rising higher, and higher, and higher within her.

The sound of the crowd was unlike anything she'd ever heard before. Her brother dropped his arms and they all quieted, until there was complete silence. Even the wind, seeming to understand the significance of this day, this hour, this minute, this second, died down.

Then, as if made of clay, the world cracked right down the middle.

A burst of blood shot out of his neck. His eyes bulged in disbelief. His body began to flicker—visible, invisible, visible, invisible, visible. The last thing she saw: a blinking sea of red.

CHAPTER 50

SHE FELL TO THE FLOOR AND TRIED TO SCREAM, BUT NO SOUND came out. Brother and Sister Blackstone had made good on their promise.

The door slid open. She expected to find a shib, or Mr. Tenmase, but whoever was there was Invisible, unpainted and odorless, their rumoya undetectable; a gold weapon floating in the air.

"Sweetmint," they said.

"Rusty?"

"Come, we have to get you out of here. *Now*." He pulled her to her feet, but she yanked her arm away.

"How could you?"

"We don't have time, Sweetmint. I'm sorry. I thought I was protecting you, our forest, and Sweetsmoke, but I couldn't protect anyone. I did what I could to watch over you, though."

"Watch over me?"

"At Minx. In Progress Park."

"That was *you*?"

"The compass I gave you. I tracked you with it. Now come."

They entered the short, light-flooded hallway. Across from her cell was another, likely Mr. Tenmase's. She knew he would be okay. This was all his own invention, and she hardly believed he planned on dying in prison.

As Rusty pulled her toward the door, passing a handful of other cells and unconscious shibs on the floor, they were joined by more floating weapons and light footsteps. Then a DP appeared, wearing a uniform similar to Hemispheric Guard Director Curts's. Her hair was a shade of fire, eyes the color of leaves. She looked familiar.

"Candace," the DP said, embracing her. "I'm so happy you're okay. I'm Hemispheric Guard Deputy Director Mund. Here, along with Kandolo and the others, to get you to safety. But we must move quickly."

The woman, an arm around Candace's shoulders, guided her out of the prison and through a maze of hallways, but then Candace stopped. "How do I know I can trust you?"

"You can't," another voice said.

Five weapons hovered in the hallway opposite them.

"It's me, Sister Sweetmint. Brother Burningwood."

The Invisibles nearest to her raised their weapons. The Children of Slim did the same.

"Don't shoot!" both Hemispheric Guard Deputy Director Mund and Brother Burningwood shouted.

The sound of heavy breathing and beating hearts filled the hallways.

"Children of Slim?" Hemispheric Guard Deputy Director Mund asked.

"That's right," Brother Burningwood replied, ready, waiting. Candace knew he wouldn't wait much longer. "She'll come with us."

"Stop all of this nonsense," Rusty said. "Ribussce and his shibs are coming. Let's go." They all turned to leave, but Candace was already walking toward Brother Burningwood.

"Sweetmint," Rusty said, grabbing her shoulder.

She looked down at him, pictured his beautiful locs with wooden beads, the many times he'd held her after Sweetsmoke left, his skin absorbing her tears. Maybe he was still that man, but he was also another, the one in front of her now. A man she didn't recognize and could never feel safe with again. Betrayal bound itself to her DNA, and she knew, no matter what she did and where she went, that it would live within her forever.

"Sweetmint," he repeated, begging her. "Please."

When she turned her back on him, no one, not even Hemispheric Guard Deputy Director Mund, stopped her.

Brother Burningwood led the Children through another hallway, arriving at a platform, where a train waited for them. Inside, hands on her knees, Candace worked to catch her breath, unsure of how many people were with her.

"It all went according to plan," a woman said from the far end of the car. "Just as Brother and Sister Blackstone envisioned."

"Mostly," Brother Burningwood said, lowering his weapon once the train began to move. "But didn't you see the Chief Enemy flickering?"

Candace remained standing near the doors. "Where are you taking me?" she asked.

"Tintaba," Brother Burningwood said. "Brother and Sister Blackstone will instruct us on what to do next. The Fundamental Flip is already underway, sister."

She walked to the back of the train, accidentally bumping into others standing in the aisle. When she reached the farthest seat, she sank into it, her head resting against the window.

The train hurtled through the tunnel's dark nothingness, and she did the only thing she could do. The only thing, at least for a moment, that would allow her to go to that sacred place inside of her where anything was possible and loss was just a word.

She let go.

ACKNOWLEDGMENTS

Man, we've come a long way. Come a long way indeed. Writing *This Great Hemisphere* was a difficult task, only made possible by the support of so many people and that which is beyond our human scope, but guides us all the same.

I'd like to begin by thanking my editor, Pilar Garcia-Brown. Pilar, I didn't know if I could do this. There were times when the undertaking was so overwhelming that I felt completely incompetent, as if I were trying to climb a mountain with two sprained ankles. But there you were, when I needed you most, with your encouraging eye, understanding spirit, and unfailing enthusiasm. As with *Black Buck*, you've not only helped me become a better writer, but also aided me in gaining a greater understanding of self. Without you, this book wouldn't be here—I wouldn't have been able to tell the story the way it needed to be told. Thank you for being such an incredible creative partner and champion. Thank you for being you.

Tina Pohlman, my former agent. Oh, Tina. How I love thee. Thank you for always pushing me, for the care you took in every aspect of our relationship. From the first time we met, I felt like I was speaking with a person who felt deeply about literature and life, and it was because of your belief in me, and your efforts on my behalf, that I'm even in this position today. I know we're no longer working together on paper, but our collaboration is far from over.

Mom, my biggest fan. You taught me how to hold a spoon and aim for the toilet bowl, sure, but the lessons you've imparted and continue to teach me are far deeper. It's easy to say, "I wouldn't be here without you," which, of course, is factually true, but you continue to be one of my best friends, confidantes, and the person I cherish more than any other on this blue and green Earth. I remember when I was a kid, how you'd say, "I love you this much," and stretch your arms wide until they couldn't stretch any more. It was hard for me to understand what that meant then, but I understand it now, because I feel your arms stretching even when I don't see you, and I hope you know how far my arms stretch for you, too. Thank you for giving me life in more ways than one.

Dad. There's so much you've passed on to me that has helped me in my pursuits. Focus, serious work ethic, a "do what needs to be done" attitude no matter how daunting the endeavor. From a young age, I saw you wake up in the early mornings without complaint, preparing your tea and packing your lunch, doing what needed to be done to ensure that your sons had a better life than you—a life where anything was possible, even if you couldn't have envisioned it yourself. Thank you for allowing us to be ourselves. Thank you for always being that hand to our backs, steadying us after the training wheels were off. Baba hamishe doostet daram. Hamishe. Kheily mamnoon baraye hamechiz.

My brothers—Darius, David, Khalik, Andy. The prototypes. The hustlers' hustlers. David once told me that he believes we've all been here before, and before returning to this world, we'd made a conscious decision to come back, together. I don't know if I believe that, but it doesn't feel that off the mark. As time goes on, I'm grateful for the fact that we continue to show up for one another, in new and different ways, understanding that love is an action, because for so many, *family* is just a word. Thank you for loving me, for loving each other, and for having the courage to ensure that we're all doing what we can to grow together, no matter what.

Thank you to all of my aunts, uncles, and cousins, including the two little ones, Theo and Zari. And my ancestors—especially Clarine and William—that have walked before me and continue to exist within me. I carry you all with me everywhere I go. You're present in each word I write, in every breath I take. When I look in the mirror, I see you in my eyes, my nose, my lips, and also in my soul. You help me keep going when I think I can't, and I pray that you're proud. I love you so much.

Q, mi hermano. Ya tú sabes. Shit, we're still here, brother. Still here, after all these years. Two hearts beating as one, flying high, chasing the sun. You've already taught me so much, about friendship, vulnerability, and selflessness. But also about what it means to squeeze every drop of juice out of this thing called life, pulp all over your hands and everything. My admiration and awe of you grows with each year I know you, and though we've already had a ton of adventures, weathered many storms, and pierced the clouds to experience that weightless feeling of cruising at high altitudes, I know it's only the beginning. Te amo.

There are so many writers to thank. Too many, really, and I know I'm going to forget some. But the three I'd like to mention first are Irvin Weathersby, Robert Jones, Jr., and Danté Stewart. You brothers already know what it is. I know you do. But just in case you need a reminder, I count you among my closest friends who just happen to write. Your guidance, your love, and your support is unparalleled. Danté often talks to me about the experience of going from playing D1 football, where he had a ton of teammates, to being a writer, where it's just us and a blank page. But it is because of this that he values those he calls his teammates in these creative pursuits even more, and I feel the same. You three continue to show up for me again and again, and I am so fortunate to know you. To witness your craft and art, yes, but also just to receive a bit of your own light and to be counted among your own brothers. I love you.

Regina Porter, thank you for all of your encouragement, advice, and friendship. Breaking bread with you is something I always look forward to. I'm so happy to be writing at the same time as you.

Jason Mott. Man, you already know this, but I have to say it: you're a real one. From the first time we met, you've had my back, made it a point to be a resource and a true friend, and helped me better understand what it means to be a holistic writer—that authenticity is everything, and staying solid through the ups and downs is the work. Sharing space with you is always a gift (cue "N.I.P."!), brother. Love.

Anna DeRoy. Anna, Anna, Anna. What a joy it is to work with you, a true master of her craft. Your willingness to always hear me out with an open ear, and then expertly explain the how or why of a what, means the world to me. Hollywood is such a strange place, full of shiny things and shiny people who love to pour milk and honey in your ear, and I would be far worse off without you beside me. I'm so grateful for how our partnership has continued to bloom over the years—to be connected to someone so kind, funny, intelligent, and hardworking. Thank you for all that you've done, and all that's on the horizon. And thank you to many of the other folks at WME, like Lara Bahr, and your many assistants, including Sarah Campbell.

PJ Mark! Being on your squad feels like the dream team. Seriously. Before signing with you, I tried to find out if *any* of my friends whom you work with had anything negative to say about you, and they had not a word! And I have some pretty discerning friends. If that doesn't speak to how revered you are, I don't know what does.

I am incredibly grateful for your energy, honesty, and belief in me and my work. I'm so excited to see what we do together.

Emma Chapnick, my first reader. Thank you for your generosity, Emma. After I reached a certain stage with this book, I knew I had to show it to someone other than my main team, and you were the first person to pop into my head. Not just because you're so well-read in the genre, but because you bring a large amount of heart and deep insight to everything literary. Thank you for your feedback, support, and friendship. See you at The West.

My people in Bellport and Patchogue—I thank you. One of the most surprising parts of publishing *Black Buck* was how many of you read and told me you enjoyed it. Teachers, friends, friends' parents. That really touched something serious inside of me, and I hope to continue making you all proud. Thank you to some of my day one homies: Geetanjali Toronto, Nick Sagginario, Lawrence Gross, and Chris Arnold.

Friends and family of the Rhode Island Writers Colony: thank you for the fellowship, love, and confidence. From Warren to the world.

Brothers of the Gentlemen of Quality. You, too, surprised me. The way you would show up to my events, spread the word of my work, send me messages of encouragement. It has been a privilege to remain connected to so many of you, and to continue growing with you all after our years at NYU. And a special shout-out to Kadeem, JJ, and Dre. Love. FYGQ.

Where would I be without the bookstagrammers? Those relentless readers and lovers of literature who take to Instagram and share their opinions on books, often in the most honest, creative, and exciting of ways? I want to thank each and every one of you for helping lift up *Black Buck* and me, not just when it came out, but to today and beyond. You were a community I unexpectedly fell in love with—the various people and personalities, affirming and sometimes diverging takes on books, your endless capacity for making books, and, by extension, us authors, cool. Connecting with you all has been a highlight of my career.

I want to give a special shout-out to Reggie Bailey. Reggie, you were one of the first people—not just bookstagrammers, but people—who saw and understood what I was trying to do as a writer. You understood that it was bigger than the words, and I can't tell you how much that meant to me—to feel seen. Your friendship is one I deeply treasure, especially our three-hour phone conversations when it feels like we've only scratched the surface. You're such a special person, brother, with a special perspective and the ability to make a difference in the lives of many, which you already have. I'm honored to be a witness to your greatness.

Various other literary homies who have sustained me in a myriad of ways since writing *Black Buck*: Nafissa Thompson-Spires, Danielle Prescod, Cleyvis Natera, Candice Carty-Williams, Marianne Tatepo, Suli Breaks, Dawnie Walton, Brit Bennett, Naima Coster, Zakiya Dalila-Harris, Yahdon Israel, Randy Winston, Jared Jackson, Terah Shelton Harris, Nana Kwame-Adjei Brenyah, Nadia Owusu, J Ezra McCoy, and Mark Cecil.

Thank you to Jenna Bush Hager and everyone at NBCUniversal. You helped *Black Buck* reach the masses, and you've continued to be incredible partners in so many ways. I look forward to our future!

A handful of extraordinary people who I'm lucky to know or have known: Julia Wendt, Julio Saenz (my breddah), Delaney Poon and the larger group of Poons and Scanlons (rest well, Nancy. I'll forever remember your smile, your laugh, and your ability to help others do the same), Gow Mosby, Antonio J. Bell, Nick Scoulios, Adam Vinson, Benjamin Franklin, Lauren Davis, Victoria Guiazul de Oliveira Ferreira, Jeb Pierce, Shanique Marie, Jda Gayle, Jennifer Ocampo, Adriana Arroyave, and Yann Gael.

ACKNOWLEDGMENTS

To all of my people in Jamaica, I thank and love you. I perpetually feel your warmth, as well as the strength of my roots rising through the soles of my feet, grounding me, keeping me stable and secure. Love to Cave Valley. Love to St. Ann. Love to the island.

Kheily, kheily mamnoon to my siblings in the Collective for Black Iranians. When you found me, Priscillia Kounkou-Hoveyda, it felt like a world was opening up right before my eyes. A home, where I found a piece of myself, where I felt understood, and where I encountered a group of dope-ass people, including my brother Alex Eskandarkhah. Dadash, meeting you was like looking in a mirror—a reflection of the physical, yes, but even more so the spiritual. Honored to be shooting beside you. To know you as my brother.

Love to all of my family, blood and extended, in Iran. I patiently wait for the day when my feet will kiss the land, when we can hold each other and begin to make sense of everything together. Until then, a chasm remains in my heart—from lost time and lost history—but I have faith it won't remain that way forever.

Big ups to the team at HMH/Mariner Books who helped launch *Black Buck*. Your efforts stick with me to this day, and I will always be thankful to have published my debut with you.

To my new home, Dutton: thank you all for being such committed individuals. I know *This Great Hemisphere* is a big swing, and I'm delighted to be publishing it with you. To list a bunch of those who have made this sophomore novel possible: John Parsley, Christine Ball, Lauren Morrow, Nicole Jarvis, Emily Canders, Amanda Walker, Stephanie Cooper, Ella Kurki (you're the best, Ella!), Jason Booher, Leah Marsh, Rob Sternitzky, David Hough (love you and grateful to work with you again, David), and Sabila Kahn.

Speaking of publishing partners, I have to spotlight Maÿlis de Lajugie and the entire team at Buchet-Chastel. Publishing the French version of *Black Buck* (*Buck & Moi*) was the experience of a lifetime. Being able to visit France not once, but twice, in one year and getting to spend such wonderful time with all of you was something I don't take for granted. Especially you, Maÿlis. I can't thank you enough for everything—the way you've worked tirelessly to position me and my work, the care you always take to ensure that even if things get tough, the difficulties are brief (like when you became my impromptu interpreter in Toulouse!), and just for being such a genuine, down-to-earth, and cool individual. Merci beaucoup. Time to do it again!

Thank you to Sally Wofford-Girand, for continuing to champion *Black Buck*, getting it into hands both domestic and abroad. You're a star, Sally.

Charles Bock. I said my friend Emma Chapnick was my first reader, and this is true, since she read the book in its entirety, but you were the first person outside of my team to really read any of this, and your advice on the prologue and first chapter helped set the tone for everything that followed. Thank you for helping me get out of my head and imbue the work with the energy it needed.

Thank you to all of the journalists, writers, and other media folks for giving my work, and me, space in this oversaturated and overstimulated world. I know your work isn't easy, and I appreciate every bit of it, especially the intention you put behind all you do.

The booksellers! You amazing individuals who make the world of words tick. Working faithfully, often thanklessly, to ensure that those who walk into your stores find the right books at the right time. Thank you, thank you, thank you for all that you do, no matter how hard it sometimes gets. There was a time I dreamed of having a book sitting in the display glass of your stores, and you made that possible and continue to do so. I will never forget that.

Before I go, I also have to recognize the work of Adam Hochschild—specifically *King Leopold's Ghost*, which I highly, highly recommend—and Chinua Achebe in helping me better understand the layers of these characters and the story I was telling as I moved from draft to draft. Roy Peter Clark's *Writing Tools* also armed me with many tools I used to breathe more life into my characters, scenes, and the novel's futuristic setting.

And finally, after these pages and pages of praise and gratitude, I have to thank you, my dear reader. Thank you for your time, for finding my words worth it, for passing them on, in some cases, and holding them near and dear to your heart, in others. None of this works without you. I love you, I salute you, and perhaps more important than all of that: I see you.

Until next time, friends. Mambonga for taking this ride with me.

ABOUT THE AUTHOR

New York Times bestselling author Mateo Askaripour wants people to feel seen. His first novel, *Black Buck*, takes on racism in corporate America with humor and wit. Askaripour was chosen as one of *Entertainment Weekly*'s "10 rising stars poised to make waves," and *Black Buck* was a Read with Jenna *Today* show book club pick. Most recently, he was named as a recipient of the National Book Foundation's "5 Under 35" prize. *This Great Hemisphere* is his second novel. He lives in Brooklyn. Follow him on Instagram and Twitter at @AskMateo.